Dear Reader:

Jonathan Luckett is a creative writer who takes risks with his novels. With *The Mating Game* (and its sequel, *The Forever Game*), Jonathan takes you on a wild ride with a trio of best friends who hop from Washington to New York to New Orleans in search of love. You may never look at the dating scene the same again.

I met Jonathan at the Baltimore Book Festival a few years ago. I listened to him read from his self-published novella, *Feeding Frenzy*. I could see that he was a prolific writer and that his style was sensual. I knew that I wanted to publish his next book, *Jasminium*. If you are looking for suspense with a twist of romance, it is surely the novel for you.

Jonathan has a passion for writing and I'm sure you will appreciate his novels. He has a knack for developing his characters and showcasing them in thrilling and adventurous situations. Outside of his writing skills, Jonathan's strength is his personality at events and signings across the country. Readers gravitate to him because of his charm.

I want to thank those of you who have been gracious enough to support the dozens of authors I publish under Strebor Books International, a division of ATRIA/Simon and Schuster. While writing serves as a catalyst for me to release my personal creativity, publishing allows me the opportunity to share the talent of so many others. If you are interested in being an independent sales representative for Strebor Books International, please send a blank email to info@streborbooks.com

Peace and Blessings,

Zane

Publisher
Strebor Books International
www.streborbooks.com

ALSO BY JONATHAN LUCKETT
Dissolve
How Ya Livin'
Jasminium

ZANE PRESENTS

JONATHAN LUCKETT

The
MATING
GAME

STREBOR BOOKS

NEW YORK LONDON TORONTO SYDNEY

Strebor Books
P.O. Box 6505
Largo, MD 20792
http://www.streborbooks.com

ISBN-13 978-1-59309-101-9
ISBN-10   1-59309-101-X
LCCN 2006928140

First Strebor Books trade paperback edition October 2006.
Originally published June 2004 as *How Ya Livin'*.

10   9   8   7   6   5   4   3   2

Manufactured in the United States of America

For information regarding special discounts for bulk purchases, please contact Simon & Schuster Special Sales at 1-800-456-6798 or business@simonandschuster.com

For Alexandra & Julian

One

Four a.m. came way too fast! The alarm shook my ass out of bed as I struggled to keep myself from falling back into the warm confines of my comforter. But today was not a day to reckon with—no, today I couldn't just lie there and hit the snooze—not on this day. Today I was going on vacation!

So I held my head that was smarting from the buzz of the alarm clock and ran the shower. Then quickly got into my normal routine—teeth brushing and shaving my face and bald head with the Braun, and trimming my thick, dark goatee. I was turning toward the shower but then thought about it for one quick second—I was heading to the islands to play, so I should spend a minute more on grooming, 'cause things like that were important to me. So, I buzzed off what little chest and stomach hair I had, used the clippers (with guard!) to trim my pubic hair down to a thin layer just the way I liked it. Then got in the shower after admiring my taut form in the mirror. I liked what I saw. Firm, bronze-colored body, tight upper body with a hint of muscles, but not overdone, like some fucking jarhead. Tattoo-adorned— a thin tribal band on my left arm above my elbow; the colorful face of an Indian chief on my right shoulder—feathers from his headdress meandering down my arm to just below the elbow; and my latest acquisition—a five-pointed star, almost snowflake-like in form, sitting on my chest above my left nipple. Well-defined legs and a tight ass that sent the women wild (I'm just repeating what they tell me, so don't hate!)

The water running down my bald head, face, chest and arms felt sooooo good, I could have stayed there for an hour. But Air Jamaica was calling my name, "Trey, everyting irie, so get ya black ass down here, mon!" I wasn't about to miss out on any of that. It had been too damn long, ya hear me! Over a year since a real vacation for me. I mean, I've been traveling on business, don't get me wrong, but it isn't the same. This was the vacation that I'd been waiting for all year long. And today was the day. By noon I'd be on white sandy beaches! I couldn't wait.

I glanced down at my flat stomach and dark cock, grabbed the razor and the bar of soap, and went about cutting off the hair around my dick and balls. I loved that feeling of little to no hair down there…and the ladies loved it as well. I'm not sure if it was the fact that it made me more sensitive or not, but all I know was that it felt good to be fucking with smooth balls. With each scrape of the razor I thought about the possibilities awaiting me on that island—all of those dark and lovely honeys…six wonderful days… my dick began to swell as I thought of the delicious possibilities…

While toweling off, I recalled the conversation last night with my boy.

"Speak!"

"What up, dawg? How ya livin'?"

"Living large and in charge," I replied to the routine that hasn't changed in over fifteen years. Vince and I are best friends, homies from way back! He's my man, the one person I genuinely look up to and love like a brother.

"So, my man, you ready?"

"Fuck no, what you think? I got my shit all over this mutha fucka—looks like a cyclone hit this place. But don't worry, my brutha, I *will* be ready!"

"I hear that."

"True dat!"

"So, my man, seriously, you gonna go down there to relax, right? Find your flow and do some soul searching?" I could hear Vince through the phone cracking up before my response was forthcoming.

"What you think? I'm gonna tag every ass that winks at me…I ain't playin'!"

"Dawg, listen to me—what you need to do is take it down a notch, find yourself one of those fine-ass Jamaican women, like Rachel on BET, with the long, dark hair, and thick like I don't know what, and romance the hell out of her. Do your thing, dawg, and she'll be like putty in your hands. Then bring her ass back up to the States and make her your wife!" He chuckled but not more so that I did.

"First off, this is *me* you talking to! Why you trying to play me like that? You know that ain't me. Shit. Wifey??? Fuck that, V. That's you, and listen, I ain't mad at ya, but that, my brutha, ain't me. Wife," I said again. "Nigga, please!"

It always amused me how two grown black men with close to seven years of post-graduate work between us still talked like we were from the ghetto—hoodlums, like rap stars or something. That's one thing I loved about Vince—put him in a work situation and he was all professional and shit, like another person took control of his voice—the way he said things, the manner in which he gestured; and his inflection sounded so damn *intelligent* and I dare say, *prophetic*. He was good at that shit—I mean, to a certain extent I am, too—I have to be in my line of work, being an attorney and such, but I'm not like Vince. He's 'da man when it comes to shit like that. I guess that's why mutha fuckas pay to hear him speak! Anyway, some things never change between us, and this was one of those things—the way we spoke and vibed when we were around each other.

"I'm just saying, if it were me and I was heading to Jamaica for six days, I would be on the lookout. There's something about the islands that gets my juices flowing...when I'm around those beautiful beaches and sunsets it makes me feel all romantic inside. Make me wanna grab a honey and wine and dine her all night!" Vince was laughing now, but I knew his words were speaking the truth. That was the major difference between the two of us—the way in which we viewed the world. Vince was a serious romantic through and through—he still got plenty of play, but his approach was totally different than mine. Me, well, I'm just a stone-cold playa! I'm in to pussy, for real! The punany, plain and simple. I don't fuck around—when I see something I want, I go for it—no long-term romancing allowed! Just not part of my rules, ya see!

"I promise you this, Vince," I said, as I closed my garment bag filled with clothes for every possible occasion—my favorite dark, Italian-cut, three-button suit for the club; black, tight leather pants and stretch muscle shirt;

a few button-downs, a thin pullover in case it got chilly; assorted jeans and shorts; and loafers and two pairs of sandals—black and tan. An unopened box of Lifestyles condoms (lubricated) lay in the upper right compartment of the garment bag. "I'm gonna relax and I'm gonna chill, but I *will* tag every fine piece of pussy I see. I ain't playing. This ole dick of mine is gonna get itself a fucking workout! Ya hear me!?!"

"You mean *more* than normal?" He laughed some more. Then we hung up after saying our goodbyes. I had to finish packing a second bag…

Both bags along with my leather carryon were currently sequestered in the trunk of my black M3. The engine was running and humming as I prepared to leave. I was dressed casual—over-dyed jeans, polo shirt—robin's egg blue, black leather jacket, and my fav Nikes, blue-tinted sunglasses perched atop my smooth dome—yeah, casual, yet stylish and fresh as only I could be— this I'm thinking to myself as I checked myself out in the full length in the hall before setting the alarm to the crib and jetting—after all, as I'm fond of saying—image is everything! No need to have the panties flying just yet. I mean, it wasn't even daylight yet. Yeah, mon!

✠✠✠

Fast forward six hours. I was forty-three thousand feet in the air and cruising above Cuba at five hundred forty-five miles per hour. How I know? 'Cause I'm a gadget freak and brought along my handheld GPS. I pointed that bad boy out the window (I was in the aisle seat with nobody beside me), got a fix on a handful of satellites (my shit got a twelve-channel receiver!) and bam! My position was instantly calculated and displayed on a small LED screen. Kind of nice to know just where a mutha fucka is at all times!

Anywho…we'd been flying for several hours and the flight had been un-eventful. Security at Baltimore-Washington International had been tight, but nothing overbearing—my designer belt buckle had set the metal detector off (what else is new!) and then they went through the pockets of my leather jacket because my Beemer key looked suspiciously fat under the X-ray machine. (Don't any of these fuckers drive a *luxury* car???) I was frisked by an elderly white guy (hourly employee, no doubt!) under the watchful eyes of a pair of National Guardsmen dressed in camouflage with their fingers on the trigger of their M-16 rifles. After that I chilled at the gate until boarding time, looking around like a hawk at my fellow passengers, trying to see if there were any fine honeys that I might get next to. Alas, no such luck. That was cool with me—I needed to save my strength for when I arrived in Mo Bay, ya know? I decided to call my other best friend, my boo, Erika, a.k.a. Sassy, even though it was before seven a.m. Shit, she hadn't even called me last night to give me a send-off, so screw her if I wake her black ass up!

"Sassy, what's up, girl?" I said, booming into my cell.

"This better be a fucking emergency, I swear to God." I could hear her turning over in her bed. *Good, I got her at just the right time.*

"What up, boo? You forgot about your main man or what? Gonna let me get on a plane without any goodbyes? You know that shit ain't right!"

A stream of expletives escaped from her mouth, and I just had to laugh out loud. I loved it when she talked dirty to me. Erika and I have been down since I don't know when. At least as long as Vince and me. Actually, we had been friends since our college days, staying tight and sharing with each other the kind of things usually reserved for same-sex friendships. But Erika was down. She was cool. One of the fellas. I let her know that every chance I got.

"Look, baby girl, sorry to wake you, but I just had to holla at you before I go."

"No, your dumb ass just had nothing else to do while waiting at the gate! Am I right?" Erika responded.

"See, now I'm hurt."

"Well, fuck you!" She laughed. "Trey, I only got one thing to say to you, since you never listen to me anyway—are you listening?"

"Yeah, Sassy. Fire away."

"Trey, use protection. You hear me???" I laughed loudly as I grunted, and disconnected her dumb ass...

Okay—here I am just ranting and raving, going on and on about this and that, and I haven't even taken the time to properly introduce myself. Where are my manners? My mother would not be proud! So, here it goes...

My name is Trey Alexander. I'm thirty-three years old, living in Chocolate

City (that's the nation's capital, D.C., for all of you who are not in the know!) I'm a divorce lawyer, admitted to the bar in D.C., Virginia, and New York. I work for a prestigious law firm in D.C.—and, no, I'm not going to tell you the name, 'cause some of you bitches just might call information and try to get my digits—I'm not having that! I'm originally from New York, Brooklyn, to be exact, and yes, that totally explains my cocky, in-your-face attitude and demeanor (fuck you, very much!) But to paraphrase what I've said habitually, "Don't hate the playa, hate the game!"

I've been in D.C. for about ten years—I came here to go to law school, Georgetown, thank you very much, and been here ever since. I love D.C.—love the atmosphere, the people, and most of all, the *ratio* of women to guys! When I got to this mutha fucka I said to myself, "This is soooooo me!" And here I am!!!! For real!

Anyway, I've lived in D.C. the entire time I've been here—right now I've got myself a stylish crib off 15th and U, a two-story condo with, check it—a doorman! Yeah! I'm moving on up, to the East side...you already know what I drive, but in case you haven't been paying attention, my ride is a sexy ass, black M3, courtesy of the firm. Yeah, late last year I won this high-profile divorce and child custody case for a prominent, white McLean plastic surgeon. The case was very complex and extremely nasty, so the Beemer was my bonus for winning. Listen, I love the ride and all, but to be truthful, when I think about it, I billed close to one hundred thousand dollars on that case alone, so that's the least they could do!

Let's see—what else can I tell ya—last year I cleared two hundred thirty-eight thousand dollars in salary. I'm not a partner, and that used to be a sore subject for me, but in the last nine to twelve months I've come to grips with the fact that Trey here does not intend to put in the hours that are demanded of an up-'n'-coming partner-to-be. My motto is and has always been—"work hard, play even harder!" And I live that maxim every day of my life. The firm gets its money's worth out of me; don't get me wrong. But when my workday is done, it is done, and don't talk shit to me about my professional gig. At that point it's Miller time, and Trey is ready to party! So, I'm cool with the salary and bennies they give me, my phat ride, crib in the city, and plenty of punany to chase after and keep me hoppin'! Now, I know the next question on your mind, so let's dispense with it right now: Girlfriend? Wife? Significant other, you ask? Not only "no" to those questions, but "fuck no!" Does that answer your question???

✠✠

Less than an hour later the clear, fresh aquamarine waters of Jamaica rolled underneath the belly of our jet as we approached Montego Bay. The lush hills of the island slipped beneath us as we landed into the wind. An ancient jeep that was painted just like the one on *M*A*S*H* (for those of you old enough—like me—to remember that show) stood off the main runway by a tin-slatted hut. As we deplaned onto the tarmac, the heat hit me square in the face and chest. Hard to believe that less than eight hours earlier, I had been in forty-degree weather. "Welcome to Jamaica," a sign proclaimed as we made a right turn and headed for the terminal and (I hoped) air conditioning. I was here. The vacation was beginning! Ah yeah!

I'll dispense with the details. Suffice it to say, it took me close to two hours by bus to get from Mo Bay to my resort in Negril (located on the western part of the island). It was hot as hell and the roads were—pardon my French— fucked up! I mean half that island was in disrepair and the roads were in the midst of a serious reconstruction. That meant that every few minutes or so our Jamaican driver would have to downshift and maneuver around pot holes large enough for a horse to lie in. Along the way we saw some interesting sights—cows and/or steer (I don't know the damn difference!) grazing on the side of the road; a Pizza Hut and KFC that our driver was so damn proud of, he had to slow down and get on the fuckin' P.A. system to announce; fishermen on the side of the road carrying fresh fish on a line; sellers of assorted fruits, beer, Bob Marley hats; bicycle tires or perhaps steering wheel covers (carried around their dark necks), and of course, ganja—yeah, these mutha fuckas actually ran alongside of our bus as we went through intersections trying to sell us this shit; a guy barefoot carrying groceries on top of his head…I thought I had died and gone to Africa!

There were five of us on the bus—two bruthas from Chicago who had gone to Howard and were therefore familiar with the D.C. area. And a nice, chatty, young, white couple named Lance and Chris from Louisiana. We got through the introductions and the normal chatter—first time to Jamaica? First time to this resort? Yada yada... But finally, we turned into our hotel complex and I breathed a sigh of relief. We were finally here. Yes, Lawd!

I thought check-in would be a breeze, but guess what? Our rooms weren't ready. I guess some things never change, regardless of what part of the world you are in. They invited us to leave our bags out front and relax in the dining room where a lavish buffet was in full effect. I was totally down with that. I sat with the H.U. bruthas and scanned the room for honeys as we ate...saw a few that definitely caught my eye. Everyone but us was clad in tee shirts, bikinis, colorful sarongs—sunglasses adorned their heads—carrying plates loaded with food to rounded tables. Open bar (this was an all-inclusive place, and I was not mad at anybody, you hear me!), so the Jamaican rum and other top-shelf shit was flowing! An hour later we were stuffed, and I was ready to lose my jeans, Nikes, and jacket, find a spot on the beach under one of them palm trees with plenty of shade and catch a snooze—after all, I'd been up since four.

I sauntered over to the front desk where my H.U. boyz had already checked in and were following the bellmen to their room. I waved goodbye and waited my turn. Come to find out, there was a problem with my room reservation. Now listen, don't fuck with me after I've flown close to fifteen hundred miles and put these six days, five nights on my Visa—I had all the proper paperwork and documentation in my leather carryon—just give me a minute to get to it. No, that wasn't it, I was told—the crux of the matter was that the resort was under renovation. Funny—no one (especially my travel agent) had mentioned that *minor* point to me...an entire section of rooms (ocean view—*my* ocean view room, btw!) was closed, in addition to the main pool and disco!

Okay...here we go! It's about to get ugly up in here! OH HELL NO! I put on my best "don't-fuck-with-me-I'm-an-attorney" face and voice, kept my composure but told the cute, but tight-lipped Jamaican woman behind the desk that she (and this place) was about to have a serious problem if they didn't produce a comparable room ASAP! She ducked into the back, presumably to consult her manager since the computer terminal at the front desk wasn't telling her shit—came out a few moments later (okay, more like five to ten minutes later), smiley face painted back on just right. This was what they were going to do—they had a sister resort literally right next door— she genuflected with a smile like she was Vanna fuckin' White—and it had some very nice ocean-front rooms that were available—I'd be transferred there—I'd retain the use of the privileges at this resort for the entire week, if I'd like—and, here's how they got me to ease up on a sistah pronto—for my inconvenience, they would comp me three days to be used the *next* time I came back here to Jamaica and to this resort!

Hmmm, three days…suddenly things weren't looking that bad…but hold up—tell me more about this other resort, I inquired. I mean, what kind of place was this; what kind of amenities did they have? The Jamaican woman with her dark, perfectly smooth skin smiled a seductive smile as she leaned in toward me, knowing that she now had my full attention. Here's the thing— this place next door was really nice—and (she just *knew* from looking at me that I'd love this part), they had a nude side and a prude side…

Nude side! Did someone say, nude side!?! My mind raced for a nanosecond—let me see, does that mean nude honeys flocking by my open window as waves crash onto the white sand every few moments, I wondered??? Hmmm, tell me more, baby, don't let me interrupt you…

Pause—since y'all don't know me that well yet, let me say this right up front—I ain't never been no exhibitionist…okay? I mean, this brutha is comfortable, *very comfortable* with his body, but that doesn't mean I get into this naked, holistic, I'm down with nature, let my shit swing free, au naturel shit! I've been to a nude beach before—hasn't everybody? Actually, when I was growing up in NYC, my parents took me to Jones Beach one day and I wandered over the dunes to this spot where there were a whole lot of wrinkled white women with droopy tits and men with little dicks prancing around like spring chickens! Please! That didn't do shit for me. But the thought of being here, in Jamaica, for God's sake, with (and here's where my mind began to fuck with me)—Rachel-looking honeys with dark and lovely hair, big butts, luscious tits—and a smile that would kill a brutha—well, I guess I was just gonna have to take my chances. After all, I was on vacation. No problem, mon! Right???

Thirty minutes later I was in my new room—ocean-front, nude side—facing palm trees, white sand, aquamarine blue water, and honeys with bare titties and shaved pussies wandering by my open mutha fuckin' window, I kid you not—king-size bed, mirrored ceiling (hello!?!—did they create this mutha fucka just for me???) Things in an *instant* were looking up. Note to self—call travel agent when I get home—curse the bitch out, then send her a dozen roses! Three extra days for my trouble? Oh, no trouble, really! OH HELL YEAH! Trey in 'da house! Time to get naked, y'all! For real!

Two

The breeze that swept in from the island beyond the beach made it perfect. It was one of those light breezes, the kind that tickles your hair and ears as it passes by, not enough to billow dresses or shirts, but with dazzling stars overhead and the full moon shining off to the west, its light cascading down onto the shore, illuminating palm trees and hammocks, it felt wonderful. The open-air disco was packed, every inch of planked floor taken up with frenzied dancers. The thump from the bass of rhythm and blues was intoxicating as men in comfortable linens and sandals, women clad in short or long flowing cotton skirts and tank tops, glistened with sweat as they twirled and dipped. The beat took control, forced movement even to those uninitiated as drinks flowed from well-stocked bars with efficient tenders.

Vince Cannon, Jr. sat on a high stool and watched from the teak bar, a long, solid, rectangular thing of beauty that butted against one wall facing the moonlit beach. A tall frosty drink with an orange and pink paper umbrella lay untouched in front of him. He observed his best friend, Trey Alexander, twenty yards away as he danced with his woman. He was overdressed, as only Trey could be—tapered, off-white sport coat and matching flat-front trousers; a thin, yellow V-neck sweater and loafers—a dark oblong stone attached to a cord that hung from his tanned neck. Trey was happy, that much was obvious. The way he smiled, his teeth shining from one end of the open-air room to the other. His woman—dressed to a tee in a thin, slinky white and red dress with leopard skin-like patterns, high-heel red sandals, hair pulled back in a bun—threw her head back and grinned as Trey spun her around, a thin, sinewy arm outstretched toward the high ceiling. They danced well together, Vince had to give them that—the way they moved in sync with each other—it was as if Trey would silently telegraph upcoming moves to her without so much as a nod or a wink, and she would follow suit. For a moment, Vince felt a surge of pang in his heart—not jealousy—he was never jealous of Trey—they had known each other far too long and were way too close for that. Looking out over the sea of bodies, an ocean of writhing forms that undulated like the sea in a storm, he felt a twinge of envy—that said it best. And mid center, almost in the glow of spotlights and lasers that cut through the smoke and perspiration that hovered like mist above the heads, he spotted those two and locked onto their flow. The look that she had on her face right then, at that very moment as Trey reached for her, pulled her into him, and wrapping his arms around her half bare back as he kissed her longingly—yes, that look—when he pulled back from the kiss, her lips wet from him—said it all. At that moment Vince felt envy. Because of that look and the feeling that undoubtedly accompanied it—the feeling of pure, unconfined love—the way their eyes locked onto each other's and no one else's—the sea continued to bubble and foam, but to the two of them, theirs was an island, deserted save for them two.

Vince shifted in his stool, took a swig of the tall drink—felt the breeze as it ran past his glasses and through his dark hair, the ceiling fans turning out of sync to the D.J.-spun music, something from an old Prince jam, back in the day—old school, when he was still funky. The kind of groove that made you want to grab onto anything in sight and move—Vince lifted his glass in a toast as he caught Trey's eyes and grin. Trey made a fist and raised it above the crowd in triumph before returning his stare to the object of his affection. Vince shook his head with a laugh and then, as he caught her eye, smiled and nodded—yes, girl, you've found someone special, I know, and I can feel your ecstasy even from here.

Then it happened—just as the music downshifted and bodies parted, making for dry land—relief from tired feet. Trey and his lady came out of a spin and slowed down, his arm finding her waist, she leaning into him and them turning a quarter turn more before stopping on the floor. Vince watched silently, almost missing that moment as he signaled the bartender for a second drink. Trey kissed her silently, let his lips fall onto hers and absorb the warmth and love as they touched. And then he wiped the sweat that had formed on his head, hiked up a pant leg with a quick tug of his hand, and sank to one knee. It was a move that did not go unnoticed. Patrons were caught off guard; the music's beat moving way too fast for this to be part of any dance ritual. Even she played it off for a brief moment, laughing for a second before the smile was wiped from her face as she looked down and saw the seriousness in his eyes. Trey was staring up, child-like, the gaze unbroken as he searched her face slowly, memorizing each curve of her smooth dark flesh. He grasped her hands lightly; Vince sat up, then got off the bar stool as the music subsided—the D.J. realizing that a special moment was about to unfold—and so he panned the sound down until the room was still—the disco patrons pointing, looking, whispering, conversing and wondering about what was about to go down. Trey cleared his throat as Vince, mesmerized by the sight of his best friend on bended knee, took a step forward, wondering like the rest of the crowd, what was going on?

"Baby," he said in a soft, yet deep voice. It carried across the room and out onto the veranda by the beach. "I've reached a point in my life where I honestly can't go on." Trey paused for a moment. He was smiling up at her, noticing the beads of fear, not sweat, that formed at her brow. "It has taken me a long time to get to this place—and so, I've got no choice but to share with you what is on my mind...Okay?"

She nodded silently.

"Baby. You make me so incredibly happy. I can't begin to describe this feeling that I've had since you've entered by life. It's a feeling that I've never experienced before. I keep waiting for this dream to end—for me to wake up and sigh, but you know what? This is no dream. This is real—you are real. And this *love* I feel is real."

Vince turned his head away for a second to catch a glimpse of the crowd, wanting to know if anyone else in the disco was hearing what he had heard. He watched several couples as they nuzzled close to one another. Then he shook his head again, as if to say to himself and the others, yeah, this definitely is one hell of a dream—to think that my man Trey here would even *consider* this kind of thing…I mean, we're talking about *Trey*…but then he saw the tear that meandered down her cheek and heard his best friend continue.

"And so, I want to say this to you in front of all of these special people here tonight, as God is my witness—that I love you with all of my heart, and from this moment forward, I pledge to be *faithful*…"

Vince had been standing by the bar, elbow on the teakwood when he processed those simple, yet powerful words. His pulse increased as the full realization of what was happening began to take shape. He shuffled forward, his eyes not able to leave the scene unfolding before him.

"I pledge to be the kind of man that is worthy to stand beside a queen." Trey was sweating, but he made no move to wipe the perspiration that layered his bald head. Vince blinked.

"And so, baby, tonight, I ask you the most important question I've ever asked anyone in my life…" The pang hit Vince again, like a left hook—it was a straight shot to the heart—powerful in its delivery. He watched as Trey's woman stood there—the look on her face said it all—that completeness that accompanies true, uncompromising love. Vince blinked again.

"Baby, I need to know whether you will be with me forever." Vince felt weak; the sweat that had popped out from his own forehead now meandered down his face through his closely cropped beard to his chin.

"Need to know, baby, whether you will consent…" Trey's hand was emerging from his pocket with a velvet-covered box. The onlookers had been dead quiet, wanting to grasp every breath, every single utterance. But when Trey produced that box there was a collective sigh that drifted throughout the room. He let go of her hand for an instant, the box was opened and at that moment a beam of light hit the diamond that was nestled inside, sending fragments of light out from the epicenter like a pebble that is dropped into a still lake…

Vince swallowed hard, felt the thump as it pounded against his chest, and blinked again…

✠✠✠

...And opened his eyes to a new dawn. He was lying on his side—a thick, pale-blue comforter pulled up to the nape of his neck. He sighed, felt his heart beating loud and clear as it danced inside his entire being. He lay still, feeling the pulse in his neck as it throbbed before settling down into a normal rhythm. He scanned the room with his eyes—first to the dark stained wooden chest where his wristwatch and thick college ring lay, then sweeping to the left and the half open bathroom door that lay beyond. He caught a glimpse of a shiny light blue bathrobe hanging from a hook on the inside. A ceiling fan turned sluggishly in the morning. An oversized tabby cat lay belly up and motionless at the foot of the bed.

Vince turned over, felt the large, thick mattress yield to his weight as he shifted to his left side and came face-to-face with Maxine. She lay on her side facing him, her eyes shut, dark, shoulder-length hair partly covering her soft face, the rise and fall from her breathing visible as the covers shifted around them. Vince loved to watch Maxi sleep—there was something so serene and peaceful about the way she slept, never twitching or moving—no, Maxi found her place and gave in to the feeling of slumber—allowing herself to be drawn into that deep, dark hole, swallowed up and consumed—a place that held not fear for her, but comfort. Maxi loved to sleep. And Vince loved to watch her doing so.

But now, on the cusp of this new day, Vince felt sadness that permeated his soul, replacing the feeling of tense anguish that had forced him from his dream state. It was slowly overtaking him—he could sense it, feeling it, the way a cup of hot tea that is drunk seeps in to stiff veins and warms one's entire being. Melancholy and downheartedness spread from limb to limb as he stared at Maxi's prone form and thought of yesterday...

It had turned out to be a wonderful day. Saturday morning spent running errands—bill paying, picking up some much needed supplies for the studio, stopping by the grocery store—much later in the afternoon, heading home, showering, changing, and then riding over to Maxi's. He took the Harley—his baby, as he was fond of calling her—a 1998 Fat Boy—purple with gray tank and trim—a custom paint job he had gotten done two years ago from a bike shop down in Richmond. He loved that thing, especially the way it sounded—eighty-eight cubic inches and Vance & Hines pipes that gave it a low growl and rumble every time he tapped the throttle. The source of much banter between Trey and him—those pipes. Trey swore his were louder. Of course, Trey was always dissing Harleys. That began last year when he went out and spent twenty-five grand on an Indian. Now it was Indian this and Indian that! The two of them loved to meet in Old Town in the evening after work, where the rest of the Hogs congregated, Trey pulling up with his beast, all of the Harley dudes stopping their conversation in mid-sentence when he downshifted to a stop—"damn, that's a fucking *Indian*!" Didn't see many of those on the road—not at all! Yeah, Trey loved that aspect—even got a tattoo on his arm—became an Indian convert for life! Vince had to admit, the bike was beautiful. But he was sticking with his Fat Boy. Nothing wrong with his girl. She would give that Chief a run for his money any day of the week!

Maxi had a small but cozy condo in Arlington by the courthouse. Vince had shown up in jeans and an oversized sweater that complemented his rich, dark skin; leather boots and jacket that together with his six-foot frame, muscles, closely cropped hair, and beard made him look rugged in a sexy kind of way. Maxi had chosen a pair of Levi's jeans and black stretch blouse that showed off her curves—she pulled her hair back and tied it down; her thin, black-rimmed glasses were set against her smooth dark face. One thing about Maxi—she didn't use a lot of makeup. Didn't have to. And Vince dug that. She splashed on some perfume, grabbed a light jacket that accentuated her leather boots, and was good to go.

They took her car into downtown around eightish—they felt like being around people but not in a dense crowd—so they settled on 18th Street Lounge for drinks—a hip, diversified place with acid jazz, plenty of comfortable couches, and great Cosmopolitans. They found a nice quiet table by the window overlooking Connecticut Avenue, ordered a round of drinks—Maxi was a Johnnie Walker Black and Coke kind of girl—and Vince was in the mood for a Cosmo. They talked about their work week and family—

Maxi was from Detroit and spoke to her family regularly; Vince still had his parents here in D.C., and visited them each week, faithfully for Sunday night dinner unless he was out of town on a speaking engagement. The conversation flowed freely and without force—they had been dating for about a month now—so they were still circling around each other somewhat cautiously, but their guard had been lowered.

Maxi really liked Vince—for the first time in a long while she was with a man who didn't play games and was sincere. That's what defined Vince for her more than anything—the fact that he was so genuine. Most of the men she had dated since arriving here in D.C. two years ago were full of themselves and so full of shit. She had gotten so tired of the dating scene—going to the obligatory happy hours with her friends from work, meeting these knuckleheads—good looking, yet overly confident men who talked a big game, but always turned out to be nothing but big liars! Then she had met Vince one night at a book signing at the Barnes & Noble in Georgetown. He had seemed almost too nice at first—confident, but not cocky, intelligent, smooth in his delivery, the way he listened when she spoke—that was clearly his gift. He made people think as if they were the only one in the room when he spoke to them.

Vince immediately had dug her, too! They had exchanged small talk after he signed his book—*Finding Nirvana: A Quintessential Game Plan for Success*, for her. She had hung back—letting the rest of the small crowd that had gathered to hear him speak go to him—but they disbursed quickly. Afterwards, he had come up to her—remembered her name—that got him points big time—and asked her to join him for a coffee at the Starbucks down the street. Nothing big, no fancy first date—just good conversation at a coffee shop on a Sunday night. She recalled how he had laughed when he told her that she had eyes just like Nia Long—and stroked her arm—that had sent chills down her spine when he did that. They had been seeing each other ever since.

For Vince—especially in the beginning, she had him all excited like a kid in a candy store—Maxi was something that didn't just come along every day. She was intelligent, had a good job, good looks—not a show stopper—

not a hottie as Trey was fond of calling them—but, and most importantly, she was drama free—a definite keeper, no doubt about that. He liked her because he saw the potential in her—it was there during that first night at Starbucks as they chatted over chai tea and a grande latte—a future with this woman. In Vince's line of work as a speaker/writer—he met all kinds of women day in and day out. Most, unfortunately, were just not all that. On the surface they were nice—but if he dug down, like a diver who dips below the surface of the waves, he'd find the baggage and the drama that inevitably would push him away. Life was way too short to settle for stuff like that. And so, Vince would move on…thanks, but no thanks.

Last night, sitting there at 18th Street, sipping a really good Cosmo, watching Maxi with her Nia Long eyes smile as they conversed, he felt good. That was the one thing about Maxi—they had fun together. Wherever they went, whatever they did, whether they decided to stay in and watch a DVD or go out to a club, they had fun. Good conversation; Maxi was not the kind of girl that bitched and complained about stuff—instead always upbeat and fun. And she was one of those self-sufficient women that impressed Vince a great deal. They weren't in each other's face 24/7, and Vince appreciated the fact that Maxi gave him his space. She had her own friends here—she hung with her girls and had some after-work activities—she was taking a photography class downtown and was really getting into that—spending a great deal of her free time with a Nikon slung around her shoulder, speeding up New York Avenue, M Street, or Wisconsin looking for stuff to shoot. If they didn't talk on the phone every day, no one had a melt down. *How refreshing*, Vince thought!

After 18th Street they went across Connecticut to Dragonfly, an eclectic sushi bar that played house and trance, and displayed weird Japanese-produced cartoons on its white walls. They finally got a table around eleven, ordered quickly because they both were famished—some really good sushi and sashimi, along with Coronas to wash the food down. The place was packed—a wacky kind of crowd in terms of dress and demeanor. But neither Vince nor Maxi paid much attention to them—they talked some more—Maxi about this project she was working on at her job—she was a software developer for a small, Internet start-up in northern Virginia. Vince listened attentively as she described some of the problems they were having with their code. Then shifting gear, talking about stuff in general—what he was working on in his studio. She had only gone there one time and watched in quiet awe as he worked on his art.

A little after midnight, they drove to The Saint on 14th. A relatively short line had formed—they waited patiently for the bouncer to let them in. Maxi recognized a few folks—they exchanged their hellos. Once inside, Vince grabbed a Corona and water from the bar and found Maxi standing by a pillar overlooking the dance floor. The Saint was packed—mostly young, college-aged folks—black, white, Puerto Rican, Spanish, even Asian up in the spot this evening. The music was bumping, and after a few minutes of small talk, Vince led Maxine to the crowded dance floor. A rapid-fire succession of really good songs came on—nice grooves and bass lines— hip-hop and rap by Jermaine Dupri, Ja Rule, and Ludacris—they danced close together, Maxi moving with rhythm the way most black girls do—like they invented the shit! Vince grinned and followed along, doing his own thing, enjoying the feeling of grooving with his lady. They had fun and got a bit sweaty as they lip-synced along with the tunes—Jay-Z, R. Kelly, and an upbeat new jam from Mary J. Blige that Maxi just loved.

By one-thirty a.m. they were heading home, Vince driving, Maxi a bit tipsy from the Black and Cokes she had downed. They made it back to her place without fanfare. When they arrived, Maxi kept the lights off and shades parted, turned on the stereo to WKYS—they were playing slow jams with little commercial interruption this time of night. She giggled softly as she shed her clothes, leaving a trail of her evening's attire around the living room. Vince watched as he undressed quietly. And then they lay down, right there on the carpet, and made love, stray flecks of warm street lighting creating patterns across their bare bodies as they moved, not as quietly as they normally do—Maxi's inhibitions being smothered by the liquor—a warm, comforting feeling overtaking her and causing her moans and squeals to increase in pitch and intensity. In the background, Aaliyah's sultry voice: ...*Rock the boat, rock the boat, work the middle, work the middle...change position...*

stroke it for me, stroke it for me... Vince was enjoying himself completely, taking pleasure in the sensation of being inside her, making love to her face-to-face, eyes locked on each other as they thrust their flushed bodies against one another, Maxi's head resting in Vince's hands. They both felt the passion build and then spill over, overflowing, Maxi crying out, and Vince covering her mouth with his as he joined her in orgasm. After a few moments of feeling the afterglow that comes from this kind of exquisite release, they lay together on the carpet for a while in silence, listening to the radio, old school songs with soulful melodies keeping them both awake. Some time later they climbed into her bed and fell asleep, Vince spooning Maxi tight, his hands covering her breasts as if they were precious gems, his pelvis nuzzling against her nude flesh, as they both settled down into that deep, dark hole, and dreamed very different dreams...

✠✠✠

In an instant, things can, and do change forever. And in this case, it was that image of a moonlit beach somewhere in paradise, Vince's buddy on bended knee—a sea of bodies huddled together, bonded in kindred spirits by this special moment—the look between lovers that would forever be frozen in time by his psyche—knowing unconditionally and without question what that look meant. What it said inescapably to him and to the others: this was the *one*. And that is what changed it, in an instant, for Vince. That knowing—that guttural, instinctual knowledge that is visceral—Maxi was *not* the one. In a sense, Vince had known that from the moment he had laid eyes on her at the book signing. Maxi was a wonderful girl—that was not even in question. She was successful, independent, and possessed good looks...also, brave, clean, and reverent! But at the end of the day, what mattered most to Vince, was that she was not the *one*. He did not love her. Not today, not tomorrow, and whether or not he *ever* could was also not the question—the fact remained—Vince needed and desired to possess that quality which he saw with pinpoint clarity in his mind's eye. Pure, unconfined love—the sea may continue to bubble and foam around him, but to

Vince—he desired a woman that to the two of them, theirs was an island all unto themselves...

And so, on the cusp of this new day, Vince once again felt the sadness infuse his being until he was consumed, his soul overflowing with its soup. He rose quietly, began the shower and stood underneath, letting the hot water batter his face and neck, massaging his shoulders and back like a masseuse. He tilted his head back and closed his eyes, not from the spray, but from the injury, the wound that was smarting. He stayed in there a very long time, going over it again and again in his mind. But Vince was no stranger to the verse that rang inside of his head. This was a movie, which was all too familiar. He knew deep down inside exactly what he was searching for. Always hoping that he'd find it around the next corner, the next one who came along and smiled at him. He'd give each one a chance—that much was for sure—Vince, the kind of man who saw beauty in everything that crossed his path. It was there somewhere, if you just knew where to look and nurture it. But, sadly, at the end of the day, beauty alone did not bring him any closer to finding the one thing that kept him rising every day with a smile to continue his journey—true, unconditional love.

Vince dressed quietly, careful not to disturb sleeping Maxi. He said a silent prayer for her and for himself—that the two of them would one day find the happiness and the passion that made life worth living. That special something that was beyond the thrill of money, sex, or power.

Before he left, Vince bent down, kissed Maxi on her cheek—she opened her eyes briefly, those Nia Long eyes watching him silently for a moment before she smiled, turned and stretched like a cat before saying: "Vince Cannon, Jr., you were soooooo wonderful last night..." Then she closed her eyes and purred back to sleep, contentment etched into her face like an ancient hieroglyphic. Vince remained for a moment more, watching her settle back down into that place, free of fear and strife, before he climbed onto his motorcycle, still damp from the morning dew, and rode off into the rising sun.

Three

First mutha fucking thing I did—no, it was not unpack! I slipped out of my clothes, took a quick shower to erase that airplane/travel smell, oiled my body up with lotion and sunscreen until my shit shined like I was in a bodybuilding competition…threw on a pair of designer swim trunks, a wifebeater, black sandals, the bad-ass sunglasses, and headed out to case the joint! Wanted/needed to get the lay of the land so to speak—I began with the open-air dining area where another lavish buffet was in full effect. I breezed through there like a movie star, head and chin up, fly shades on, pausing at the bar to order a Sangaster's original Jamaican rum cream. The dude behind the bar filled my glass with ice and rum cream—I took one sip and suddenly felt the reggae vibe as it coursed through me. Yeah, mon! Strolled around the grounds, checking things out—a few restaurants and bars—a 24/7 gym with free weights, Nautilus, and machines, duty free store, tennis courts, squash courts, and basketball courts. I passed by this fine, Jamaican honey dressed in tight, pink bellbottoms and a matching, low cut top that proudly displayed her lovely tits in a push-up bra! She said, "Welcome to Jamaica, mon!" I smiled while eying her lovely curves.

"Just get in?" she asked while sneaking a peek at my chest tattoo.

I smiled back. "Yes, I did—and loving it already."

"Prude side or nude side?" she inquired while resting a hand on a waist that was no more than twenty inches in circumference.

"Nude side," I exclaimed proudly, thrusting my chest out like it wasn't any big deal to me! "You gonna come by for a visit?" I asked all cockily.

"Oh," she said, softly, licking her lips seductively, while thinking of a comeback. Her nametag was attached to her flimsy top, but I was having a hard time concentrating on the lettering. "*They* gonna have fun with you!"

"Bring it on, I ain't *scared*," I replied, pronouncing the word "scared" like "scurred," the way Mystikal, that fly rapper from the Dirty South had made famous in his song, "Shake Ya Ass." Then as she walked away with a wave of her hand, I was left standing there observing the rise and fall of her ass cheeks in those pink pants, thinking to myself, who were *they*????

✠✠✠

A sign proclaimed, "Nude Beach—No Photography!"—alrighty then! I had walked down to the beach, prude side first, observed the folks: black, white, Europeans, Jamaicans, and whatnot, baking in the sun. Folks looking good, I'll give them that. Walked past the watercraft—sunfishes, catamarans, kayaks, bicycles with huge oversized tires for use in the water, past the Jamaican locals who were selling wood carvings, trinkets, and jewelry on tables under the shade of palm trees—past rows of white plastic lounge chairs filled with holiday travelers lying out and just chillin'—until the sign slowed me in my tracks. Okay, here we go…

Walking past, I observed a number of couples lying about, butt-naked, mostly white, a few with some pigment to them, bushes neatly trimmed. Saw a lot of silicone—you can guess that I'm a self-proclaimed expert on titties, and can spot the fake ones a mile away—not that I'm mad at any of these ladies—do your thing, girls, I am not complaining!

The beach curved slightly to the left, and at the end off to the right was the pool area. I walked up the stone steps slowly eyeing those around me. The place was fairly well packed. A bunch of people, all butt-naked in the pool and by the swim-up bar area, checked me out as I strolled by looking for a place to chill and lay my things. I was still in my trunks and tee, but that was about to change. Through my shades I observed tits and much ass, and a few dicks, how could I not, and I have to say, I was impressed (with the tits/ass, *not* dicks)! Most of the women here, okay, let me say this—close to seventy percent, looked damn good! I mean, there were a few pigs; I'm not trying to be mean, just telling it like it is…but seriously, most looked okay in my book. The women were an average age of thirty-five I would say, and in good shape. The guys on the other hand were a mixed bag—some were fit, but most were carrying around a beer gut. I saw one brutha over by the edge of the pool sitting alone, lost in thought. Didn't pay him any mind. Past him was a hot tub the size of most YMCA pools. In the middle, was a whirlpool that currently held about eight people, all shaded and drinks in hand or close by.

I slowed my already unhurried gait and found an empty lounge chair with a good view of the festivities. My heart was thumping as I readied to remove my clothes—not from fear, just the opposite, in fact—my mind churning from the possibilities…endless possibilities. Bending down, I pushed my trunks off like they were an afterthought, balled them up and lay them under my lounge chair. The tee came off next and finally the sandals. Mutha fuckas were watching, I kid you not—oh yeah, they were checking a brutha out—seeing what I was packing. Now, let me stop you right there and keep it real. I ain't no Long Dong Silver; I ain't packing eighteen inches, no, not hardly—but my shit is nice; I've been told I've got a beautiful cock. It doesn't hang very low, but trust me, when you awaken that bad boy, that mutha fucka inflates to a nice length and solid girth. And that's when the ladies hold their hands over their mouths (and pussies) and exclaim, "Oh *my!*"

I glanced left, spied the towel rack behind the enormous hot tub that was empty this time of day. I casually walked to get a towel, shades on and nothing else, my shit tight and on-point! Mutha fuckas were clocking me, I swear to God, as I grabbed a towel and slowly sauntered back to my lounge chair. A few smiled, but most just *watched*…I gave them the show I knew they were craving…doing a very slight pimp roll, you know how *we* do…not too much leaning, but head up and chest out; stomach tight; arms flexed; a thick, expensive Breitling Blackbird on my left wrist; a thin, sterling silver bracelet on my right, each jingling as I walked by the onlookers. I flung the towel onto the chair without missing a single stride; cut to the right and pool edge, bent down, one arm on the concrete and in one fell swoop, I gracefully entered the cool, refreshing water. Took my shades off for a moment as I submerged my head, then quickly returned the shades 'cause it was bright out! Swam over to the swim-up bar, mutha fuckas making a path for me as I went. Yeah, buddy! Who's mutha fuckin house is 'dis???

The bartender was a dark, Jamaican brutha with black shades on and a Hawaiian shirt. He was bopping to reggae music emanating from a boom box behind the bar. I nodded to a few couples as I edged over, ordered a rum punch, and said a few "Waz ups" to people who eyed me cautiously. Got my drink, took a sip and touched the bartender fist-to-fist, giving him dap. I nodded. "Respect," he replied.

I turned and headed back to my chair, being clocked by the women as I went. It felt real good. I mean, I hadn't been here five fucking minutes yet and mutha fuckas already knew I was the shit! Wait 'til I told Vince about this. I suppressed the thought of running back to my crib (a.k.a. my room) and hitting him on the cell—naw, not right this minute, I'm a bit preoccupied...

A woman with a tight-ass body; deep, rich tan, and big titties that were obviously fake ('cause they defied gravity) was sitting on the side of the pool, while her man (or *someone's* man) massaged sunblock into her skin. He ran his hands over her neck and then descended to her mammoth tits, massaging those bad boys like he was a professional masseuse! She smiled as I went by, drink in hand.

"How you doing?" she asked in a New York accent, looking down over the rim of her designer shades. One leg was up on the edge of the pool, her perfectly shaved pussy was within spitting, or, more accurately, licking distance! The guy continued his massaging like he was on a mutha fuckin' mission! I was not mad at him!

"Livin' large. How YOU doing?" I replied as I stopped in front of her.

"Everyting irie." She threw her head back, long brown hair flowing down her back as she laughed.

"Oh, I didn't know you was Jamaican. Damn, girl!" I laughed with her and sipped my rum punch. Damn, that shit was good! "Listen," I continued with a grin, "if dude here misses a few spots, holla at me...Okay!?!"

"Damn," he said, removing his oily hands from her erect nipples to look at me for the first time, "been here five minutes and already working!" He was grinning; not that I was worried. Dude had a gut and would need a few of his buddies to take me on.

"You know how we do!" I responded while eyeing his honey. One thing about me, one lesson I learned long time ago—look a woman straight in her eyes when you're talking to her. Don't half-step it—none of this glance here, then there—no, that shit just doesn't work. Women love a brutha that will stare them down while he's speaking. Look right through them to their very soul. That shit turns them on. And that's just what the fuck I did— stared straight through this honey while I spoke to him, as if I was saying, "Yeah, I hear ya, my man, but it's *you* I'm talking to!"

"Just might do that," girlfriend replied, licking her lips in a way that I just know was done automatically, without conscious thought—like her lips had a mind of their own and were speaking directly to me.

"You do that, sweetie! I make house calls, too!" Taking another sip I moved on, feeling her eyes as she followed me away. I left the pool damn near the way I entered, with a flex from my upper body and a quick exit. I strolled back to my chair in slo-mo, drops of refreshing, pool water cascading down this bronze brutha's tight body, the weight of dozens of pairs of eyes upon my firm back, sexy tattoos, and ass. My package was right, ya hear! And it felt so damn good to finally be in Jamaica, on vacation. Yeah, mon!

✠✠✠

You know, y'all, I probably should pause right here to explain something for a moment; a clarification, so to speak. One thing you need to know about me, when it comes to women, I am colorblind. I love women—all colors, shapes, and sizes. To me, the only color that matters is the color pink—that's 'cause pink is the mutha fuckin' universal color, ya hear? It may be different shades on the outside—white, black, dark, light, and whatnot, but it's all pink on the inside. Now, some of you are haters—you know who the fuck you are—yeah, I'm looking straight the fuck at you!

And you're sitting there thinking to yourself, well, Mr. Big Shit over there thinks he's too good for sistahs. Naw, it ain't that at all. Don't get me wrong. I love me some sistahs. I've got nothing but love for my Nubian Queens; I'm serious. But at the same time, give me a blonde with big tits and a black girl's ass and I'm all in that shit, ya hear me??? I mean, I'm gonna fuck that pussy like it is going out of style. So don't hate 'cause I push up on a Latino, an Irish chick, or some corn-bread country thing with big tits and thick hair. I ain't mad at any of them. Long as they got pink pussies...I'm there! Enough said!

By now, the sun was beating down and attacking this black man's body from all angles. Okay! Every few minutes I had to leave the confines of my deck chair and immerse myself in the pool. My bald head was roasting, regardless of the sunblock that I had massaged into my skin. I had refreshed my drink a few times too many I thought already—them rum punches were kicking into overdrive, let me tell you. And it wasn't even dinnertime yet!

I had (mistakenly, I would later learn) taken a book with me to the pool. I rarely got time to read during my "normal" life in D.C. as an attorney and with my busy social commitments, I mean, hey, who has time to read? So I was viewing this vacation as a way to play catch-up on my fiction. I had picked up a few paperbacks at the airport Barnes & Noble, and the one I had begun on the plane now lay on my lounge chair. It was funny, but I had noticed that I was the only mutha fucka in the pool area who had brought a book with them. The book I was reading was entitled "White Teeth" by Zadie Smith—a black woman from England. I remember her from Oprah or some show like that saying something like, "Readers were better than sex!" I'm not sure what that was all about, but I'll tell you this—the book was all that! Anyway, I gotta give this chick credit—the book was damn good—I had totally gotten into the first seventy-five pages on the flight over, so naturally I took it to the pool with me...I mean, why wouldn't I? It had a distinctive red cover with bold white lettering on it. People kept glancing at the book when they walked by me. At first I assumed it was the cover that they were attracted to. Then I realized they had never seen a book in a nude pool area before!

For the first few hours I think I got about two pages read! I kept restarting the same paragraph over and over again. Just when things got interesting (in the book, that is), something in or around the edge of the pool would catch my eye! First it was Ms. Biggums with her Massage Daddy. Then I caught some activity over in the whirlpool—a few honeys were playfully splashing each other's tits with water while their boyfriends watched enviously! I mean, it was getting hard for a brutha to concentrate! And the heat was fucking with me. I decided to take a break and head to my room—time to put on another coat of sunscreen before I baked to a crisp, and see what I could see on the beach side…but before I left, I went to take a quick cool-me-off soak in the whirlpool, and do some quick intros to get acclimated…

I climbed in and over a few folks. Most nodded in approval as I joined them. The fellas and I exchanged some "Waz ups," while the ladies looked on. I caught each of their gazes in turn and said, "Waz up, girlie? My name's Trey," or some variation of that theme as I got out of harm's way from one of the powerful whirlpool jets (that shit was way too close to a brutha's asshole, know what I mean?!) Small talk was exchanged: Just get down here? How you like it so far? (Wink, wink, grin, grin!), you know, shit like that, yada yada yada. A well-built middle-aged guy named Randy from Indiana with a shit-load of tattoos over seventy percent of his body was doing most of the talking at this point. He was loud, but totally cool. His wife, Cathy, was by his side, large tits with pierced nipples and a large tattoo on her navel plunging below to her shaved cunt (I didn't know it was shaved at this point, but trust me, I'd find out this little tidbit later on that evening.) Randy and I vibed right off the bat—he was a regular guy who dug his wife and was down here chilling and enjoying the sunshine, T&A, and reggae music. They owned a restaurant and tattoo parlor back home. I was not mad at them!

"Dude," Randy said in between sipping some kind of banana cream concoction that looked like cum, but smelled a whole lot better, "are you down here with the Lifestyles crew or what?"

"Hmmm?" I responded. Not clear on what he was talking about, I thought maybe he was referring to the condom company—perhaps they were down here doing a promotional bit, giving out condoms and shit…free samples? For real? Hit a brutha up 'cause I'm gonna be fresh out by nightfall!

"Lifestyles," Randy repeated slowly, moving closer to me to be heard over the two honeys across from us who were cackling like a bunch of black crows. "You know, the group?"

"Naw, never heard of 'em." I shook my head while watching the dark nipples surrounded by large, jiggling tits of the brunette in front of me.

"Lifestyles," Randy repeated, "they're a kind of national swingers group—they sponsored a trip to this resort for the past two weeks—you lucky guy, you happen to catch the tail end." He smirked as he checked my reaction over his dark sunglasses. His wife, Cathy, on the other side of me nuzzled against my side and her hand found my leg. She had a smirk of her own.

"You don't say?" I said, smirking now myself. At this point, everyone was just a smirking! "Swingers? You mean most of these folks here are…" I gestured with my hand while lowering my voice and keeping one eye on Ms. Jiggletits, letting the sentence finish itself.

"Oh, yeah," Randy said with a harsh laugh that I would learn was his trademark. He grinned and showed his teeth. "Oh yeah!" he said again while Cathy stroked me, knee to thigh. *DAYUM*, I thought to myself. Things keep getting better and better in this piece!

✠✠✠

I walked slowly back to my room, taking the scenic route. There was a tarmac-covered walkway that cut behind the beachfront and in between the two-story rooms, nicely littered with tall, shade-covering palm trees. A few chickens ran through the underbrush as I sauntered along, following the meandering path, my sandals and sunglasses the only articles of clothing on my person. This actually was a totally new feeling for me—the sense of ultimate freedom, the sun on my exposed flesh as I walked, talked, shook another's hand, took a sip, slept, read—feeling totally relaxed and at ease, as if I was a natural, and had been doing this for years. I admit I was a bit tired (jet lagged, in a sense), but the rum had kicked in and mellowed me the fuck out. I felt the reggae vibe inside of me—it coursed through my limbs and veins even though I heard not a thing—but that was irie with me!

There were a few couples, mostly nude, who walked past me, nodding their welcome. I nodded back, caught up in my own little world. Farther down the winding path was my room. My room key jiggled on an elastic band around my dark ankle. The path wound to the right. I followed, suddenly noticing up ahead a splash of pink. My senses were heightened immediately, on alert—Defcom Three! It was the lovely Jamaican honey I had spoken with hours earlier. In her elbow she carried a metal vase filled with what appeared to be champagne. Two wine stems were curled between long, slender fingers. She was heading toward one of the rooms and it took her a moment to look up and see me. She smiled when she did, glanced down slowly (admiring the package), and then back up. We had stopped at the same place, in front of the same room. My room!

"For little ole me??" I said, batting my eyelashes.

"Doesn't look that *little* to me," she threw back. I laughed as I watched her observing me with a grin. "Just our way of welcoming our newest guests to our fine resort," she said, thrusting the vase in my direction. Her eyes sparkled, and I concentrated on them for a moment, letting my gaze seep in before lowering my stare to her wonderful dark breasts that strained against her tight, sequined bra. Barely covering that was her pink top. I glanced at her nametag—Jackie.

"Well, Jackie," I said, feeling myself growing, enlarging, engorging as I imagined that luscious, tight black ass covering my face and neck, tasting her luscious juices, "it's a good thing you are here," I remarked, lifting my sunglasses onto my bald head so she could see my eyes. I leaned against the doorframe and set down the champagne. Her face changed to a frown as if something was out of place.

"Is something wrong?" she asked, pursing her full lips together. She had on a pair of dangling earrings that sparkled in the sunshine. A thin, matching chain was around her neck. Complementing these, her belly was pierced with a single, knobby piece of silver that winked at me every time I peered down. Trick of light, I presumed.

"Most definitely there is, Jackie," I responded in my serious, attorney voice that I had perfected over the years. "And you arrived not a moment too soon. I was just getting ready to call the front desk." I unlocked the front door with my key and pushed on it, held it open, and gestured for her to enter. "Please, this way." Jackie looked at me for a moment; her eyes sparkled as she sized me up, trying to see if this was a ruse, a ploy to get her into my room. She stood her ground until I lightly touched her thin waist, ran my hand along her back and exerted small amounts of pressure. In unison, we crossed the threshold to my room. I set the glasses down on the dresser as her gaze swept around my room. I held the cold bottle of champagne by the neck in one hand, letting the cold drops of ice water run down my wrist.

"I'm sorry, Mr. ..." Jackie paused.

"Alexander, Trey Alexander," I responded lightly, taking her hand in mine.

"Mr. Alexander then. Is it something with the accommodations?" she asked, twirling around the room to take in its contents. I used this moment to admire her beautiful ass. Two perfectly shapely balls packed in light cotton—I was about to lose my mind! She glanced toward the bathroom, then popped her head in for a brief moment before returning to the side of the bed. I let a moment of silence invade the space before responding.

"Isn't it obvious to you?" I asked, brushing my dick with the bottom of the bottle. The coldness made me flinch. I noticed that Jackie followed my movement with her eyes before responding.

"I'm sorry, Mr. Alexander, you're going to have to be more specific."

"*Indeed*," I said while moving within a foot of her body. She was quite beautiful. I glanced down into her sparkling eyes, which held my attention for a brief moment. "Actually, Ms. Jackie—the problem simply has to do with this bed." I paused while she looked over my shoulder to the well-made bed. She moved around me, tested the bed with her palms before straightening up and staring at me helplessly.

"I fail to see the problem. I'm sorry."

I sighed for effect. "The problem, Ms. Jackie, is *you*. And the fact," I exclaimed, moving within six inches of her, "that *you* aren't in it..."

In the time that it took for her brain to process that information I was on her in an instant—my mouth covered hers as I grasped her small waist, bringing her the remaining distance to me. She struggled (if one can even call it that) for a brief moment—her arms raised up to my smooth chest as if in protest, ran her hands along my nipples and down my forearms—but that ceased as my tongue slipped into her mouth. She groaned as I wrapped my arms around her waist, taking a handful of ass with me along the way. My cock was fully hard now. I pulled her closer to me. Felt her warmth as she came to me, body-to-body, my pulsating dick against the thin fabric of her pink pants. My free hand went to her mouth, touched her face and traced the outline of her lips while I continued to kiss her. She pulled back.

"I…can't…" I gave her enough air to breathe before I ran my tongue around the edge of her mouth and then stuck it back between those divine lips. She licked at me, playfully at first, hands on my arms, as if trying to decide whether to pull me closer or push me away. "Seriously," she said, exhaling forcefully. I glanced down and could see her hardened nipples. I stroked her waist with my free hand, moved it up her belly, lightly touching the piercing before moving to the sequined bra. I ran a fingernail across the material, tracing circles over the exposed top part of her breasts, kneading the flesh with my hand. She moaned again and pulled me into her as she sucked at my tongue. Yeah, there wasn't going to be any further problems with this one…

My hand grabbed her tit and squeezed. Felt those lovely mounds of flesh. She let me squeeze and probe for a moment before she pulled back and ran a hand through her hair.

"Trey—seriously, I can't be doing this. I mean, I work here and…"

Okay—under normal circumstances I might have been tempted to hear this honey out—you know, it can be quite amusing to watch a woman all turned on and shit, pussy dripping, nipples distended, trying to explain why she shouldn't sit on your cock right this particular minute—but today's situation was different. Here I was fifteen-hundred miles from home, in paradise, I swear, standing, with not a stitch of clothing on, beside a beautiful, young Jamaican honey, with my dick harder than high school trigonometry—I wasn't about to let this shit get out of my sight! Nope. So I did what any playa in my situation would do. I pushed up on her; she backed into the closet that housed my clothes and the room safe—until there was no place left to go. I ran a hand down to the valley between her legs and felt for the damp space. It was there, just like I knew it would be. I bent down and kissed her harder this time, taking her upper lip in my mouth and sucking at it like fruit. I kept a firm grip between her legs, my fingers outlining her pussy through the fabric of her tight pants. My dick was pushing against her leg and she couldn't help but feeling it. But on the off chance she had a case of tactile insensitivity, I reached for her hand and brought it to my cock. She inhaled quickly and looked down as her fingers curled around the girth.

"Dayum! That…," she said, swallowing hard, "is one beautiful piece." (See what I mean, I don't make this shit up!) Her hand grasped the shaft and she squeezed it before moving to the head, which she massaged with her palm. "It's sooooo hard!"

"Yes it is, Jackie…look what *you've* done." I smiled while pulling her toward the bed. The door remained open. She glanced to the right as I let go of her hand. She went to the door and slid it shut, locking the bolt in place. I lay back on the bed, checking myself in the ceiling mirror the size of the bed itself. Slowly, Jackie moved back to the bed, a seductive grin on her face. My right hand held the champagne bottle while my left slowly stroked my cock.

"Damn," she exclaimed again, "boy, does that look good. *You* look good. Tattoos and all!" She leaned over me, one hand on the bed, and the other on my stomach. She lightly fingered my nipple, ran a hand across the newest acquisition—the star tattoo, spent a bit of time tracing the outline of the Indian Chief and his headdress—all the while licking her lips seductively. My cock was throbbing; I swear I could see that bad boy pulse!

"Stop playing, girl," I said with a smile. She tugged on my dick, ran a hand down to my clean-shaved balls, lightly squeezing the sacs. I managed to get the bottle open without too much effort. The cork flew off with a loud pop, startling Jackie, who bent down on the mat in front of the bed. Grasping my cock with her hand, she moved closer, lightly blowing on the shaft of my dick with her mouth. My eyes rolled back into my head, but not before I caught a shot of her and myself in the mirror. Damn, wish I had brought the camcorder! Her tongue touched the tip of my dick—she traced the outline of the head, leaving a trail of saliva in its wake. Then down the shaft she went, holding it gingerly, licking it like a child does a lollipop, reaching the base and my balls, giving them a playful tug before heading back up along the other side. With two wet swaths she painted my cock with her tongue, and I was not mad at her! She was incredible. I groaned and held her hair in my hand.

Jackie moved up, kissed my tight stomach, probing my belly button with her tongue before plunging her mouth, without warning, onto my dick. Her warm, wet mouth met my cock and it slipped inside effortlessly, parting lips and pushing her tongue aside in one fell swoop. She kept going down, my hand tightening the grip on her hair as her mouth took as much of me in as deep as she could. I hit the back of her throat, she paused, her eyes opened and she stared back at me, my cock buried to the hilt in her mouth. I took the bottle and ran it across her face. She flinched, but didn't lose any dick in the process—and then she went back to sucking.

"Yes, love, you are so amazing. My God!" I said, as she sucked my member with abandonment. "Shit, don't make me come yet, you hear me?" My words were lost in the sounds of her sucking—slurping, slobbering, suckling sounds that made me twitch in excitement. I reached behind her and unfastened her bra—her tits were fantastic—ripe, soft melons of fruit—small dark nipples that stuck out at attention at least a half-inch. I tugged at them with my fingers, squeezed the fruit, enjoying the feeling of natural flesh (no preservatives or enhancements here)—just 100% woman, soft, spongy titties that fit in the palm of my hand as if they were custom made just for me. Dark lovely nipples, hard as I twisted them between my thumb and forefinger.

"Your cock tastes so damn good!" Jackie exclaimed while leaning back to admire my taut, reclining form.

"You like?" I asked, knowing the answer. "Do I taste good, honey?" I said all baby-like. She glanced up and smiled, her eyes twinkling as she watched me.

"Oh yes, I love the way you taste, the way you smell. I could do this all day."

Hmmm, now there's a thought!

I took the opened bottle of champagne and poured some of the cold liquid onto my cock and stomach. Grabbed her hair and steered her mouth onto my champagne—laced cock. Have some bubbly, I thought to myself with a chuckle! She took it like a good woman should—without any complaints, and sucked me like this would be the last time for both of us. I felt myself stirring—that feeling, that pre-come sensation, which begins like a storm, deep in the bowels of my balls. I forced her off of me.

"What?" She had this look of disgust on her face, but I stroked her face and bent forward kissing her hard on the mouth.

"Jackie, you need to slow down. You are gonna make me come *hard* if you keep that shit up."

"Isn't that the whole idea?" she said, standing up and slowly unbuttoning her pants. Dayum!!!—Can I package this bitch up and take her ass back with me to America like Vince said, I wondered. I watched her perform a slow striptease. She slid her pants down, revealing a black g-string.

"Turn around," I ordered her. "Let me see that ass." Jackie was a soldier who knew how to follow orders. She turned seductively, her eyes never leaving mine. Her ass came into view—and what a sight it was to behold. Better than my wildest imagination: her black skin was flawless, without marks or blemishes. I held those lovely mounds of flesh, kneading them in my hands. Ran my fingers over her skin and to the cleft, then downwards, following the thin cotton fabric that disappeared as it reached around to cover her cunt. My fingers moved down and under, feeling her mound, which was wet with pussy juice. I pulled the cotton to the side, slipped a finger around her sticky pubic hair and then plunged inside, Jackie sucking in a breath as I entered her. A moment later I pulled a glazed finger out. She turned to me as I held my finger in front of my face, examining it for a quick second like a doctor would, before slipping it between my lips. I closed my eyes as I did this, for effect, of course, sucking on my finger hungrily before opening my eyes and offering up a single moan.

"Girl," I said, my eyes locked with her, "you taste *so* fucking good." Jackie's face melted right there. Putty in my hands!

I pulled her on top of me, running my fingers over her ass, tight thighs and knees before up her back and around to her lovely tits that hung inches from my face. I took each one into my mouth, licked them all over, paying special attention to the nipples that I bit lightly. She threw her head back and closed her eyes—I know this because I was watching her in the mirror—watching that ass that rotated as I massaged her cheeks, thrusting my hardened dick into her pelvis.

"Come here, Island girl. I've gotta taste you before we go any further."

I grabbed her by the waist and lifted her off of me, my muscles twitching and flexing as she slipped beneath me. She spread her legs and my mouth went to her stomach for a brief moment, ran a tongue over her belly before tracing a swath down to her canyon. Her dark skin glowed under me—then I came to her pussy. It was lightly covered with dark, curly hair. Her pussy lips were not overly big or fleshly, but she possessed a meaty clit that was presently elongated. I teased it with my mouth, blowing on it and then brushing against it with my closed mouth. Moving downward to her thin pussy lips, I twisted my head around her thighs, pressed my nose in between her wetness, then stuck my tongue straight out and let it forge a path. It found her cunt; she opened up with a groan as I probed her—licking voraciously as if I was a man who had been without a meal for far too long. Jackie was incredibly wet—her pussy juice meandered down her thigh before I caught it with the edge of my mouth, sucking the juice in and swallowing the liquid down in one gulp.

My head shook from left to right, her clit in between my lips. I tugged at it with my teeth as her lower body—hips, thighs, and ass—all began to shake. I had been eating her for thirty seconds before Jackie grabbed her ass with both hands, lifting herself off the bed as she came—her whole body trembling as she groaned.

"Ohhhhhhhhhh fuuuuccccckkkk!" She pushed my head—then ground it into her pussy—grabbed my ears and tugged left and right—commanding my mouth to do her bidding, and I obliged like the good soldier that *I* was. When she was fully spent she collapsed exhausted onto the bed and held my head on her pelvis. My face was covered in love juice, nose and cheeks glazed with her cum, but I was happy, so damn happy.

"Damn, Trey, you suck a lady good!" I moved up her body and kissed her on the mouth. She sucked at my lips, tasting her own sap on my skin. Then I pulled away, leaving her wet and spent on the bed, legs parted and pussy pulsating in the afterglow of orgasm, as I went into the bathroom to grab a condom.

Trey came back ready for action. My shit was on-point and hard—encased in latex. Jackie had this glazed look on her face as I went to her. Her legs lifted and her arms found my ass as I guided my cock into her pussy. I threw my head back and sighed heavily as I entered her—what a lovely feeling, her tight pussy constricting around my cock—pulling me, sucking me inside. When I hit bottom I paused, kissed her lips and enjoyed the feeling of *not* moving, but just feeling us as one, me in her, her around me—her cunt tight like a glove, my cock buried to the hilt like treasure, deep inside of her fine body. And then I began rocking in and out, slowly at first, pulling that bad boy out until just the tip was showing, then plunging back in and to the hilt, hitting rock fucking bottom. My hands found her ass and grabbed her cheeks as I fucked her, first slowly with long, full strokes that made her shudder, then with increased momentum until I was jackhammering that hole, squeezing her ass as I pummeled her, the entire bed shaking as I worked my shit, Jackie grasping my ass as it blurred in a frenzy of fucking above her—her eyes rolling back into her head as I worked my shit!

"Yes, yes, yes, yes, yes, yes, yes…" she repeated over and over in time to my fucking. I could feel her cunt constricting on the down stroke. Her heart was beating; I could feel it, too, when my chest slapped against hers, our sweat mingling as one. I paused for a moment, placed my weight on top of hers, and hungrily devoured her mouth and lips.

It was time to turn her over. "Let me take you from behind, baby," I said gingerly. She grinned—no problem, mon!

I placed both hands on her ass, glanced up at the ceiling, loving the scene that met my gaze. Her head was turned to the side as she watched me. I rubbed my cock against her pussy lips and ass before slipping inside again.

"Oh, yeah," Jackie moaned as I quickly found my stroke again. I began rocking against her again, all the while glancing down to watch my large cock appear and disappear among the lips of her cunt. Jackie was moaning now, her chest flat against the bed, her entire back and ass a thin layer of beaded sweat that turned me on as I moved. I continued to fuck her, ass cheeks firmly entombed in my hands. I slowed slightly, rotating my ass and hips so that my cock pushed against her cunt walls at different angles. This drove her crazy. She began to hum and moan, softly at first, then exploded with a yell as she came again, her hands reaching between her legs and rubbing the blur of flesh that was my cock and her pussy. In seconds I felt the storm winds blow and combine to hurricane strength—rising from the base of my cock, a tornado about to unleash its carnage. I raked her back with my fingers, twisting a nipple before gripping each cheek in hand and pumping with abandonment as I worked that thing, grunting as I went along. My head tilted back and I caught a glimpse of myself as I came—a split second of pain on my face as I unleashed into Jackie's lovely orifice—then the scene was erased as my eyes scrunched shut and my brain went on auto-pilot—I slammed in and out of that cunt as I continued to come—my mouth hanging open and something completely unintelligent emerging from my lips. The storm passed slowly. I felt myself spasm over and over again, Jackie's hand reaching up to grab my ass and pull me into her. I collapsed on top of her as the tide ebbed away.

"Oh my God!" I exclaimed, panting like an asthmatic, "that was so fucking awesome, I…" and then, for once, I was speechless, unable to continue the discussion. I rolled off of her and kissed her silently. She nodded to me and snuggled against my sweaty frame. No words were needed. Thank goodness. For once, I didn't have the energy for simple speech or dialogue.

Four

It is amazing what the smell of coffee will do for some people. For Vince, a good cup of coffee was worth the trip across town any day. He knew all of the coffee shops within a twenty-mile radius by heart. And he made sure that part of his daily ritual included stops at the various coffee establishments—sometimes only for a minute or two to sip at a cup in between tasks—other times, for longer periods of time, perhaps an hour or more, where he would take a legal pad or his laptop, prop up his feet on a chair or on one of the comfortable couches and get a solid amount of work or creative energy expended, all the while the scent of ground coffee permeating the air.

He took the Fat Boy across the Memorial Bridge, which was relatively quiet this time of morning, down Constitution Avenue past the State Department, Fed, White House, and museums, then across Seventh Street to Independence Avenue. He loved riding through D.C. on his bike—the feeling of the open air and wind against his dark skin as he rode—something he found hard to describe. In a vehicle, one felt contained—protected—cut off—in a sense, from the road and what was occurring there and beyond its boundaries. But on a bike, you were immersed in the totality of the road and the elements—the smells, rolls of the earth, and its vivid colors—all of this, the very essence of life that jutted right up to the asphalt, suddenly attacking all five of your senses—the wind and sun on your face and skin as you rode; the vibrant colors not filtered by a windshield, doors, or windows; sounds not dampened; scents and odors, raw and uncut. Riding through D.C., Vince experienced people in their natural element as he roared by, catching them, photograph-like, stuck in mid-stride, mouth hung open, a dribble of syllables trickling out as he leaned into a turn and passed them. Owners walking their dogs, sniffing the air and barking as he moved swiftly past. Up Independence, beyond the various government buildings, the Capitol on his left as he increased throttle to maintain speed up the hill, loving the Boy as it hummed and groaned beneath him, the Vance & Hines singing their rumbling bass tune in the morning air.

Into Capitol Hill and near the various restaurants and bars like the well-known Hawk and Dove that catered to Hill staffers, and finally to the place which he frequented several times a week. The Cosi coffee and bar stood on the corner of Pennsylvania Avenue and Third Street, S.E., a two-story building with a bunch of tables and chairs that were arranged around the entrance. Vince pulled to the curb and cut the engine. Several patrons glanced up from their Sunday paper—*Washington Post* or *Times*, as he climbed off and strolled in. Cosi was one of those places, especially this Cosi—hard to describe—but you knew it when you waltzed in—it was the airy, down-home, comfortable feeling. Call it atmosphere, or what have you, but it was something about the colors—warm earth tones—tall ceilings, eclectic art, which hung on brick walls, small tables and oversized couches, and heavenly smells that kept Vince coming back. He strolled up to the counter, helmet and gloves in hand, and smiled at the black girl behind it.

"Hey, beautiful, how goes it this fine, fine morning?" Vince asked, placing his helmet, a black half-shell littered with dozens of stickers—some nasty, but mostly just funny—a thing with bikers—on the counter.

"I'm fine—kind of tired—hung out last night with my girls until real late," she replied, moving a strand of hair from her eyes. "I knew I shouldn't have, but damn, there were some hotties up in that joint!"

"Yeah, where was this?" Vince was pulling out his money from his jeans, and she was ringing him up, all without either of them uttering a single word concerning his order—they both had done this many times before.

"This club up New York Avenue called Love. You should see it, Vince; I swear to God, this place is so awesome!" Her face lit up as she genuflected and spoke. "I mean, check this—this place has like, three levels, this huge dance floor, and two or three VIP sections—I can't remember which!" Vince grabbed his cup of coffee from a dark-skinned brutha with dreads whom he merely nodded to behind the counter.

"Yeah? Haven't heard of Love."

"Oh my goodness—you need to check this place out. Vince, I swear! It is soooo nice. Wood and nice shit everywhere—I mean, this brutha, Marc Barnes, the owner, same guy who did Republic Gardens, put it down! Spared no expense. Everyone was up in that spot last night. All kinds of Ballers! I've never seen so many fancy rides in my entire life!"

"Really, Lisa?" Vince sipped at his coffee but made no move to leave.

"It's okay, go drink your coffee in peace. I'll holla at you later." The young girl shooed him away. He grinned at her, placed the change in a tip jar on the counter and headed for the couches in the back by the small bar.

There were only a few others in the bar this time of morning. He nodded to a white couple as he passed by, found a comfortable couch that faced the front counter. He planted himself in it, placing his things on the low coffee table in front. Vince sipped his cup, flipped through the paper that lay splayed on the table. Nothing much of interest caught his eye. He used this time to kind of decompress and chill—to just think—Vince was a cerebral kind of guy, his mind was always ticking, things coming and going, information catalogued, stored away for later reuse—calculations and processing being conducted in the background, even during conversation. Vince noticed everything about someone—his or her dress, hairstyle, the fact that one eyebrow had been plucked a bit more than the other—the way a shirt hung just a bit too much over a waist. His eyes took in his surroundings, his mind trying to block the inevitable out of his brain, but it was hard—Maxi was there, just below the surface, and if he wasn't concentrating, or if he let his guard down for a second, she came bubbling back up to the surface. He let thoughts of her and last night invade his psyche; there was a part of him that missed her already, wondered if he was doing/feeling the right things—but then he shook his head—No, he was not going to do this to himself—he knew what he was doing and feeling was indeed correct. And so, he pushed Maxi and their short-lived relationship back down, below the waves, and concentrated on the present, the here and now.

Vince got comfortable, took off his leather jacket and leaned back. Then he decided to run to the bike and grab his artist pad from his saddlebags. He always carried around a pen and pad of some sort—there was just too many things swirling around in his head that he needed to jot down. And on mornings like this—Sundays, when there were few people up and about to bother or interrupt his thoughts, he worked best—whether composing his thoughts for an upcoming talk, or just sketching out some ideas for an upcoming art project.

He returned to his favorite couch, took a swig of coffee, leaned his head back, and stared at the ceiling. The piece he was working on at his studio required finishing. Vince was a sculptor of sorts—he took casts of people's faces, arms, or legs, made plaster castings and then painted over them. He had stumbled into this by accident years ago—he had always been creative and loved to spend hours as a kid in his parents' garage creating art from things most people threw away. He had come up with some pretty creative pieces and his parents encouraged him to take art classes and hone his skills. So he did—first, drawing classes, then on to pottery, which really didn't hold his fancy, although he did enjoy the feeling of working with clay and other malleable material. Then, almost by accident, he came across a plaster of Paris cast of a person's face—it was laying around in a bin at his art school class—his teacher told him he could have it. Vince took it home, stared at it for hours—the contours, bas-relief in each square inch of tissue—and then he had pulled out his paint set, grabbed a brush, and used his oil-based set to paint alternating swaths of color diagonally across the cast. When he was done he had a vibrant, colorful mask—something that came right out of an African tribal headgear—his teacher, parents, and friends loved it—his dad had had it mounted and framed; it still hung in the foyer of his parents' home today, a reminder to all of their son's creativity.

Over the years Vince had experimented more and more, pushing the envelope, not content to stay within the confines of "normal" art. What was normal anyway? The whole idea of being creative, the essence of why he did what he did—was to create things out of random nonsensical things— order out of non-order, and make them beautiful. And so, Vince discovered his passion—spending time in his studio huddled over castings of strangers or acquaintances—adding touches of paint and shadow to create something unique—a mask that told a story.

When he had first met Maxi a month ago, he had wanted to do a casting of her. She had agreed—reluctantly, at first, until he brought her to his studio and showed her his work. The process, while not painful at all, was messy, and required that a gel-like substance be applied to the subject's face and neck. You then waited for it to harden, and then it was pulled carefully off. Maxi was lukewarm to the idea of being his subject, but warmed when she saw his collection of masks—a assortment of colorful faces—caught in various expressions and effervescent shades of tint—some hot and exciting, like the subjects and their personas, others more subdued, shadowed, or darkened. Vince had done her casting about two weeks ago. The thing laid on his worktable at his studio, yet remained untouched. He had sketched out a number of color schemes to match her moods and facial makeup. But his work and travel schedule had precluded him from spending any real time on completing it. With the sudden turn of events—he wanted and needed to bring closure to this piece. One thing about Vince—he was constantly sketching out new designs and seemingly wanting to move on, but he hated to begin a new project until the others were completed. And now, as he sat in Cosi sipping his coffee, he thought about Maxi and the plaster cast sitting on his worktable surrounded by newsprint, and resigned himself to bring this part of his life to completion. Finish it, he told himself, and then mount it with the others—a collection of faces, many past lovers, those, he was sorry to say, who took *his* test, and had failed...

✠✠✠

The sound of the door opening caused Vince to glance up. He had been deep in thought for God knows how long—perhaps thirty minutes or longer. His pad lay on his lap—a woman's face, neck, and shoulders coming to life— the woman from his dream—Trey's woman—Vince attempting to capture those eyes, the look that spoke to him—the one that reached right under his skin, tugged at his insides until it reached the inner sanctum of his heart, and pulled on his heartstrings… Get it down on paper, if it were indeed possible, what was in his mind's eye. Difficult—even now, for the image was fading from the confines of his mind, evaporating like misty tendrils of smoke which are exhaled, and drift off into the ether.

A tall, dark-skinned woman stood at the counter—a shock of thick, black hair emerging from the back of her gray baseball cap. Dark-blue sweat suit and Avia running shoes. She ordered; turned for a moment in his direction, looked to the far end of the bar—where Vince was the only patron left; the white couple had left over fifteen minutes ago—and then turned back. Got her coffee—a tall, steamy thing, and a bagel, and took a seat at a table across from the long counter. Vince noticed a University of Maryland tee shirt underneath as she unzipped her jacket and pulled it off, placing it on the bar stool across from her. Vince spotted her long, yet muscular arms—they weren't overly big—but he could see that they were firm and without any traces of fat. She glanced in his direction for a moment, looked past him and then down to her bagel. Vince watched her as she began to eat it, forgetting for a brief moment the pad that lay in his lap. The woman pulled off her cap, took the ponytail holder out of her hair and shook her head, letting her hair go wild before tying it back up. The woman had high cheekbones—they were edges to her cheeks, and Vince found himself staring at her—not out of disrespect, or because he thought she was overly beautiful—but because she had an interesting face, and it intrigued him from an artist's point of view. He glanced down at his pad, flipped to a fresh new page, and quickly began to sketch the outline of her face, a dark face with well-defined angles to it—distinct lines that cut from the V in her chin to the edge of each cheek. Vince became mesmerized by the symmetry, the geometry of her face, glancing up as he drew—trying to capture and put on paper a vein of an idea that had formed in his mind…

She caught him staring. It was one of those awkward moments when a woman senses someone looking at her and glances up to find someone staring back. At that moment, Vince had been paused from what he was doing, mechanical pencil hovering over the coarse paper, as he stared at her chin, focusing on it and its lovely curves. Then onto her eyes, which in direct opposition to her strong facial lines were soft, oval orbs that shone when she paused from eating, and wiped away a crumb that had stuck on the edge of her lip. Yet, Vince wasn't smiling—he missed the opportunity for that fleeting connection—that microsecond of dead space—silence—before two people whose eyes had locked, turn away. For Vince, his mind was on a different plane—he was studying her, the way a scientist researches a particular subject—no, that wasn't quite right—in this case, that clinical detachment was missing—he was intrigued—and quite interested—but his intentions were about to be misunderstood.

The woman glanced down at her food and continued eating. She was reading something, Vince couldn't tell what—she sipped at her coffee—letting small mouthfuls of the hot liquid go down her throat with a single gulp. She was young. Vince put her in her early twenties—twenty-three at the most. She, obviously, was in good shape. He could tell from the way she sat, her fit and trim arms, the lines of her neck—he hadn't paid much attention to that before, but now as he looked closer he could see. Yes, she had wonderful lines in her neck—those ropy muscles and tight skin—sinewy, that's the word that came to mind as he stared at her neck—the way those lines plunged downward, toward her breasts—his eyes descended, following the lines, observing the rise of flesh, her breasts, pausing for a moment, watching with a sort of clinical detachment, then moving down again to her stomach and waist. She glanced up again, caught him staring for the second time—her stare remained—longer this time than the last. Vince, his mind in artist mode—mind racing, thinking of the possibilities here, yet once again on a different level than hers. Vince smiled at the woman—but her facial expression did not change. She shook her head—it was ever so slight, and then she went back to eating and reading.

Vince glanced down at the sketch on his lap. It was crude—in no way, shape, or form would anyone think this was a "good" sketch, but it wasn't meant to be—Vince was capturing ideas—the lines and symmetry of her face—chin and cheeks—the yin and yang between her lines and those soft, oval eyes—wondering all the while how to imprison all of this in plaster—confine it forever in the construct of a colorful mask. His mind sprinted with the possibilities—like a freshwater stream that rushes over slippery rocks—yes, he could use color here and splashes of hue there—he pointed to the sketch, and made a few impromptu notes. And then suddenly, he was rising from the couch as he finished the last of his still warm coffee in one gulp, slung the sketchpad to the table, and walked over.

She glanced up as he stopped in front of her table. Vince was smiling.

"Hello," he began, "I don't mean to bother you, but I've been sitting over there…" He gestured to the couch. "And I just wanted to say hello." He paused for a split second and then stuck out his hand. "I'm Vince Cannon, Jr." The woman watched him silently. Her eyes broke away from Vince's stare and glanced at his dangling hand. She let it hang there for a moment before speaking.

"I noticed you staring. Didn't your mother tell you it isn't polite to stare?" There was no trace of a smile on her face, nor a warming to her voice.

"Yes, she did, as a matter of fact." His hand rose a few degrees; he tipped his head to the side a bit and smiled, letting her see all of his perfectly straight white teeth. "So, touché! Now, are you going to sit there and not show this brutha any love??? Gonna just let my hand wave here in the breeze? That is definitely not right, is it?" He laughed. That got her to soften up just a bit.

"I'm Desiree." She placed her palm in his and they shook.

"Desiree. That is a lovely name. I apologize for staring. It's just that you have a very interesting face. Has anyone ever told you—you have wonderful lines?" Vince crossed his arms to his chest. Desiree cocked her head to the side.

"Wonderful lines? I'm not following." She put her coffee down and gave him her full attention.

"Yes, wonderful lines. Your face is very angular. I find that very distinctive—not something you see every day. The symmetry of your face is *intriguing*."

"Intriguing?" Desiree asked.

"Yes. And then there are your eyes—which are in direct contrast to your hard lines—I don't mean hard in a 'bad' way. On the contrary—your eyes have a very soft, almost dreamlike quality to them. Very distinctive."

Desiree stared up at Vince, watched him for a moment while she said nothing. She nodded slowly.

"Thank you."

"May I join you?"

"Listen, Vince," Desiree said touching her ponytail, "you seem like a nice guy and all, but here's the thing. It's Sunday—I'm sitting here chilling, enjoying the peace and quiet of the morning, not trying to get into anything with anybody and…"

Vince cut her off with a wave of his hand. "Oh, let me stop you right there—I'm not trying to pick you up or get your number. Actually, I'm an artist—what I am interested in doing is getting you to pose…"

"Listen, Vince," Desiree said again, "can I keep it real with you?" Before Vince could answer, she continued. He dropped his arms to his side and exhaled slowly. He could already see where this was leading. "See, this is what I never will understand—bruthas and their wack-ass pick-up lines. I mean…" And here she began to raise her voice. Lisa, leaning behind the counter, was watching her silently like a hawk. "I don't get it. How come bruthas can't come up with anything *original*. Damn! You know how many times this week *alone* some dude has offered to take my picture, hook me up with a portfolio, or make me a star? Damn, you bruthas need to get some original lines before you step to a sistah!"

Vince had listened to her without comment. He stood still, letting her say her piece. He was calm—no reason not to be.

"Obviously, you have the wrong impression about me, but that's cool. I was not trying…" Vince paused, then sighed. "You know what?" He shook his head forlornly. "Desiree, have yourself a very nice day. Sorry to have disturbed you."

He turned on his heels and went back to his couch. He picked up his sketchpad in one fluid motion—didn't even pause in mid-stride as he grabbed it, and exited out the side door. Desiree was watching him silently. She finished the last of her coffee, scrunched up her cup and got up to walk to the trash can, shaking her head. Lisa observed her, elbows on the counter, a women's magazine splayed in front of her. Desiree passed her by, paused, and then turned.

"Tell me something, sistah," she said to Lisa. "Are you feeling me on these wack-ass niggas who don't got no game?" Lisa nodded sullenly. "I mean, I got nothing against a good-looking brutha who can converse, but if he don't have no rap, don't even waste my time!"

"I hear you," was all Lisa said in response.

"Listen, I'm not trying to disrespect these bruthas out here. But, damn, do you have to use the same ole tired-ass lines? 'Oh, baby, let me take your picture—you know you look like a model?—let me hook you up with my cousin, he's a director for MTV. For real.' Damn! All I want to do is come in here, get my coffee, sit here and chill, relax, not deal with that bullshit, you know?"

Lisa backed up from the counter, closed her magazine, and eyed Desiree carefully.

"I do hear you, my sistah, and it's none of my business, but you did come on kind of strong with my man there," she said, gesturing to the side door. Beyond the glass, Vince had finished donning his gloves, goggles, and helmet, and was firing up his Harley. The two watched him in silence for a moment.

"Please, he's just as tired as the next…nice-looking and all, sexy smile, but please! Get some brand-new lines!" Desiree grabbed the remains of her half-eaten bagel and tossed it in the trash. She donned her jacket—zipped it up and turned to leave.

"Like I said, none of my business," Lisa said in Desiree's direction, "but you might want to take a look at that over there," she said, pointing toward the far wall by the door. Desiree's eyes followed, stopping at a piece of art hanging on the wall. It was a mask set in the middle of an off-white canvas, with a thick, black lacquered border—with vibrant splotches of paint adorning the face—red, orange, green and blue spots that covered the surface—underneath, a reddish, brown stain that seeped below the surface and gave it a phantom-like sheen. The expression was one of joy—the lips were upturned, and accentuated—the eyes—although holes, burned bright with touches of brilliant acrylic paint—an eyeliner of sorts that rimmed the orbs and brought the mask to life. Desiree stared in silence—gathering her stuff and without breaking her stare moved toward the piece. The beauty of the mask drew her in—its raw, surreal quality was poignant. In the distance,

Vince gunned the throttle, let in the clutch and rode away, the low growl from his engine suspended, like particles in the morning air.

Lisa let Desiree get within six feet before speaking: "A moving and very powerful piece, wouldn't you say?" She eyed Desiree, whose entire demeanor had changed. "He calls that one, 'My Secret Redeemer.'"

"Who?" Desiree asked even though her body shivered with the recognition of the answer, which loomed directly in front of her own face.

"The brutha who just walked out of here—the brutha with the tired-ass lines." Lisa eyed her for a moment more and then turned toward the back, leaving Desiree to stand in front of the mask, and contemplate its meaning, and its maker, alone...

Five

Say what you want about a brutha, but after cutting a damn fine slice like Jackie, I had no choice but to sleep like a baby! I mean, Jackie and I had lain there a few moments after our lovemaking session, staring up at our reflections in the ceiling mirror, her finger tracing a meandering course along my sweaty thigh. A light rain had begun to fall—Jackie informed me that at this time of year, it rained on a regular basis for short periods of time almost every afternoon in Jamaica—usually for less than an hour. So, I closed my eyes, catalogued away this wonderfully delicious image of the two of us, legs intertwined, her sexy body covered with a thin layer of sheen, the afterglow that comes from being totally fulfilled and spent, her straight white teeth that formed a beautiful smile as she waved to the mirror while holding my wilted cock, and that pierced navel, which continued to wink at me as her stomach rose and fell from her breathing.

I awoke a few hours later. Jackie was gone and the rain had stopped. And I was hungry! Checking the Breitling, I saw the dinner hour was upon us. So I took a quick shower, washed away the remnants of lovely Jackie from my body, and put on some fresh, clean clothes after buzzing my head and face for the second time that day. I decided that for my first night at the resort I needed to look fresh—you know I had to rock a phat outfit just in case there was any doubt as whose house this was for the next five days. So, I decided to slip on (and leave unbuttoned) my light/dark colored silk shirt along with a pair of shorts. I rounded out this ensemble with my black sandals. Dabbed on this new cologne that I was totally feeling. Grabbed my rose-colored shades and headed out to dinner and the promise of an adventurous evening.

As soon as I rounded the corner and walked into the open-air dining room I heard my name shouted. I felt like Norm from *Cheers*. *Damn, it's good to be me!*

I found Randy and Cathy sitting with some folks at a large round table. Randy for some reason high-fived me, as if he already knew what I had been up to before dinner. Cathy winked at me as introductions were made. They asked how my first afternoon had gone. I leaned in to Randy and quickly provided the high-level on my encounter with Jackie. I left out the juicy details, 'cause I'm just not one of those bruthas who kisses and tells—ranting and raving all over this mutha fucka about what went down. Never done that shit, at least not to casual acquaintances. Randy freaked out, began laughing really loud and patting me on the back. Cathy leaned in to participate, but Randy just shooed her away with his hand. "He's telling me about that real cute Jamaican he just fucked!" The rest of the table, men and women alike, bobbed their heads rapidly as if I was the man—like, damn, we've *all* been trying to get with that fine piece since we first got here… how'd you turn that out so damn fast???

The food wasn't bad at all. It was served buffet style—fresh fish that was blackened or grilled, jerk chicken (you can't go anywhere in Jamaica and not get jerk *something*!), roast beef, a lot of pasta, various cooked vegetables, bread, salads and whatnot on separate tables, and desserts. One thing about me—I had been on a low-carb diet for a few months now—not that I needed to lose weight, but I liked to look my best, and watching my carb intake allowed me to stay lean and tight. I had decided long time ago, I would not reach mid-life with a gut or paunch—oh hell no! I was not gonna carry no beer belly or anything other than a tight bod. So, I loaded up on meats and fish, left the starches and breads alone, grabbed a separate plate for a nice salad, and drank about three tall glasses of ice water.

About halfway into our eating, Randy leaned in to me to explain the *rules* to me.

"Trey, it's real simple. You see something you want while down here, you simply ask. I mean *anything*. And here are the rules—no means no. And yes, well, that means hell yes!"

I decided to play dumb and to make sure I absolutely got this part down pat; that there was no confusion on my part. "You mean, with respect to these 'Lifestyles' folks?"

"You got it!" Randy ratcheted down his voice, which was a real stretch for him. "Me and the ole lady came down here last year for the first time—met up with the 'Lifestyles' folks. We were kind of curious back then—you know, we'd talked about it, the whole idea of swinging..." He bent forward and lowered his voice a notch further when he said the word, "swinging," then flowed back to normal volume. "We'd never actually tried it until we came here. And boy, let me tell you..." He let the rest of the sentence hang in the air, as if it didn't need finishing. His wicked grin said it all—use your fucking imagination...

"Yeah?"

"Oh fuck yeah—Trey, let me tell you, it's so fucking easy down here—you literally just *ask* for it. I mean, how much simpler can it be?"

"Are you serious?" I had been scanning the crowd—my honey radar had been sweeping and beeping non-stop since I'd sat down. Women had been walking by with their sexy-ass selves, most wearing something seductive—something you couldn't really get away with back home. But here, it was a different story, no rules applied, and so they strutted around in their see-through tops, titties half exposed, booty shorts that showed plenty of ass, lingerie and body wraps that left little to the imagination. All grinning to each other as they took a second helping of food, smiling at cuz as they went by, checking out the silk and the shades, admiring the tattoos that peeked out from underneath my Versace shirt; some of them undoubtedly had witnessed the package at the pool and were now *fans*—just recognizing a brutha! Yeah, I was smiling and nodding to most of them, letting them know that I was down while giving Randy my full attention—that I was approachable— don't be *scurred*!

"You're telling me I can just walk up to these women even with their man around and ask them if they wanna fuck?" I had this incredible look on my face, like *damn, this has to be a dream, or have I really found heaven? Punany heaven???*

"That's what I'm telling you! And no means no, remember that—don't take it personally at all; but yes, my man, means yes!" Cathy giggled at that last comment. She knew what we were talking about.

"Damn!" That about said it all. I was anxious as hell to try out these new rules. I mean, here I was—six hours into my first vacation day down in Jamaica—in fucking paradise, and things were about to get *live!* "Bring it on!" I exclaimed to Randy. He high-fived me again. I laughed and high-fived him back for good measure! All the way *live!*

✠✠✠

Don't ask me how, but we ended up at this piano bar much later on that evening. We had been laughing and carrying on at dinner, until I suggested that we check out the rest of the resort and see what we could see—so we headed out, Randy, Cathy, and me, a few others that I had met at dinner in tow—a caravan of sorts, going here, then there, to the beach (prude side), the various shops and restaurants, the disco (but it was way too early for anything to be jumping off in there yet), tennis/basketball/squash courts, before making it over to the nude side and the hot tub. This was where (I was told) everyone went later on in the evening.

We shed our clothes and got in. The hot tub was packed—probably a good fifty or sixty folks in there. The water felt damn good. We found an available corner where we could chill and take in our surroundings. People were hanging out under the stars, drinks in hand, laughing and carrying on, talking among themselves, touching, feeling, probing, and kissing. I spotted Lance and Chris, the couple from Louisiana whom I had met on the ride over to the resort. They, too, had had their room switched here. Quick introductions were made, and I was mesmerized by Chris's wonderful tits. They were large ripe melons with dark, taut nipples. Her body was a tight package with a nicely manicured pussy. Randy wasted no time and asked if her tits were real. Chris proudly proclaimed that she had just gotten them done less than six weeks ago. Everyone was impressed. They really did look life-like, I have to say. Randy then asked if he could touch them. Chris was fine with that. So we all got a turn squeezing her newfound friends, and let me tell you, those puppies were nice! Lance stood around all proud, and I could see why. I was not mad at him!

A few minutes later, Randy and I found ourselves on either side of Cathy, who wasted no time reaching for our cocks and stroking us to hardness under the water. My fingers quickly found her shaved pussy while Randy played with her pierced tits. Small rings were on the ends of each nipple. Randy tugged at them playfully, while I finger-fucked her in the water. Cathy arched her head back and came with a grunt as Randy kissed her neck. Cathy then returned the favor by taking my cock in her mouth. A few people turned, and conversations paused to watch this delicious act in the making. I lay back on the side of the hot tub, water dripping from my dark body while this chick took my dick in her mouth. It felt damn good. Randy was egging her on: "Go on, girl, take that snake in your mouth!" I just closed my eyes and enjoyed the moment. A friend of Cathy's came over to interrupt us, a small woman with dirty blond hair and perky tits; saying something about how good my cock looked from over there, and proceeded to take over, deep throating a brutha! I grabbed her wet hair as she sucked me, then Cathy moved in and together they licked the side of my shaft in unison, each taking turns putting the head in their mouth, licking and squeezing my balls, while a crowd of admirers watched the scene unfold. This to me was the ultimate, having two women servicing me at once. I have to say, as freaky as I can be, I've never been in a situation like this before—two women on me *and* in front of a crowd. It was a definite turn-on—the other guys who were paused in conversation, watching with envy as these two ladies went down on me, the look on their face said it all—you lucky bastard! Even the other women were checking out the scene—watching my dick get stroked, the shaft getting licked like a piece of sweet candy, witnessing it grow and blossom, my flat stomach, tight upper body, and tattoos moving/flexing as they worked me. And then I found myself pulling at Cathy's friend, a woman as yet un-named—she got on the edge of the hot tub and silently sat on my face. I reached for her perky tits and squeezed them while consuming her loveliness in my mouth. I tasted her sweetness, licked at her pussy lips and sucked her insides; Cathy grabbed my cock and jackhammered my dick with her mouth. The three of us; water bubbling underneath our hungered bodies that writhed as we touched, licked, and fed; bodies slicked with water, love juices, and desire as we played under a Jamaican moon; an envious crowd that longed to join in, but didn't dare interrupt this feast. I was the main course. And I had found heaven. No other way to describe it...

Later still we donned our clothes and made our way to the piano bar. A nice size crowd had assembled there, a few nice-looking ladies standing at the wooden bar being served by Jamaicans as folks sang along with the dreaded piano player. Randy sashayed up to the bar and ordered shots for the entire lot of us—a nasty concoction called a Flaming Bob Marley. Don't ask me what was in it—I sure as hell couldn't tell you. But I do recall that you had to light that mutha fucka on fire and drink it rapidly through a straw. Five of those later (Cathy made me do it!) I was feeling no pain. I was in rare form—I'm pretty sure of that—laughing, carrying on, and talking more shit than I normally do, but I don't remember the details. I know I didn't get up and sing, 'cause no amount of alcohol is gonna make me do that! But other than that, I can't say with 100 percent certainty what else did or did *not* happen. I do know this—at some point close to twenty-four hours since that alarm clock had shaken my ass out of bed in a world that now seemed blurred—long ago and far away—I managed to drag myself away from the Flaming Bob Marleys—"dragged" being the operative word here—back to my room where I collapsed in a heap on the oversized bed, and slept long and hard. Who knows what I dreamed of—it could have been of the lovely dark-skinned Jackie—her wonderfully unblemished ass that spoke to me and made my dick quiver; the two women who licked and sucked me while I lay back on the smooth tile under a colorful moon; or the hot Jamaican sun that sizzled my skin and turned me to a ripe, golden brown. All I know is that I slept, deep and without tension, the stress being sucked lovingly from me by new friends in a place that defied explanation but made life worth living—with a smile that I wore straight until morning...

Day two! Mon, what can I say? The vacation had paid for itself twice over, and yet I hadn't even spent a full day on the island. What a place! I had assumed that I would enjoy myself once I got down here—I'm the kind of brutha who pretty well adapts to any given situation, like a chameleon that can change colors depending on its surroundings. I knew I was gonna have fun on this vacation—I mean, sun, fun, reggae music, rum, and dark 'n' lovely women! Come on! But what I experienced my first twelve hours on the island was not something I had planned for. But Trey always goes with the flow—never a problem, mon! When you think about it, most people have never (and will never) experience what I just experienced. So, what was it— was it my good looks, sexy body, engaging smile—seriously, was it those things that put me in these situations? Or was it my attitude, my carefree way of taking advantage of a situation and creating a very positive outcome? I thought about my encounter with Jackie: fucking her with abandonment, my caramel-colored body slapping against her lovely, chocolate skin until I had come *hard* in her cunt, and then onto the threesome in the hot tub, and how I had laid back while those ladies had grasped my shit, each one taking a fistful in hand and tag-teaming the head, licking me up and down as my eyes rolled back into my head from sheer fucking *delight*—how many people could only dream about something as wickedly good as that? And then I realized what I had always known—that there were those who meandered through life like a leaf floating in a stream; they were carried along by the current, never truly knowing where they would end up—and then there were those who *took* control—grabbed hold of the reins and told that pony where the fuck to go! That had always and forever would be me: directing, controlling, commanding, leading—and making things happen! Yes, Lawd!

So here I was, day two, sun streaming in through the open window, a dark-skinned Jamaican with thick forearms and a colorful hat placing wooden carvings on a table in between two palm trees, setting up shop for the day. My head was pounding, like a hammer that smacked my bald head every few seconds with no let up. Those fucking Flaming Bob Marleys. Did I mention that I never wanted to see a flaming drink again as long as I live? Did I? Please don't ever mention that brutha's name around me, again! Okay?

So, I decided to deal with my hangover head-on, like a man. I pulled on some running shorts and a tee shirt, threw on my Nikes and shades and walked to the open-air gym. There I proceeded to sweat every drop of that fucking liquor out of my body for the next thirty minutes. I ran on the treadmill—two miles until I thought I was going to throw up or pass out, whichever came first. But as I cooled down, I actually began to feel better. My stomach was growling, a good sign. So I came back to the room, took a shower, shaved, dressed, and headed to breakfast.

I ran into Randy and Cathy on the omelet line. I bitched about my hang-over and how I was holding them personally responsible for all of the pussy I had missed out on the previous night. Randy just laughed his loud laugh and told me not to worry; that everyone drank way too much their first night down here and then passed out. Anyway, as far as he was concerned, I was already *way* ahead of the game, so stop bitching!

I had to agree with him on that one. Yeah, mon!

✠✠✠

The rest of the day passed uneventfully. I can say that without any sense of disappointment. I had a wonderful day. Relaxing on the beach, getting some reading done, enjoying the water as it lapped at my ankles while I walked along the shore, consuming large quantities of rum punches made by my man behind the bar who said "respect" whenever I nodded at him, talking with folks, and just watching the festivities. Yeah, it was a great day!

I met another nice couple—Raul and Gabrielle, a South American couple from the D.C. area. Raul was a middle-aged man who owned a construction company, and constantly smoked Cuban cigars. Gabrielle, his wife, was a good-looking woman with olive skin, full tits, and dark nipples, rounded out by thick thighs and a full ass. She had a cute accent that fucked with me—most women with accents do. She was sitting with a bunch of naked folks at a picnic table under the shade of several palm trees. She didn't do a lot of talking at first—just kind of sat there and watched me as I was intro-duced to the group. I had walked by with my shades on when someone called my name. Apparently, I had been introduced to somebody there the previous night in the piano bar—but of course, all of what transpired after the Flaming Bob Marleys was just one big fucking blur to me!

I had gone back to my beach chair after chatting with them for a while. Lance and Chris were also on the beach chilling. I hung with them for a bit, just talking and enjoying the view of Chris's lovely new acquisitions. I was actually getting a fair amount of reading done when out of the corner of my eye I noticed some activity in the water. Gabrielle and two of her girlfriends were splashing around on a raft in waist-high water not far from where I lay. I put my book down to watch as the three of them decided to have a pussyfest—each one in turn eating out the other while a bunch of us watched them in earnest. At first I wasn't that interested—I've never been the kind of guy who gets into watching lesbian activities, whether in porno or in person—but when Gabrielle climbed onto the plastic raft and spread her dark legs for this black woman with a J.Lo ass, I definitely paid attention. Perhaps it was something about the way she threw her head back, dark hair dangling into the water as she moved her hips, the other feasting on her dark pussy lips—I don't know. But that shit turned me on! What can I say?

I spent a fair amount of time in the pool area as well, just getting a lay of the land, so to speak, seeing who was there, and whom I wanted to pursue. This real fine white woman with an hourglass body and wearing a frayed white cowboy hat drew my attention. She was lying in the shallow part of the pool on a lounge chair by the grotto or cave area. A bunch of men and women, all damn good-looking (I have to say), were with her. I walked by several times on my way to refresh my drink, and smiled or winked at her, checking out the thin patch of blonde hair just above her pussy, her nipples that spoke to me as I walked by—just profiling at this point, you know how we do—not being overly pretentious, didn't have to, really, but letting her know that I was interested.

I spotted Jackie walking by, clad in a white tennis skirt and lavender polo shirt. Damn, she looked fine! I got up from my chair and went to her, my dick tingling in excitement as I recounted those delicious images from the previous day. I grabbed her hand and asked if she was gonna stop by later to see me. She just gave me a seductive smile as she let go of my hand, told me that she was working and that I would just have to wait and see. I feigned disappointment, but she stroked my cheek and told me that I'd be okay. I told her I know that's right!

At some point in the afternoon (I can't tell you exactly when 'cause I left the Breitling in the room safe) it began to rain, just like Jackie said it would. A bunch of us ran for cover—I headed for my room and a nap while others waited it out in the hot tub. When I returned it was blue sky and fiery sun again, and I joined Raul and Gabrielle who were talking about this toga party that everyone was attending after dinner. I didn't even know how to tie a fucking toga, but the thought of all of us drinking, dancing, and carrying on, clad only in thin, white sheets turned me the fuck on! Gabrielle informed me that one of the Jamaican resort girls had been showing people the proper way to tie a toga over at the pool. I guess I had missed that during naptime. I swear, if I ran into Jackie again, I'd take her back to the crib and have her show me exactly what to do!

Guess what I learned—there are over a thousand different ways to wear a toga! I stood in front of the mirror for over a half-hour getting mine just right. You know I had to rock this party—and so, I made sure my shit was tight. First off, I didn't want the sheet to hang down very far past my balls. Oh hell no! I wanted to give honeys a show tonight. Let them see a bit of the snake as it sneaked a peek from under my toga. Also, it was *key* that my tattoos were prominently displayed. So, I managed to tie the two ends of the sheet together onto my left shoulder, draping the rest of the fabric down across my lower chest, and around my hips and ass. When I was done, I threw on my sandals, dabbed on some spankin' cologne, and walked into this mutha fucka like I owned the joint.

White folks got creative—I will give them that—some folks wore their shit in some whacked-the-fuck-out ways, but it was all-good. Ladies were the most creative, coming up with these designs that showed off their titties and asses. Some obviously decided to just say "fuck it" and not even attempt to cover much up. One skinny guy, for example, walked in wearing only a sock covering his dick. I got to give homeboy credit—his shit was on point—but not as tight as mine!

I cruised around the dining area where the toga party was being held, met the gazes of a few ladies who clocked me as I walked by. I grabbed a drink from the bar—at this point I was pretty much a rum punch-only kind of guy—and chilled. A few honeys walked up, showed me some love as they waited to be served. I was enjoying myself when I spotted Gabrielle and Raul. Raul had his shit hastily tied, like he really didn't give a fuck. Gabrielle had bikini bottoms on covered by some see-through flimsy thingy—her tits were bare and she wore high heels—that's about it! She came up to the bar and without fanfare reached for my dick underneath of my toga. Gave it a quick tug as she smiled hello. One of her girlfriends from the afternoon came up to us, and Gabrielle told her to check, in her words, "my nice package," which she promptly did. I was just standing there; drink in my hand, minding mine…two bitches feeling my shit. And it wasn't even nine p.m. yet! DAYUM!

Gabrielle was whispering in my ear that she wanted to fuck me. She had this kind of devilish/seductive look on her face—an interesting glow in her eyes and full lips that pouted when she wasn't saying anything that made my dick hard. I leaned over and asked her what her husband would say. She told me to wait a moment and waltzed over to this table where Raul was sitting smoking a cigar, chilling with another couple. They conversed for a second and then waved me over. I shook Raul's hand and sat down. He leaned over to me and said in between puffs from his Cuban:

"You wanna fuck my wife?" I looked at him for a split second before responding. Gabrielle had taken a seat beside me and was watching the scene in silence, her lips turned into a sexy kind of pout.

"Matter of fact—I do." I was thinking about Randy's Rules as I replied. "But only if that's cool with you."

"It's fine with me. I ain't going nowhere. Go handle your business." He offered me a Cuban, which I politely declined. My mind was spinning, contemplating this place where folks were so *casual* about another man fucking their spouse. Not that I was complaining, you understand!

Ten minutes later (I would have made it five, but I didn't want to seem desperate, 'cause Trey is *never* desperate), Gabrielle and I were heading back to my crib. It was a beautiful night outside—just a light breeze coming in off the water, temperature just about perfect. No clouds in the sky, a nicely shaped moon rising. I took Gabrielle's hand as we descended the steps toward the beach and our rooms.

A bonfire on the beach beckoned us near. It lit up the night, spitting sparks up into the darkness. Over to the right of the fire were a bunch of hammocks strung out every ten yards or so between palm trees. Amazingly, the beach was empty, most of the resort guests at the toga party. Silently, I led Gabrielle to one of the white hammocks that swung lazily in the nighttime breeze. As soon as I stopped, Gabrielle was on her knees, and pulling my cock out from under my toga. She put my growing member in her wet mouth, and began sucking it as I hastily untied my sheet. She had a wonderful mouth; strong cheeks that sucked me in, swallowing almost my entire length. I enjoyed looking down while she sucked me off, her dark lips constricting my cock, while I grabbed a tittie in my hand and squeezed. Pinched her nipples as she worked on me. She paused, coating the side of my dick with her saliva as she glanced up.

"You have a big cock!" She stuck it back inside her mouth with a slurp, getting it all wet and engorged. At this point the toga was down around my ankles, and I was watching the shadows from the bonfire reflect off our bare skin, her head bobbing up and down, my one hand grasping her dark hair, guiding her rhythm, the other fondling her firm tit. I lay back onto the hammock, getting comfortable, adjusting my weight so that my cock was at mouth-level. Her bikini bottoms were still on, so I snaked my hand down around her ass and pushed the rayon fabric to the side. My fingers found her cunt: thick, dark, pussy lips that glistened with juice. I stuck two fingers inside. She sucked at me harder, one hand solidly wrapped around the girth of my dick, the other cupping my balls. She kept squeezing and rubbing my smooth sac lightly as she slurped and sucked on my dick. Her hand moved down to my asshole and lightly played with the hole. I felt myself tense and spasm in her mouth as she did that. I pulled out and laid her back on the hammock, the ropy material making imprints on her ass cheeks as I spread her thighs. Kneeling down on the still warm sand, I pushed the bikini to the side; I attacked her cunt with my mouth, wetting her hole with my spit. She moaned as I ate her thick pussy lips, which I tugged at with my teeth while her eyes rolled back inside her head. Her pussy tasted good—it had a musky kind of pussy smell that got me off. I dug that. I licked her from ass to clit, while sticking my thumb in her crack and pressing it around. Pushing her legs back and up into the air, I concentrated on her ass, probing the hole with the tip of my tongue while my thumb massaged her clit and wet pussy lips. She reached down and tugged on my fat cock, and I knew I needed to get inside her quick.

She was so damn wet, that slipping inside was the least of my worries. I glided in lusciously, hit bottom and then pulled all the way out, using the hammock's swing as my cadence. I paused again, bent forward, and grabbed the back of her head with my hands as I settled into the hammock, shifting my weight on top of her. I began slowly, letting her feel the full thrust of my cock as I fucked her, her hands tightly gripping my firm ass, then increasing the speed of my stroke, fucking her without tenderness, her head thrashing from side to side as she yelled out in that damn accent that made my dick spasm.

"Oh, fuck yeah, fuck me!"

"You like that?" I asked while sweat formed on my brow and nose. Off in the distance I could hear the bonfire spit and crackle as logs shifted in the sand. "You like my cock?" As I asked this I rammed her pussy hard and fast. The hammock rocked back and forth, powered by our movement—animal sex, primeval, raw, and powerful. Her cunt responded by contracting and pulling me into that sloppy, squishy cavern. A smile was painted across those sexy, dark lips. The limbs from both trees bowed inward as I fucked her with *determination*.

"Oh, yeah! Don't stop!"

But I did.

I paused in mid-stroke, pulling my shit out until just the tip was showing around those sticky, thickset cunt lips. Shifting to the side, I carried her along until she was on top of me, careful not to upset the balance and fall out. We giggled together, like kids in a schoolyard passing around a tiny joint, then I was grabbing her full ass and pulling her down on top of me, stuffing my cock deep inside of her hole once again.

"Oh, fuck yeah!" Gabrielle exclaimed again. She was sweating, her upper body and full tits swaying in unison to our rhythm, her dark nipples erect as I twisted them hard between my fingers. I pummeled her vigorously from below, arching my back off the hammock net to meet her pelvic thrusts. My body was writhing underneath hers, hands kneading her ass and swinging tits, grabbing at her mouth and sticking my fingers inside, her sucking at them hungrily like sugarcane as I stroked her pussy with my black cock.

Flipping her around, I just *had* to get a shot of that big, fine ass. She spread her legs wide, holding onto the hammock for support and balance as I stood by the edge of the net; her pussy lips hanging in front of me, all inviting, that fleshy aperture beckoning me in to play. I rubbed my latex covered cock all around her ass cheeks and hole, oiling her up, before thrusting into her waiting gap. She grunted as I filled her in one fluid stroke, one hand gripping her ass cheek, the other reaching forward and grabbing her hair, pulling her head sharply back. The sight of my large, dark cock slipping in between her butt cheeks was more than I was prepared to bear—several seconds after I entered her—a good ten strokes or so of good thrusting and fucking, the hammock vibrating as I worked her, palm trees on either side rustling in the gentle wind, I was pulling out, my hand reaching for my cock as the latex came tearing off, my other hand grasping for her chin and pulling her down onto the sand. I felt myself erupt and come almost suddenly, and I desperately wanted to see it on her face.

She opened her mouth; her eyes sparkled in the firelight in that devilish way that made my toes curl in the sand. I grunted as I came, spurting my hot, white cum onto her waiting face and parted lips. A stream of cum hit her on the tongue, shot straight to the back of her waiting mouth and went down her throat. A second shot splashed onto her full lips and formed a broken line between her chin, cheek and nose. I jerked my cock rapidly, base to head, the tip of my dick inserted into her cum-covered mouth as I continued to spurt my load, cum overflowing, not contained, and running down her chin in a delicious kind of way. She swallowed some with a smile, but the rest meandered down the valley of her full tits, coming to a final resting place on her belly. I looked down at the glazed path my cum had made on her damp skin: face to stomach, and bent down to kiss her on the mouth. She reached out and tongued me, sperm mingling between mouths and tongues as my cock slowly began to sag like an aging flower.

Behind us I heard applause—lightly at first and seemingly far away, then eruptions of sound: whooping, hollering, and plenty of high-fives. I turned around, seeing for the first time the crowd that had gathered by the edge of shadows, men and women alike, clad in togas, many gripping each other and tall drinks in hand, grins on their faces, thumbs upturned in the air. And as I reached for Gabrielle and took a bow, I spied in the midst of the crowd, Raul, her husband, clapping away with the others, a grin spread across his face as puffs from his Cuban rose into the Jamaican sky.

Six

No matter how many times Vince spoke in front of a crowd, he always had butterflies before getting on stage. His father, an orthopedic surgeon at Children's Hospital in D.C., always commented how that was a good thing—the day you stopped getting nervous—that was the day you put down your microphone and found something else to occupy your time.

Vince stood behind the curtain staring out at the four hundred or so folks who had assembled at the Le Pavilion Hotel in downtown New Orleans on a bright Friday morning—hard-working people just like him who had shelled out good money and taken off work to hear him speak. And regardless of where he was, New York, Atlanta, Boston, San Francisco, or The Big Easy, as he was right this very moment, he always felt the same pressure prior to getting on stage—these folks had come here today to hear something *profound*. They were here because they needed help in finding that one thing that eluded so many of us, regardless of race, creed, religion, or national origin—happiness and success. Therefore, Vince didn't do the mental calculations to come up with how much money he had just earned—no, instead, he did what he always did before walking on stage—he bowed his head, said a short prayer, and asked for the power to *inspire*…

A tall brutha dressed head to toe in Kente cloth stepped to the podium. The lights dimmed, conversations hushed.

"Good morning, my bruthas and sistahs. It is my distinct honor and pleasure to bring to the stage a man who among his many talents inspires, encourages, stirs, arouses, and motivates folk to do their very best. This is a man who has assembled all of the elements of leading a fulfilling and passionate life, and distilled it into a message that all of us can understand and learn from. Vince Cannon, Jr. hails from our nation's capital and has written the book *Finding Nirvana: A Quintessential Game Plan for Success.* He is the president and CEO of his own company, a motivational speaker, avid motorcycle enthusiast, and accomplished artist. Please give a warm New Orleans welcome to Vince Cannon, Jr.!"

The stage grew dark. A jazzy rhythm began to take hold, softly at first, and then rose in volume as a barrage of lights and images bombarded the front screen. An African child; a sleek Learjet; a giraffe foraging for food in a tall tree; an air traffic control tower; a baboon and its mate; the interior of a high performance racecar; the winding, meandering Nile River shot from overhead; the World Trade Center in New York City; an enormous mansion; the Sphinx in Egypt; a pair of lovers walking hand-in-hand through Central Park; a rainstorm somewhere in the Midwest; a row of expensive cars, a crowded beach—thousands of other images—all cutting at breathtaking speed from one scene to the other—seemingly without any theme, rhyme or reason. And then as the music rose to a crescendo, a single image remained—a breathtaking sunset, fiery reddish orange—a fireball that consumed the entire screen. The crowd began to clap, softly at first, then more loudly, as they searched left and right for the speaker to emerge. And then, after waiting a few extra long seconds, Vince Cannon, Jr. walked on stage, dressed in a dark-blue, wool-and-silk, six-button, double-breasted peaked-lapel suit, pale-gray silk shirt and matching silk tie, black leather lace-ups, thin, rectangular lens with wire-thin frames, hair and beard trimmed by the hotel barber an hour before. He strolled to mid stage to the enthusiastic applause of the crowd. He smiled, stuck his right hand in his pocket and waited for the applause to subside. *Okay*, he thought to himself as he flicked on the wireless mic attached to the lapel of his jacket...*here we go.*

"Morning!" he said, his voice bellowing across the high-ceiling ballroom.

"Morning," the crowd responded in unison.

"That's what I'm talking about! Folks wide-awake and raring to go! Welcome everyone. Before we get started let me say how delighted I am to be here—you are a good-looking crowd—I always love coming here, to New Orleans—there's something about this city that I find *magical.* The music, the food, the people…" that got more applause, "Yes, especially the people—there are some good-looking folks here today! So forgive me if I lose my place from time to time; I will try to stay on track!" Laughter, then settling down. Vince put on a serious face.

"Let me ask you this—how do you define success?" He paused, took his hand out of his pocket and touched his finger to his lips as if deep in thought. He began to pace the stage, looking out over the crowd. Most were women, young and middle-aged, all colors, shapes, and flavors—no different than most of his workshops and seminars—he catered to women mostly, the backbone of the family who were searching for answers to improve/enhance their lives.

"What is success? Is it happiness? Is that it? If you are happy, have you made it? Are you then deemed a success? Are you? How about owning a fancy car—does getting a new Cadillac Escalade, with a ten-CD changer, in-dash DVD, On-Star computer, and blazing steel rims make you successful? Huh??? Don't laugh, you know there are a bunch of you out there right now saying, 'Damn, how'd he know that's *exactly* what I want?'" Vince paused for the laughter, stared down at the tables, nodding at the folks who smiled back. He lumbered off the stage and began walking through the crowd, touching folks on the shoulder, nodding in greeting, smiling, shaking a few hands as he walked and continued his talk.

"Seriously, if that's your definition of success, that is fine with me. I did not come here to judge you or anyone else, so whatever you decide is fine with me. So, I ask again—what is success? Does it mean owning your own business? Finishing that degree you put off long ago? How about having two or three lovers at your beck and call? Is being a playa what success is all about? Huh? How about this? Are you successful if you earn three-quarters of a million dollars a year? Is that what happiness is all about?"

Folks were nodding their heads as if in church. Some were yelling out: "NO!" or "YEAH, that's what I'm talking about!" Vince encouraged that kind of thing—he wanted his crowd to get into what he was saying—this was what it was all about—interacting with folk—bringing the message to the masses—and having a healthy debate about the topic at hand.

"Making seven hundred and fifty-thousand dollars a year—is that how success is defined for you? By the way, if any of you *do* make that kind of money, please see me during break—I need to get you my room key! I'm serious!" That elicited laugher from the entire room. Vince high-fived a woman upfront. She giggled and whispered to her friend nearby.

"Folks—I hate to break it to you, but I've got bad news—and you can write this down! I honestly don't know what success is. Why? Because success is measured differently by each person. So what is success to me might not necessarily be success to you. I will tell you this much, and you better pay attention to this, because here comes the profound part of my lecture—are you all—or as we say down here in N'Awlins—are *y'all* ready for the profound part?" Vince paused, hiked a leg on the seat of an empty chair, and stuck his hand in his pocket—*strike a pose,* he thought. He grinned and the crowd grinned back, nodding in agreement.

"Are y'all ready? I don't think those folks in the back are ready for the profound part yet." He dropped his head to his chin. In the back, folks were vigorously nodding their heads and shouting. Vince used the time to smile at the crowd, make eye contact with as many people as he could. He let his stare find each one—linger for a moment and seep in—give each one a moment of private time, his way of sharing himself with the audience. They responded and loved him for it. You could feel the energy and enthusiasm in the air.

"Okay!" Vince spun on his heels and made his way back on stage. He moved to the center. The crowd hushed. "This, my friends, is the most important part of my lecture—so pay attention—in the packet of materials in front of each of you, there is a blank pad of paper. Take that out and a pen. On a blank page I want each of you to draw a large circle. Go ahead; draw a circle on the paper, and don't be stingy—take up the entire page. Okay. Now, divide the circle into three equal parts—you can either draw a large "Y" inside the circle or an inverted "Y," like a peace sign—I don't care which you choose—just make sure that all three sections are the same size. Okay—everyone done?" Behind him the image of a large circle with an inverted "Y" inside—a peace sign—took up the entire screen.

"I don't know what success means to each one of you—but I do know this—

there are three aspects or facets to being happy and successful. Without these three aspects to your life being in balance you will never succeed and find happiness. This, my friends is a fact—we don't have time to debate it here this morning, but as you can see, I've taken the liberty of giving each of you a copy of my book, where at your leisure you can read at length my thesis and arguments.

"The first aspect to a healthy, successful existence is one's professional life—select one-third of the circle and write in 'professional life.' This part deals with the professional aspects of our lives—whether we are a mathematician, CEO, astronaut, or executive assistant, each of us has a professional life—this aspect of our life deals with the things we do to earn a living—it includes all of the relationships that accompany our professional life, such as our boss, our assistant, if we have one, our colleagues, etc. Okay? Everybody with me so far? Good.

"The second aspect of a healthy, successful existence is one's personal life—select a second section in the circle and write in: 'personal life.' This part of our life deals with family and friends. Personal relationships—it includes marriage, children, parents and grandparents, and siblings. If you are single—it deals with searching for one's soul mate—the whole dating scene, looking for love, etc…Oh yeah, and sexual gratification falls into this area. Can't forget that part, can we?" The crowd members shook their heads.

"Last, but definitely not least is the third aspect to a healthy, successful existence—Self! Go ahead and write 'self' in the remaining space in your circle. Self deals with the care and feeding of ourselves—it is the mental, physical, and spiritual facets of our lives that we do to strengthen and enrich our own selves. It includes staying healthy—and that means, eating right and exercising. It also includes finding one's passion—whether we mean hobbies, or things that we are good at, things we love to do: things that stimulate us. Make us want to wake up the next day and do it again! Finally, it includes keeping one's mind and soul healthy—however you choose to do that—whether through prayer and/or positive thought.

"There you have it, ladies and gentlemen—three aspects to a healthy, successful life: professional, personal, and self. All three must be developed and in balance. Without exception." Vince paused to let his words sink in. He climbed off the stage and meandered among the crowd, which was silent, contemplating this idea.

"We all know people who have great jobs, and great home lives, but don't make time for themselves—they haven't concentrated on the 'self' aspect—and are they truly happy? NO!

"We all know people who have great relationships with their family and friends, have invested heavily in themselves, but not in their careers—are they truly happy? Have they made it? Do they consider themselves success-ful? NO!

"We all know people who have great jobs and wonderful hobbies, in fact, many times these hobbies consume their personal lives—but their home life suffers as a result—are they truly happy?" Vince shook his head gloomily.

The crowd answered in unison. "NO!"

"And many of you out there are parents, some of you single parents. Am I right?" Light applause. "And, Lord knows raising children, either with a partner, spouse, or alone is one tough job! But, let me keep it real for a moment—I know some of you out there are *consumed* with raising your children—hey, I know parenting is a full-time job, but some of you—and you know who you are—can't or *won't* find any time for yourselves. Are you truly happy? Are you successful? Answer it truthfully, y'all. The answer is NO!

"I challenge each and every one of you here today…" Vince said, pointing to the crowd and sweeping his finger from side to side in a wide arc, "choose any successful person you know, either now or in the past. Anyone—and I guarantee that they have these three facets of their life—professional, per-sonal, and self, in balance. That, my friends, is the secret to success. *Define* these three elements in your own life—*develop* and nurture them—and *balance* the three—and you, my friends, will find success and happiness!" Vince walked to the center of the ballroom underneath a huge, ornate chandelier. He held his hands up.

"Today we will accomplish great things—today, with the help of my assis-tants and me, you will draft a game plan for finding and sustaining a healthy, successful existence. You will a) define these three elements as they relate to your life, b) develop them so that you know exactly what areas you need to concentrate on, and c) begin to comprehend and understand how to balance all three. At the conclusion of today's session you will possess your own personal game plan, ladies and gentlemen—a game plan for a healthy and sustained successful life!"

Vince held his hands at arm's length, palms out to the crowd and smiled. The audience began to nod and then clap—lightly at first, then erupting into a booming thunderous applause, which swept through the large room. Vince nodded to the crowd as he smiled, touching a few folks in turn, as he made his way back to the stage.

✠✠✠

A short movie was shown while Vince stood at the podium taking a sip from some bottled water. The movie was a testament to his program—he didn't want to seem like an infomercial, or like something out of an Atkins Diet—some woman who had lost over sixty pounds and was standing there in Spandex going, "This program changed my entire life!" But the reality was that people responded to others who had lived through the program— had followed the steps outlined in his book and seminars, constructed a game plan, learned how to strike a balance, and were now reaping the benefits. So, instead of standing there telling people how great the program was, he showed these short testaments—that did the trick—got them enthused and ready to work.

A movement off to the side caught his attention. It was like a flash of lightning from a midnight storm—the sudden crack of light draws your attention in. Vince followed the movement—someone making their way to the front of the darkened room. The person didn't move as much as sweep in, like a rushing stream. He could see the hair—highlighted from the spotlights—it was long, frizzy, and wild; unkempt like a vine. A bronze color that seemed to change like the seasons as it moved—bronze, to golden brown, to a reddish brown. And then the figure stopped at a table with an empty chair to the left of center stage, and Vince was able to get a good look. The woman wore a white-lace blouse, bare at the shoulders; light brown; laced-front suede bell-bottoms with an elaborate embroidered pattern on the front; tan sandals, and a large Spanish suede-fringed shoulder bag. She found her seat, brushed her hair from her face with a quick flip of her head, stared at Vince on the podium and smiled. He smiled back, the movie ended, and the lights came up.

Vince moved to the center of the stage as the spotlight shone on him. His eyes swept out over the crowd—yes, they were ready, and he could see it in their eyes. They longed to soak up his knowledge like soft earth, and begin their own journey. He began to speak, tell them of how the rest of the day would shape up. How they would break into groups, facilitated by one of his assistants—and Vince himself would hit each group in turn, spend some time with them—give them a chance to develop their plan, share them with each other if they'd like—or with him.

The woman with the frizzy, wild hair who had just joined them crossed her legs, flipped through his book rapidly before setting it back on the table in front of her. She was nodding her head, as if she was moving to a tune that only she could hear. Vince snuck a glance in her direction—she caught his stare, glanced up and turned her head to him, matching her stare with his for a brief moment. Vince found himself studying her as he spoke to the crowd before they launched in to the next part of the workshop. She seemed very interesting—her look was one that reminded him of Lisa Bonet from *The Cosby Show*. She had that same sultry-sexy look. Her eyes never remained in one place for very long—always moving, searching, probing—except when she met your stare with hers—then she stopped and stared—didn't bore her eyes into you, but searched your innards, the window to the soul. Her clothes, too—bohemian in a sensuous kind of way. He was glancing at her every few moments—actually trying *not* to—he was taking questions from the crowd—just a few hands had gone up, when he had asked if anyone had any questions, but his concentration was on her—the bell-bottom suede pants—tight-fitting that showed off her contours. She bent down to get something from her bag, her blouse rode up her back, revealing the top of dark, g-string panties. Then she was upright, giving Vince her full attention once again, smiling once more, aware that he was looking at her.

Vince was thinking about the conversation he and Trey had had many times before—there were two kinds of good-looking women out there—those who had beauty and good looks—and both men agreed that there were many of those around. And then there were those who possessed sensuality. Not everyone who possessed good looks was also sensuous. In fact, there were many good-looking, even fine women out there—but only a small subset were sensuous—being sexy wasn't something you were born with—it was something you learned, practiced, mastered, and then lived—this woman, whomever she was, had sensuality that she hoisted around her wherever she went. It was there in her eyes, and her smile that held a bit of deviousness to it. Her tongue that flicked out to wet her lips every so often. And regardless of her unkempt hair and funky clothes, Vince found himself aroused by her—not just in a physical sense—but because he could sense a whole lot more to this person beneath the surface. Like an iceberg. Yes, she was an interesting one…he'd keep an eye on her.

✠✠

The rest of the day flew by and before he knew it, Vince was wrapping up his workshop. It was close to four o'clock in the afternoon on a Friday in New Orleans—the day had been a good one—lots of folk had gotten something out of his seminar—he could see it in their faces as he walked around talking, shaking hands, looking at the personalized game plans that each participant had developed. The breakout sessions had gone very well—a lot of good discussion and dialogue—he had facilitated a number of them, moved between the different groups, meeting folks, spending a few minutes in private, getting to know individuals and the particular issues that had brought them here. At lunch, he had dined with about twenty participants, and had conversed with them about a number of issues—mostly personal but of value to everyone around the table—motivating oneself, how to make time for those goals that always seems just out of reach, and more personal questions—how did he, Vince Cannon Jr., keep it all together?

After lunch and during the afternoon sessions, he had looked for an opportunity—an opening—to try and get close to the bohemian woman, but it hadn't happened. Not at lunch nor afterwards. They had exchanged glances several times over the course of the afternoon—he had joined her group and fielded several questions. He was hoping she would speak up—at one point she looked like she was going to—moving around in her seat, poised to raise her hand. But, alas, it hadn't happened. And now, they were coming to a close—Vince was thanking them for their participation—urging them to continue on their journey toward sustained success—to keep in touch with him over email, to let him know how they were progressing. And then he stood and bowed to the crowd's lengthy applause before exiting the stage, determined to make his move—and not let the woman get away without grabbing a few moments of conversation.

The Kente-clad gentleman returned to the stage—told the crowd that a wine and cheese reception would immediately follow with Vince Cannon, Jr. available to sign his book and answer any questions that they might have. The crowd began to adjourn to the dining area where lunch had been served. Vince was standing backstage, watching the crowd from his vantage point. When it began to break, he moved—not wanting his movements to seem too hurried or frenzied, but quick enough to ensure that he got to her before she left. He advanced on the woman, who was gathering her things, scooping up the materials before her. He approached from the side as she bent down, rummaging through her shoulderbag, the sight of her lovely bronze shoulders and a hint of her breasts peaking out from the white-lace blouse, made his spine tingle. He touched her shoulder lightly. She flicked her head up quickly, sending her wild mane flying, a frown replaced by a smile as recognition seeped into her.

"I'm sorry," Vince said, "I didn't mean to startle you."

"That's quite all right."

"I was hoping that we could talk for a moment before the workshop ended. Are you planning on staying for the wine and cheese reception?"

"Yes. I was going to introduce myself if you hadn't come over…" The woman stood and Vince inhaled the scent of her perfume. He couldn't place it, but she smelled wonderful…the scent of flowers and other nameless things, intoxicating. The emcee touched his arm, and Vince turned, the spell, for a moment, broken.

"We'll be ready for you shortly. Would you like to freshen up before we begin? We have a few minutes."

"Yes, thanks." Vince turned back to the woman, the interruption a mere annoyance. She had collected her things and replaced her bag on her shoulder. She stood there, looking up at him silently.

"You need to go." It was a statement.

"Yes." Vince touched her elbow. "Don't go anywhere. Okay?" He was staring into her eyes, mesmerized by their color—hazel like that of her hair, which seemed to change in hue every few moments depending on the light.

"Wasn't planning on it." She smiled and he grinned back.

Vince ran to his room to freshen up and check his messages. When he returned, the reception was in full effect. Folks were mingling, glasses of California Chardonnay and Merlot in their hands while they nibbled on crackers and various cheeses. A table had been set up at one end of the reception hall for Vince. He took his place after shaking the hands of participants and began signing his book. It wasn't tedious work at all—even though it had been a long day for him, for Vince, this was what it was all about—being able to interact one-on-one with his fans, his readers, his seminar participants—spend a few precious moments with them alone—even if for just twenty or thirty seconds—hearing folks tell him what they thought of his book and his workshop, and how he helped to inspire them. The look in their eyes, the smiles on their faces, when he signed his book—writing out their name and some short, one-line message—'Shoot for the moon'; 'Don't stop until you're completely there'; 'Be proud of your accomplishments'; or his personal favorite—'Be passionate about everything you do, and amazing things will come…' And so, he was thrilled to see that most of the four hundred or so participants formed a line and waited patiently for their time to pay their respects and get their copy of *Finding Nirvana* signed.

By six the reception was winding down. A short line remained. Over the past hour or so, he had glanced up several times from scribbling his name and conversing with people to look for the bohemian woman. He felt like an adolescent back in high school—this was silly, he told himself, but the butterflies were fluttering around in his stomach when he spotted her off to the side, deep in conversation with two other women. He watched her for a moment, observing as she sipped her glass of Chardonnay before he resumed the signing of his book for the next participant in line.

Shortly after six she got in line. There were less than a dozen folks whose books were left to sign. When it was her turn she walked up to the table, clutching her frilly shoulderbag and his book in one hand, her wine glass in the other. She smiled as she set the book down.

"I'm pleased to finally meet you, Vince—I've been a fan since your book came out." She grinned, showing him her pearly white teeth and contagious smile, as she wiped her hair from her face. Vince grinned back and found himself stealing a glance once again at her lovely shoulders. It was their color and her smooth, creamy skin that he found eye-catching.

"Hello, it is always a pleasure to meet an old fan!" He smirked and she laughed. She stuck out her hand.

"My name is Angeliqué. I enjoyed today's workshop very much." Vince took her hand, enjoyed the feeling of touching her, the way it felt when their palms connected.

"Vince Cannon, Jr. It is my pleasure. What a lovely name. Angeliqué. That is…different. Very classy…with an air of mystique to it."

"Thank you. My mother named me after a voodoo priestess whom she was very fond of."

"Now that is something I find quite interesting. And are you continuing the tradition of practicing voodoo?"

"Well, that's a long story…" she replied as she smiled down at him. He began writing out her name and then paused, wanting to come up with something profound to inscribe. He glanced up.

"A voodoo priestess—hmmm…" He shook his head; she smiled as he composed a short note to her. He signed his name with a flourish, glanced back at her and passed the book delicately back to her. She read the inscription: *I sense intense passion in your veins—channel that and you will go far… Best regards, Vince* She nodded her head silently and smiled before looking over at him.

"You are very good at what you do. You obviously have a gift for reading people and helping them on their way."

"Thank you. I hope you found today's session helpful. At a minimum, I hope it has given you much to think about."

"That it has. Listen, let me not take up any more of your time…" She glanced behind her at the line of remaining participants. Vince felt his pulse quicken. Their eyes exchanged a short burst of silent messages. His mind raced—there was much more to say to this mysterious woman with the voodoo namesake—but ten or so people remained in line—he couldn't do them a disservice by disrespecting them, focusing all remaining energy and attention on her. Yet…he didn't want it to end like this…it was now or never, he told himself. Seize the moment…

"Listen, you seem very interesting. I'd like for us to talk further. Can you wait a few more minutes—let me finish up here—we're almost done. We could grab a cup of coffee or dinner somewhere, if you don't have plans…"

"Yes. I'd like that."

"Good." He extended his hand and she took it. Again, he savored the feeling as their hands touched—the electricity that seemed to flow between their fleshes.

The next person, a black woman with short hair, wide eyes, and a smile came up and excitedly shook his hand. Vince beamed at his fan while he watched Angeliqué walk away, his thoughts not on this new person or what she was saying, but on the woman who lit him up…

✠✠✠

He found her to the left of the lobby twenty minutes later, standing alone by an oversized clay pot of wildflowers—their colors and fragrances, feral, like her hair, but beautiful nonetheless. She smiled when he approached her.

"I hope I haven't kept you waiting long," Vince said, relieved that she had decided to remain.

"Not at all," Angeliqué retorted.

"Wonderful! I have a few thoughts about dinner if you are still…"

"Can I interrupt you for a moment—before we get to that, I should let you know my, uh, fee—it's two hundred dollars for half 'n ' half; three hundred dollars for 'round the world…just so we get that part out of the way…"

Vince's face turned ashen; his jaw dropped, and he found himself speechless. "I'm…sorry. 'Half 'n' half'? Are…you…" Vince was having a hard time conjuring up the words. Unconsciously, he shook his head. It wasn't possible. It couldn't be. The thought of her as a—Vince couldn't even let the thought reach completion. Angeliqué let the silence invade the space between them for a moment before a wide grin overtook her face.

"IT'S A JOKE!" she said, pronouncing each word carefully. "Calm yourself! I am not in *any* sense a two-bit whore—besides, my stuff is way too *delicious* to be going for a mere two-hundred bucks!" Vince stared for a moment more before he broke into laughter; nevertheless, he wiped his forehead with his hand.

"Damn, woman, you got me that time! You don't know what just went through my head."

"I'm sure!" They both laughed, their gaze never straying from one another. "Now, you were saying?" Angeliqué continued.

"Okay, let's try this again—I was saying before I was so rudely interrupted…" Vince paused for effect and to grin before continuing. "I was hoping I could interest you in dinner with me—I have several ideas, not that I'm by any stretch of the imagination an expert in Creole cuisine—but I hear there are some good places around here."

"Actually, I took the liberty, while waiting for you to finish up, to make reservations. Hope you didn't mind. We've got an eight o'clock table at Brennan's, one of New Orleans' finest…I hope that's acceptable to you?" Vince stared down at Angeliqué, her fine features—frizzed hair that moved like the wind as she worked her neck, amazing bare shoulders, golden brown, like desert sand, those suede bell-bottom jeans with the embroidery on the front, hint of tan, flat stomach, her in-your-face-attitude—refreshing, like newly fallen snow—all of this swirling around him, his senses taking all of it in, inhaling all of her in one big gulp as if she was clean, invigorating air. Vince fought the overwhelming desire to reach down, scoop this lovely lady's face into his hands, and kiss her. Instead, he merely smiled and said, "That, my friend, is wonderful with me."

Seven

One would think that after a workout like the one just experienced with the lovely Gabrielle, I'd be spent! But for some reason, I felt completely revitalized—as if someone had injected *me* with a shot of adrenaline, instead of the other way around. I went back to my room, showered, to get that fuck-smell out of my pores, buzzed my head again (gotta keep the dome clean, ya know?), splashed on some more cologne, massaged a fair amount of lotion into my skin so that my shit would be *aglow*, then decided on what I was going to wear. The toga party was still in effect, however, my toga was sand-filled and nasty, the sheet having been used to wipe the cum off of Gabrielle's pretty face and body. So, I searched through my closet for a half-hour (like a girl) trying on this and that, just not being satisfied until I decided on a simple outfit to blaze. I chose my stone blue shorts as the foundation, and then turned my attention to a shirt. That took even longer—I mean, I went through six or seven different ones before I just said, "Fuck it!" and left my shit bare. Kept the top button to my shorts unbuttoned—kind of like inviting the honeys in without actually doing so—slipped on my brown sandals, the Breitling Blackbird, my silver necklace and bracelet set, a sharp pinky ring, and headed on out. It was still early and I planned on getting into some *more* fun before midnight!

I waltzed into the toga party feeling like a king. I mean, things were going so wonderfully well for me, I couldn't believe it. I felt so revitalized—really good sex always did that to me—like cleaning out the system, one felt completely refreshed and rejuvenated. I had come *hard* with Gabrielle, my favorite way to come, and my dick and balls still carried that totally spent feeling that would stay with me for hours. I was feeling good, on top of the world. And my first full day hadn't even come to an end yet!

A bunch of toga partiers were sandwiched together on the small dance floor while reggae music blasted out of ceiling-hung speakers. As soon as I walked in, the crowd spotted me (how could they not—I was one of the only mutha fuckas in there *not* wearing a toga!) A few rowdy partygoers started yelling and screaming, pointing my way—in seconds the entire crowd was cheering me. There was a small stage up front—the D.J. had positioned his equipment off to one side—when he saw me, he grabbed his mike and moved to center stage while calling for me to join him. I was playing it off at first, just standing back, smiling and waving to the crowd, my gleaming chest heaving from the play I was getting, my arms shining and flexing, tattoos looking good against well-tanned skin. But then I thought to myself, I'm the star of this show, so why delay any further—and so I rolled onto center stage. The roar became louder, almost deafening as I moved to the middle. Bitches were clocking me as I went—I waved to the moving, sweaty throng while grinning at Randy who was raising his fist into the air screaming my name—"TREY, TREY, TREY, TREY, TREY!" People were being worked into a frenzy. And I was not mad at any of them!

I reached for the mike and gestured for the crowd to chill. The sound fell quiet on my cue.

"Yeah…y'all," I said, all Barry White-like, dropping my voice down several notches in pitch—the crowd went wild again. Again, I gestured for quiet and they responded.

"I'd like to thank God and the Academy…" Laughter erupted as I grinned and nodded silently to the toga-clad pack. A few women showed me their tits. I winked and licked my lips to each one in turn.

"But most of all…let me thank my co-star," I put a hand to my forehead to search the crowd, "where the fuck's she at?" A pause. "Y'all seen my CO-STAR?" My voice rose to a crescendo as I completed the sentence. Mutha fuckas were pointing to Gabrielle who was seated with Raul and another couple about mid-way from the stage on the right. I grinned, pointed to her and told her to get up. Reluctantly she stood and curtsied for the crowd. Gabrielle remained standing for a moment more while applause erupted around her. She threw me a kiss. The mob then went wild as I raised my fist in triumph, the heavy reggae beat began to rise, and I turned to exit the stage gracefully, like the star that I truly am!

✠✠✠

That's when I spotted her. And literally, in the time that it takes to blink, the blood drained from my face. Far back, but unmistakable among the toga-clad revelers—she stood there, distinct from others by her short dress—orange, low cut, and hugging her sensuous curves like a tight, leather glove. But it was the high cheekbones, distinctive even from where I stood, frozen in mid-stride—and her long hair, perfectly straight and jet black, running halfway down her back like that of a model—that caused my heart to miss a beat and jaw to drop like a stone. I knew I looked ridiculous up there on stage—the entire *congregation* watching my every move, the pain that formed at the top of my bald head and flowed like an avalanche down my face, neck, shoulders, and chest—and onto my firm legs that suddenly felt like Jell-O and began to tremble as such.

My knees buckled; I faltered and began to sway—the D.J., thankfully sensing that something was terribly wrong, reached out with his dark arm to right me—and I took refuge in his grip, flashed a fake smile, trying to play it off. Some might have assumed it was the booze taking control—that being the norm at a party like this, but the vast majority of the crowd knew something was indeed wrong. It was the look—I could see it on their faces—their smiles wavered, laughs and catcalls waned as their eyes locked onto mine, everyone in the room trying to comprehend the shift, the sudden drop in temperature. Our eyes locked for a moment, hers and mine—and like flipping a switch, the pain appeared: severe and concentrated in my heart, like a knife, which is thrust into flesh and twisted in a sinister, grue-some way, ensuring maximum collateral damage. My throat constricted, I felt the air being extinguished, the lights dimming, fading fast, and for the first time in a long while I was *scared*, utterly terrified; my heart was thumping, reverberating in my ears so fucking loud I swore every partygoer in the place could *hear* my pulse. So many thoughts and images invaded my brain in that split second—like a movie jammed on fast-forward—they flashed by, details blurring as they raced by—and yet, I knew what I was seeing. And then the *realization* hit me like a crisp slap to the cheek—was this my punishment for living large on a cloud too high, consuming way too much, more than my slice? Down here for less than thirty-six hours and living *dreams* that only a fraction of us ever get to realize—who the fuck did I think I was—was that it? Was this God's way of letting me know I had gone *too* far—pushing me back down, and into place?

And then the wave passed—as quickly as it had surfaced—with the sudden awareness that the object of this unexpected ache was a delusion, like a desert mirage—it was not *her*. The pain dissipated into thin air, like tendrils of Cuban smoke—I was breathing once again, vision clear and focused, legs working as advertised—I displayed a smile to the crowd, once again raised my fist in a puny attempt to correct any misconception that had begun to form—this was *still* Trey's house, wasn't gonna let mutha fuckas think even for one quick second that it wasn't—these bitches were still sweating me like I was going out of style—yeah, in the blink of an eye, I was back—okay, sixty percent and rising—batteries recharging…

I found myself at the bar, a steady stream of fans stopping by to high-five me and say, "Waz up!" At this point, every mutha fucka in the spot knew my name. But I wasn't basking in the *glow* of the limelight. No. I stood there anxiously, wiping away the sweat that had formed on my smooth dome, ordered a drink after a few minutes of indecisiveness—finally deciding on a Bob Marley, and told the bartender to light that mutha fucka up if he dared—cause at this stage Trey needed *anything* with strong liquor in it. The bartender placed the shot in front of me and stroked his lighter—I sucked heartily at the straw, oblivious to the blue flame, and motioned for another. Out of my periphery I could see Randy and Cathy making their way over to the bar—Randy's boisterous voice leading the way—hand on my shoulder—"Dude, everyting irie? You look like you've seen a ghost!" I flashed another fake smile, grabbed the second shot before the Jamaican could reach for his lighter, and downed it, splashing some on my cheek.

"Naw, I'm fine…" I elbowed my way out of the bar crowd that was getting thick and annoying. I needed space and fresh air to breathe. Randy had this funny look on his face; I was putting distance between the two of us, but Cathy reached for him as he tried to go after me. I turned to him and gestured for him to stay. "Everyting irie, mon," I said, flashing a weak smile. "Trey back in control…True dat!"

Randy stopped and nodded. He seemed to believe it. I turned to leave. The question was, did I?

✠✠✠

Back in my room, I splashed cold water on my face and tried to think—and will myself to calm down. This was out of character for me, and that's what really bothered me. The fact that my mind was on a separate path, not going with the flow—not with the damn program. That wasn't right, but nothing I could do would change the way I felt. And so, I stood in front of the mirror—stared at the image that reflected back. Took deep breaths. Patted my face with a towel and pushed the thoughts that were welling up inside of me away, like an annoying child.

A knock at the door broke my spell. I froze—listened to the sounds—movement on the other side of the wall, white noise and other distractions that made it hard to focus—but Randy's voice was unmistakable, cutting through the air like a knife. I made my way to the door, knowing with certainty that he was not going away.

"Dude, open up! Someone's here to meet you!" Banging, incessant knocking—and that deafening/raunchy voice that I had come to know—now the last thing I wanted to hear. I paused at the door, taking a deep breath, wiping my head with my hand as if that would somehow transform my appearance.

When the door opened I found myself face-to-face with *her*—orange dress no more than twenty-four inches away, smiling, her perfectly white teeth shining as her eyes sparkled, lighting up the darkness. She was gorgeous, no, that didn't even do her justice—her beauty, and in particular, her sensuality, was unparalleled—high, sculpted cheekbones; perfectly shaped nose; bright, unwavering eyes; dark, unfathomable hair; long, curved eyelashes; perfect breasts that peeked out from the confines of her dress...

"Trey, mon, this fine young lady was inquiring about the star of the show! Hope you don't mind, my man, know you wouldn't..." Randy was interrupted when she stepped forward, invading the narrow space between the doorframe and where I stood, thrusting a hand forward—I had no choice but to take it—electrons flying between us as our hands touched, I could feel the electricity surge, and under any other circumstances my whole aura would be glistening and shimmering, yet I could feel the temperature dropping again.

"I'm Cinnamon, undoubtedly your biggest fan!" She flaunted another smile—meanwhile Randy stepped up, a few drinks under his belt/toga, and feeling no pain.

"I'm sure you are, baby; all sugar and spice!" he replied, wrapping a tattooed hand around her lovely waist.

"...And," she said, eyes blinking, waving Randy's comment off like it was an annoying insect, "I just wanted to say how much I enjoyed your show."

I stood there, taking this all in, mind spinning, the normal Trey-comebacks being plucked from the far recesses of my crammed databanks and compiled, but at half-speed, way too fucking slowly. Randy, sensing my discomfort, stepped in, taking control.

"Trey, meet Cinnamon. Cinnamon, this is Trey. Mon, Cinnamon's visiting—only here for this one night—and guess what? She's heard about our nightly hot tub party—said she's definitely game, but only if *you* join the party tonight..." Randy was grinning ear-to-ear as if he had just delivered news that would save the nation. Cinnamon made no move to back up—her eyes sweeping over my bare chest and arms, taking in the tattoos, my unbuttoned shorts and tanned legs that gleamed under the night-lights. Cathy, standing behind her, locked her eyes on Cinnamon's scrumptious ass, licking her rouge-touched lips, and undoubtedly thinking of the possibilities here...

"Give me a minute," I said finally, delivering the best that I could do under the circumstances. The pain was there, just under the surface, like a jellyfish—its long, perilous tentacles paralyzing every living thing in its path—"I just need to *freshen* up." Randy cocked his head to the side, pursed his lips as if this notion didn't compute. "Need just a minute…is that cool?" I asked, smiling at Cinnamon. As an afterthought, I reached out to stroke her forearm, as if this would add some sense of potency to my words.

"Oh yeah, that's *way* cool with me, Trey," she answered. Under any other circumstances, I swear to God, I would *deposit* my tongue down the throat of this goddess-bitch—this was a no-brainer; the woman was sweating me; them panties were *soaked*, that much was obvious, I had already won the prize. And yet, just reaching out to touch her had left my right arm feeling beaten and bruised. I smiled regardless, shielding my trepidation, closed the door slowly as Randy, Cathy, and our new companion, Cinnamon, withdrew to the hot tub and the prospects of another made-in-heaven connection.

I could hear their retreat: their laughter and footfalls echoing in my ears long after they had left. With the lights extinguished, as if that would some-how shelter me from harms way, I slid down the whitewashed wall, gradually to the bare, cold floor. At some point I fell asleep, my figure remaining in that spot—not moving, harried breathing, until this new anxious self—one that I hadn't seen in a long, long time—met the new dawn…

Eight

Angeliqué left Vince to go change and freshen up, with the promise to meet him at Brennan's at eight. For the next hour, Vince could barely contain himself. Images of her—her form, the context and content of her words replayed themselves a thousand times in his head. He practically ran from the elevator to his room, stripped off his clothes and jumped in the shower, the excitement and adrenaline coursing through his veins like a drug, intoxicating, warming his spirit. He thought about bringing flowers for her—pondered the thought for close to thirty minutes, even reached for the phone to give the concierge a call, then thought better of it. Didn't want to seem too excited. But then again…no, he decided…not yet…

Vince arrived at Brennan's by taxi at seven forty-five. The restaurant was located on Royal Street in the French Quarter, a block up from the famous Bourbon Street and a short walk from the Mississippi River. Antique shops and art galleries framed it on both sides. Angeliqué arrived a few minutes past eight—swept in, again, like the wind, looking sensational. She had showered and changed—with a renewed glow to her features. She wore a long flowing skirt of vibrantly colored tie-dye patterns, a matching blouse with oversized sleeves and a plunging neckline—her hair had been washed, conditioned, and combed back—it shimmered and shined halfway down her back. She wore large, silver hoops in her ears, and an Ethiopian cross dangled from a thin chain around her neck. She greeted him with a hug and Vince stole the opportunity to inhale the fragrance of her hair and skin—once again the desire to kiss this woman was overpowering; instead, he savored their moment of closeness, before she pulled back and looked him over. He had changed into dark slacks and a camelhair sports jacket—with a dark turtleneck underneath; comfortable yet stylish loafers on his feet—Angeliqué's gaze swept over him before commenting on how good he looked. Vince returned the compliment, adding that he was dizzy from her perfume and scent of her hair. She displayed her wonderful smile as the hostess led them up the stairs to the second floor.

Their table was in a cozy room off from the main dining area—dark-red wallpaper, a few portraits in ornate frames, a fireplace, dual windows overlooking a garden courtyard below, just two other parties besides them already seated. An attentive waiter got their drinks—Angeliqué was staying with white wine—she made an off-handed comment about how mixing liquor with wine brought out the wildness in her—Vince made a mental note to file that precious info away. Vince, too, settled on a nice glass of not-too-dry Chardonnay. They began to talk, Vince giving Angeliqué his undivided attention.

"So, tell me about yourself?"

"Not much to tell," Angeliqué began.

"I find that hard to believe." Vince grinned.

"Well, I was born here in New Orleans—my father was French Creole and my mother is Cuban. I've spent my entire life here and love it—the people; my roots are here—the music, cuisine, and arts. I'm not a big-city kind of girl—I like to be left alone to do my thing. Here people let me do my thing…"

"I hear that. Go on."

"Like you, Vince, I'm an artist—painter mostly. I have a studio that is close by—walking distance actually—right smack in the Quarter, which I just love!" She paused to take a sip from her wine glass. "I run an art gallery—a small place, but it pays the bills, mostly my stuff and some friends—paintings, some sculptures, a few glass-blown pieces, stuff like that. But, I'm happy here—I am a social person—I love to go out and listen to live music—and if you're into live music, New Orleans is the place to be!"

"Tell me, Angeliqué, what brought you to the workshop today?"

"Well," she said, shifting in her seat and raising her glass again to her lips. Vince used the occasion to gaze at her features. He found himself mesmerized by her stare—those eyes seemed to look right through him—yet he was not uncomfortable by it—just the opposite—he felt himself warming every time her eyes found his. "I read your book shortly after it was released—happened upon it by chance one morning while strolling through one of our local book shops. Read it and became fascinated with the entire premise—this concept of yours—this holistic approach to happiness—using the circle as a metaphor—and the idea of balancing each of the three portions. It was definitely something I related to.

"For one, I found myself intrigued with the story—your story—your description of how you came to this place where balance rules your life—your journey with your art, your passion for motorcycle riding and writing; how you were not content to live the typical nine-to-five routine and took steps to break from the mold—I found myself drawn to you in a way, and your story. You see—I would like to think that I'm cut from the same piece of cloth as you—we share a passion for life—that much is evident—and balance is something I strive for every day of my life."

"You sound like a very together woman," Vince said. He reached for her arm, stroked it without thinking. Let his touch linger for a moment. Angeliqué smiled, enjoying the contact.

"Thank you. In one sense, I guess I am. I am fiercely independent, passionate about many things—but there is a side of me that is in need of development—that, Vince, is why I came here."

"The fact that you recognize this…shortcoming…for lack of a better term—and you are ready and willing to tackle this head-on, and improve yourself—speaks volumes to who you are and where you are going. I am very impressed."

The waiter returned. Food was ordered—Angeliqué told Vince of Brennan's—they were famous for their turtle soup, which he had to try, and Bananas Foster—a dessert consisting of fried bananas dipped in rum and lit—world famous and to die for!

"There's another reason why I came."

"And that is…?" Vince asked.

"I was hoping for help in making sense of a relationship that went bad—a year and a half ago I was involved with someone. It lasted for close to a year. It ended suddenly and I'm over it—but I guess I've been searching for answers—what went wrong—why is it that two people who love each other can't sometimes find the strength to stay together—is it something about me that I need to focus and work on? I thought this workshop could help—after all, relationships are a big part of your circle." Angeliqué stopped, pulled at the bread and ate silently. Vince nodded while watching her, sipping his wine.

"Indeed. Tell me about this relationship." His voice softened, drawing her in. And Angeliqué smiled and began to talk, sensing his compassion and being okay with her wanting to vent her feelings, as if she were discussing her relationship problems with an old friend.

Angeliqué had met a man—a Creole from the north side of town at a gallery showing. He was handsome, educated, and married. He had courted her for a while—she was standoffish, having no desire to get in the way of an existing relationship—especially a marriage. But he was persistent, and well, he intrigued her. He seduced her—slowly through romance, flowers, late night phone calls, notes left on the steps of her studio—in the end, she gave in to the passion and her desires, and had an affair with him. She told herself that it would only happen once—but it was so good and intense, that she found herself going back for more. She became swept up with the *idea* of this relationship—this thing that never could be what she ultimately wanted it to be—but that didn't stop her from fantasizing about the two of them being together for more than just a few fleeting moments.

She turned to voodoo—a religion and way of life for her since she was small—the charms, rituals, deeply spiritual practices as a way to enrich her life in the ways of love. To assist her in getting what she desired more than anything else—to possess what she needed to feel complete—this man—Angeliqué dug deep, called on the spirit of Ezili Freda, the goddess of love to help in this endeavor. She erected an altar of her favorite offerings—pink and pale-blue candles, jewelry, sweet cakes, perfume, cigarettes, images of white doves; took a lady bath using basil, sweet peppers, *zo-devan* powder,

Baume du commandeur, and Florida water—the inside and outside of her tub basin traced in chalk with the *veve* or symbolic drawing of Ezili Freda. The bath, preceded and followed by an offering of a sweet dessert—rice cooked with milk and a sprinkling of cinnamon—then she withheld from bathing for three full days in order to allow the lady bath to take full effect. Afterwards, she fashioned a charm lamp made from a coconut shell, in which she placed a piece of sheep's brain (which took her a painstakingly long while to obtain), immersed in olive oil, cane syrup, honey, and petals of jasmine— the attributes of the sweet ingredients, Angeliqué explained, used to enhance the properties of attraction. A wick was then threaded through the center of a Queen of Hearts playing card, which was then floated on top of the oil. The lamp was refreshed daily, and burned continually until the charm worked...all of this Angeliqué did, with the single, unifying purpose of making her lover hers. And yet...

The food arrived—Angeliqué fed upon fresh redfish that was served blackened and with turtle soup. Vince ate a medium-cooked filet with horseradish sauce and cooked banana—it went against his better judgment and palate sensibilities, but once tasted, one single bite, and he was a convert for life—the meeting of sweet banana, creamy sauce, and beef was pure pleasure on his tongue. The conversation slowed, due to the food—it was wonderful, and both Angeliqué and Vince savored the silence, and the opportunity to stare across the white tablecloth at one another, watching as each ate silently, not afraid of the gaze—nor the bond that was rapidly being forged between them this evening.

After they had finished, Angeliqué made Vince order the flaming bananas dessert. While they waited, they sipped glasses of Chardonnay topped off by their waiter, and she continued with her story. She and her account captivated Vince. He couldn't help it, but the desire to reach out and stroke her forearm, grab her hand, and kiss her was overpowering.

"For close to a year, I practiced my voodoo, the craft that had been handed down from generation to generation—I was a serious practitioner and truly believed that my baths, altar offerings, and charm lamps would bring me what I desired. But, in the end, it did not happen. My rituals did nothing to deliver to me the man whom I desired, away from his wife. They rekindled their waning relationship, and moved away from here, as if this place and I were a curse."

Vince swallowed and took her hand. "I'm sorry," is all he said.

"Don't be." She made no move to let go of his hand. It felt comfortable between them. "I grieved for a period of time—blamed myself for all the wrong reasons—analyzed it from every angle—in the end, what suffered most of all was my craft—I became disenchanted with the whole concept of voodoo—as a religion and way of empowerment. I took a step back from that part of my life—that was hard, it's been with me my entire life…but I had lost my faith."

Dessert came, lighting up their faces as a match was struck and the rum ignited. Vince enjoyed the sweetness—Angeliqué nibbled a bit but let him consume the rest of it. They finished their dinner with rich smelling coffee. Hot and good tasting.

Vince spoke: "Angeliqué, you've shared something very special and personal with me tonight—thank you for that. Thank you for trusting and confiding in me. I wish I could provide you with a succinct answer—something poignant and prophetic that would take all that you have gone through and make sense out of it. Alas, I don't have such answers.

"In a sense, we all are searching for what you seek—completeness that we hope will come from finding that special one—our soul mate—I confess that I suffer from the same malady as you do—I, too, long for that special person. I'm still searching—and hopeful that she is out there and that I'll find her."

The check arrived. Vince paid while Angeliqué excused herself to the ladies room. Vince watched her exit the room, feeling her more deeply than he did a few hours before—the opening up, like a flower, causing him to see beyond her physical self—her beauty—to the deeper core—her strength, her essence, her being.

When she returned, he watched her silently as she moved—the colorful patterns of her tie-dye skirt shifting like a sea storm, the hint from her breasts—rising flesh that caused his skin to tingle, and her lightly colored hair bouncing seductively under the light of dimmed chandeliers.

"I have an idea," Angeliqué said to Vince as she rounded the table, touching his back, letting her fingers graze his neck and shoulders briefly. "Let's continue this conversation, that is, if you're up to it, in a more *intimate* location…someplace where we can finish this in peace…"

Vince caught her hand that had alighted from his shoulder blade. He found it in mid-flight and took hold, stopping her from moving away. She glanced down into his eyes. He returned her stare, passion smoldering under the surface of his corneas. "Nothing, Angeliqué, would please me more…"

✠✠✠

They walked along the streets of the Quarter—past the antique shops and art galleries of Royal, avoiding Bourbon Street and all of its clamor— the loud music, inebriated tourists gripping potent Hurricanes from Pat O'Brien's, bead-laden young folks, stopping to gawk at the female impersonators, strip-club dancers who hawked their wares on dirty, beer-drenched sidewalks, or out-of-towners who dared to bare their breasts for a pair of cheap, beaded necklaces, past the thumping bass of Cat's Meow, or one street down to the gay clubs where patrons slipped dollar bills into the tiny g-strings of male dancers. Angeliqué and Vince avoided all of this, choosing instead to take a more tranquil route, enjoying the peaceful night, and the moment where their shoulders and arms met, quite by accident, leading to an intertwining of fingers and hands. They remained this way, enjoying the connection, the joining of each other's warm flesh, and the sensation of being in close proximity to someone new, the feeling, electrifying and invigorating. Past Toulouse, St. Peter, Orleans, and St. Ann; then over to Dumaine and finally St. Philip. A quiet, residential block, an eclectic collection of colorful two-story homes, shutter-covered windows, balconies with ivy reaching up to the roof. Hushed conversation or the sheer beauty of relaxed silence—the excitement of just feeling each other as their clothes brushed up against one another.

They came to a two-story, newly painted building that sat on the corner, the first level taken up by an art gallery with wide panes of twin glass divided

99

by a single oak door. The second level featured a wraparound balcony with wooden ceiling fans positioned every ten feet. A single gas lamp hung from the base of the iron balcony down to the front door, its flame wavering behind beveled glass. Off to the right, several yards before the building curved along the edge of the street, a side entrance, enclosed with a wrought-iron door. Angeliqué silently led Vince past the entrance to a garden hidden from the street. It was rectangular in shape, a courtyard of sorts that was surrounded by the building's four sides. Directly in front of them was a brick wall, with thick ivy clinging to red stone. Below the wall, an oval pond trickled water, lit from an overhead spotlight. Goldfish swam in between damp lily pads that sheltered a spotted bullfrog. On either side of the pond, medium-size trees had been planted. And beneath them, a concrete bench and wrought-iron round table and chair set. Vince was speechless.

"Please make yourself comfortable," Angeliqué ordered. Vince chose a wooden bench on a wall overlooking the pond. Across from him, light from the back windows of the gallery illuminated the garden. Overhead, windows cut into the second-floor brick were dark.

Angeliqué returned moments later holding twin stems of white wine. They toasted each other silently. She pulled up a lounge chair and reclined in front of him.

"My God, this place is beautiful," Vince remarked.

"Yes, it's been in my family for years. I'm very lucky to possess it. I love the fact that it's smack dab in the middle of the Quarter. So close to the action, so to speak, yet far enough away from prying, nasty tourists."

Vince laughed. "It's wonderful. I'd remain here day in and day out if it were mine."

"So, Mr. Cannon, your turn. Tell me about you and your art?"

Vince took the opportunity to tell Angeliqué about his passion, explaining his evolution as an artist. Most of it she knew already; he had covered this in his book, so he concentrated on what he had been working on recently—the life casting process, and the making and painting of masks. Angeliqué sat still while he spoke, mesmerized and intrigued by his creativity.

He then asked her about her art. She indicated that she had been an artist, specifically, a painter for most of her adult life. She had always gravitated toward representing the *veve* of the various voodoo spirits—normally traced on the ground during ceremonies using cornmeal, wood ash, powdered red brick, or even gunpowder—the elaborate designs creating geometrically complex and intricate patterns. Instead, she took these designs and put them on canvas, using the colorful hues and shades of the Haitian art as a backdrop. Soon, she tired of this and branched out, explored the creation of *veve* on alternate medium—settling on painting the detailed, highly structured patterns on the human body.

Vince sat enthralled as she spoke about her craft.

About six months ago, after experimenting with various patterns and colors for months, she held a show at her gallery. Word of her work spread quickly through the New Orleans art community—the painting of these intricate, hieroglyphics on moving, breathing flesh garnered her some interesting reviews, to say the least. A few months later, she held a second show—this time to a sold-out audience. Folks from as far away as Dallas/Fort Worth came to see her *veve*-covered bodies and live art.

Vince had a million questions. She smiled at him, as the words rushed from his mouth. As an artist, he was intrigued by her creative spirit and hungered to understand her process. As a man, feeling the connection between them, he longed to soak up more of her.

For hours they spoke in hushed tones, about everything—their childhoods, growing up, school, adult life, failed relationships, likes, dislikes, favorite foods and colors. Angeliqué refilled their glasses several times over the course of the evening. The evening was perfect, the temperature just right—the glow from the city arcing above them created a comforting blanket of radiance. Before long, Vince was stunned to learn from his watch that it had passed one-thirty a.m…the time racing past them like a flock of bluejays.

Vince stood. He drained his glass and set it on the stone ground. Angeliqué stretched, her feet having long since abandoned the confines of her sandals. Spontaneously and without thought, he pulled her to him, wrapped an arm around her lovely shoulders and back, moved in and kissed her lightly on the lips. She responded, reached for his face with both hands and returned the kiss. For a moment, they did not move, simply savoring the feeling of their lips pressed together, as one.

They parted and smiled.

"Thank you for a lovely evening," Vince said, his hands dropping down her forearms, fingers interlocking.

"Yes, it was wonderful to meet and spend time with you," Angeliqué replied. "I like you, Vince. I'm not afraid to say what is on my mind. You stimulate me, in more ways than you might think. I'd like to see you again."

"That, Angeliqué, would be my pleasure." He tipped her chin up with a finger and kissed her again. This time, their tongues met for the first time. She slipped a card into his palm. He glanced at it. It was for her art gallery.

"Come visit me tomorrow. I've got a show to do at seven. You can come early and watch me work. That is, if you'd like to?" The beam on her face was so seductive and sexy that Vince could only stand there and exhale slowly.

"I'd like that."

After he had left—she had offered to call him a cab, but Vince insisted on walking, the beauty of the evening and all of its glory invading his senses and giving him time to replay every delicious detail concerning their time together—Angeliqué went upstairs. She slowly removed her clothes, stood naked by the altar not far from her bed and made up her mind—no contest really—Angeliqué was determined that she would make love to Vince, felt the desire stirring in her, vibrating her body from the insides on out.

And for the first time in over a year, Angeliqué bent over her altar, whispered a short prayer to Ezili Freda, the voodoo goddess of love, and lit a pink and pale-blue candle before slipping into bed, and falling gently asleep…

✠✠✠

Vince awoke at noon, feeling more revitalized and refreshed than he had in a long while. He felt recharged and invigorated, as if every pore on his body had been scrubbed clean, leaving him brand-new. He remained in the king-size bed, covers pulled up to his chin, staring at the ceiling, recounting last night. He closed his eyes and memorialized every detail of the lovely

Angeliqué—her hair, skin, face, smile, arms, legs, and toes; the way her lips curled up when she smiled and laughed, her gaze—deep, strong, and unwavering.

His thoughts were on flowers this particular morning, the desire to send Angeliqué a bouquet so overpowering that he could think of nothing else; the thump in his chest, overbearing. He slipped out of bed, booted up his laptop and went on-line, checked a few floral web sites for ideas, then turned to the hotel's concierge. He was on the phone with her for over half an hour, discussing arrangements and delivery options. His first thought was to get her a vase of rustic wildflowers—something from a country meadow that would denote her spirit—gerbera daisies, alstomeria, delphinium, lavender, stock—or perhaps a colorful arrangement of lilies, snapdragons, carnations, and solidasters. On reflection, he began to consider a branch and plant arrangement—pussy willows, forsythia, kalanchoe, and ivy; or perhaps the striking snow-white calla lilies with their beautiful flowers and rich, green stems, a symbol of grace and elegance. Roses—another consideration, but one he quickly discounted…ordinary men bought their women roses—he was no ordinary man and this, my friends, was no ordinary occasion…

In the end, simple beauty won out and said it best—tulips—crisp, brilliant petals, stems that lifted and curved, soft pastels and bright hues—a vividly mixed color combination that the concierge personally guaranteed. Vince had them sent over to the gallery shortly after one.

And then he was on his cell—a longshot, he knew, but maybe, just maybe, Trey would pick up. He knew his best friend was tearing up the island of Jamaica this very second, leaving no stone, that is, skirt, unturned…

The call went to voicemail, and he hung up, disappointed. Vince knew what Trey would have said anyway. He could see his friend this very minute yelling into the phone—"Dawg, you mean to tell me you spent all that time alone with her and you didn't *HIT IT*????" Vince laughed out loud.

The next call was placed to Erika. It was early afternoon—hopefully, she was up. He desperately needed to tell *someone* about his evening and this amazing woman with the voodoo namesake. All about the astounding connection between them, their common interests, and approach to life. Unfortunately, this call, too, bounced over to voicemail. He hung up, crest-fallen; suddenly he was famished—he showered and got dressed.

The rest of the afternoon was a blur—eating breakfast/lunch at the hotel's restaurant, getting an hour of running in, then relaxing, walking through the streets of New Orleans and the French Quarter, shopping at River Walk, and preparing for his second evening with Angeliqué.

He returned to the hotel, spent close to an hour selecting his suit—finally deciding on the dark wool pinstripe suit—simple and elegant sometimes said it best; a thin, black, crew-neck sweater he had picked up that day; and the black lace-ups. By five-thirty, he was ready.

✠✠✠

Vince arrived at the gallery at six. He went in and spent a few moments admiring the artwork. A number of paintings adorned the wall—most were Angeliqué's work—and for the first time, Vince was able to observe the *veve* rather than imagine them—the intricate, replicated patterns of the voodoo gods/goddesses on canvas—interpreted by Angeliqué and her brushes: the sailboat motif of Agwe and Lasiren, king and queen of the ocean; bulls head and horn patterns of Bosou, associated with the fertility of the soil; serpent lines of Danbala and Ayida Wedo, snake spirit and mistress of the skies; heart shapes of Ezili Freda, love goddess; cross and coffin figures of Gede, guardian of the dead. Wonderful stuff—the motifs back-dropped by vibrant colors—Haitian influence—reds, blues, greens, purples, and oranges, swirling around canvas, creating powerful statements.

A thin woman with short hair and dark vibrant skin walked up and touched his elbow. "You must be Vince. I've heard a lot about you. Angeliqué is ex-pecting you." Vince beamed at the thought of the conversation between these two concerning him.

She led him to the back, where he could see the garden, displayed in its entire splendor in daylight through French doors, down a short hallway and up a set of stairs. At the top, a narrow hallway ran left and right. Vince was led to his right and he at last found himself in Angeliqué's studio.

Angeliqué was bent over a nude form on the floor. She glanced up and smiled when he entered. Off to the side, on the far wall, in the forefront of a large, six-foot square colorful painting, sat a nude man with well-defined muscles spread across his body. He was covered bald head to toe with light-red paint—the *veve* interlocking across every inch of his decorated skin.

"Hey, stranger! I'm glad you are here." She stared at him and grinned, then stood, her denim cutoffs layered with splotches of drying paint. A white tee shirt bunched at the waist was similarly covered with speckles and splotches. Her hair was tied back with a band. "I'd come over and give you a kiss, but I'd hate to mess up that fine suit of yours—check you out!"

Vince just laughed.

"Thank you soooooooo much for the beautiful flowers—I absolutely love them!" Angeliqué exclaimed while pointing to the tulip-filled vase on a coffee table.

"You are very welcome," Vince replied warmly, but his attention was drawn to the young woman on the floor. She reclined; head back, brown hair inches from the floor. Her darkly rimmed nipples were erect; trim body, firm legs and thighs, auburn skin also covered with a different pattern of *veve*. Her eyes roamed over his clothes and to his shoes, silent while Angeliqué stood over her, brushes in hand. Thin lines of wet brown and black paint were visible on her stomach—a star radiating out from her navel done in the design of a snowflake. Vince was stunned into silence by a shard of recognition that flowed through him. He couldn't put his finger on it, but something about this woman reminded him of…something…he just couldn't quite place it.

"Vince," Angeliqué said, "I'd like you to meet Jacques, over there, one of my male models, and this pretty thing here is Amber." Vince nodded his head to Jacques before turning back to the lounging Amber. She was staring at him while his gaze swept over her.

"Amber, a pleasure," Vince said with a smile. "You look vaguely familiar, it is possible that we have met before?" The woman continued to stare at him for a moment before responding.

"No, I don't believe so," she responded softly. Amber turned her head, glanced up at the ceiling as Angeliqué bent back on her haunches and began applying paint to Amber's thighs. She worked silently for a few minutes as Vince stood and watched.

"You can take a seat if you'd like," Angeliqué remarked. We are almost done here—then I've got to get ready. Not much time before show time!"

Vince took a seat and let his gaze sweep across the room. It was large, airy and free of clutter. A number of paintings of various sizes adorned the walls. Off to Vince's right side was a large wooden worktable covered with paints, brushes, and artist's tools. Behind it, a picture window looked out on the courtyard garden below. In one corner was a small, dirty sink. Over by the male model, Vince noticed an altar of sorts—a small wooden table covered with a pyramid of lit, scented candles, of various sizes and colors. Several cloth dolls were propped up, along with a myriad of assorted things—coins, incense, cigarettes, playing cards, and sequin-covered bottles, one containing a doll's head. In addition, dozens of beads and beaded necklaces were strewn about the surface of the altar and adorned the dolls; a large metal cross and *paket kongo*—cloth packets bound with ribbons and other decorations, topped with feathers. A large embroidered rug covered the floor. An old brown leather couch and an oak coffee table were set against a wall facing dozens of paintings, some unfinished, which leaned against a bare wall. Vince noticed a copy of his book was sitting on the coffee table near a pair of burning candles and the colorful and fragrant tulips. The scent of incense filled the room.

"Angeliqué has been talking about you, Vince," Jacques said, shifting off of his stool. Vince's gaze swept to the man's large penis and testicles, which were shaven and painted with red *veve* of Papa Legba, guardian of the crossroad between the sacred and mortal worlds—the repeating patterns of red, intricate crosses, keys, and walking canes. He quickly looked up to the man's face.

"All lies, I'm sure," Vince replied with a smile. He unbuttoned his jacket and took a seat on the couch, stealing a quick glance over at Amber. From his vantage point, it was an unobstructed view to her painted thighs. She, too, was shaved, the thin, swirling lines of the *veve* decorating her sex in a manner that Vince found enthralling. Amber had dropped her gaze from the ceiling, checked Angeliqué's work and glanced over at Vince. She seemed totally at ease and carefree as her lips curled into a tight smile before returning her stare to the painter.

"I doubt it," Jacques continued. "We heard all about the workshop and your subsequent dinner at Brennan's. Actually, that's all we've been talking about." Jacques laughed and snorted.

"I know that's right," Amber said softly.

"Oh, the two of you need to be quiet and mind yours…both of you are just jealous." Angeliqué pivoted on her haunches and stole a quick glance at Vince while she grinned. "Wish you could be with a finely dressed man like Vince. Ain't that right, Jacques?" Jacques just smirked.

"Oh I know that's right!" Amber proclaimed, giving Vince a seductive smile.

"Okay, we're done here. Stand up, Amber, and you too, Jacques. Let me see the two of you together." Amber stood and stretched. Vince stared at her perfect form, her shapely hips, ass, and firm breasts. She was young—Vince judged her at no more than twenty-two. For the second time, a vein of recognition quivered in his mind, but once again, he couldn't seize it.

Jacques walked over to join Amber on the rug, the *veve* covering his skin undulating like a serpent. He reached for Amber, slid his arms around her thin waist; their hips joined and Vince was astounded to see the new pattern that emerged as their skins converged. Angeliqué was hovering around their bodies checking her handiwork, touching and probing with her brushes, ensuring everything was perfect. Amber's gaze swept around the room, not focusing on anything in particular. Then she settled on Vince sitting on the couch and smiled—it was an innocent grin—her standing there, her body bare, taut skin covered with the *veve* of a voodoo goddess, and yet, Vince felt something stir in him. He brushed the thoughts quickly from his head.

"It's show time," Angeliqué exclaimed, before exiting quickly from the room, as if she were riding on puffs of air…

✠✠✠

Four hours later he found himself standing with Angeliqué in the courtyard garden, the glow from the gallery bathing them in shadows. Angeliqué looked sensational in a pair of thin, form-fitting black satin pants, a see-through black top with solid sleeves and embroidery-like designs across the front, and a pattern-filled belt with a large, oval buckle made of silver. Added to this ensemble was a pair of hanging earrings of tiny stones strewn together in the shape of a pyramid, matching necklace; hair combed down her back. In her hand she held a flute of champagne. Vince toasted Angeliqué as her hand slipped around his waist.

"I'd say the show was an unqualified success!" Vince remarked. She grinned up at him and squeezed his side.

How to describe the show—close to five-hundred, well-dressed people had shown up. There were five models, including Amber and Jacques. Each had been painted with a different, distinct *veve*. The models had been positioned in different corners of the gallery, lit from above by track lighting, and for the first hour they remained in unmoving poses for ten to fifteen minutes apiece while folks crowded around, watching, staring, and admiring the body art. Angeliqué had moved between the crowd, Miles Davis' "Kind of Blue" playing softly in the background, encouraging the participants to touch her artwork, feel the *veve*, experience the *veve* as it moved and breathed—and people did not have to be told twice—fingers met bare *veve*-covered flesh, felt it as the models moved and breathed, while waiters served champagne and seafood hors d'oeuvres. Excited women and a few men drew their clammy palms across the taut chest and thigh muscles of Jacques as he stood there, his stare unwavering. Then later, pairs of bare models drew together for joint poses, male-female, female-female, male-female-male combinations that were strikingly erotic. Face-to-face, breasts and nipples covered with paint touching, or face-to-back, bodies pressed together, the crowd bearing down on the models, anxious to run a finger or hand across painted flesh. At one point Jacques reclined on the bare floor, Amber climbed on top of him, and lay her sleek festooned body over his—they remained there, flesh upon flesh, the ending of one *veve* creating the beginning of another, a sea of decorated, undulating flesh, erotic, seductive, and enthralling to all who witnessed this performance.

To say the least, the crowd loved it!

Afterwards, Angeliqué stood mid-center of her models and bowed, said a few words about her art, the flashes from cameras of local newspapers and television stations reflecting off of gallery walls and ceiling. Her gallery assistants worked the crowd, and sold a number of pieces. Throughout the evening, Vince watched with deep admiration, enjoying the show and the closeness to Angeliqué who was never far from him. She introduced him to many of her friends and artsy acquaintances as a big-time author from up North, and he enjoyed mingling and networking with the crowd. All in all, everyone agreed, it was a very successful evening.

"So, Mr. Cannon, Jr., tell me honestly what you thought of my show," Angeliqué asked, nuzzling against Vince. He wrapped an arm around her shoulder, and gazed down into her eyes.

"It was incredible, Angeliqué. I've never seen anything that stirred me as much as what I saw here tonight. You have an amazing talent. There is no doubt that this is just the beginning of where your creativity can take you." Vince kissed her lightly on the mouth. His tongue invaded her mouth and she tasted him, grabbed hold and devoured him as if he were a piece of succulent lamb, marinated with heavenly spices. In the background, the sound of running water gurgling from the pond infused with the darkness.

When they finally parted, she held him by both hands and said, "Let's go back to my studio. There's something I want to do to you." Her eyes sparkled with mischief and of untold things to come.

"It's not gonna hurt, is it?" Vince asked with a smirk.

"That…is what I should be asking you…"

Nine

I'm back y'all…Yeah, Trey in 'da house! Livin' large and in charge! But, hold up—I see some of you haters out there—yeah, you know who you are—just standing there with your hand on your hip snickering—"last time we saw that fool, he wasn't talking very much smack!" Well, let me tell you something, *dickwad*—Trey is in control and back on the scene, ya heard? Back from a wonderful, crazy, mind-blowing, better-than-I-ever-could-have-imagined, sex-laden vacation that left me purring like a damn kitty! DAYUM! That shit was 'da bomb!

But, enough about the past! Fast forward to today. A lovely Wednesday morning and I was on top of the world. Just got back into town late last night. Felt like I hadn't been home in a month! My shit was all strewn around my crib—lots of dirty laundry, unopened mail, and shit to put away. But I left a message with Mrs. Feathers, who cleans and does my laundry, to swing by. My crib would be sparkling clean and my clothes laundered and put away by the time I got home from work tonight!

So, there I was…driving down 16th on my way to work feeling totally refreshed and rejuvenated—top down, the drone from the M3 invigorating, permeating every nerve ending, Lenny Kravitz's jam—"Dig In"—playing on the in-dash CD player—the twelve Harmon/Kardon speakers cranked so that I could hear that mutha fucka's guitar wail as only he can! The thumping in your face rhythm from Lenny, my fingers hammered against the leather-clad steering wheel like a bass player. Me, shaded, in an auburn-colored, two-button, single-breasted suit, a light-blue cotton shirt, yellow and blue spotted silk tie, and leather lace-ups. One word said it all—*sharp-sophisticate*! Okay, smarty pants, that's two words! Just singing away as if there was nobody sharing the street with me ...*once you dig in, you'll find you're coming out the other side...*

I downshifted as I pulled up to a red light. Off to my left, a lovely honey in a tight mini and vibrant yellow top with her titties jiggling underneath her sheer blouse came off the curb, watching me with a curved smile. Her hair was light and frizzy, standing off her head like an eighties fro, but I was not mad at her! She was looking good. Sistah was clocking me, I kid you not! As she got even with my bumper her smile was replaced by a frown as she *processed* the music and wrinkled up her nose at the rock-infused song. She shook her head slightly. I lowered the volume via the controls on the steering wheel.

"What's the matter, baby?" I said, clearing my throat and speaking above the engine noise. "Don't like my music?" I flashed a smile, showing her my teeth as I ran a hand over the lapel of my jacket.

"All that money," girlfriend replied, still shaking her head from side to side, the flash in her smile gone, "nice ride, threads, yet brutha-man still ain't got no sense!" She made it to the other side of the street, glanced back once more before turning her head and moving on, swaying her hips and fine ass 'cause she knew I was watching.

I swear to God the words: "Fuck you, be-yatch!" were forming on my tongue when I checked myself. Instead, I calmly replied, "Sorry, baby, if I'm not your *style*...but to each his own..." I guess she was expecting me to be sporting some hip-hop shit like Busta Rhymes or somebody. Pu-leaze! I tipped my head back and laughed as my eyes sparkled with mischief. I cranked Lenny back up while watching her sashaying up the street, attitude dripping from every pore of her being. My philosophy was simple—your loss if you don't dig my style. No harm, no foul. I put the M3 in gear and peeled away, leaving that sweetness on the sidewalk alone, with something to think about...

A few moments later I pulled into my spot in the garage on Pennsylvania Avenue. It was a quarter 'til eight. I breathed deeply, listened to the electric whirl as the soft-top unfolded itself from the trunk, settling in overhead, and locking down. I grabbed my briefcase from the back seat and walked to the elevator that took me to the eleventh floor and my office. I was glad to be back, actually. Work didn't stress me. I loved what I did and was damn good at it. And so, I walked with a skip in my step, pushed the "up" button as I hummed softly and checked myself in the steel reflection. "Once you dig in, you'll find you'll have yourself a good time!" Trey back in the saddle, y'all. True dat!

❊❊❊

I flashed my signature smile as I swept into the reception area like a storm. Becky was at the front desk, headset over her blonde hair, smiling as I waltzed in.

"What's up, baby girl?" I said, running my palm over the teak reception desk. She glanced up, desire in her eyes as mine traveled down the front of her blouse to where those lovely mountains rose.

"You're back!" she exclaimed. "How was your vacation? Did you miss me?"

"Baby, it was wonderful, but you know I did. I couldn't help but thinking, how much better it would have been if you had been there with me…Oh, the things we could have done, my sweet Becky!" I replied, pursing my lips and then grinning.

"You are too much," she glanced around before lowering her voice as her stare found mine, locking on, "and *so* full of shit. But I'm glad you're back. We missed you around here."

"I'm sure," I said confidently.

"Perhaps you should invite me to lunch to *catch up*…"

I leaned over the desk and scanned her curves slowly before replying, "perhaps I should…" And then I had a sudden epiphany—a wonderfully, delicious thought of sweet, sultry Becky sprawled across my sheets, butt naked—and I felt myself getting hard at the thought of my chocolate-covered Johnson sliding between her smooth, white thighs. But then I caught myself—Trey's Rule Number 28—Don't fuck the help. Or put another way—

Don't shit where you eat! I sighed heavily, my smirk replaced with a look of disappointment.

I strolled on, passing folks who welcomed me back and commented on my tan features. I just grinned and high-fived a few partners who were in the hallway conversing, coffee in hand. I came to another reception area—this one a bit smaller than the main one. My assistant was hunched over her desk, head between her legs, her dreads spilling across the white top.

"Whatchew looking at, girl?" I asked. She quickly popped her head up, sending her hair flying.

"Well, well, look what the cat dragged in…"

"Good morning to you, India!" I said.

"That's Ms. Jackson, to you!"

"Pardon. Morning, India Jasmine Jackson! Better?"

"Much." India smiled while wiping the dreads out of her face. "So, Trey, how was it? And don't leave any details out. You know you gotta give a sistah the *full* 411."

"India, all I can say is that it was off the chain! For real. It was all that and a bag of chips, I kid you not! Off the rocker!"

"For real?"

"For real. I'll fill you in later." I walked into my corner office with India trailing in tow. My office was large and spacious, and had a wide view of the street below. In the distance the Capitol could be seen to the left. A cream-colored leather couch was set in the middle of the room on a patterned throw rug. Across from the couch was a pair of thick upholstered chairs. A low, glass coffee table stood between the chairs and the couch. On the walls were various paintings—a large African plains scene on one wall and two smaller framed prints done by local black artists on another. Behind the chairs was a wide bookshelf with hundreds of books, mostly from my academic years. A high-tech-looking Bang & Olufsen CD player/tuner was sandwiched on the top shelf—the remote laid at the corner of the coffee table. I loved my office. It was very much a part of me. It made me (and my clients) feel comfortable, and that was important in a job where I sometimes spent many hours walking them through the ins and outs of divorce court.

I put my bag down on the couch and went behind my desk that was situated in front of the large picture window. I sat in my chair, swiveled around to boot up my computer and glanced through my messages that were neatly arranged on the corner of my cherrywood desk. "So, what have I missed around here?"

"Not much. Oh, Calvin wants to see you as soon as you get settled."

"Yeah, okay. Tell him I'm on my way up in five." India retreated. "Oh, by the way, I got you something." I rose and went to the couch where my bag laid. India waited by the door with an excited look in her eye. She was dark skinned, about five-six, nicely shaped with thick, long dreads. India possessed a great smile. She had been with the firm for eight years. She knew her shit and could keep up with the best of them. She talked shit in front of me because I allowed it. But she was strictly professional. That was until she tried to nose into my business and I had to tell her where to step off!

I opened my briefcase and rummaged inside. "What the hell?" I exclaimed with a puzzled look on my face. "Where did I put that thing?" I paused for effect while watching her out of the corner of one eye. India squirmed around like a child.

"Stop playing, Trey!"

"Oh, here it is." My hand emerged, holding a small box wrapped in colorful paper. I handed it to her. She wasted no time ripping off the outer cover.

"Oh my goodness, they are beautiful!" She held up a pair of wooden earrings, dark triangles with intricate carvings on the face, done by hand by one of the natives.

"Yup, one of the locals carved those on the beach by my hotel. Saw them and thought of you."

"Oh, Trey, I take back every nasty thing I've ever said about you." India came over and hugged me. I feigned revulsion for a moment but then hugged her back.

"Don't get mushy on me, Ms. Jackson, or I'll fire your black ass. Now, listen up: I need an eight p.m. reservation at bluespace for this evening, table for three, our usual spot, and then give Vince and Erika a call reminding them of our little get together. Oh, and call that chick over at BET, what's her name? Oh yeah, Alicia something…tell her I need a pair of tickets to the Brian McKnight concert that they just announced on the radio—I need really good seats, like first couple of rows—if she can't deliver those I'm not interested…tell her there will be something real good in it for her if she does—something that involves lots of oral sex!"

"You so nasty!"

"I know."

"So, who you taking to that show?" India inquired.

"You so damn nosy. Anyway, who the hell knows? I've got two weeks to decide," I replied as I swept out of my office, leaving India standing there, admiring her earrings in one hand, and shaking her head. "Tell Calvin I'm on my way up!" I yelled as I rounded the corner, quickly out of sight.

✠✠✠

Calvin Figgs, ESQ., was my boss and 'da man. A managing partner with the firm for the past fifteen years, he had personally recruited me out of Georgetown, mentored me while I prepared for the bar; helped me to get a clerkship at the D.C. District Court under Judge Henry Jackson, Jr. before moving me over to the firm. That was five years ago. He had made sure that his pick worked extra hard—and hard work is what I gave him back. For the past five years I've been one of the rising stars at the firm, taking on the difficult and complex cases, many involving high-profile clients and celebrities. The hard work had paid off. Calvin, who is legendary in Washington as a shrewd attorney, art collector, philanthropist, and an "A-List" kind of guy, had taken me under his wing. I got to know his family and spend some time with him at his home. Now many of the sweet cases were passed my way, or at a minimum, I had been given the right of first refusal.

I took the steps up to the twelfth floor and found him in his corner office. Calvin's office was three times the size of mine and could have come out of the pages of *Architectural Digest*. The amount of teakwood amongst these walls alone would make any grown man cry.

Calvin looked up from his phone call, smiled and waved me to a chair. I took a seat in the red leather wingback chair facing the floor-to-ceiling windows. A number of art pieces littered his office—a few bronze sculptures, colorful paintings, and knickknacks that Calvin had picked up from his journeys around the world. He signed off, removed his headset and got up to shake my hand. I stood as a sign of respect.

"Good to see you back in the office, Trey," Calvin Figgs said, his voice clear and steady as the morning air. "How was the vacation, son?"

I smiled affectionately. "It was wonderful, good for the soul, Calvin. Just what the doctor ordered." Calvin grinned and went to the door, shutting it softly. He was tall and a well-built man, mid-fifties, in excellent shape, with short dark hair that was peppered with flecks of gray. A thin, closely manicured beard adorned his dark face. He had smooth lips and an engaging smile. A pair of designer reading glasses was perched on top of his head.

"Bullshit. Don't play an old school playa, Trey. Tell me how it really was!"

"Okay, you always were the man…"

"Damn skippy, and don't you forget it!" Calvin remarked, taking a seat across from me. He folded his legs, and ran a hand down the crease of his pants. Calvin's suit was immaculate. He was dressed as only Calvin could— dark Armani suit, crisp white shirt, silk silver patterned tie, and leather loafers. The man could put me to shame when it came to dressing—in fact, he's the one who taught me everything I know in this world about clothes and fashion.

"Well, Calvin, what can I say? I found paradise. I kid you not!"

"Go on." Calvin leaned forward, elbows on his knees while he steepled his hands in front of his face.

"I can't describe this place and do justice to it. All I can say is that…"

"Trey, brevity was never your strong suit. Just tell me how many?"

"Actually, sir, I lost count." I grinned.

"Hot damn! That's my dawg!" Calvin remarked. He high-fived me, then sat back. "You know I've got to live vicariously through you, since the Missus wouldn't appreciate me whoring around town."

"Don't even think about it, Calvin; you've got yourself a fine woman there."

Calvin and I chatted for a few minutes, but I could see that something wasn't quite right. He wasn't his normal jovial self. I cut to the chase.

"Calvin, what's up? You've got something on your mind. I *know* you," I said gently.

Calvin's look took on an air of seriousness. "Trey, we've brought in a new managing partner." He paused, letting the weight of that sink in.

"WHAT?" I said incredulously. Suddenly everything, including the trip to Jamaica was a distant memory. "You're the managing partner of this firm. Have been for fifteen years!" I wanted to fucking scream, but I kept my composure. Something was definitely not right here.

"His name is Bernard John Marshall. He's a rainmaker from Briggs McPherson out of New York City. A good guy. Lots of connections in the right places."

"You're a good guy with *loads* of connections in the right places." I stood and paced his office, never taking my eyes off him.

"Trey, it's not that bad. Things will change somewhat—they always do when a new partner is brought in, but you have nothing to worry about. Your assignments won't change. And..."

"Calvin." I stooped down on my haunches to be eye level with him. I spoke softly but distinctly. "Listen, this is me you're talking to. We go way back and you're like family to me. So please—tell me what the *fuck* is going on?"

✠✠✠

A knock at Calvin's door broke the spell. Both our eyes turned in unison. Calvin cleared his voice and said, "Come in." In walked Bernard John Marshall.

I fucking knew it was him, and instantly I hated the man. They say first impressions are everything. Bernard John Marshall strode in, and the first thing that I noticed was the grayish-black hair that swept back from his forehead, coated with a layer of gel. He reminded me of a gangster. *Goodfellas*, for God's sake. His face was thin and angular, not an ounce of fat anywhere on his cheeks or chin. He was jacketless. Thin body and tall; a flat stomach—obviously, he worked out. His white shirt was impeccable. His tie: Neiman-Marcus, Private Collection (I know; I shop there.) He came to us, extended his hand to me as he grinned, showing me his perfect teeth. "You must be Trey Alexander. A pleasure. Bernard John Marshall." I watched his eyes as I took his hand. They were jet-black, motionless, and lacked any depth. They just stared back—this dead/dull kind of expression that spoke volumes. That's when I was sure I hated the mutha fucka. He was going to make my life a living hell. I could sense it.

"Calvin, morning to you." He smoothed out his tie with his bony hand. Calvin waved him to a seat.

"Morning, Bernie, I was just telling Trey that you had joined the firm."

"Wonderful. I've heard a great deal about you. I'm looking forward to us working together." I smiled and nodded, but said nothing.

"Calvin tells me that you've got an interesting deposition coming up." He paused while turning his head in my direction, those lifeless eyes neither darting left nor right. "Quentin Hues, Washington Wizards forward."

I took a breath. "Yes. Settlement agreement. Tomorrow morning if memory serves me." I knew exactly when the fucking meeting was and what the particulars of it were.

"Sounds interesting."

"How so?" I kept this deadpan expression on my face. I wasn't gonna give this mutha fucka shit. Not until Calvin and I finished our one-on-one. "It's your typical agreement. Division of property, etcetera, etcetera…not too terribly exciting," I said.

"Yes. Except for the fact that the property in question is valued at over five million dollars." Bernard was pokerfaced and I didn't like that one bit.

I shrugged. "The guy's a professional athlete. Been in the league for five years. What can I say? He signed a sweet deal with the Wizards. With New York before that." Bernard had been snooping around in my files, that much was clear. "I'm sure you knew that," I added scornfully. Note to self—have a *chat* with India, ASAP. We need to lock down the fucking office! I glanced at Calvin. He, too, was pokerfaced. At least his eyes were *alive* with movement.

"Sounds like you have things well in hand. I'll look forward to hearing how things turn out." Bernard John Marshall stood and shook my hand. "I'll let you two get back to your business. Again, good to meet you, Trey."

I stood. "You, too, Mr. Marshall."

"Please. Call me Bernard. Calvin."

"As you wish," I said ever so softly as my eyes flicked over to Calvin who merely nodded, yet remained silent.

Ten

A ngeliqué was not about to waste any more time. She went to her altar, lit the candles and incense, returned to the couch where Vince had chosen to sit, lit those on the coffee table as well and extinguished the light. Warm air swirled in through an open window, causing the flames to flicker. Angeliqué silently handed Vince a wine stem, went to her worktable, grabbed her brushes and paints, and returned to the center of her studio where hours earlier she had worked on Amber. Shadows of her lovely form wavered on the surrounding walls.

"Take off your jacket and sweater," she commanded. Vince stood, removed his jacket and placed it on the ends of the couch. She watched as he took off his sweater, noticing the well-developed muscles of his stomach and upper body. He started for her but she spoke. "Come to think of it, take off your pants, too. We certainly don't want to mess up a perfectly good suit, now do we?" Her eyes had closed to mere slits, but Vince could still see the twinkle in her stare as she kneeled on the rug. He obeyed—came to her, the fabric of his black boxers pulled taut. His heart was fluttering. She reached for him, pulled him down onto the carpet and began adorning his chest with color.

At first, she used light delicate strokes, and then she abandoned her craft, deliberately cutting wide, uneven swaths across his neck, nipples, and stomach. Vince laughed, grabbed his wine stem and took a healthy swig; the amber-colored liquid spilled and meandered down his bearded chin to his chest. It mixed with the still-wet paint. Angeliqué laughed. She pulled the wine away from him and took a wild swig. Vince reached for her blouse and pulled upwards—her arms raised without indecision and it came off. Underneath, she was braless. Next the belt and pants were removed. She was still painting him, applying red, brown, and orange paint onto his legs and thighs, the thick brush sweeping past his boxers, lingering for a few moments so that she could feel his flesh. He grabbed the brush from her hand, dipped the tip in red wet paint and applied a swath to her swaying breasts. She giggled and he repeated the movement again, applying circles until her entire upper body was covered.

Angeliqué began to wrestle him, attempting to pry the brush from his grasp. Vince was far more powerful, and won easily, although Angeliqué didn't give up without a fight. He directed the brush to her lower region, painting a wide path from one thigh to her knee. She had her head back and was laughing; suddenly she kicked out at him as he reached behind her and felt her ass. Vince maneuvered over her, and she reclined into a prone position; he placed the freshly dipped brush between his teeth and ran it across her neck, shoulders, and chin. Simultaneously, and without warning, he grasped each end of her g-string between his fingers. Her eyes widened briefly as she felt the fabric moving down her legs. And then she was naked, frowning because he was still covered. She thrashed out, attempting to reach for him, but Vince was too quick, squirming out of her reach. During the lull in the excitement, Angeliqué grabbed a bit of blue paint with her fingers, tricked him into coming near her—not that he needed coaxing—smeared it over his back and ass, before catching the rim of his boxers with her cupped hand and yanking *hard*. The boxers came off, Vince yelping as they tore down his legs and ankles.

And then Angeliqué was on him in a flash, her body moving like that of a cat, firm breasts hovering over his chest, her hair in her face and his, Vince's hands reaching for her, feeling the ripened mounds of flesh and squeezing, twirling fingers about her nipples, and consuming her mouth with his. Angeliqué savored the feeling of their mouths and bodies pressed together as one, the current that surged from her insides, pushing outward until she felt as if she were about to burst. They tasted each other, no holds barred, giving into their desires, exploring each other with their mouths, tongues, hands, and fingers. Vince moaned under Angeliqué, his sex fully engorged and feeling as if he was ready to explode from the passion and excitement. Her thighs rubbed against his, her hips seductively rotating against his muscular legs, the heat between hers overpowering. Vince closed his eyes, desperately wanting to ensure that this was no delusion. Before he could open his eyes, Angeliqué impaled herself with Vince's hardness—riding him bareback, Vince a beautiful, black stallion, her legs splayed wide across his wonderful, decorated body, gripping the reins of his flesh, her head back, eyes shut, skin dripping with acrylic color and blending with their sweat as the candle flames flickered and fluttered, and Vince and Angeliqué gave in to their fervor…

They made love, intensely and passionately, the way true lovers do. Vince shut his eyes and concentrated on *feeling* Angeliqué, every nerve tip alive and dripping with sensitivity. His entire being seemed to be swallowed up by her, she riding him slowly, enjoying every delicious inch of his manhood, Vince smiling as her pelvis ground against his, and his arms reached around to hold her, feel her delicate flesh as his fingers glided across her paint-covered skin.

"My God, you feel so incredible!" Vince managed to say in between lunges of his hips. She smiled, then giggled, reached for the paint tray, swiped at the pile of bright orange paint with her fingers, and smeared it all over his chest, circling his nipples. As she continued to squirm against him, her hand snaked down his stomach to where they joined, and on her upstroke, she grasped hold of his member, wrapped her hand solidly around him and decorated it with the paint, before plunging back down on his stiffness. Vince grinned as she coated him with the sticky dye, reaching for her taut nipples as she threw her head back and laughed. Then she tilted to the side and they came undone, Vince following her lead, scooping her up in his powerful arms and laying her gently underneath him. She glanced down, wanted to witness him in all of his glory. She touched him, wrapped her hand around his penis again, and felt his pulse as she guided him back into her wetness.

"Oh, YES!" Angeliqué shouted, her voice rising in pitch as he slipped into her, his forearms resting near hers as he bent down and kissed her lips.

Then his muscles flexed as he pushed up and moved arm's length from her, his hips and ass below a frenzied array of movement as he unleashed his vigor into her. Angeliqué thrashed underneath him, her sweaty hips and thighs a blur of activity in response to his thrusts. She reached for his face, tugged at his closely cropped beard that she found so damn sexy, and gripped the back of his head as she watched him make love to her, the exquisite feeling of him alternately filling then draining her, so intense and overshadowing, that she felt herself flush. And then Vince paused, pressed his body against hers, the sticky pigment from his chest, stomach, and legs mingling with hers. They remained this way, quiet and frozen, the only sound coming from their harried breathing, each feeling the other's heart-beat, powerful and strong, as they listened to the wind as it rustled in from the open window.

Vince came off Angeliqué, knelt before her and let his gaze sweep from her tousled hair to her painted toes. How lovely she was! He reached for her, turned her over gingerly until she was on her stomach, her lovely ass rising like a crescent shaped moon above the now sticky carpet. He scooped up a handful of red paint from the tray, and silently lathered up her thighs, ass, and lower back until a solid coat of paint was evident. Angeliqué turned her head to the side and laid it in her hands while she watched him work his art. When he had smoothed out the coat of paint, smeared it around her flesh and massaged it in to her skin with his fingers, he reached for the bright blue acrylic, scooped up a small mound and applied a wide swath in a circle around her ass. Next, he grabbed some green paint and did the same, draw-ing a smaller, inner circle, closer to her canal. Lastly, he reached for the black paint, measured out two-fingers' worth as Angeliqué moaned and spread her legs sensuously for him. With the candles flickering in the background, creating dancing shadows on the walls, Vince smeared the black coloring over and around her sex, the tips of his fingers gliding in between the slip-pery folds of her molten core. He sat back finally, admired his handiwork, as Angeliqué lay there panting, a bull's-eye on her lovely, fine ass. Vince smiled a wicked grin, before guiding himself back inside of her.

He thrust against her decorated ass with abandonment, the passion within both of them riding high until it crested like a giant tidal wave—and they cried out, in tandem, consuming each other until there was nothing left to give, the passion wrung out, spent—the relief oozing out from pores and orifices like sap from a tree. And Angeliqué lifted her head slowly, turned toward her altar of burning candles and incense, recited a quick prayer of thanks to the love goddess of voodoo before closing her eyes and losing herself in this ecstasy of this man named Vince...

✠✠✠

The chime from the cell phone awoke them—Vince at first, then Angeliqué, who was nestled in his arms, paint-coated back to him, and under the warm confines of a blanket. The chime stung his senses—at first he was unaware of his surroundings, but one look at the disheveled bronze hair on his chest told the story—he smiled as he felt Angeliqué stir, stretching her legs and flexing her backside, which was nuzzled against him on the carpeted floor.

Vince extricated himself from the still half-asleep form of Angeliqué, rose and moved, naked, to the leather sofa where his clothes and cell phone laid. He answered on the fifth ring; his eyes stretched wide open as he scanned his paint-clad body, and recalled delicious images from the previous night.

"Hello?"

"Hey you." A woman's voice. Vince was staring at Angeliqué who had turned toward him, and was staring admirably at his nude form, her eyes not roaming but fixed in one position.

"Hey..." Vince did not recognize the voice.

"I'm...not...calling at a bad time, am I?" The voice raised in pitch. Angeliqué's stare had elevated to his eyes. She watched him silently, as he stood there naked, cell phone in hand. She knew it was a woman on the other end of the phone. No doubt about that. None whatsoever.

"No...not really." Recognition came to him and he unconsciously frowned. It was Maxi.

"You haven't called." A statement.

"...I've been busy with my workshop..." Vince was beginning to get uncomfortable. He attempted a smile at Angeliqué, but it came out flat and weak. She sensed his discomfort immediately.

"...Which was over Friday night. It's *now* Sunday morning. Forgot how to dial, or just busy?" Maxine was pissed and she made no attempt to hide her blossoming irritation. Vince had turned his body toward the still-open window. He glanced down at the garden-courtyard, which was bathed in sunlight. The trickling pond shimmered in the morning light. Angeliqué watched him as he moved toward the window, his back to her. She slipped out from beneath the blanket, rose, nude, like him, her body adorned with the battle-scars from last night's lovemaking session. She smiled with the recollection of them falling asleep with Vince still inside of her, the two of them on their sides, spooning each other as Vince held her tight and nuzzled his face against her warm neck. The feeling—indescribable. She had been in heaven. Still was...

"Listen, I'd prefer not to get into this right..." Vince paused as he felt Angeliqué's hand circle his waist. Before he could pivot on his heels, her warm body was pressing against him, and he felt her soft breasts bear down on his painted back, her pubic hair rubbing against his ass. He began to harden.

"Oh I see!" Maxi said, loud enough for Angeliqué to hear. "I guess this *isn't* a good time after all!" she said, all indignant. "Let me not hold you up, Vince!" He turned to Angeliqué, wrapping an arm around her waist and pulling her into him, relishing the warmth from her naked skin. He was fully hard now, as Angeliqué had taken his member in her hand and was slowly squeezing and tugging on his sex, a wicked grin spreading across his face.

"We need to talk, Maxi," Vince replied, taking a moment to exhale forcefully, his hand dropping from Angeliqué's waist to her lovely round ass. He took hold of it and squeezed. She moaned involuntarily. Vince turned away; concerned that the sound could be heard on the other end of the cell phone. "I will call you when I get a moment to talk—I'm heading to L.A. this afternoon, so it may be later on in the evening."

"Fine. Whatever." The phone went dead and Vince sighed, snapping his phone shut. Angeliqué moved in front of him, positioned herself dead center and in his space. His manhood was snuggled decisively between her painted thighs. She looked up at him with an iniquitous grin.

"Problems at home?" she said, faux-innocence dripping from her baby-girl voice like maple syrup.

"Good morning to you, too!" Vince said, his pulse slowly returning to normal...

✠✠✠

They showered together to remove the paint from their bodies. While the hot water pounded against their freshly scrubbed skin, they made love again, Vince taking her from behind as Angeliqué stood in the shower stall, her palms pressed against the dripping white tile, her head thrown back in complete utter delight, and her lovely bronze mane dangling down her back in a single coil of wet, stringy hair. Vince's hands went to her breasts, massaged her nipples and soft mounds, and held on as their bodies slapped together underneath the rush of steamy water.

Afterwards, they dried each other and dressed, and Angeliqué prepared a hearty breakfast for Vince—an oversized Creole omelet with cheese, tomatoes, and fresh crawfish that she had picked up from the market the previous morning; bacon, and strong coffee. He had to get back to his hotel—pack and get ready for his trip—his flight to Los Angeles left that afternoon, four p.m. to be exact, and it was close to noon now. And of course with security being what it was these days, he needed to give himself plenty of time at the airport. It was time to go...

And so...Vince and Angeliqué stood out in front of a closed art gallery on a brilliantly lit Sunday morning, on a quiet street named St. Philip, in the decadent French Quarter of New Orleans, a short, lovely walk from here to the Mississippi River, a wonderful breeze catching the leaves and causing them to quiver as Vince kissed Angeliqué tenderly under the flicker of an overhead gas lamp. No words were spoken; nothing further needed to be said. Sometimes, the language of lovemaking is more than enough...

✠✠✠

And later—much much later, Vince found himself staring out at the sprawl that is known as Los Angeles. His mind was racing—shuttles, hotels, food, business at hand, book signings, workshops, speaking engagements—and just as the flight attendants were preparing the cabin for landing—his mind pushed all of this irrelevant stuff to the side and made way for the *new* object of his affection—he was staring at the business card that had "Angeliqué Malevaux—Artist" in embossed lettering; his fingers rubbed the inscription as if doing so over and over, like Aladdin and his magic lamp, would somehow bring her to him this very instant; transcending time, and, more importantly, space—and he desperately wished that he could remember the voodoo god/goddess of love—Freda *somebody*—wished that he had been paying better attention when Angeliqué had mentioned these deities by name, so he could issue his request in prayer right now...

✠✠✠

And then, in an instant, Vince found himself running through the white terminal, the steady stream of luggage-clad passengers a nuisance on his corneas as he dodged old ladies and children holding Pokemon and Barbie dolls. Outside, sliding into a taxi and slinging his bags in behind him, shouting orders to the turban-clad cabdriver, rolling, and the city-side a blur as his foot tapped incessantly with mounting impatience. Eyes moving, shifting like sand in a storm as he glanced ahead, willing cars, trucks, and buses in front of him to part around him like the Red Sea, annoyance and irritation boiling under the surface, like a fighter ready to strike. Subsequently, he was descending into a tunnel and running along the tracks before the wind suddenly shifted, and the subway car arrived, its gleaming doors opening with a whoosh. In-a-rush passengers, pushing and shoving their way out like tuna trapped in a net, before the dust settled and he could see again. Vince breathed heavy, entered the train, moving again, from car to car, searching the backs of heads, necks, and shoulders, some all too familiar, until he was within arm's length, striking distance. Running now, knowing she was near—he knew it, could feel it, his skin tingling, synapses firing, and the smell of her, invading his senses, overpowering everything else, his legs weakening, blood pumping, rushing to tiring limbs, trying to hold up, under the escalating pressure. And Vince reaching out now, almost haphazardly, from one agitated individual to another, the snap of their head all-telling, yet Vince not giving up, knowing in his heart, that she was here...close at hand...

Finally onto the street—cool, refreshing air invading his lungs, away from the darkness and dampness that was making his skin *crawl*—turning the corner and yelling out in anticipation, the desire building like a tremor that metamorphoses into a rumbling earthquake. In the distance, a lovely form, hips and untamed hair swaying to an untold beat, synchronized with his rapidly beating heart, that in its own way, was attempting to break free from the confines of its chains.

And Vince finds himself reaching out, his fingers splayed, brushing against her hair as she turns, recognition lighting up her smile like the dawn. Vince falls to his knees, the tears erupting from his eyes as he comes face-to-face with his desires, opens his mouth to speak as she smiles, those perfect teeth and dazzling, sparkling eyes—and he begins to articulate his feelings to her, knowing that she may not comprehend—or worse, that she will be frightened, but having to go on nonetheless because Vince simply has no other choice...and so on bended knee he opens his mouth...prepares to say those simple, yet powerful words...yet nothing...*nothing* escapes from his lips...

Eleven

I arrived at the restaurant at quarter past eight. Pulled up to the front by a small crowd that had already formed under the signature sloping awning that rushed at folks from on high—plunging down like a ski slope before turning upward at that final moment and fanning out over the street; an awesome contraption of steel, mesh, and canvas, with neon blue at the tips spelling out the name of this eclectic establishment—bluespace. Me in my sexy-ass black M3, top down, clothes unchanged from earlier in the day, D'Angelo on the box—yeah, y'all, I was in *that* kind of mood—didn't want to hear nothing but old school funk, "Chicken Grease," to get me out of my own funk. The braided, *swoled* brutha did just that—I was singing along with the lyrics as I rolled up to the valet, checking out the patrons from behind light-purple shades even though it was dark outside, (you *know* by now how we do!), *Let me tell U 'bout the chicken grease…*

I handed the attendant a fifty, told him to keep it and my shit right out front. I pointed to a coned-off section that lay beyond the front door. He nodded rapidly as he squeezed into the heated leather seat. "Don't mess with my ride, *Holmes*," I remarked before heading inside.

A beautifully elegant Ethiopian woman named Nikki greeted me once inside the door. We hugged, I pecked her high cheek, commented on how damn sexy she looked, told her that if I had a piece of *injera* on me right now, I'd sop her up and eat her like a succulent mouthwatering portion of *zil zil…* Nikki just laughed, shook her head, and pointed upstairs to our usual spot.

How to describe bluespace? Art meets food. Jazz, colorful, vibrant images, and luscious dishes all coming together under one roof. Inside, the walls were whitewashed and curved, floor to ceiling. Multiple levels, with a balcony that ran the circumference of the place and allowed the patrons an unobstructed view of the floor below. A freestanding fireplace stood mid-center of the hardwood floor, open on four sides, a translucent chimney that carried the sparks and ash up to the sky. Multiple skylights were cut into the concave-shaped ceiling. Tonight they were open to the nighttime air.

The owner/designer, Scott Chase, had fashioned a unique light show and choreographed it to jazz. A ring of track lighting adorned the walls, midway between the floor and ceiling. Their beams were directed back onto the walls to display a vibrant show of patterns, colors and shapes. Scott Chase, a talented brutha with an eye for color and a taste for wonderful food, had married the two in bluespace. The place received rave reviews shortly after it opened. Reservations were hard to come by. Folks came from all over to see his light shows and sample his great cuisine. On the weekends, after twelve or one when the last of the patrons were gone, they'd clear the tables and turn bluespace into D.C.'s hottest after-hours spot—playing house, trance, acid-jazz, hip-hop, or old school, depending on the mood of the D.J. and the crowd.

I waltzed in, feeling my playa-vibe take over. That always happened when I was around well-dressed folks. Plus, the shit at work today had fucked my head up—left me with an annoying buzz going on inside of me—like a hunger that couldn't be satisfied; it hung just below the surface, out of reach, but letting me know that it was there.

I heard the sound of raindrops—slowly, imperceptibly at first, and then changing to a driving rain. The lights dimmed and for a moment winked out. Off to the right, a splash of purple and blue splayed across one wall. From the left, a swath of red and orange shot across the wall/sky, combining with the purple/blue in an explosion of color. Simultaneously, the beginning of a sunrise—a red hot/orange/indigo-colored horizontal line, bowed slightly, that rose slowly to the sounds of Boney James and his sax. Then, when it had risen almost to the top of the structure, the music changed, shifted to classic Pat Metheny Group—"Are you going with me?" The soulful, wind-inspired synths of Lyle Mays increasing in volume slowly until everyone was grooving along with the sound, as patterns erupted onto the walls from all directions—blue/greens, the colors of a Brazilian jungle, and its rich sounds—then shifting to the reddish brown and bronze earth tones of a California desert at twilight, the background noise of a rainstorm soothing and frightening at the same time. I had to pause in my step and watch, like everyone else, the scene mesmerizing and awe inspiring.

I reached the top step, folded my shades and put them away, and scanned the crowd, making eye contact with a few choice honeys who were seated with their men. Erika and Vince were already there. I grinned to them as I made my way over. Vince stood and hugged me. It had been a while—only a few weeks, actually, since I'd last seen my best friend in the flesh, because our schedules took us out of town, but it seemed like a lifetime. I missed my homey, and our drawn-out embrace told me he felt the same. He was dressed in a dark sports coat, tan slacks and loafers. He looked impeccable as usual and I told him so. I then turned and hugged Erika, kissing her on her cheek. What can I say about my home girl? Erika is the bomb, and she looked damn good as usual. Erika was tall, about five eight, thin, with smooth, caramel skin, black curly hair that she wore pulled back and resting on her shoulders. She wore a light-blue tank top, which accentuated her small, yet firm breasts and showcased her thin arms, an off-white knee-length skirt, a thick tan leather belt, and matching open toe shoes. Her face was beautiful—the suggestion of Asian descent, sculptured nose, thin lips and eyebrows, high cheekbones, and finally, just a hint of a cleft chin. We hugged affectionately. I had missed my girl, too! I pulled back, looked at her up and down admiringly while making animal noises. "Ummm, ummm, ummm! Damn, Sassy, you look fine. Don't she, Vince?"

"You know it. Classy as usual," Vince said, grinning and grabbing a sip from the wine stem in front of him.

"Fuck that, Holmes," I said, turning my attention once again to Erika who had taken her seat. "Baby girl, can a brutha getwithchew?" I licked my lips and she replied by swatting my arm. I just smiled and sat down. Trey's Rule Number 13—don't fuck your friends, no matter how fine they are. For real!

The waiter came and I ordered a drink. Vince and Erika hadn't been seated more than five minutes. We got down to business.

"So, how ya livin'?" I asked around the table.

"Large and in charge," Vince responded.

"Me too!" Erika chimed in. We both shot her a nasty look.

"What?" She playfully hit me on the arm again. "I can't live large and in charge like the big boys?"

"Anyway…Damn, y'all," I said, kicking things off. "It feels like a lifetime since we've all gotten together."

"I know," Erika mused. "If you two would stop gallivanting all over God's green earth then maybe we could catch up on the *regular*."

"Oh no she didn't, Vince," I said, a feigned look of surprise on my face. Vince just shook his head silently. "Don't she know someone's gotta do it?"

"I guess she didn't get the memo," Vince remarked.

"Whatever," Erika said. "Anywho, I gather from both of your calls that there is a lot to cover tonight."

Erika, Vince and I had been doing this thing for over a year now—we'd come here to bluespace every other Wednesday to catch up, to find out what's going on in each other's lives—a lot easier having the three of us in one room as opposed to having separate conversations—not that that still didn't occur, mind you. I loved these times with Vince and Erika—they were my true friends—the ones I could share my innermost, deepest, darkest secrets with, and know that they would not judge me, regardless of my actions.

"So, whose turn is it anyway?" Erika asked. Vince and I turned to one another and said simultaneously: "Mine!"

"See," I said, placing my palms flat on the table. "This ain't right. You know it's my turn to go first this time." I looked to Erika for support; her face was scrunched up in a frown.

"I don't think so," Vince said calmly.

"Don't even try it, my man, you know it's my turn. Erika, help a brutha out, please?"

"Trey, you *always* try to weasel your way into going first. Damn, can't you let someone else go for a change?"

"That is not true. Vince, that's not true, right?" I looked to Vince for moral support, a man-to-man, brutha-to-brutha thing.

"True dat!" he said. "Now, can everyone kindly shut up, you especially, Trey, so I can say my piece? We're wasting valuable time here…" Vince said, looking at his watch.

"Sassy," I said, cutting my man off, "you notice how Vince always tries to act all grown up and shit? Like he's somehow a cut above the rest of us?"

"Yeah," Erika responded, eyeing Vince cautiously. "Who he think he is, anyway?"

"Exactly!" I joined in. Vince pressed his mouth shut and shook his head silently.

"Y'all are *so* damn childish! Anyway, as I was saying before being so rudely interrupted…I met *someone*…" Vince's eyes were sparkling and the table became silent.

"No shit?" I said, looking at Vince dumbfoundedly. Surrounding us, the light show was in full effect. Colorful strobes danced on and off to the sounds of Acoustic Alchemy, something upbeat and funky that left patrons tapping their hands and feet as swaths of colors—green flashes, orange strobes, and yellow pulses danced and meandered across the ceiling and curved walls.

"Her name is Angeliqué, I met in her New Orleans during a workshop, and guys, she stole my heart…"

"Wait a second," Erika asked, holding up her hand. "What happened to Maxi? Am I missing something?"

Vince cleared his throat and for the next fifteen minutes proceeded to give us the details—beginning with his dream that led him to question his relationship with Maxi, onto his trip to New Orleans where he met Angeliqué, and their subsequent, whirlwind romance.

He spoke of their wonderful, romantic dinner; intense conversation in the courtyard of her gallery/home; the passion of this mysterious, voodoo goddess; her art, subsequent show, featuring *veve*-covered flesh; the way they made love on the floor to candlelight—painting one another with colorful hues, smearing each other's flesh with paint, and fucking with abandonment, the way new lovers often do.

Erika was enthralled. I sat there, asking questions when Vince got to the juicy part.

"That's my dawg!" I exclaimed, high-fiving Vince. "Dude, hope you captured that shit on video…please tell me you brought a copy home to a brutha?"

"Sadly, the tapes were confiscated at the airport." Vince looked dejected.

"Damn, I hate when that happens. But, dawg, sounds like you did okay— I guess my mentoring finally paid off!"

"Please," Erika said. "Vince, I'm happy that you met this woman. It sounds like the two of you hit it off immediately."

"Sassy, that's what excited me the most," Vince said, his eyes lighting up with remembrances of Angeliqué. "The speed at which we vibed. I mean, you know, I meet women every other day of my life, but something about her struck me as truly special."

"Here we go," I said, downing the last of my Corona.

"Ignore his ignorant ass, Vince," Erika mused, scooting closer to Vince and rubbing his shoulder. "I, for one, am very excited for you. I just have two questions for you: one, are you going to see her again, and two, what are you going to do about Maxi?"

"Dawg," I added quickly, "You know I'm happy, too, for you. Damn, you go, boy! Sounds like you got a tight woman on your hands."

"Thanks, man," Vince said. He turned to Erika. "To answer your questions—hell yeah! I'm gonna see her again. If I have my way, real soon. And two, I gave Maxi a call when I got home. She knew something was up—she called when I was just waking up with Angeliqué…not a good thing…"

"Damn!" I exclaimed. I didn't know which turned me on more—the sex or the drama!

"Yeah, but I was honest with her, as usual. Perhaps too much so. I told her that I wasn't feeling the relationship anymore. That while she was a wonderful lady and someone I had a lot of fun with, I just didn't see things panning out the way I wanted them to. She didn't understand—asked a lot of questions for which I didn't have a lot of answers." Vince paused to take a sip of wine and to rub his beard. "I don't know, Sassy—I know I'm doing the right thing. I can't put into words exactly how I'm feeling, but I know what I want…and Maxi, unfortunately, is not it."

"I hear you, Vince, and you should be commended for being a man and telling her how you feel—not dragging things out the way some bruthas do just so that they can get some every now and then. No woman wants to be led on and have things dragged out, trust me."

"Yeah, I guess." Vince was quiet, deep in reflection.

"Listen," I said, steering the conversation back to a more positive vibe, "all this talk about naked painted women, hoodoo-voodoo, and wild monkey sex reminds me, I've got a shitload to spill. So if the gentleman from the District is finished, I'd like to go next…"

"I can't believe this mutha fucka," Erika remarked, getting all indignant and thrusting her finger in my face. "Can't you see that your boy over here is both excited and hurting? Seems all you want to do is get to the blow-by-blow sexploits of your incredible vacation. Trey, that's low, even for you." Erika got up abruptly and excused herself to the ladies room. I was left staring at my boy Vince, who eyed me curiously from across the table.

"Dawg, you know I got your back on this one?" I said, hoping Vince wasn't angry with me. He smiled, giving me that grin that was his signature trademark, like a photo taken from his book jacket, and in that moment I knew everything was a-okay with us.

✠✠✠

The food arrived. I was famished. Erika was working on an oversized Caesar salad with fresh cheese and healthy-sized chunks of dark jerk chicken. Vince was in the midst of consuming thick, honey-glazed pork chops, alternating between admiring the presentation and remarking on the ease at which his knife cut through the meat as if it were butter. I had opted for the grilled Norwegian Salmon—I loved the way Scott Chase prepared this dish, with spicy mashed potatoes and fresh asparagus, which had been stir-fried in hot oil and spices. I know y'all will find this hard to believe, seeing how I'm a true playa, but with my interest in culinary delights—yeah, you *heard* me right—I had spoken with Scott months back, compared recipes, and was constantly trying to improve and share my new creations with him via email or in person.

Around us, laser beams of hued light danced across the whitewashed walls to the soulful voice of Billie Holiday's "God Bless the Child," while the bright faces of children from over two-hundred countries beamed overhead, a celebration of life, its most treasured gift.

It was my turn. Finally! And this brutha waited not one second more to dive into the carnal delights of my trip to Jamaica. I talked for forty-five minutes, sparing no minutiae as I recounted every deliciously sinful detail—from my getting down there, the problem with my room that turned out to be a blessing in disguise, from my chance encounter with the lovely Jackie, and her first taste of *Trey Steak*, an African-American *delicacy*, to me in the hot tub with mutha fuckas watching, green with envy as two ladies went down on me under a blanket of stars. Onto the days spent lying by the warm waters of the Caribbean watching a pussyfest unfold, or by the pool getting my dick sucked by some honey with fake tits and a shaved pussy—then fading to the toga party and the late night entertainment featuring Gabrielle, the South American honey, and yours truly in a hammock by a bonfire, while dozens, including her own husband watched and cheered us on. Yeah, Sassy, I kid you not, her mutha fuckin' husband!

Girlfriend and Vince just shook their heads while their mouths hung open…

And as I talked on, the lights around me strobed and pulsed as if alive. Swaths of orange fire burned high overhead while Erika and Vince were mesmerized by my recount. The melodic pianos of Jim Brickman, Keiko Matsui, and Joe Sample played on, while I found myself transported back to the shores of Negril and to paradise, where this Stella *definitely* got his groove back. The rest of my mind-blowing vacation became a colorful blur, running at high speed—bits and pieces, those lusciously delectable tidbits, which I'm sure will come to me from time to time in the future, but I swear the fine points are lost forever.

I closed my eyes, bringing to mind the white cowboy hat lady with the hourglass-shaped body. Her name was Montanna; she and her husband, Chad, were out of Houston. Chad and Montanna, I explained after taking another swig of my Corona, took me to another level of Lifestyles pleasure—they taught me the difference between raw animal pleasure of the flesh, and connections that lead to a deeper, fulfilling lovemaking—that feeling of total, uncompressed passion that is expressed as a storm—one which wells up inside of you, and ejects itself from every pore during the severe explosion we all know as orgasm…

I recalled my final nights in Jamaica as memorable and special. At that point, I was a man wholly satisfied and at peace, the tranquility that comes from total fulfillment—I had been enjoying the pleasures of numerous women, but I had toned it down, no longer needing to go non-stop like a freaking Energizer Bunny—I had reached the summit, the Mount Everest of fucking; my mark was indelibly left on that special place—mutha fuckas whispered my name, pointing to me as I swept by, my dark cock swinging in the Jamaican breeze. At this juncture, *everyone* knew my name!

And then I recounted for Vince and Erika that final morning where I found myself in the whirlpool surrounded by my friends and lovers—old and new, as I waited for the Breitling Blackbird to turn one p.m., signaling my departure home. The sky was overcast—a telling sign, a rainshower was coming in from the west. New faces lined the pool and bar area—a lot of the folks whom I had come to know intimately were gone, back to their normal lives, the treasures experienced at this out-of-this-world resort packed away in the special recesses of their minds…never to be forgotten…

And yet, in a sense, nothing had changed. Those last moments by the pool when I exited the whirlpool for the last time, hugging my remaining friends, strolling back to my chair to collect my things, drops of refreshing pool water cascading down this sexy brutha's tight body, the weight of dozens of pairs of eyes were once again upon my firm back, sexy tattoos, and ass. Yeah, they were clocking a brutha, one last time…And I was totally feeling it—life and all she has to offer. I was livin', y'all. Livin' large!

✠✠✠

I finished up, took a deep breath, sighed, and sat back, a satisfied look on my mug. Erika was speechless. Vince was shaking his head slowly from side to side, a grin painted across his dark features.

"Dude, you should write a novel with that yarn," he remarked. We pounded fists. I downed the last of my Corona and signaled for another.

"Trey, that shit is incredible, even for you," Erika said finally, breaking her silence.

"Yeah, what can I say? You're right, Sassy. It's gonna be hard topping that shit. But you know this brutha's sure as hell gonna try!"

"True dat! You wouldn't be my dawg if you didn't," Vince exclaimed.

I paused for a moment, reflected on the one part that had been hidden from my recitation—and as I checked my friend's faces, I weighted whether or not I should mention that one, small yet indelible bit of info…realizing that I would be grated over the coals if it came out later that I had held this important fact back. And so, after pushing the lime into the bottle of my fresh, cold Corona, and tipping it upside-down as my thumb covered the opening, I took a long swig, wiped my mouth and sighed deeply before speaking. "There's one more thing I need to mention." I paused. Both eyes were locked on mine. Unintentionally, my voice dropped a notch in volume. "Something freaky happened down there; I need to share." That got Erika's and Vince's attention but quick!

✠✠✠

How do I say this—where do I begin? I found myself suddenly perspiring and wiped the beads that had formed on my brow. My dawg, Vince, and my boo, Erika, watched me silently.

"I, umm, saw someone down there…or I *thought* I saw someone." I paused and took another hit of my brew.

"Trey," Erika remarked, eyeing me curiously, "the suspense is fucking killing us!"

"Okay. Damn." Another breath taken. My mind whirled. Fragments from *that* night raced along the corridors of my mind, but at half-speed—me on stage, toga-clad, at the top of my form, my game, the crowd whipped into a frenzy and chanting a mutha fucka's name over and over again as I stood defiantly center stage—"TREY, TREY, TREY, TREY, TREY!" And then, I spotted her, and…that feeling…sinking…

"What up, Dawg?" It was Vince speaking. "You okay?"

"Yeah." I cleared my throat. Raised my head and scanned both sets of eyes before continuing. "I thought I saw *Layla* down there."

"No...Oh shit." Erika's hand had involuntarily gone to her face. Her mouth hung open.

"Yeah. *Layla*." I let the *significance* of that sink in. And sink in it did. Like a big-ass rock! I watched Vince, whose face had twisted and taken on an air of deep concern. He said nothing, but the apprehension showed in his brown eyes. My eyes flicked over to Erika, whose own face was painted with distress. "They say," I continued, holding the table's rapt attention, "that everyone has a twin somewhere. Well, let me tell you something, I found Layla's twin, and she was *her* to a T, I kid you not!"

"Damn. Where and when did this happen?" Sassy wanted the facts.

"Remember I told you about Gabrielle, the honey I fucked on the beach in a hammock?" Once again I found myself transported backwards in time as I closed my eyes, back to that night, the ocean breeze on my face, sweaty chest, and withering cock, the applause from the crowd behind us, the eruption of sound: hooping, hollering, and plenty of high-fives, thumbs upturned in the air, and smiles, while Gabrielle and I took our bow. Then a dizzying fast-forward to the toga party, and me onstage, the crowd scream-ing and carrying on, and I standing there with this cocky, shit-eating grin on my face thinking: *There's no one on this planet right now who is feeling more alive and in control than I am.* The power that comes from having mutha fuckas throw their hands in the air because they *respect* your style...yeah, ride this beautiful shit for just a minute, while honeys whisper your fucking name...

And then, in an instant—like a car careening out of control, over the median, and into oncoming traffic—the wind was snatched from my lungs, the blood drained from every inch of my tanned skin, when I spotted *her*. A spitting image of her, of Layla, the woman I had once loved more than life itself, the one person I would have gladly lain down and died for. Without question...

Once again, Vince and Erika were speechless.

"For a moment, y'all, it was her. Same hair, same face, same eyes. I swear to God, I would have bet all of my 401K plan on that shit; I ain't playing!"

Short dress—I recall it well—some things you don't forget—orange, low cut, hugging her curves like a tight, leather glove. Curves I had once upon a time gotten to know like the back of my own hand.

"What did you do, Trey?" Erika asked softly. Her arm had come up and was massaging my back. The waiter had cleared our plates and refreshed their drinks. I had waved him away without a second thought.

"I stood there—frozen on stage—I couldn't breathe. I felt…how can I describe this…sick, yeah, I felt sick, off-balance, like I was going down. But then, the feeling passed, thank goodness." I drained the Corona and set it down hard on the table. "I'll tell you this, I wasn't any good for the rest of the night."

"Layla," Vince said breaking his silence. He shook his head slowly. "Did you speak to her?"

"Yeah, well, I had to get the fuck out of there. Got back to my room where I could think. But my friends showed up at my door…with her." I shook my head in remembrance. "Her name was Cinnamon. And, God was she beautiful. Cinnamon wanted to party. Was there at the resort for only one night. And she wanted me."

"Damn."

I looked around the table. Just the thought of that moment had taken a toll on me. My shoulders sunk down as I felt the weight of something just out of reach pressing down on me. The added burden of my situation at work added a vicious blow to my already bruised self. I shook my head sadly.

"The funny thing—as fine as she was, I couldn't bring myself to be with her. I remember her standing at my door, with that look of sheer fucking desire blazing in her eyes." I paused, shuddered involuntarily as I recalled the scene in vivid detail. "She wanted me, Dawg, no fucking question about that. Those panties were *soaked*, you hear me?" Vince nodded silently. "But I had to leave it alone."

"It's understandable," Erika said, rubbing my back again.

Yeah, I thought to myself as I tried to emit a cocky laugh. But it came out more like a shrug and a groan.

I *had* to leave it alone…

Twelve

They finished up at bluespace by ten and left to run home and change. Trey and Vince swung by Erika's place in Silver Spring, and together they rode down 16th Street to the waterfront, like wingmen from a fighter squadron. The night was perfect for riding—the temperature had not yet begun to dip into winter zone.

It was after eleven by the time they roared up Maine to H20. Insisting they make a grand entrance to the club, as only they could do, Trey rode point on the Indian, decked out in soft brown leather from jacket to boot, Erika gripping his waist, adorned in a pair of tight jeans, black leather jacket and boots, her hair swept back by a faded yellow bandanna underneath her helmet. Vince held the rear on the Fat Boy, shaking his head as Trey wove in and out of downtown traffic, the stars shimmering and shining overhead as they rode.

By the time they had arrived, a crowd had formed on the sidewalk in front of H20, a rare sight for a Wednesday night. But Erika had remembered from listening to Donnie Simpson, the green-eyed bandit on WPGC earlier that day that someone famous—she just couldn't recall who exactly—was gonna be there for some kind of reggae after-party.

Trey downshifted, gunned the throttle for show, making a few women jump from the sharp rapport, smirked behind his shades, and turned toward the sidewalk. All eyes were on them as he dropped his boots to the ground—and this was the part that excited Trey and Vince the most—when folks stopped in mid-conversation as they rode by—wondering just who those wild boys were—decked out in their leathers and fly shades, the rumbling of hot chrome between their legs. Trey steered his machine past the now silent crowd that had parted to let them through, up under the awning where they came to rest, all eyes upon them. Normally, this space was off limits for any kind of parking, since it was directly in front of the club's front entrance. But Trey knew the owner fairly well, and had been here with the Indian and the Fat Boy too many times to count—so the bouncers became familiar with their motorcycles, and allowed them to park there. Plus, it was good for business. The owner knew from experience that folks loved to gawk at those two machines. They always attracted a crowd.

Erika dismounted first, taking Trey's hand to maintain balance as she swung her leg over the Corbin seat. Once both feet were back on solid ground, she smoothed out her jeans and removed her helmet, retying her bandanna tightly behind her. Trey and Vince also wore bandannas over their heads, and looked sexy as hell, she had to admit. Trey waved to a few acquaintances as he stowed his gloves and set the disc-lock. He then walked over to the bouncer who had let them through, hugged him briefly and slapped his back as he palmed a fifty into his hand. The brutha pocketed the bill and gave Trey dap. Erika just had to smile. She had to give her boy credit; he knew how to work it, no question about that.

In the few moments that it took to waltz into the club—there was a line, but Erika and company damn sure weren't about to wait to get into this place—she surveyed the crowd and had to smile. It never ceased to amaze her; she thought to herself while scanning the mostly dark faces—a source of much discussion between Vince, Trey, and herself—how women always had the same look on their faces when they spotted guys on their bikes. What was it about being a roughneck, possessing that living on the edge wild-streak that drove women crazy? It was funny—most women talked non-stop about wanting an educated, well-dressed man. Hell, they all knew that from personal experience, especially Trey—his ass worked downtown, he knew! Just waltz around 7th Street, F Street, or K Street (Lawd, have mercy!) at lunchtime, shaded and Brooks Brothers-*down*, and watch the women as they stared at his fine ass! Them ladies loved them some well-dressed niggas! No doubt! But then, let Trey or Vince sport a leather jacket and pants, bandanna and shades, face unshaven, and come roaring by—oh, hell no, and sistahs would just about lose their minds! It was that sense of excitement mixed with danger—it could be seen in their eyes…

"Oh, I see, you ain't just any old nine-to-five man, you *ride?*"

"Oh, hell yeah, Shorty, I live to ride…"

"Hmmm…I've *always* wanted to get on the back of a bike…"

"Baby, I'd just *love* to get you on the back of one right now! Girl, you just don't know…"

Erika grasped both Trey's and Vince's hands—the three of them loved to do this when they went out—kept folks guessing just who Erika was with—this one…or that one—or was that fine sistah with them both??? Dayum!

They waltzed into the club that served up Caribbean-inspired food and the best music Chocolate City had to offer (that is if you dug *anything* besides hip-hop and rap), up the winding stairs to the second floor, past the large dance floor, and raised upper-level area to the back VIP section and bar. Past hundreds of patrons who were sweating and grooving to the funkin', throbbin' sounds of the D.J., who had Cameo on the box—"Single Life," its bass line thump-slapping against their chests like heavy heartbeats. Trey grabbed Erika's hand and pulled her into the sea of bodies while belting out, *I'm living a single, single…life…* Folks parting around them like a waterfall surrounds suntanned flesh, watching them closely, wondering just who in the fuck was this leather-clad couple, colorfully bandanna-*down*, painted-on jeans (fellas, Erika was working them jeans!) while everyone else was dressed conservatively—as Erika and Trey moved to the rhythm as if tethered, yeah, they moved *that* well—her thigh slipping in between his legs as his arms wrapped around her thin waist, head thrown back, eyes closed, fingers and hands reaching toward the ceiling. Vince pulled in behind her into *his* slot, as if on cue—now mutha fuckas were really losing their minds—watching him slap against her ass with his pelvis as if he were fucking her right on this very dance floor, his hands on her hips as the three of them fell into their own sync-groove, like pistons on a well-oiled engine—the trio making a writhing sandwich, Erika being the *meat*, one hell of a sight—everyone in the club straining their necks to get a glimpse…

And then the music shifted, D.C.'s own Me'Shell NdegéOcello, "If That's

Your Boyfriend (He Wasn't Last Night)," her sultry, sexy voice rapping over a bass-infused jam.

Folks who were tiring and beginning their exit from the dance floor turned in mid-stream as they recognized the melody and yelled, "That there's my song!" The floor filled again quickly, as Trey, Vince, and Erika disengaged and moved over to the VIP bar overlooking the harbor. The bouncer shook Trey's and Vince's hands in turn before turning his hooded eyes toward Erika. They sparkled briefly as he looked her over. She was used to that and didn't pay him any mind. He waved them past and they took a seat at the bar, Erika between them, and ordered drinks from a Rasta bartender.

It was late, they all had to work in the morning, but there was still much more to discuss—Trey had just begun to touch on the newly unfolding drama at work, and Erika hadn't even shared any of her stuff yet—that was just like them too—usually, Trey and/or Vince spent most of the time consuming their precious bluespace-time reveling over their own exploits, rarely leaving enough time for her—actually, that was okay with her—she didn't possess the same need as they did to spill her guts and glory all over the table…but still…once in a while…damn…and as it turned out she actually had something of her own to share this time…

When their drinks arrived they toasted to each other, and Erika glanced around. The VIP section wasn't crowded—just a few well-dressed folks lounging on couches behind them, and a few seats at the bar taken up by well-dressed women. Erika smiled at them while watching Trey and Vince from the corner of her eye. Vince, to her left, was chatting with the bartender about some reggae star who had just completed a set downstairs. Trey, on her right, was swiveling around on his bar stool, nodding silently to the women at the bar, while simultaneously checking out a group of women on couches off to the side. He had caught the eye of a particular white woman; Erika noticed that immediately—Trey was grinning his usual grin, showing all of his perfectly straight white teeth, and tipping his glass in her direction—Erika was surprised that he was still sitting in his chair when she felt a tap on her shoulder. She pivoted around and looked into the eyes of a familiar face. Without warning, she felt herself flush.

"Erika."

"James." Trey and Vince turned in unison and glanced up at the man who stood behind Erika. They stared at him, synapses in their respective heads firing rapidly—Trey's smile was replaced by a frown as he looked the brutha up and down—sharp, two-button, single breasted wool suit and leather lace ups, gotta give him credit—whoever this mutha fucka was, he sure knew how to dress! And then recognition exploded in front of him—Trey knew this guy—saw him on a regular basis—on television—the local news.

"How are you? You look great." James bent down and pecked Erika on her cheek. She smiled but wondered if her boys could sense her discomfort.

"James, these are my close friends Trey Alexander and Vince Cannon, Jr. James works for Channel Four here in town."

"Nice to meet you two," James remarked, sticking out his hand to Vince first, as if sensing that Trey might not take it. Vince smiled ever so slightly and shook James' hand before dropping it quickly, as if he might catch a communicable disease from this guy. Trey made no move to shake James' hand; rather he just continued to stare into the brutha's eyes.

"Where you two know each other from?" Trey asked, his vision a laser point equidistant from James and Erika. James began to speak, but Erika raised her voice, signaling to James and everyone else within earshot that she was going to take this one.

"We met a few weeks ago at an embassy function that I attended recently…"

"Since when you attend embassy functions?" Vince had turned on his stool and was staring at Erika, boldly ignoring James who hovered closely behind her.

"Yeah, embassy functions? That's a new one on me," Trey quipped.

"Listen to you two—acting like my damn daddy!" Erika smiled and James laughed. He was the only one. "Anywho—we met, had a drink together, and got together a few times after that." She stared at Trey who was eyeing her curiously, and then over to Vince whose drink lay untouched beside his elbow.

"Got together a few times…" Trey repeated. He had cocked his head and was looking at James curiously.

"You have to excuse these two—we go way back and they tend to be a bit possessive—like I'm their little sister or something."

James swallowed involuntarily as he eyed Vince who was shifting in his bar seat. Vince placed his palms flat on the bar deck and used the opportunity to flex his large muscles. The moment was not lost on James.

"I understand." A pause followed by a short laugh.

"Do you?" Trey said, turning to face James fully. "I mean, we take Erika here very seriously. We don't let just anyone get close to her—I'm sure you know what I mean."

"Of course." James stepped back a bit as if to remove himself from within striking distance. He placed a hand inside his pocket and shifted uneasily in his shoes. "Well, I'm going to leave you alone. It was nice seeing you, Erika. Give me a call—I'd like to take you out again, that is, if it's okay with your protectors here?" He smiled and backed away before either Vince or Trey could respond.

"Mutha fucka," Vince whispered. "Sassy," he said while following James with his stare, "you better come clean right now! What's the deal with you and James?"

"I was going to tell you guys when my turn finally came around."

"Whatever, trick! Don't play us like that," Trey exclaimed. "What? It just conveniently slipped your mind that you're dating the fucking anchor from Channel Four news? I think not!"

"Both of you need to take a sip of your drinks and chill. Damn, I have nothing to hide. And I was going to tell you tonight. But Vince here's falling for a voodoo priestess, and Trey—well, with all of your monkey sex-acts, it's extremely difficult to get a word in edgewise!"

"Don't make me bitch-slap you!" Trey exclaimed, but his eyes were softening. Erika took a breath. "K," she said, "Here it goes..."

✠✠✠

And so, for the next fifteen minutes, it was Sassy's turn to tell her tale—what she had been up to since they all had last met. She began with the embassy function—a fund-raiser that Caren, one of her friends from the hospital, dragged her to several weeks ago. Erika had been standing around a bunch of stuffy, uppity folks—pontificating about this and that when she spied James

148

across the room, deep in conversation with a mixed group of people. She caught his eye as he was genuflecting with his wine stem—he smiled, she returned the smile, then turned her back on him. He disengaged himself from the group ten minutes later and came up to introduce himself.

"James was very confident in his approach. I liked that. I think it had to do with the fact that there weren't too many of us there," Erika said, rubbing her brown forearm to make the point. "We chatted about superficial stuff—I asked a few questions about news anchoring, 'cause I knew exactly who he was as soon as I spotted him."

"Cut to the chase, Sassy—you fucking him?" Trey asked, signaling the bartender for another round. Beyond the VIP bar the main floor was packed as Usher sang in the background.

"Did I interrupt your monkey ass when we were at bluespace?" She didn't wait for the answer. "Anywho, before I was rudely cut short…" She cut a quick glance at Trey who was pursing his lips and eyeing her inquisitively. "That night we had a very stimulating conversation. I was very much attracted to James and the fact that he wasn't trying to impress me with his 'hey, I'm on TV and I've got my own driver' bullshit. He is intelligent and can carry on an intellectual conversation. I like that. Plus, look at him." She smiled and patted Vince's forearm. "Homeboy is fine, you've got to admit it—he was wearing that suit!"

"Whatever!" Trey and Vince spoke in unison, then turned and high-fived each other.

That first night, forty-five minutes into their conversation, James pulled out a business card, scribbled his home and cell numbers on the back, and handed it to Erika. Without being asked, she had reached for his pen, requested another one of his cards, and written her home number on the back.

"Call me, James, and we'll go out," she had said while staring up into his clear brown eyes. And then she turned on her heels and exited the large room, leaving James with this shit-eating grin on his face!

Two days later, James called. They met at I Ricchi on 19th for dinner the following night. Spent two hours over some of the best Italian she'd every had, conversing about everything from where they grew up, gone to school, dating in the new millennium, African-American politics, and the hip-hop culture. They left I Ricchi and walked over to Ozio, an eclectic cigar bar on M Street, which caters to Washington's chic and elite. James got them into the third-floor VIP section where they lit up a pair of fresh Cubans, ordered Cosmopolitans made extremely well by a bartender named Nick from New York, and danced to hip-hop music. By eleven-thirty, after they had been dancing for thirty minutes straight (they were the only ones in VIP who were dancing, but Erika didn't care—she was thrilled by the way everyone was checking her and her new beau out, plus she loved the way James moved when he danced, especially after he had shed his suit jacket and loosened his tie)— she made up her mind right then and there. She was going to sleep with James—that night...

"WHAT???" Trey yelled, almost knocking over his drink onto the wooden bar and spinning around to see if James were still in the vicinity. Thankfully (for James) he was not.

"You've got to be kidding, Sassy," Vince remarked. "At that point you had been with the guy what, four maybe five hours? And you were already consenting to having sex with him?"

Erika took a sip of her drink slowly and then put her glass down. She eyed Vince first, then Trey before speaking. "This shit is hilarious! The two of you have got to be the world's biggest hypocrites! You, Vince—with your voodoo lady—how long did it take you before you were fantasizing about spanking that ass? Huh? I'd estimate no more than an hour—tops! And Trey. Don't even get me started on you—I mean, when you fucked that Jamaican girl the first day on your vacation, exactly how many *minutes* had gone by since you'd first eyed her? Five? Ten? Surely no more than that!"

Both were, for a moment in time, lost in thought.

"I can't believe this double standard our society has—I'm not stupid; I know it's always existed between men and women, but this is me we are talking about. Erika—and I'm a woman who has the same wants and desires that you men do. Well, maybe not the same as Monkey-ass over there," she said, cutting a sharp glance over at Trey. "But I get just as horny as you both do. I have sexual thoughts. A lot. And I want to get mine just like you do.

And like the two of you I sometimes choose to act on my emotions when I want to. This is twenty-oh-six. I'm a big girl. And If I wanna fuck a brutha I just met, I'm gonna!"

Trey was snapping his head from left to right and back again, eyes closed, repeating the words, "no, no, no," over and over again.

Vince tried… "Sassy—I, we understand what you're saying…"

"No, we don't," Trey interrupted.

Vince sighed. "Sassy—I understand how you are feeling. But you know, it's different for a woman to be out there doing that kind of thing."

Erika cut him off. "Oh, I see. If a man sleeps with a woman he hardly knows it's okay, but if a woman does it, then she's a ho."

"Excuse me, Mr. Bartender," Trey said loudly. "Do you have any ho cakes for this ho right here?" Erika's hand rose up without warning and slapped him hard on his shoulder. Trey yelped and immediately hung his head.

"If I'm a ho, mutha fucka, then you are one bitch-ass slut puppy!" She had her fingers in Trey's face, and everyone in the VIP section, including the women at the bar had ceased their conversation to partake in the new drama going down. Vince calmly (and gingerly) took her hand away from Trey's face.

"People, let's not let this situation degenerate. Trey, if Sassy wants to get her groove on, then that's her prerogative. Okay? Look at it this way—she could have picked a worse nigga to ball. At least we know who he is and where to find him. He ain't going to do anything stupid or risk his precious career over messing with a woman, ya know?"

"Whatever. I can't believe you gave that nigga some. Damn!" Trey rose off his bar stool, grabbed his beer from the bar, and walked away.

"What's his fucking problem?" Erika asked, turning to Vince.

"He's very protective of you, Sassy, you know that. Always has been."

"Yeah, I guess." Erika's eyes began to soften. Actually, she found the whole scene kind of cute. A slow song had come on: Brandy, from one of her more recent CDs. Couples rushed toward the center of the floor for a chance to slow dance. "Oooh. I love this new jam. Dance with me, Vince. I need someone to hold me."

Vince smiled and reached for her. "Lead the way, Sassy, you sexy-ass ho!"

They were walking toward the dance floor as the lights dimmed and lasers began to strobe when his cell phone vibrated. Vince reached for his hip, flipped the phone open, glanced at the screen and grinned. "Uh, one moment, Sassy, I've got to take this." He took the call, and Erika watched his face change—a slow transformation, like candle wax dripping or slow-going molasses—Vince's eyes lit up along with his smile. "Hey you…" he began. Erika knew it was Angeliqué, the voodoo priestess—who else these days would make Vince beam like that? And so, Erika walked away to give Vince some privacy, and stood by the side of the dance floor. There she witnessed couples hold each other as if it were their last night on earth, while listening to that Brandy slow jam, the one she just loved, alone…

Thirteen

"Guess what I'm wearing?" That sultry, sensuous voice transported Vince back to the Quarter and the courtyard of Angeliqué's home; a light breeze, the steady trickle from the oval pond lit from high above by a crescent-shaped moon. *Veve*-covered flesh that undulated to his light touch. A kiss, a tongue, a hard, distended nipple, and hair that bounced to Miles, *A Different Kind of Blue*. He had no choice but to smile.

"I can't imagine…," Vince said, cupping the phone to his ear and heading for the balcony outside where he could continue his conversation in peace, "and the suspense is damn near killing me!"

"I'll give you a hint, baby," Angeliqué teased. Her voice rose and fell as if in singsong. Vince found himself aroused and closed his eyes for a moment to experience the full effect. "Not much. I'm in my studio—lights off, my favorite jazz piece playing softly in the background, pink and pale blue candles burning, sweet cakes and a pack of unlit cigarettes on the altar, an offering— the spirit of Ezili Freda permeating the air like thick wonderful perfume…"

"Ummmmn, wish I was there." Vince found a spot overlooking the street. He could see the line of folks that extended beyond the overhang—party-goers, young folks, oblivious to the time of night, who were still waiting to get inside H20.

"If you were here, lover, you'd see that I've painted myself, my breasts that ache for your touch and your hot tongue; my forearms, thick with red paint and yellow dots; my pussy, which I shaved an hour ago after a long hot bath of basil, sweet peppers, and *zo-devan* powder—shaved her clean so that I could lather her with vibrant colors and feel every stroke of my brush—God, that's what did it, you know…that tiny little brush stroking my freshly shaved pussy—my eyes closed, thinking it was you stroking and eating me with your wonderful tongue. God, I'm so fucking wet, Vince. I'm sorry, baby; I know it's late, but I had to call you and let you know that I was thinking of you…"

Vince turned away from the patrons who were sitting at tables on the dimly lit balcony, enjoying the nighttime air. Turned away so that he could hide his growing erection. That's what he admired—no, loved about her, his Angeliqué. The way she was at peace with her own sexuality—and the way she could communicate her thoughts and desires to him as if they had known each other for ten-thousand lifetimes. His thoughts whisked back to weeks ago, when the two of them had lain there on the carpeted floor, the light from a half dozen candles flickering off their naked forms, as Angeliqué slid on top of him in a flash, her body moving like that of a cat, her firm breasts hovering over his chest, her long wavy hair in her face and his, as he consumed her mouth with his—savoring the feeling as their tongues and bodies pressed together, the current that surged within until they were about to burst.

Vince could only imagine her there now, alone, and sighed.

"Vince Cannon, Jr., if you were here with me right now I'd give myself wholly to you—rub my shaved, *veve*-painted pussy against your bearded face until you tasted all of my voodoo love juice. And then I'd make love to you so good like I did that night, let you take me the way you did when we were together. Do you remember that, Vince?"

Vince was fully hard now and dizzy with the liquor of sensual dreams. "Oh, God, Angeliqué. What I wouldn't do to be there with you right this very minute…"

Angeliqué's voice softened. "I spoke to Ezili Freda tonight, Vince, 'cause I couldn't take it one second longer—told her I needed you back here, inside me where it's safe and warm. I heard her, Vince, heard her speak to me in the hot, scented bathwater, among the vapors and candle wax that dripped onto the porcelain lip of my tub." Vince heard Angeliqué take a long drag from a cigarette. He imagined her standing there, nude and painted, thin tendrils of smoke drifting upward as a dozen set of button-eyes from cloth and sequin-covered dolls watched her with their unwavering gazes. "She told me you'd be coming." Vince could hear Angeliqué's voice shift—it became hushed and far away. "Tell me Ezili Freda speaks the truth, Vince. Tell me you are on your way soon?" Vince heard the pleading in her dithering voice.

"Yes, Angeliqué. Ezili Freda is a wise ole voodoo priestess." He paused for a moment to look up at the clouds that were forming over Washington from the west. His heart was beating fast, and his penis was fully engorged. But this came down to more than raw sexual desire or the longing for soft warm flesh. Vince felt his muscles constrict, tightening around his chest walls. "Baby," he said softly, in a tone that surprised even him, "I am on my way soon…"

✠✠✠

Trey Alexander sauntered around H2O, attitude permeating from every pore of his black body. Part of it had to do with his conversation with Erika—Trey knew he was being overprotective and a bit childish, definitely a double standard when it came to Erika and himself—but damn it, they went *way* back—they'd been friends for God knows how long, and so, it was okay if he was a bit overbearing at times. Besides, he knew that deep down Sassy loved it! But this was only part of the reason for his demeanor…

The other reason…Trey was dressed for attitude. He had donned his brown leather pants and matching boots before heading out on the bike. Underneath his leather jacket he wore a caramel-colored, tie-dyed, ribbed tank top that was tight-fitting and showed off his tribal band and Indian chief tattoos. And this was exactly the reason why his jacket was presently resting on the back of the bar stool over in the VIP section. So, he wasted no time strutting around the club's floor as if he owned the place—stopping to speak to whomever glanced his way. He wasn't getting very far considering all of the stares…

Folks, mostly women, were getting to observe him in all of his glory. He was feeling good—the few drinks that he and friends had had over dinner earlier had presented him with a nice warm buzz. Not that Trey needed anything to converse with folks…

He made it down to the first floor and navigated around the dance floor that was packed with dancers vibing to thumping, heart-pounding reggae. He headed for the bar, got the attention of another dreaded bartender, a sistah this time, and ordered a beer. He saw her checking out the "tats" and his soft leather pants, flirted with her for a minute, before moving on…

Back to the second floor, Trey circled the area, checking out the talent—not much this evening, it being a weeknight; a lot of folks though were staring and whispering as he walked by, bandanna still tied about his bald head. He loved this rough-cut look—so distinctively different than what he was used to—always suit-and-tie-down! This felt good—*because* folks were talking about him. He knew exactly what they were thinking: damn, he looks good—wish I could pull that shit off!

Trey made his way back to the VIP section where Erika was sitting alone nursing her drink. He moved behind her, stroked her hair and back with a light touch. She glanced over her shoulder and smiled when she spotted him. They didn't exchange words. The look between them said it all. He downed the rest of his beer and set the empty glass on the bar.

"I just hope that nigga's treating you well," he said.

"Yeah, James is cool. He's treating me just fine. No complaints so far."

"You know, Sassy, if it was just dick you were longing for, you could've come to me. I mean, what are friends for?" Trey smirked as Erika spun around and gave him a dazed look.

"Trey, have you forgotten how hard I slapped you the last time you pulled that shit?" She had a scowl on her face, but Trey could see that it was rimmed with a smile. He recalled back to the very first time he had ever laid eyes on Erika. That was almost fifteen years ago…

Trey recalled it vividly. He was standing on the main floor of the university library waiting for the elevator to take him to the third floor. A blue knapsack half-filled with textbooks hung over his left shoulder. The elevator was taking forever to come. He was exasperated and almost decided to huff it up the stairs (located across the way on the other side of the stacks) when the indicator pinged and the doors opened. Trey stood aside to see if anyone would exit. When no one did, he entered the cramped elevator and pushed the button for the third floor. As the doors slid shut he raised his head and noticed her standing there. What he saw took his breath away— tall, creamy skin, wonderful dark hair, and a lovely curved mouth, but most importantly, firm, round breasts under a thin cotton polo shirt the color of lavender that clearly exhibited her taut nipples. Trey stepped back to the wall, faced her and stared. Even back then he was cocky, and while his mind whirled with something profound to say, she just stood there, glancing down at her sneakers. Erika felt his stare and slowly raised her head. Big mistake! Trey had a grin on his face the size of a football field! He was staring directly at her breasts and erect nipples; gazing upon them; fantasizing about their color, feel, and texture; wondering why on earth they were at attention in this elevator? Trey made no attempt to conceal the object of his affection. He took a breath and began to speak, seeing that he had her full attention now.

"My goodness. Aren't those puppies lovely? Are you a bit nippy or just glad to see me?" He thought he was being charming—and that women actually found this kind of shit appealing. Erika stared in disbelief at him for a split second, shock and anger written all over her face. Then her hand came up from seemingly nowhere and slapped him in the face so hard Trey's bony frame spun around, causing his forehead to crash into the steel back wall. His knapsack went flying as he yelped in pain from the sudden contact of Erika's open-fingered hand and the elevator's frame. The imprints of her digits were easily discernible on his light-skinned face, and would be for at least the next twenty-four hours. Not good, considering he had a track meet in four hours…

"Obviously manners are not your strong suit," she exclaimed calmly as the elevator door opened and she exited without so much as a backwards glance.

They became friends fairly quick after that first encounter…Erika felt guilty because of the mark that had been indelibly left on Trey's malleable face…And for his part, Trey never again tried anything fresh with his friend…

They both smiled with the remembrance…

"So, are the two of you regular *fuck buddies* now?" Trey asked, still standing. "James looks like he's already whipped!"

"What can I say," Erika exclaimed. "My shit is 'da bomb, you hear me?"

"Whatever. Just watch your back, Sassy. I don't want to have to bust a cap in some anchorman's ass, but I will if I have to. Just say the word!"

"Thank you, boo, sometimes you can be so sweet and endearing."

"And—other times?"

"Trey—you know you can be A-Number-One asshole without even trying." She smiled and reached for him, kissing him on the forehead. Trey returned her smile but said nothing.

"To be honest, we've only hooked up only twice—not that it hasn't been nice, because it has been—Stella got her groove back, ya know! But I'm just not trying to get all serious right this minute, you know?"

"I hear that."

"Besides," Erika said, rubbing Trey's forearms for a moment, and lowering her volume, "James is acting kind of weird when it comes to sex."

He was preparing to sit down when he glanced around and caught the eye of the white woman from earlier in the evening.

"What did you say?" Trey asked, eyeing the woman, his thoughts shifting into high gear.

"Nothing much. Just that James is acting a bit weird about sex, that's all…" A frown had replaced her smile. Trey, unfortunately, was no longer paying Erika any attention.

"Sassy, watch my drink; I've got to take care of something for a minute." She nodded silently, looking beyond to the couches where the woman's party had congregated. It was okay with her. Trey probably wasn't the best person to talk to about this particular issue…now, if Vince would get the hell off the phone and come back…

Trey walked over, confidence exuding from his being like a blinding white light. The woman, who was sitting with four other women, glanced up and smiled as he arrived. In the background, the music was rocking, and the D.J. had just put on a record by Fat Joe and Ashanti, a jam that Trey just adored.

"Let me ask you a question," he said, without so much as a hello.

"Yes?"

"You know how everyone has that one song that they just love—that's their song, the one that makes them stop and groove regardless of what they're doing or where they are?"

"Yeah, definitely." The woman was gazing up at him, a sensuous grin on her face. She wore her brown hair shoulder-length, a beige skirt, knee-high black boots, and a tight, blue and tan striped shirt that was low-cut and showed off her ample breasts. Trey enjoyed standing over her and glancing down at her cleavage.

"Well, this here's my groove. So, I have no choice but to dance. Understand?"

"Absolutely." The rest of her friends had paused in conversation and were watching him closely, amused by his introductory line. Where was he going with this, they were wondering.

"So, my question is this—if you and I go out on the dance floor over there," Trey said, pointing to the packed area beyond the bar, "are you going to show this crowd how it's done, D.C.-style, and make me proud, or…" and here he paused for effect before continuing, "are you just going to move like a typical white girl and mess up my image? Hmmm? Baby, I need to know before we go any further!"

The woman was speechless and taken aback for a split second. At first she couldn't believe her ears, but the laughter and the "Oh no he didn't!" from several of her girlfriends told her that she had heard him correctly. She set her drink down on the coffee table in front of her, got to her feet slowly, smoothed out her skirt, and looked Trey square in the eyes.

"I guess we'll just have to find out exactly what *this* white girl has to offer, won't we, darling?" Her friends began to giggle and high-five each other. "You go, girl," one of them said. "Don't let that fool talk trash to you!"

Trey stared back, not in the least bit intimidated. He smiled, showing her all of his straight, white teeth. "Well then, whatchew waiting for, girl?" he said, holding out his hand. "Show me what you got!"

They walked hand in hand to the dance floor, past Erika who merely rolled her eyes when they went by. Trey led her to the floor, excused himself as he parted bodies to make way toward the interior of the dance area. They made it about ten feet in before he stopped and turned to her. The music was blaring and folks were shaking, sweating, and grooving. They began to dance and immediately Trey was impressed. The woman didn't dance like any of the white girls he had known. No, she moved like a sistah! He grinned widely; she smiled but said nothing, concentrating instead on showing this man how she moved. Trey admired her—here girlfriend was, in a sea of black folks, gyrating her hips and ass to the beat, moving her upper body, shoulders and neck with attitude and style like she was one of them. Trey increased his movement, determined to stay the course with her. She leaned in, grabbed his shoulder and pulled him to her.

"How's your image holding up so far, darling?" she said over the din of the music.

Trey grinned. "So far so good. Damn, I'm impressed. If I didn't know any better I'd swear you were a sistah. You damn sure move like one!"

"Things are not always what they seem. So watch yourself. You might learn something!" She pushed back, twirled around and dipped. Flipped her hair backward while positioning her ass against his pelvis. Her arms extended to the ceiling as she glanced back and gave Trey a seductive smile—it spoke to him—it said, show me what you can do! He reached for her hips, pulled her into him, feeling her ass cheeks make contact with his awakening cock. They moved together, in unison, while his hands moved upward from her hips, past her ribs and toward her breasts. He paused when he felt the flesh begin to rise. She reached for his hands and squeezed before pulling away and spinning back to face him.

Trey observed her closely as she danced. She was enjoying herself, lost in the rhythm and thumping sounds. Then the song changed, Fat Joe to J. Lo and Ja Rule—and Trey and his newly found friend continued to dance. For three more songs they grooved, until the sweat was visible on her face, neck, and the valley between her breasts. Trey was having a hard time concentrating on little else. Plus, he was sweating as well. He could feel the drops of perspiration form under his bandanna and on his arms. So, he grabbed her hand and led her off the floor. She was grateful for the reprieve.

"Well, that wasn't so bad, now was it?" she said in his ear. Trey turned to her and grinned while placing his hand around her waist and pulling her into him snuggly.

"Not at all. I love the way you move."

"Thank you."

"No, thank you. My reputation remains intact!"

They moved back to the VIP section. Vince had returned and was chatting with Erika.

"Saw you out there, dawg. Looks like girlfriend was giving you a run for your money!" Vince said, smacking his bare shoulder.

"Yeah, Trey. It's a good thing you quit when you did—she was about to hurt you!" Erika added.

"Trick, please!" He bellowed. Trey turned to his dance partner. "Don't pay these haters any mind. Okay?" He patted his empty bar stool while grabbing a stack of square napkins. He gently dabbed the woman's forehead and neck. She watched him in an amusing kind of way, but didn't stop him until his hand descended toward her bust.

"Okay, I think I'm dry now."

Trey eyed her. "You sure? Any other *wet* spots?"

"You are something else, you know that?"

Trey just smiled. "What are you drinking?"

"Apple martini, thank you."

Trey ordered. "I don't even know your name—forgive me."

"I'm Allison." She stuck out her hand.

"Nice to meet you, Allison. These two knuckleheads here are Vince and Erika. Oh, and I'm Trey!"

Allison was reaching out to shake Vince's and Erika's hands when she heard Trey's name. She turned to him, the curve in her smile momentarily flattened ever so slightly. Erika noticed it.

"Uh oh, Trey, seems like your reputation has preceded you *this* time."

"What?" Trey was gazing down into Allison's face and upper body, his eyes sparkling with a million desires. Her breasts were right there...he was thinking, so close and looking so damn yummy...

Erika began to laugh. "I saw that look, Allison—if Trey would stop eyeing your boobies, he'd have seen it, too!"

"No..." Allison tried to speak.

"Hold on, Sassy," Trey said, breaking his stare from Allison and giving

Erika the evil eye. "I was just admiring Allison's lovely frame. Besides, you know I'm a gentleman. Why you trying to go there?"

"Because, she knows you! Or she's heard about you. Isn't that right, Allison?"

All eyes turned to Allison who sipped her martini slowly, the drink weighing heavily in her hand.

"No, we've never met. The name's familiar, that's all."

"Bullshit," Erika quipped. "You may have never met him, but something caused the light bulb to glow bright."

Trey ignored Erika by moving closer to Allison. Erika snorted and turned her attention back to Vince. "So, Allison, have we met before? Seriously, I just *know* I would have remembered someone as lovely as you."

"Nope, honest." Allison glanced toward her friends and their table.

"So, what do you do for a living, Allison, besides looking so damn fine?"

Allison laughed while rolling her head back. Trey watched her thick brown hair as it glided down her back. He also noticed her ropy neck muscles go tight, watched her full breasts as they rose, then fell. He felt himself becoming aroused, and imagined her on his mattress at home, legs splayed, body laced with sweat from their intense lovemaking—wanting to bed this woman in the worst way.

"Trey, do we have to talk about work? I spend twelve to fourteen hours a day busting my ass—I'd much rather talk about something else right this minute, if that's okay with you."

"Baby, that's cool with me." Trey reached up to stroke her shoulder and play with her hair. Allison involuntarily shut her eyes for a brief moment before turning to him.

"Listen, I have to get back to my friends, but thank you for the dance and for the drink."

"Hey, so soon?" Trey asked, his palms held outstretched like a preacher. "I'm just getting to know you, and there's more ground to cover." He flashed his trademark smile and Allison returned it with one of her own, thinking to herself, this one is really smooth...be careful...

"Tell you what, let me go check on them and I'll join you in a few. Okay?" Trey stood over her and watched her eyes as they swam back and forth following his stare. He dropped his gaze again to her breasts and waist. Continued the vein of a thought concerning the two of them in his bed. Tonight. Jamaica and all it had to offer was a distant memory. He needed to move hurriedly.

"Sure, but don't keep a brutha waiting too long…"

"Gotcha. Be back…" She slid off the bar stool and strolled back toward her table leisurely, knowing Trey's eyes were on her ass, but no way to avoid it, so she smiled to herself, and gave him the show he longed to see…

Fourteen

"How's Angeliqué?" Erika asked excitedly.

"How'd you know I was talking to her?" Vince asked.

"Nigga—please! I only had to look at those puppy dog eyes that drooped as soon as you said hello!"

Vince smiled as he rubbed Erika's shoulder. "Angeliqué is doing fine. She misses her boo. Can you blame her, all that good lovin' I threw down!"

"Nigga, *please* is right!" Trey said, turning in his stool after completing his stare of Allison's slow stroll. Vince ignored his best friend and continued.

"We spoke about me coming back down to New Orleans real soon to see her." Erika noticed the fire in his eyes—the way they blazed as he spoke of her, the voodoo priestess whose fire had stoked his heart, melted his core like molten lava.

"You go boy," Trey said, giving Vince dap. "Go handle your business, ya heard?"

"You know that!" Vince was nodding his head slowly, a decision already made. He turned his attention back to Erika.

"Sassy, you were saying about James?" Erika turned to glance at Trey who was eyeing her curiously.

"What, why you all up in my business?" She smiled and then laughed. "I was just saying that James and I are cool."

"You had mentioned something that wasn't quite right." Vince encouraged her to go on.

"Naw, everything's cool."

"Obviously *not*," Trey interjected.

"Do we have to have this conversation right now?" Erika asked, suddenly feeling self-conscious.

"Yeah, we do! What's the matter—cat got your tongue now that I'm present?"

"Trey, shut the fuck up and let Erika say her piece—without *commentary* from your black ass!" Vince's speech was forceful, but the glint in his eye let Trey knew he was asking for some understanding here. Trey nodded silently. Erika sighed.

"All I said was that James was acting kind of weird when it came to sex." Erika paused, realized that it was much more difficult to discuss *this* thing that had been bothering her for over a week now with both of them staring her down—individually, there was no problem. She could talk with Vince about this, no problem, and even with Trey, one-on-one. The difficulty arose when both of them were present. But, there wasn't a whole lot she could do about it now. So, she pressed on.

"We've only hooked up a few times so far—two to be exact."

"Go on," Vince said.

"I really enjoyed myself with him. James is a good lover—he takes his time, is romantic and knows how to please a woman."

Trey was sitting there thinking to himself, *well, what's the fucking problem then*, but decided to keep his thoughts to himself.

"That first night when we went to dinner, then over to Ozio, I was, for the first time in a really long time, *feeling* a man. James wasn't pretentious like most niggas I meet—he wasn't trying to impress a sistah. He was just being himself, and I dug that. A lot. I found myself letting my guard down with him and just decided to go with the flow. And I wanted him. And I knew he wanted me."

Trey turned uncomfortably in his seat.

"We left Ozio and went back to his place 'cause I told him I wanted to go there. Decided that night I wasn't going to play any games—I told him what I wanted. *Him*."

"You go, girl!" Vince exclaimed. Trey said nothing. Erika felt herself loosening up as she recalled the details of her night.

"Yeah, I remember us dancing up in the VIP section, smoking cigars, drinking Cosmos, and just chillin', having a grand ole time. I put my lips to James' ear and whispered that it was time to go—back to his place. I've never seen a nigga pay a tab so damn quick!"

Vince and Erika high-fived each other.

"When we got to James' place, he was very much the gentleman. He already knew by this point that he was going to have me—that was a foregone conclusion. Homeboy could have just waltzed into the crib with lil' ole me in tow, grabbed my hand and pulled me into the bedroom. Honestly, fellas, at that point, I would have gone. Willingly."

Erika paused, and checked Trey. He looked at her, eyes unblinking as he mouthed the word "ho" slowly. They both grinned.

"Takes one to know one, be-yatch! Anywho—as Trey here is fond of saying—'them panties were *soaked*,' ya know? But James was playing it cool; he put on some smooth jazz, lit a few candles and some incense and dimmed the lights. Very romantic. I wasn't expecting that."

"Damn," Vince exclaimed, "that nigga does have some sense. Maybe he's salvageable after all. So, Sassy, wherein lies the problem?"

"Well, Vince, as I said, James took his time. He undressed me very slowly and sexily, taking the time to touch me and not rush things. I was very turned on."

"Yeah?"

"Oh yeah. Homeboy had skills! We began kissing and groping, you know, and then he started to…you know…perform oral on me."

"You let a nigga you don't even know go down on you, Sassy?" Trey belted out, then immediately regretted it. Both Erika and Vince eyed him with disdain. He quickly lowered his head.

"And here's where the problem began," Erika said softly.

"What happened?" Vince asked tenderly.

"Don't get me wrong. James was good. Very good. No, damn *spanking* good—okay? I mean, he made me come *twice*. Tongue and all. I am not mad at him!"

"Doesn't sound like a problem to me."

"Hold on—after that, of course a girl's gonna reciprocate. I wanted to give him pleasure. I mean, he was still fully dressed. I tried to take off his pants, unbuckle his belt, but James stopped me…"

"Uh-oh, that brutha's a faggot—see I told you!" Trey shouted.

"Shush!" Erika whispered. "James is no faggot—I could tell he was aroused—damn, I could see his dick sticking up straight through the fabric of his suit pants. I wanted to feel him, wanted to taste him the way he tasted me. Wanted to feel him inside of me. I told him so."

"And?"

"James said that he wanted to focus that first night on pleasing me. I thought that was sweet, but honestly, all his tongue had done was make me want his dick even more. Does that make sense?"

"Yeah, it does," Vince said, with caring in his voice. Trey rolled his eyes.

"I swear to God, I was tugging on his shit for five minutes—we practically were wrestling on his couch before I finally gave in—he wasn't going to let me fuck him."

Vince cleared his throat and thought for a moment. "Sassy. I don't necessarily see a problem in James' actions. When you think about it, there is nothing wrong with what he did—wanting to focus the evening's attention on pleasing you. Actually, what he did was down right admirable—letting his pleasure take a back seat to yours. In a way, he was sealing the deal for the next time, not that he needed to do that—but in his own way, he was saying to you, baby, pleasing you is my first priority. Not a bad thing, if you ask me."

"I hear you, Vince, but think about this," Erika said. "Sex is about communication and connections between two people. What makes lovemaking so special is that it allows two people to touch each other in a very intimate way. The whole point is not to make one person *come*; it's not a task to complete; it sure ain't no damn competition, like a fucking race, but a way of bringing two people closer together in mutual pleasure and a flurry of passion."

"Okay, point taken. But so far I don't agree with your assessment of there being a problem. So go on. What happened next?"

"Well, it was late and James was done, as far as he was concerned. He cleaned me up, kissed me tenderly on my lips—damn, I still remember how good that shit felt, and took me home." Erika paused to remember the sweet details. "I got busy at the hospital; James was tied up at the station, so a few days went by. I wanted to put some space between us anyway, so that I could figure things out. James was calling almost every day, but we didn't hook up again until the following week. Our second date was very nice— James prepared dinner for me…" Trey snapped his neck so quick both Vince and Erika flinched.

"Oh no he didn't!" Trey declared, getting off the stool to make his point. "Nigga's gonna mooch off my shit—I knew I should have *copyrighted* that play—now everybody's gonna try that shit at home! And fuck it up! There is only one chef supreme pussy-licking big daddy connoisseur playa in this mutha fucka, you hear me!?!"

"Yeah, Trey, you 'da man. Everyone in Chocolate City knows that. Even Allison!" Erika quipped.

Vince howled.

Trey spun around in his seat to check out Allison, who was seated on the couch, engaged in laughter with her friends. She caught him staring, glanced his way and smiled. He waved sheepishly.

"Anywho—as I was saying before being rudely interrupted—James cooked me dinner—nothing that would compare to one of Trey's mouthwatering masterpieces, but the brutha was trying—can't fault him for that. We ate, drank some very nice wine…"

"Where this nigga live anyway?" Trey asked.

"Reston."

"Figures," Trey retorted. Erika glanced at Vince, then continued.

"Alrighty then. We drank some nice wine—more of the same, candles, incense, and smooth jazz. He had gotten me some really pretty flowers…"

"Isn't that special!" Trey quipped. "Mutha fucka's a regular Martha Stewart with balls—well, that remains to be seen!" He sneered. Erika was not amused.

"Trey, fuck you!" She swiveled in her stool and faced Vince who was silently shaking his head. "Once again James was the perfect gentleman, but this time, after dinner and a few more drinks, he led me upstairs to the bedroom. We undressed—both of us, simultaneously. It was an incredible turn-on. Then we made love."

"Cool," Vince said. "So far so good!"

"Yeah, it was wonderful. It felt really good to be with a man who was that romantic. As I said, James wasn't the kind of lover who rushed himself. He took his time, attended to my needs first, but this time, afterwards, he let me have my way." Erika had a devious look on her face. Vince grinned and even Trey had to crack a smile.

"Go 'head—handle your business, girl!"

"Yeah, but here's the thing. I don't know if I should be making an issue of this or not, but…" Erika's voice trailed off.

"What? Sassy, as you're fond of saying, the suspense is fucking killing us!" Vince said.

"I know." She chuckled. "The thing is, James didn't *come*. Not once. Not during me giving him a blowjob, which I damn sure know how to do, thank you very much! Not during sex, which incidentally involved several positions besides plain old missionary." Trey eyed her curiously. "What? You don't think this here girl got skills? Please! I know how to do the *do*!"

"All right. So did you talk about it?"

"Well, I mentioned it. I mean, there we were going at it for close to an hour and he still hadn't come. He finally stopped after I came God knows how many times, and proceeded to wash us off. He apologized, stating that it was the condom, which was 'interfering'; I think was how he put it. Under normal circumstances I wouldn't have thought twice about it—but with what happened the first time, I became suspicious. After that evening I found myself thinking about it a lot. Don't get me wrong. I'm enjoying the hell out of sex with James. But until I figure out what the deal is, I'm not sure I want to mess with James any further. I just don't want to start something that might spell trouble down the road." Erika downed the remnants of her drink and sighed, placing her palms on the shoulders of her two best friends. "Whatever the case, the nigga's been calling me every day like clockwork. You know my shit is 'da bomb!" Erika grinned and nodded like a boxer who had just knocked down his opponent.

"I don't know, Sassy; sounds like a faggot problem to me," Trey quipped. Erika cut him a nasty glance.

"Sassy, don't pay that nigga any mind. I think everything's cool—just give the brutha a bit more time. I have a feeling things will work themselves out," Vince reasoned while stroking Erika's back.

Erika sighed. "Well, we'll see…"

✠✠✠

Allison was gone. Trey noticed it as soon as Erika had finished telling her tale—the thing between her and James—the "sexcapades" of Sassy—damn, what was the world coming to? Sassy getting her groove on???? Who would've thunk it? Anyway, more pressing matters were upon him. Trey jumped off his stool, grabbed his half-empty Corona, and headed for the main floor.

Trey walked slowly, yet confidently, scanning the crowd for the white girl. He wanted her. Something about her smile—the way her hair fell on her shoulders and back when she laughed; and those titties—firm, masses of warm flesh that he desired between his fingers and lips.

He came to the winding, curving staircase. Glanced downward, watching folks as they sauntered up and down, taking their time, the reflection from the mirrors ensuring everyone had a view. He started down, gripping the metal as he took a swig. He came to the bottom and saw her, Allison, her back to him as she donned her coat and headed out the front door.

Trey hit the bottom step with both feet, ran past the large, thick dark-skinned brutha bouncer who eyed him with curiosity as he hit the glass door with his palms. It swung open and he was suddenly outside, the midnight air feeling wonderful on his skin.

"Allison!" he yelled. She had gotten about fifteen yards when she turned, and Trey had to smile. The way she pivoted in those black boots, her dark hair swinging in an arc, ass tight within the boundaries of her short skirt, her breasts held within the confines of her blue and tan top, jiggling with the movement made by her sudden turn—made him appreciate being a man. He jogged over to her. Her friends waited a short distance away.

"Hey, girl. Leaving so soon?" Trey flashed a smile and ran a hand over his bandanna. It was damp from sweat so he removed it. Allison gazed up and admired his handsome face and bald head.

171

"Yeah, gotta get ready for the a.m. You know I'm not as young as some of those folks in there—girl can't hang like she used to."

"Please, I bet you'd give them all a run for their money." He moved closer. "Listen, I know it's late and all, but I was really hoping we could spend more time together. I like you, Allison, you've got...spunk...I dig that." Trey looked down into her eyes and smiled, gave her that look—can Allison come out and play with me—the one he had perfected over the years...innocence with a touch of mischievousness tossed in for good measure.

"Trey, I wish I could...honestly. Perhaps another time." She turned to move. Trey caught her arm gently with his hand and stroked her forearm. He was taking in the whole package—form, fly clothes, hair, eyes, scent, everything. He wanted her. Now. Time to go to general quarters...

"Let me take you home, Allison. My ride's parked right here," he said, gesturing to the hunk of engine and gleaming chrome. The Indian made a statement and he watched her eyes brighten. "Allison," he said, dropping his voice and moving in, as close as they had been earlier on the dance floor, "I really want to get you on the back of my bike—you just don't know!"

"Is that right?" Allison said, enjoying the closeness and the raw sexual energy that pulsed in the air. She glanced up, admiring the bald head, his pretty eyes, that engaging smile—damn, he was fine, no question about that, but off limits...

"Oh yeah. You, me, those sexy black boots—I could keep mine on if you'd like..."

"Really? Hmmm. I think I'd like that." Her voice had dropped to a whisper as she glanced down at his leather pants and boots, noticing how well his clothes fit him. Trey still held her arm. His fingers were splayed—feeling her skin through the shirt; eyeing her breasts—couldn't help himself—not that Allison seemed to mind. In fact, Trey was convinced that she was thoroughly enjoying this exchange. He moved in—maneuvered his thigh next to her ass, extended his leg and connected. Let her feel him, know that he was engorged, inflamed, excitement in the air like electricity during a storm. She stood her ground—making no attempt to move, staring up at him and his eyes as he watched her, enjoying the fact that his gaze roamed all over her body, the flirting between them delightful, like the midnight air. She was no fool—Allison knew what he wanted. "Trey, darling. It's late—I'd love to stay here with you, but I really can't." Allison twisted to her girlfriends who waited patiently for her to finish up. "I've got to leave—my girls gotta go."

"Like I said, giving you a ride is no problem. In fact, I'd thoroughly enjoy it!"

"Another time—another place." Allison disengaged herself, ran a hand through her hair, and made ready to leave.

"Then give me your number. Let me make sure you find yourself home safely tonight."

Allison bit her lip. Indecision was written on her brow. She glanced back at her friends. "Tell you what—do you have a card, Trey? I'll call you."

Trey was already reaching into the back pocket of his leathers—he *always* carried a card. Like condoms. Shit, Trey never went anywhere without them. He handed one to her. Allison took a moment to read it.

"Trey Alexander," she read, "Esquire. I like that. Can I call you 'counselor'?"

"Please do—real soon—tonight preferably." He bent down and kissed her cheek—let his lips linger on her skin a little longer than necessary. Allison made no attempt to pull away. Then he straightened up, flashed her one more smile before spinning on his heels and heading for the front entrance of the club. He left her the way he liked to do all of his women—leave them quick—standing there, contemplating him, this man of mystery with the dazzling eyes, great looks, tattoo-adorned brown skin, and a devilish smile that drove most women (and some men) wild with the possibilities…infinite possibilities…

Fifteen

All six-foot-six, two hundred thirty-five pounds of dark chocolate-complexioned Quentin Hues, Washington Wizards forward, graduate of UConn, former resident of New Jersey, husband and soon-to-be divorcee turned and smoothed his three-button blazer when Trey swept into the reception area. Quentin had been bent over the reception desk, preferring to wait there as opposed to being ushered into Trey's office directly, a ploy, Trey knew damn well, to give Q. time to chit chat with Becky, the blonde receptionist with the pretty teeth, smooth shape, and fake titties. When he strolled in, Trey hugged him, brutha-style, and gave him one of those, "Dawg, I'd hit it if I were you" looks and winked at Becky before ushering him down the hall. While walking they exchanged small talk. Q. and Trey had known each other for a little under a year now. They had been introduced to each other at some bourgeois function held at Jordan's Restaurant over in the new Ronald Reagan Building. Trey loved to attend those soirées—it gave him an opportunity to network with folks—an absolute necessity in his business—plus, and far more importantly, pussy adored sports, money, and power—and Trey *treasured* pussy above all else.

They came to a wood-paneled conference room door. Trey had briefed him on the agenda on the way over…negotiating a property settlement between a client and their spouse could be a nasty business—especially when it involved big items such as mansions, speedboats, and penthouse suites. Luckily, Quentin hadn't amassed that kind of property in his short NBA career. Plus, he had only been married a little over a year. This wasn't going to be too difficult. All in a day's work for Trey Alexander, Esquire, no doubt!

Trey pushed the heavy door open and strolled in first. He stared over at the oversized window, where a white woman wearing a smart navy blue suit stood with her back to him. Her brown hair was tied back with a single blue band. He cut his gaze over to the immense mahogany conference table. At the very end sat a thin, extremely attractive young woman. Trey took in her russet-colored skin, her half-black, half-Indian features, and the dark hair that wound down her back in a single braid. She was twenty-three years old. Her eyes were fixed not on Trey, but on Quentin, her husband, behind him. Her mouth was set in a firm arrangement. She neither gave off positive nor negative vibes—she just existed, in this time and place, a necessary evil, unfortunate that it came down to this—waiting patiently for this meeting to commence and be done with. Trey thought to himself: *Damn, Dawg, you let that honey get away?* And then he remembered the maxim—regardless of how fine a woman thinks she is, somewhere, someplace, there's a man who's tired of her shit!

At the exact moment that Quentin walked in behind him, his eyes fixed on his young wife, soon-to-be ex, the woman at the window turned. Trey's heart skipped a beat when he recognized Allison, the woman from H20, the night before.

"Morning, Counselor," Allison said, extending her hand and staring into Trey's startled brown eyes. "I'm Allison Matthews, attorney for Mrs. Aponi Hues. I trust you are well-rested and are ready to get down to business!"

✠✠✠

Vince kept his eyes closed, the large mug of steaming coffee held under his nose as he inhaled the scent of the freshly brewed liquid. He imagined the vapors as tendrils of smoke, which raised up like cobras, winding like a mountain stream before finding their home—his nostrils, slipping within as he took a breath—meandering through his insides, gliding downwards as they headed for his center, feeling his core heat up with each mouthful. And then he placed the mug to his lips and took a sip—instantly warming as the liquid shot down his throat like a raging waterfall, and Vince shook his head slowly, thinking to himself, the old adage is indeed true: wake up and smell the coffee—it would do all of us some good…

Vince opened his eyes and set the mug down on the coffee table. It was Sunday morning, about elevenish, the Cosi coffee and bar on Penn and Third a hubbub of activity, folks streaming in and out, business booming, tables and chairs both inside and out filled to near capacity. Luckily, Vince had arrived before the morning "rush" and was able to get his favorite spot— the low couch in back—a yellowish-green eclectic thing that was clean and comfortable. Vince leaned back, observing the ceiling before glancing around at the patrons, magazines or Sunday papers tucked under their arms, then scanning outside to his gleaming Fat Boy that was parked out front like a pit bull, guarding the entrance.

Vince was in a great mood—the week had been a good one—productive; his book, *Finding Nirvana*, was doing well, not bestseller material…*yet*, and Oprah wasn't banging down his door…*yet*, but okay for someone who was new to the publishing game. He pulled out his Blackberry and made a few notes—next week, he'd concentrate of getting *Nirvana* reviewed in a few more papers—that was important. Plus, he had yet to take his seminar to Philadelphia or Boston—he'd work on that in addition to trying to set up a book signing or two while he was in town. Then there was his trip back to New Orleans. Vince smiled to himself as he thought about Angeliqué and the conversations that had been heating up between the two of them lately. She was some woman, Vince mused. He definitely needed to get back down there soon—he missed Angeliqué, her touch, kiss, and the whole *vibe* that surrounded her like a thick fog. That voodoo vibe—electric, mysterious, eerie, and yet, comforting. She was something else—that was for sure.

Vince glanced up and saw Lisa, the Cosi cashier, walking toward him. She looked tired.

"Coffee okay?" she asked as she cleared a few empty cups from the table next to him. They had spoken when he had first arrived.

"Fine, as usual. Business is kicking, I see."

"Yeah, I wish it would calm down; I'm tired as hell." She produced a weak smile as she used a rag to wipe down the table.

"You look it, Lisa. What's up? Burning the candle at both ends again?" Vince asked, grinning at her.

"Vince, you know how *we* do. Shoot—last night, my girls and me checked out this spot called the VIP Club. Have you been there yet?"

Vince shook his head.

"Oh, Vince, this place is the bomb! It's on F Street across from Platinum. This place is all that! I'm not playing. Check out who was in there…" Lisa said, her eyes becoming animated as she spoke. "Jermaine Dupri and Jagged Edge. Supposedly, they're in town shooting some video. Ummn, then Lisa Raye was there and also Missy Elliott, but we didn't actually see her. But the rest of them we did."

"Damn!" Vince exclaimed. "Sounds like it's the new hot spot. What happened to Love? I still haven't made it there yet."

"Oh, that place is still the bomb, too. Especially on Friday nights—shoot, you can't even move in that place, it's so packed." Lisa chuckled to herself.

"So, what time did you get in this time?" Vince asked with a smirk.

"Vince, you don't even want to know—all I got to say is that it is a damn miracle that I'm here right now!"

"I hear that."

"Oh, by the way, your secret admirer keeps asking about you." Lisa turned toward the front, saw the line of customers growing and groaned to herself. "Shit, I gotta go, Vince."

"Wait," Vince exclaimed, reaching for her arm. "What secret admirer?"

"Tell you in a minute—let me handle these folks before my black ass gets fired!"

Vince sighed and let go of her hand. She winked at him as she skipped away toward the front. *Ah, to be young again*, Vince considered. Staying out to all hours of the night and then having the energy to get up and go to work the next morning—he had to hand it to Lisa. He couldn't do that shit—not anymore. He, like Lisa, had lived that life, once upon a time—when hanging out in trendy clubs and new joints was the most important thing in his sphere. But that was then, when one could survive on three hours of sleep. And this is now—Vince had grown, matured, gotten to the point where going to the club wasn't the end-all. There was more to life than drinking Cosmos, doing shots, and exchanging numbers in dimly lit, smoky, D.J.-infused spaces. Then his thinking shifted to what Lisa had last said before scampering away—he had a secret admirer. Vince wondered whom she was talking about. He hadn't been here in a few weeks with his travel schedule and everything else going on. One of her friends or perhaps a customer?

Vince shook it off—Lisa would fill him in later, when she had the time… if she could remain awake long enough to tell him…

✠✠✠

Vince had been reading for a while and had lost track of the time. He glanced up from his book, a new Eric Jerome Dickey urban-drama that he just loved—picked up his coffee mug, stared down into it and saw shiny bottom—empty—and put it down with a sigh. His eyes lifted toward the front. A line of customers formed all the way to the door. Lisa was busy ringing up orders. The Fat Boy remained where he had left it. Folks were reading their papers, in no hurry—a lazy kind of Sunday—the best kind, Vince considered. No place in particular to go—nothing of importance that required his immediate attention. This was the way Sundays were supposed to be. A good book, a great cup of coffee, and a comfortable couch…

Vince scanned the line of patrons as he stretched his legs and yawned. A young woman stood out from the rest of the pack—baseball cap, dark hair emerging from underneath her hat, navy blue leggings, running shoes, white Nike tee shirt, and smooth dark skin. Her turn to order just then, she moved up, spoke briefly to Lisa, glancing up at the menu while laying her wallet on the counter top. Her head turned in his direction and Vince recognized her from the last time he was in here—the woman whom he had spoken to briefly. The woman whose face he had sketched—strong, angular lines, the geometry of her face that he had found intriguing…her name, however, escaped him.

Vince watched her collect her bagel and steaming cup of coffee. Lisa glanced

179

at him, nudged her chin in the woman's direction before turning back to the next customer. Vince was momentarily caught off guard—was Lisa trying to tell him something? It seemed that way. And then the woman was strolling toward him, eyes locked on him—Vince looked away, not uncomfortable, but confused for a moment. Was she coming to talk to him?

"Hello. May I join you?" she said before Vince had an opportunity to process the rest of his thoughts.

"Yes, of course. Please have a seat," he said, smiling. The woman took a seat opposite him in a small, yet comfortable chair. She put down her bagel and cup and proceeded to hold out her hand.

"Hi, I'm Desiree. We met a few weeks ago—actually, I was quite spiteful to you, and I wanted to apologize."

Vince took her hand and shook it. "Vince Cannon, Jr." He watched her break apart her bagel, popping a sliver into her mouth.

"The artist. I've been admiring your piece over on that wall," she said, gesturing toward the far wall by the door.

"One of my favorite pieces." Vince smiled.

"It's very good. You're very good. I had no idea you were actually telling the truth." Desiree eyed him and smiled. "About being an artist—sorry, but it's true." She took a sip of her coffee and laughed. "Do you know how many bruthas I've met lately who *aren't* full of shit? Zero or very few— you're in the minority, Vince, let me tell you. You should be proud."

"Thank you. I am. I've always thought that telling the truth gets you farther along than telling a lie, even a little white one."

"I hear that—can you tell some of these bruthas out here, please?" Desiree took another sip of coffee before continuing. "Anyway, I wanted to apologize for my behavior last time—you were being nice and I wasn't…I'm sorry for that—you seem like a good guy and obviously a very talented brutha."

"Apology accepted. And I do understand. There are a lot of full-of-shit folks out there—it's really too bad because it gives those of us who are genuine a bad name." Vince closed his book and put it down. He eyed his coffee cup forlornly, frowning because it was empty but not having the desire to stand in that long line up front. Desiree continued to consume her bagel and sip her coffee while watching him silently. Vince looked up as one of the Cosi people walked over carrying a large mug of steaming coffee. He set it down on the table and said to Vince, "Compliments of Lisa and the house." Vince thanked him and glanced over to Lisa who was ringing up a customer, but smiled briefly and winked. Vince waved and mouthed, "thank you," to her.

"Wow, that was nice," Desiree said. "You've got the hook-up around here."

"Pays to know the help, you know?" Vince said.

"I guess so."

Vince took a sip and savored the flavor of the strong brew. "So, Desiree—you know what I do—I can't say the same." Desiree wiped her mouth with a paper napkin and Vince watched as she raised her hand to her lips—smooth dark skin, fine lines, strong, yet not overpowering muscles and ligaments and she worked her arm in the simple act of reaching for her mouth.

"Well, let's see—I guess you can call me a perpetual student—I'm about half-way through a part-time master's program in early childhood education, and I also work at a Montessori school in the District."

"Very nice!" Vince exclaimed. "A woman who extols the virtues of higher education while giving back to society. I dig that."

Desiree smiled while picking at the crumbs of her half-eaten bagel.

"Yeah, for a long time finding what I wanted to do was a struggle—I thought I wanted to do something in marketing or advertising, but after taking Marketing 101 I decided to look somewhere else."

"Many people spend most of their adult lives meandering around—lost—trying to figure out exactly what it is that makes them feel good—what is the perfect job that gives them that absolute joy. Most people, unfortunately, never find their true passion."

"True. Have you? Found your passion?"

"Hmmm…that's a good question—and be careful—because I'm known for not giving concise answers." Vince smiled and sipped at his coffee.

"Meaning you like to talk?" Desiree quipped.

"Exactly!" Vince said. "Anywho, to answer your question, yes, I believe that I'm one of the lucky ones—I've discovered my passions."

"And they are???" Desiree asked with a wicked grin.

"Well, my art, for one—being creative—developing something that is beautiful and lasting with your hands is something that provides me with endless joy. I know that sounds clichéd, but it's true."

"Yes, I can see that just from looking at that piece over there—one can tell it was done with lots of love."

Vince nodded, his thoughts whisked back to the creation of that piece, "My Secret Redeemer," the vibrancy of colors—reds, oranges, greens, and blues mixed with the chestnut reddish-brown stain that seeped below the surface of the mask, the upturned lips, and eyes that burned bright with excitement, anticipation, and passion…

"Art can be a true enabler—it allows one to go beyond the normal bounds that hold us back—it facilitates the creation of something truly amazing and in many cases, transcending…it allows us to speak in a tongue which is universal, and that is what gives art its power—the ability to transcend cultural and language barriers, cut through the political morass and speak to us here…" Vince paused to point to his chest. "In our hearts."

"I feel you, Vince." Desiree nodded while studying his face.

"Yeah, my art is without a doubt my passion. But it's not the only thing."

"Wow—more than one passion in life—you *are* one of the lucky ones!"

"Yes, I am. I also write and talk to folks about things—I guess you could call me a motivational speaker, although I really don't like that term because in my mind, it limits what I can do. I have this vision of Les Brown or Anthony Robbins doing these infomercials, and that's *not* what I'm into!"

"That's deep—motivational speaker. So, what do you speak on?"

And so, Vince proceeded to tell her about his life's work—when you broke it down, deconstructed it down into the various piece parts, what Vince was truly about was helping folks find their happiness. Through his seminars and workshops, his book, *Finding Nirvana*, and talking to people like he was doing now, Vince was helping folks, one step at a time. Defining those three important aspects of one's life—*professional, personal, and self*—developing and nurturing them, the way a gardener tends to soil, and balancing them so that no one element pushes any other too far out of whack. At the end of the day it was all about balance, baby…

Desiree listened intensely. She found herself enjoying the conversation with someone who had something positive to say. Lately she found it the exception to the rule to come across a black man who could carry on a conversation without staring at her breasts or commenting on her looks—don't get her wrong—Desiree was like most women in that she enjoyed compliments as much as the next gal—but there was a time and a place for that, ya know?

She told Vince about her family that still lived out west in Southern California, and how she had come East to be on her own and nurture herself. Vince talked about his move from working for the *man* to being in charge of his own destiny—and the joy and pain of working for oneself.

"Anything else, Mr. Renaissance Man?" Desiree asked, beaming her broad smile around the interior of Cosi. "I mean, you are an accomplished artist, writer, speaker—damn, most bruthas out here can only list their ride as their claim to fame!"

Vince for a moment was taken aback—he was ready to open his mouth and respond, but found himself pausing, almost by accident, as he stared across the space at Desiree, drinking in her features—flawless skin, those angular facial lines, warm, sensitive eyes, and the striking dichotomy between her dark chocolate complexion and her straight white teeth.

"Uh-oh," Desiree said, putting her coffee cup down with a thud as she felt the pause in conversation open up. "Maybe I spoke too soon—are you about to prove me wrong, Vince?"

"What?" Vince asked, using the interruption to sip from his mug.

"I mean, the way you were staring and all—and after I just concluded you were different." Desiree shook her head and finished the last of her coffee. She gathered her trash as she eyed him curiously.

"Desiree." Vince said her name slowly. "I see you are sensitive around this issue, and that's too bad—I was looking at you thinking how first impressions can be deceiving." Vince reached for the newspapers, folding the sections within themselves before sliding his book inside of the papery folds.

"How so?" she asked.

"Honestly? You're more than a pretty face, Desiree—you have considerable depth to you, and I find that appealing, especially in, and don't take this the wrong way, one so young. That's something you don't find every day. But my first impression of you—at least what I came away with from that first exchange we had weeks ago—was of a young, attractive, street-smart, but shallow woman. But as I talk to you here today I see that I was wrong. You are more than just a pretty face—and I am enjoying talking with you; please don't read more into it than that. I'm sorry if my thinking about that caused you some discomfort. It was not my intention." Vince smiled as he ran a hand across his closely cropped beard. Desiree watched his movement in silence for a moment before speaking.

"Thank you, Vince. I enjoy talking to you, too. I hope that we can con-tinue to do this. And I'm sorry for overreacting. It's just I get tired of men having nothing more to let loose than comments about my looks."

"Understood. Tell you what—I promise not to say anything further about the way you look as long as you keep your comments about my good looks to yourself. Deal?"

"Excuse me, but what comments? I haven't said anything about how good you look…"

"See," Vince interrupted, "that's what I'm talking about right there!" Vince exclaimed, while pointing at Desiree. She swatted away his hand as she laughed.

"Whatever—I can say whatever I want, Mr. Vince, whatever your last name is…"

"Cannon."

"Yeah, I can say whatever I want, Mr. Cannon, Jr. so there!"

"Alrighty then!" Vince checked his watch. "Damn, where has the time gone—it's close to two p.m."

"Are you kidding me?" Desiree asked, checking her own timepiece, as if Vince's were telling lies. "Damn, boy. You sure can talk!"

"Whatever!" They made ready to leave, grabbing their things and deposit-ing their trash. Vince winked at Lisa who was eyeing them as they headed for the door. She wore a smirk on her face and Vince just knew that he would owe her the full 411 next time he returned.

Outside, the sun was high in a cloudless sky. Desiree donned a pair of sunglasses and glanced up, feeling the warmth nuzzle against her skin the way a cat does its master, as Vince made his way to the Fat Boy.

"Oh, no, you don't ride a *bike!*" Desiree cried out. Vince feigned injury.

"What? A renaissance brutha like myself can't be down with a hog?"

Desiree ignored him while circling the machine, gawking at the gleaming chrome, fat pipes, and wide leather seat.

"Oh, cat got your tongue now?" he inquired.

"Damn, Vince—you don't know what a Harley does to me," Desiree said, continuing to stare the way a kid does when a jet plane passes overhead. "It makes me all squishy inside!"

Vince grinned. "Squishy is good. Very good, Desiree."

"I'll say!"

"Perhaps I'll give you a ride one day."

"Damn, Vince, don't play with me. You give me a ride on this thing and there's no *telling* what I might give you!"

"Oh really? What makes you think you got something I even *want*?" Vince added wickedly.

"Oh please—I see how you look at me—don't even front, Mister. You know you want these goods." Desiree cocked a hand on one hip and lowered her stare so she could give him the eye.

Vince sucked his teeth as he swung his leg over the seat. He adjusted his goggles, donned his helmet and fired up the Boy as Desiree watched him silently. He gunned the throttle several times causing her to jump back. He was playing with her and loving it. He nodded to her and prepared to leave.

"Hey, wait a minute, Vince—aren't you going to ask a girl for her digits?"

Vince removed his hand from the throttle, lowered his goggles and leaned toward Desiree. "Right now I'm having impure thoughts concerning you and my ride—and so I'd rather leave it alone. Keep that perfect gentleman image of me inside your pretty head instead. Okay." He grinned.

"No, not okay," Desiree said as she rummaged through her wallet and pulled out a card, handing it to him. Vince took it and glanced at it before stuffing it into the back pocket of his jeans. "Call me, Vince Cannon, Jr. Okay? I want to collect on that ride, damn it."

"Oooh, I really dig it when you talk dirty to me, Desiree."

"I'm serious—in fact, hold up…" Desiree reached for a flip phone that was attached to her hip. She opened it and looked at Vince. "Okay, boy, give me your digits."

Vince sighed, glanced around at the patrons who were swarming in and out of the Cosi coffee and bar.

"Come on, I don't got all day!" She grinned at him. Vince pursed his lips and gave her the info she was requesting. She punched his number into her phone, bit her bottom lip while playing with the cell, storing his name along with the number. "Cool—so now if I don't hear from a brutha in a reasonable period of time, I'll just call him my damn self! See about collecting that ride."

"You do that."

"I'm gonna."

"Later, alligator!" Vince let out the clutch while throttling up. Desiree stood on the corner shaking her head, muttering to herself, "I can't believe he just said that…"

Sixteen

The night air was crisp and clear. Erika fell in step next to James silently, glancing upwards at the tiny pinpoints of stars that blazed down upon them as they ran. Out here, away from the bright lights of street corners and neon-lit establishments, one could truly see heaven. Erika sucked in a lungful of fresh air and exhaled forcefully, pumping her arms as she extended her legs to match the rhythm of James' stride. They ran together, side-by-side, past huge, aging oak trees that towered over wide asphalt streets, James' idea actually, he having called her on her cell about three hours ago, as he was finishing up at the station.

"Hey, beautiful—here's a thought—a quiet relaxing evening at my place—some Thai takeout, perhaps a DVD movie, we could get a run in, then take a shower together…whatdayathink? Bring your stuff and you can stay over. Cool?"

"Way cool!"

Erika smiled to herself. It really didn't take much to make a sistah happy. A good man with a sense of humor, intelligence, good conversation; a romantic, good in bed—scratch *good*, make that *great* in bed, God-fearing, mom-loving man—that wasn't asking too much, was it? James was different than so many of the men she had been dating lately. He didn't try to impress her with rides in his fancy car, taking her to the hippest spots, and working the VIP *thang* every damn day—no, the point was, James didn't have to do that. He possessed a sense of humor, was a great listener, always asked about her day and what was going on in her life—and didn't pontificate on and on about how he was a celebrity. He talked about things that were important to her, and not how much *cabbage* he made or how big his dick really was…Thank God!

They ran on in silence. This was something that they had discovered they enjoyed doing together. It was important to Erika to work out on the regular. Sistah-girl wasn't getting younger—none of us were—and the only way to maintain a tight body was to work it every chance she got. But with a j.o.b., especially with her insane hours, it was increasingly difficult. James, it turned out, had the same problem. His hours were unpredictable, to say the least, so he tried to get to the gym when he could. But to be in great shape required discipline and commitment. The proverb, "I'll get to it when I can," was just not good enough.

And here was another thing that made her smile and thank her lucky stars— she and James could run together without having to make conversation. Sometimes it was nice to just be in one's presence without all of the dialogue that accompanied most relationships. After a long day at the hospital, tending to patients, running around doing this and that, dealing with those damn doctors (Lord, they were worse than attorneys, Erika knew that for a *fact!*) this was exactly what the doctor ordered—peace, a little space, and tranquility out here among the elements, her man at her side, jogging a few miles, working her muscles, feeling her heart throb with every step and breath, pumping her arms as she pulled ahead of James with a grin, then settling into that rhythm that all runners strive for—that point in your run where you forget about the pain in your legs and chest, overlook the fact that your ankles may be starting to swell, disregard the heaviness in your arms—and just let your stride carry you onward, your breathing becoming regular like a smooth sine wave, the stress from the day escaping from your pores like puffs of air whisked off into space. It was just her among the elements, wind in her ponytail-tied hair, stars navigating overhead as her feet touched ground to a beat only she could hear. It was comforting and restful. And having James there was the perfect end to an otherwise ordinary day.

They turned onto an even wider street, felt the incline pull at them as they increased their pace, James glancing over to Erika and winking before directing his attention straight ahead. Erika glanced at her watch and saw they had been running for close to forty-five minutes already. She was jazzed, feeling good, her heart pumping loud and clear, the blood that rushed through her veins and arteries was clean and fresh. Anticipation of the coming evening tugged at her insides, directing little pin pricks of enchantment to that spot between her thighs, the form-fitting Lycra shorts which she wore accentuating the sensation. She stole a glance at James—his firm body snug in a pair of tight-fitting running pants and tank top, the sinewy muscles of his arms and torso covered with a thin layer of sheen, and looking good enough to eat. Speaking of eating, Erika felt her stomach bark. James must have heard it rumble.

"I'm hungry," he said.

"Me, too."

"Cut left at this next intersection—we're less than a half-mile from home."

Five minutes later, after sprinting the remainder of the way, they were bent over and panting on the back upper deck of James' palatial home—a large, five-bedroom, multi-level brick home with manicured lawn, three-car garage wider than her own living room and dining room *combined*, upper deck that spanned half the length of the house, feeding to a mid-tier deck that housed a circular wrought-iron table with matching chairs and an enormous gas grill—which in turn led to a lower deck that housed a twelve-person hot tub. A gentle rolling hill led away from the deck to a thick tree line several hundred feet away. The space was dark save for a few halogen spotlights that shined their light on the deck surface. Erika stretched her legs while James did squats to keep his muscles from seizing up. A moment later he led her inside to the kitchen where he dialed a local Thai restaurant that delivered. He placed their order—chicken with chili sauce, pad Thai noodles with curry shrimp, and an order of grilled calamari. Forty minutes until. Perfect. Time enough for them to shower and to play...

James' bedroom was upstairs and at the far end of the house facing the tree line. Erika undressed silently while James stepped into the master bath—a huge room with dual skylights, a step-up Jacuzzi tub with so many jets she needed a calculator to count, shower stall with twin brass shower heads and clear glass doors. She heard him start the water as she slipped out of her Lycra running pants and glanced at herself in the full-length mirror in the corner by the obscenely wide flat-screen plasma monitor and stereo cabinet. James, like most men, was an electronics freak—he loved him some gadgets— and he had it all here—satellite receiver, DVD, VCR, dual cassette deck, 33-band graphics equalizer, Dolby 5.1 tuner and preamp, home theater speakers, remotes too numerous to count. And this was all in the bedroom—you should see his set-up in the family room downstairs! The lights pulsed and flashed in different colors and hues as she scanned her figure from top to bottom, her naked flesh rosy from the recent workout. James called to her from the bathroom.

"Shower's ready…"

Erika joined him. He stood with his back to her, head tilted back, letting the water pummel his face, neck, and shoulders. He felt her move behind him, he reached down and behind, pulling her into him. Squirmed against her pelvis, running both hands along the contours of her thighs and ass. Grinning with delight.

"I'm so glad you are here," he said gently.

"Me, too, thanks for the invite."

James turned to face her, glanced down while reaching for her breasts and giving them a tug. Erika closed her eyes, tipped her head back and into the stream of hot water, and let the water cascade down, dousing her hair. James reached for the body wash, this citrus and basil smelling gel that according to the label, "turns a shower into a wonderful pampering experience…" It came out as a gel, but turned into this rich foam shaving-like cream. Erika had brought it over a week ago and left it there, consciously marking her territory—letting any other bitches that might come around know that she had been there. James loved the stuff—he used a loofah pad to soap her up until not one square inch of caramel skin showed through—beginning with her ankles and thighs, working his way upwards, spinning her around to get at her back and ass, then back around again, to her stomach and breast area, neck and face—stopping just below the eyes. Then he used his fingers as if he intended to massage each molecule of foam into every single pore, circling around her areolas, tracing the outline of each clavicle, feeling the rise of flesh as it transitioned from thigh to buttocks—James fully hard now, his member swinging against her foam-covered stomach, and Erika, eyes still closed, reached out to take it, covering it in the palm of her hand, and rewarded him with a playful squeeze.

"Turn around, baby," James commanded. Erika did not have to be told twice. Pressing her elbows against the large square tile, she rested her head against the wall and felt the water beat against her skin. It felt so damn good. The smell of citrus and fruit was in the air. Her skin tingled. Her muscles relaxing with every second spent under this waterfall. And then James silently spread her legs, ran the back of his hand from the crack of her ass to her vulva, flipped his palm up and retraced his steps, allowing his fingers to linger among the slippery folds of her sex.

"Ohhh, James," Erika whispered, "That feels really good." James was silent in his response as he pressed himself against her warm backside, the foam layer between their skin providing ample lubrication. James rotated his hips slowly while moving his hand around and cupping her breasts, pinching the nipples that stuck out like thumbtacks. He used his fingers to feel her, and this is what Erika really liked—most bruthas went straight for the promised land—gave the nips a quick hello before traveling south and aiming for the wet spot. But Erika—like most women, dug foreplay. That meant, knowing not only where the spot was, but more importantly, how to get there…

James had wonderful hands—he used them wisely, always taking his time, playing her body with his fingers as if she were an instrument, never rushing, never ever in a hurry. He always got to where he was going, and when he did, Erika was ready. He touched her there now, the epicenter of her womanhood—felt her open to his touch, slipped a finger inside while his other hand reached for her neck and played with her thick hair. Erika moaned. James worked his finger inside of her, slowly at first, then, sensing a change in her rhythm and feeling her drive against his pelvis with her ass, he increased the momentum, using his thumb and forefinger to grasp her clitoris, tugging at it, pulling it from side to side, spreading her lips, pulling them apart and then to one side, all the while kissing her along neck and wet cheek.

It didn't take Erika long—in moments, after the anticipation of seeing James again after a short hiatus of several days, *knowing* the pleasure that was in store for her, awaiting his touch as they ran side-by-side, expecting the release but not knowing exactly when it would occur—finally feeling him totally as he explored her sensuously, doing to her precisely what she liked to have done, and at the tempo that was right for her—Erika arched back and felt her entire being vibrate as she *came*. That wonderful feeling of discharge, the expulsion of everything that is *bad* and infusion of everything that is *good*, all in the same breadth—the sensation that is undeniable and indescribable, an orgasm which is intense, all consuming, and satisfying... Thank you, Lawd!

✠✠✠

They lay on his wide bed with the thick bluish-green comforter—this fluffy, wonderfully feeling bedspread that reminded Erika of what it must look like beneath the waves—muted colors of sea green that morphed into bluish-black—that kind of out of focus sensation that one gets when immersing themselves underwater—vision blurred, but color and hue lovely and discrete.

James was still wet, clad in a thick white terry cloth robe with the initials JWC on the breast. Erika wore a matching robe that hung to her ankles, her dark hair unencumbered and still wet from the shower moments ago. She lay near him, her hand propping up her face; the folds of her robe open, allowing an unobstructed view of one breast. James' robe hung open, too; a light coat of chest hair lay wet and matted against his cinnamon skin. Boney James played on in the background, his sultry sax sounds permeating the air like fog. Several scented candles burned, creating the only light in the bedroom, save for the cockpit-like glow from the electronics on one wall and the sliver of light that seeped from the bathroom door, making an angular statement on the off-white carpet.

Erika reached for James, lightly played with his chest hairs, before tracing a path with her fingernail down his torso to his stomach, circling his navel, untying the loose belt that held the folds of his robe in place, spreading the terry cloth apart, like butterfly wings, setting him free. Silently, as James watched from a half-sitting, half-prone position, she reached for him, felt his already engorged state, and slipped him into her waiting mouth.

Erika took her time, in no rush, tasting the head, nibbling at it like it was a tasty strawberry, enjoying the flavor, then running her tongue along the shaft, circling this piece of manhood that was strong and firm. She backed away, the sheen from her saliva noticeable even in the dimly lit room, grasped him in her hand, studied it from her close vantage—marveling at the way no two looked identical—James had one that was of average length, but was beautiful, a true work of art—the head, smooth and not overly bulbous—and Erika enjoyed rubbing the spot where the soft piece of skin downturned into a generous lip of flesh with rounded edges. The girth was something she enjoyed, too—big enough to fill her up, but not overbearing in a way that made things uncomfortable. The most enjoyable thing she thought was the way his penis laid on his stomach now, curving slightly upward like that of a banana, not enough curvature to cause discomfort—just the opposite in fact, she loved the way it felt inside of her, especially when she was on top and leaning in to him, that probe of manly comestible, curving inside of her and rubbing against her womanly walls in a loving and comforting sort of way.

Erika returned her mouth to him, sucking him in quickly with an audible slurp, and gripping the shaft, hearing him wince. James shifted and lay back, face to the ceiling, eyes closed, enjoying this feeling that overtook him. She sucked him good, using long, full strokes, allowing James to go as deep as he could before reaching the back of her throat—and then pulling back out—James controlling the motion with his hips, Erika holding on and directing the show with her glazed hand. She very much enjoyed the sensation of fellating James—knowing as sure as there was a tomorrow that this was a feeling that he truly loved. As she continued along with this rhythm, Boney James in the background on a groove that made her toes dance, she matched her beat to his own, and closed her eyes, taking pleasure in making him feel good. A nagging thought suddenly appearing in the annuals of her mind without warning—tonight would James *come*? Would he finally come, once and for all? It had been close to five weeks. That was a long time not to have an orgasm. They had talked about it—briefly—James telling her not to worry—once again reassuring her that it was the condoms. But there had been a lot of sex within those five weeks. But no orgasm for James. And then, before she could make sense of these thoughts, lay it out for full inspection, and analyze further what was really going on, the doorbell chimes rang, a low-pitched, electronically enhanced sound that floated up to the bedroom. James, who had been squeezing her damp hair between his fingers as she sucked him, gently pulled her away, and sat up.

"Hold that thought, beautiful," he said, catching his breath and closing his robe quickly, "dinner's about to be served…"

Five minutes later he returned with the food. Loaded onto a large wooden tray, the three entrees were set on fancy china, the fragrance of curry shrimp and piquant chili sauce suspended in the air, tall glasses of Coke filled with ice, cloth napkins, salt and pepper, utensils, everything they would need to commence their little feast. James arranged the plates on his comforter, telling Erika not to worry—*whatever* got on the sheets, he said with a sneer, could be washed off.

Erika inquired if his fat erection had subsided by the time he made it to the door. James smiled and replied that, no, the delivery guy, who just happened to be gay—gay and a Thailander, imagine that—did indeed notice his "pickle in his pocket" as James put it, and after handing over the brown bag of food to James, cocked (no pun intended) his head to the side and asked if he could be of *further* service. James politely declined and closed the door. Erika squealed with laughter!

The food was tasty and hit the spot. The calamari was perfect—grilled, not fried—not too spicy, but with a kick that made Erika's mouth tingle. They lay on the bed, still clad in their robes as they ate, James occasionally feeding her with forkfuls of the chicken immersed in chili sauce—he had given up on using chopsticks after seeing that it took far too much effort to keep from dropping the morsels of food onto his comforter. Erika chowed down on the pad Thai noodles with shrimp, one of her favorite dishes, washing the seafood down with her Coke. Boney James had been replaced with Norman Brown's CD—his soft guitar licks inhabiting the room like an old friend.

They made small talk as they ate—James talked about his day at the studio, and a story he was working on that intrigued him—a piece about a black kid, high school age, who had just been accepted to Stanford University on a scholarship. The rub was that the kid and his family were homeless—the piece would primarily be about how the family had come to be in this predicament, and more importantly, how in this day and age, people from all walks of life still lost their homes every single day. Erika listened as he talked; then they switched gears, and she spoke about her day—as with many people Erika talked about what was bothering her at work—mostly office politics and such—this person trying to backstab another to get ahead. How petty some folks were—how personalities made or broke many situations—and turned one's experience at work into something pleasurable or something that was dreaded, like surgery. Erika thought about Trey, and how in the blink of an eye his situation had gone from wonderful to extremely shitty—with his mentor being replaced by some slicked-back newbie, trying to get in everyone's business and upset the balance of the firm.

When they were done about thirty minutes later, James cleared the plates, loading everything up onto the wooden tray and carrying it back downstairs. Erika seized the opportunity to stand and stretch her legs, run her fingers through her still drying hair, and re-tie her bathrobe. She was full, feeling good—the combination of run—shower—orgasm—food had left her feeling peppy and totally alive. She pranced over to the stereo, changed CDs again—this time to something a bit more uptempo—selecting Donnell Jones, snapping her fingers as the first jam came on. She began to move her hips, mouthing the words along with the singer. She bent down, examining James' collection of music and DVDs. Several titles caught her eye—a few blockbusters—*The Matrix*; *Training Day*; *Gladiator*, *M:I-2*. Next to those were a dozen or so DVDs that were placed in the shelf backwards, their titles not showing. Erika pulled a few out and studied their covers—*Indecency*; *The Uranus Experiment 2*; *Devil in the Flesh*; *Shag-A-Rama!* A frown replaced her smile. *Shag-A-Rama?* Her fingers went to other titles—*Anal in the*

Amazon; Black Cocks, White Pussies; Assume the Position; and *Unusual Objects.*
Erika stared in awe at the explicit cover photos. James—a closet freak? This
was totally unexpected. She heard him enter the room, spun around, feeling her face flush from embarrassment. His eyes met hers and he smiled.

"See you found my collection," he mused. His fingers fumbled with the
sash at his waist. He unloosened it, letting the folds of his robe hang free.
Erika could see his penis swinging free, but beginning to swell.

"Yeah. James, what is this stuff?" she asked, anxiety filling her voice.

"What's the matter, baby? A little porn scares you?" James' tone had changed
and Erika shivered involuntarily. He went to her, wrapped his arms around
her terry-cloth-clad frame and pulled her into him. He kissed the top of
her head and she immediately felt warmth. He glanced down at her.
"Everything cool? If it bothers you I can put it away."

"No, it's just…"

"I thought it might be fun to watch one. Together." James pulled back
from her and smiled, untying his sash as he went. His robe fell to the ground
and Erika saw he was fully hard. "Anyway, don't we have some unfinished
business to…uh, finish?" She nodded silently, her mind spinning, wondering what James was up to. She had seen him this excited before—hell, he
was always excited when *she* was around—but something about this time—
she couldn't put her finger on it exactly—but it just seemed different.
Silently, she watched as James selected a DVD and inserted it into the
player. He lay back on the bed, holding out his hand for her to join him.
She did, keeping her robe on as she knelt by his waist, reaching for his
penis. James placed a pillow under his head so he could remain propped up,
facing the large screen. Erika ran her hand around his shaft, cupped him in
her palm and began to jerk him, feeling the thickness expand with every tug
she gave. Her mouth reacquainted itself with his member, taking him in
her mouth, as much as she could stand, as her eyes scanned the TV set, as
James worked the remote. Scenes flew past rapidly, and then he settled on
one, as Erika continued to blow him. James massaged her shoulders and
neck with his left hand, then reached for her hair and grabbed it, letting her
mane slide in between his fingers. She increased the tempo, her head slid-

ing up and down as if on a string, a puppet, her eyes never leaving the screen.

The scene was of a thick black woman, equipped with a killer body—large, firm breasts, J. Lo ass, strong legs and strong arms—an equally impressive brutha underneath of her—the woman and man sixty-nining each other as they wriggled and moaned for the camera. His cock was being consumed by the woman on screen—she was taking him entirely in his mouth until only his testicles showed; for his part, his face was completely covered by her lower body, which thrashed around as he ate her voraciously, his fingers spreading her ass cheeks apart so he could reach and consume more of her.

James bucked his hips slowly; spoke softly to Erika, letting her know how much he was enjoying her doing this to him. He reached again for the remote, pressed a button or two—the scene fast-forwarded to where the black woman had returned with a white vibrator, the brutha lying back on the bed, legs splayed wide, matching the grin on his face. Erika watched with a detached sort of fascination—on the one hand enjoying the fact that her man was so excited and stimulated by what was going on—on the other, bothered by this scene—not that it was disgusting or anything—but it struck her as somewhat odd that *her* man would find this sort of entertainment stirring.

The black woman on the screen reached for the bedside table and some lube—spread some on her fingers and proceeded to rub the gel on the brutha's ass and around the dildo. Then she, without any fanfare, inserted the tip of hard plastic into the brutha's orifice, while stroking his dick with her dark hand.

At this point James had taken a hold of Erika's head with one hand, and using the palm of his other to push her downward, increasing the tempo of her sucking. He was moaning incessantly now, not attempting to conceal his pleasure. Erika increased her grip, lightly gnawed at the head, teasing him with her tongue and teeth before rubbing his balls with her fingers and brushing against his ass with her digits.

On screen the brutha was in heaven—back in the real world James was, too—both women fellating their men deeply, except on screen the girl was plunging the white vibrator in and out of the brutha's ass while she worked her oral magic. Erika found the scene disturbing, to say the least. What, she wondered, did James find erotic, about a man with a dildo up his ass???

And then, James issued a low growl, his legs and the rest of his body tightening, and Erika felt her mouth fill with semen. It caught her completely off guard, but she did her best not to show her surprise. James was holding her head in both hands as he spasmed, and Erika had no choice but to let him fill her mouth with his seed. She jerked his penis with her hand, her mind on autopilot, feeling the waves recede as he began to wither between her lips.

"Oh God!" James moaned. His head fell backwards, and Erika moved off him, bringing her hand to her still closed mouth. She glanced at him while heading for the bathroom. His eyes were fluttering rapidly, eyeballs rolling back and forth in their sockets, lost in their own little world.

Once in the bathroom, she ran the water, spit his seed down the sink, and washed out her mouth. Rinsed again before she ran the hot water, grabbed a hand towel, and lathered it up. Returning to the bedroom, Erika cleaned up James in a loving sort of way, washing him with the warm cloth. He moaned softly, but was otherwise silent. She took the remote from his limp hand, shut down the television set and went back to the bathroom. When she returned, James had crawled underneath the comforter, turned on his side and was snoring peacefully, his chest rising and falling slowly with every steady breath.

Erika blew out the candles and slipped beneath the covers, coming to a rest behind him. She ran her tongue inside of her mouth and swallowed a taste of James—thinking about the scene that had just unfolded in real life and on screen…wondering to herself as she wrapped a leg and arm around his sleeping form—was it she who had made him come tonight—or was it the couple in the video? This was the single solitary thought that would haunt her until daybreak…

Seventeen

I couldn't believe my freaking eyes—Allison, lovely fair-skinned Allison, homegirl from the night before—same honey who barely nine hours previously was allowing me to dab little droplets of sweat from between her luscious breasty melons—across from me—in the flesh! Now here I was, my jaw dragging against the goddamn floor—not a pretty sight, considering I was decked out in my usual smart office attire—a four-button robin's-egg blue suit, crisp white cotton shirt, navy blue silk tie with thin slivers of yellow meandering down the face of the fabric, and to complete the *coup de grace*, light-brown lace-ups—the kind of ensemble I usually reserved for those upscale social settings, but it just so happened I was in one of those *moods*—you know how *we* do, when you feel like making mutha fuckas snap their heads around as you walk by—don't even trip, y'all, you know you get that feeling just like I do every so often…and so, I quickly shut my trap, smiled at Allison and Quentin's wife (whom I had never met), and gestured for my client to take a seat.

I was giving Allison the eye, all the while grinning but thinking to myself—bitch, I can't *believe* you pulled this shit on me last night—playing me like I was some kind of fool, but before I could let my thoughts go to completion, she was introducing me to Quentin's wife, soon-to-be ex, Aponi Hues, a tiny little thing, lovely as she could possibly be. I took her all in as she stood to reach out and shake my hand—thin waist, tight body, no traces of aged fat here—that's what I'm talking about, y'all, medium sized firm breasts that didn't need the support of a bra underneath her button-down white blouse, a sculptured face, dark hair in a single braid, dark eyes that stared right through you—all-in-all a very nice package! Quentin, you go, boy, I am not mad at you. Dawg, if that were mine, I'd hit that ass every fucking chance I got! And as I gripped Aponi's hand, smiled, and thought about what she must look like naked, I had to check myself—Trey's Rule Number 4—never, ever, fuck your client—that, my friends, is a no-no. That shit can get you disbarred! But then, in the blink of an eye, I analyzed the situation, examined it from all angles, as if I were a physician probing the innards of an anxious patient—and came to the logical conclusion that in this *particular* situation, Rule Number 4 did *not* apply! Lawd Have Mercy! After all, Aponi was not my client! Ah, sookie sookie now!

Allison was bending down to open her briefcase and scatter some legal papers across the shiny conference room table, and I was clocking her every move. Her navy blue suit looked damn good on her, hair pulled back, girl-friend trying to look all business-like, and *succeeding*, and I'm sitting there thinking about last night at H20 and how damn good she appeared, titties spread before me like a pair of succulent fruit that were waiting to be snatched off a vine and devoured. And then my lips downturned into a frown—was Allison off-limits also? Did Trey's Rule Number 4 apply to opposing counsel as well? I'd have to check the rulebooks for a decision, y'all—let me think...naw, Allison and *any* opposing counsel were cool, I hastily concluded—and so I wasn't about to let this stop me from tagging that ass. Just then Allison looked up, her gaze meeting mine for a brief moment—and in that instant an encoded message for me and me alone seemed to transmit across the ether that hovered between us silently, and my smile was quickly erased—it was clear that whatever had transpired between us in the club the night before was *past tense*...and would stay in the past—Allison was about to get down to business. Strictly business.

Damn it, y'all, I just *hate* when that happens!

Allison cleared her throat and ran her palm over an ink-filled legal pad. "Good morning, gentleman. As you know my client has filed for divorce in the District of Columbia. One of the first matters that needs to be attended to is the separation of marital assets and property. Per normal legal procedure, I've asked Mrs. Hues to take an inventory of said assets and property in the hopes of speeding up this process." Allison proceeded to pass out several sheets of paper that were stapled in the upper-left corner. "Of course, we expect that Mr. Hues will review this list, or if it is counsel's wish, he can generate a list of his own for our review." Allison paused and smiled at Quentin who merely nodded silently. Her gaze flicked over to me—I let my stare find the bridge of her nose and hover there for a moment without saying shit. I wanted this little huzzy to feel my indignation over last night. I still could not believe that she played me! Girlfriend knew all along who I was—that's what Sassy had been referring to when we made our introductions—she had seen the way Allison had paused for a split second when I told her my name. She had known I was opposing counsel. So that's why she had decided to leave the *dick* alone. Okay, two can play that game. I decided to play tough with her—spare no punches—was ready to say, "of course we will be furnishing our own fucking list—you think we're going to take the word of some skanky ho?" —but then decided that this probably wasn't the most appropriate thing to say in front of my own client, considering the "ho" in question was still his wife…

"That's fine, Ms. Matthews, let my client review this. If there's a problem or if he'd prefer to produce his own list then we will, of course, let you know." I sat back, satisfied. Looked at Quentin who was studying the list with a furrowed brow, deep in thought. I glanced over at Aponi to my left— she remained motionless, her eyes moving between her attorney and me. Her breath was steady—the slow rise and fall of her breasts was mesmerizing to me. *But*, I told myself, *this is business—and business comes first.*

Allison grabbed a pair of thin reading glasses and slung them on while flipping to the second page. Damn, she looked sexy in those black frames! I imagined her lying in my oversized bed, the *Wall Street Journal* strewn around her naked form, save for those sexy glasses…

"As you can see, gentlemen, while there are lots of items on this list, my client is prepared to make this process far more palatable for Mr. Hues. She is *only* interested in the deed to the primary residence…" Quentin sucked in a quick breath and exhaled forcefully. I involuntarily reached out for Q.'s hand. Allison paused for a moment and glanced up before continuing. "The residence in question located in Raritan Township in New Jersey being turned over to my client."

"No fucking way!" Quentin spoke low and with a growl. He had turned his body to face his wife. Ignoring Allison, he reached out past me and pointed to his wife. "You've gotta…"

"Hold it!" I said forcefully, while gently pulling Quentin's arm down. I had spoken to Q. on the way over here about the possibility of this happening. It always did. Quentin was like most youngbloods in the NBA—he had made mad loot quickly—he was still young—twenty-seven—and rapidly had gone about making his mark by amassing a small collection of material things—a jet-black Land Cruiser ($68,000), a silver Jaguar XKR convertible ($90,000); two twenty-thousand-dollar Harley Davidson motorcycles (which he rarely rode); a top-floor condo overlooking the Georgetown Harbour ($1.6 million); and a three-million-dollar mansion in New Jersey that his wife had just put her dibbs on. Not to mention the jewelry, video, satellite, and high-fidelity electronics, mounds of CDs, matching Jet Skis, furniture, a small recording studio—probably costing over one-hundred grand in equipment alone—because Quentin (like many of these niggas out there) thought he could rap, and a small mountain of cash for God knows what. Quentin had gone over his own list three weeks ago with me, item by item— so I knew exactly what was what—and I had told him in no uncertain terms—in situations like these, the wife usually goes for the main home— fuck the cars, the bikes, the boats and rest of the shit—electronics weren't invented for women anyway—they don't know the first thing about using a remote! I had briefed Q. that this might happen. Asked him to maintain his cool if it did…let me take the helm…I was ready for this shit—had rehearsed it many times…so I took a breath and went on.

"Ms. Matthews—I fail to see how your client has any legal right to this home. If my memory serves me," and here I paused just to make a point by glancing up at the ceiling for a brief period of time, "Mr. and Mrs. Hues were married two years ago in May. Unfortunately, Mr. Hues had purchased the home in question back in September of 1998, several months after he signed with the New York Knicks. That was 1998, Ms. Matthews, two solid *years* before he married Mrs. Hues here." I paused, gave her one of my "how ya like me now" smiles before glancing over at Aponi who remained tight-lipped. I had to give homegirl credit—she was playing things way too cool—she was calm and held her demeanor a little too well. This concerned me—I expected her to go "ghetto" on us at any moment now—break out of the seat, pointing, spitting, and telling us just what the fuck she and her posse were gonna do—that's what was usually the case with some women—but Aponi seemed to be different. This would require further thought.

"My client," I continued, "has every legal right to continue to own the main residence, live in it, sublet it, or do whatever he sees fit. Your client, regardless of the fact that she was married to Quentin, unfortunately has no legal right to it."

I took a breath before continuing. Allison stared impassively at me. *Good, I got your fucking attention now, be-yatch.*

"My client," I continued, "Ms. Matthews, is prepared to split all assets and property that was amassed *during* the marriage, amicably and equitably, but not one day before. That is not only fair, Ms. Matthews," and here I sat forward, pivoted left, and gave Aponi my full attention, "and Mrs. Hues...but that *is* the law." I sat back, confident and satisfied, giving my client, Quentin Hues, Washington Wizards star forward, a quick clutch of his forearm while I grinned my ass off at Allison!

✠✠✠

Like in the movie, *Titanic,* I was on top of the world!!! But Allison Matthews, counsel for Aponi Hues, was about to bust my bubble. The skanky ho wench!

"Mr. Alexander," she said, way too calmly, while glancing around the room, smiling that devilish smile that had made my dick quiver last night. "Do you happen to have a laptop handy that I could use?" My eyes narrowed—a laptop???? Just what the fuck did she want/need with a laptop?

"I'm sorry?" I said gingerly, buying time to allow my analytical mind to run scenarios through my brain at gigaflop speeds. Quentin was searching

Aponi's eyes for a clue. There were none, and this, more than anything, bothered me.

"A laptop—do you have one handy?" Allison asked again, producing a shiny CD-ROM from her leather briefcase. She held the disc case in her hand, moving it ever so slowly between lovely fingers. My mind was pounding in anticipation—this was the Yin and Yang of law that gave me the adrenaline rush that was as good as sex (well, *almost* as good as sex)—the not knowing what was to come next—sparring with an able partner and learning to antic-ipate their tactics—like a tough game of chess where the most able players think eight to ten moves ahead—pawns overtaking rooks when one isn't expecting it...

"Hold on. Give me a sec." I reached for the PolyCom in the center of the conference table and quickly dialed India's extension. She picked up on the first ring.

"It's me—can you bring a laptop over to the Peace Room? Yes, thanks." I smiled at Allison and Aponi. "Aptly named, don't you think?" I sat back, took a moment to compose my thoughts, cut a quick glance over at Quentin who was sitting at the table quietly, save for the vein in his temple that throbbed to some hushed rhythm. Allison smiled, took a moment to jot down a few notes on the pages of her legal pad. Aponi, on the other hand, took the opportunity to get up and stretch her legs by moving to the large window. I used the occasion to check out her ass—it was nice, round and firm, no hint of jiggle, momma's been good to her, that's for sure—the package wrapped up in a pair of tight, shiny black pants with a thick leather belt with an oversized ornate buckle. Under any other circumstances I would have zeroed in on the contours of her sexy young flesh, the kind that hadn't begun that decomposition of sensuality that ultimately brings every woman down—the sexy curve of her ass cheeks which intersected the cleft where her (undoubtedly tight) pussy lay—but not today—today, at this exact moment I *needed* to know what the fuck was on that CD...something wasn't right. That was for sure.

India arrived three minutes later. She set the laptop down in front of me, smiled and departed silently. I flipped the clamshell open, powered it on, and swiveled it around for Allison to use. She nodded to me while inserting the CD into the drive.

"Mr. Alexander," she said softly, as she waited patiently for the computer to boot up, her full attention directed on me, "are you aware that the only reason for the demise of the marriage between Quentin and Aponi Hues is your client's *infidelity*?" I felt the weight from a steel I-beam that is used to build skyscrapers come crashing into my solar plexus, knocking the wind out of me. While I couldn't see my bald head, I knew without a shadow of a doubt that beads of sweat were bursting forth from my pores. I felt myself turning pale.

I managed a weak, "excuse me?"

"Infidelity." Allison said the word with fluidity, style, and grace. Like she had practiced it a million times before this morning's meeting. I snapped my head over to Quentin who was holding his breath and looking straight-forward. *Oh shit*, I thought to myself, *this is going to be one fucked up day…*

✠✠✠

Allison had finished fumbling around with the laptop and swiveled it around to face Quentin and me, her index finger poised over keyboard. She checked her legal pad for a moment—as if she needed to be reminded about what was to come next. Without preamble she unleashed on us.

"Mr. Hues has on at least three occasions that we are *aware* of, committed adultery…"

"What?" Quentin yelled. I put my hand on his forearm and gestured for him to be silent.

"Yes, adultery—and memorialized it onto digital format for all of eternity. Not too smart, considering the fact that his wife found the evidence on his laptop." Quentin was turning ashen. Aponi's mouth was frozen into a tight curve. "Yes, his laptop." And with that Allison hit the <Enter> button with her manicured index finger—and in a split second the screen was filled with moving images of Quentin and his extremely well-hung cock being pampered, licked, and sucked by some nameless white girl. Allison turned the sound up with a flick of her thumb so we could all hear him talking his dirty trash to this little slut. I blinked and all I could think about was R. Kelly and other stupid mutha fuckas who filmed their own versions of home porno, and then lived to regret it…

Now it was Aponi's turn to unleash.

"You mutha fucka! I thought you loved me!" she exclaimed, rising out of the seat as she extended her hand in his direction. I was already out of mine, forming a human shield between her and my client. "Instead you were fucking these *bitches*? You dirty mutha fucka!" Traces of spittle were deposited at the corners of her mouth. Her nipples were hard, that was apparent, and even in the midst of her fury, she was still quite beautiful. Quentin had pushed back from the conference room table and was standing, staring down his wife. He was silent for a moment before it was his turn to go off.

"Bitch, if you weren't always shopping and spending my goddamn money trying to be Gucci-down, perhaps I'd pay more attention to you!"

"Calm down, Q.," I told him, raising my hand to ensure he didn't decide to charge left toward his wife. Allison had risen and had gone to console her client, who stood her ground, and was huffing and puffing like a raging bull.

"Fucking bitch!" Quentin hissed, loud enough for everyone in the room to hear. "Why the fuck don't you go back to Limited Too where I found your dumb ass…"

"FUCK YOU, nigga!" Aponi spit, flinging her hands in the air. "You're the dumb mutha fucka here—taped your stupid ass and left it on the computer for me to find?" Aponi's face turned into a snarl. "Who's the stupid mutha fucka now, huh, nigga?" Her arms were across her upper body as if she were hugging herself. Quentin was a mass of rage that I would have trouble controlling in a moment. The boy was huge.

"Quentin," I said, calmly, looking first at him and then at Allison, while punching redial on the PolyCom. "India, please come escort Mr. Hues to my office—NOW." I pointed my finger toward him and glared at his eyes. "Quentin!" I repeated. Quentin bowed his head as he backed up toward the door. India flew into the room like a storm. She knew from my tone what was up. This wasn't the first time a meeting between feuding couples had turned ugly. She reached for Quentin's arm and gently nudged him toward the door. His eyes flicked from Aponi to Allison to me. I nodded silently as he left the room. The door closed and I spun to face Allison, who was still touching Aponi's shoulder.

"First off, that was a stupid stunt, counselor!" Allison opened her mouth to speak but I raised my hand and cut her off before giving her the opportunity. "That was really great for drama, but it didn't serve either of our clients' interests. Secondly, that disc doesn't mean a damn thing, and you know it. That could be anyone on that tape! Hell, nowadays anyone with a camcorder and some low-cost editing software can make a pretty convincing movie."

"You saying that's not Quentin on that screen?" Aponi yelled.

"I have no idea, Ms. Hues. But that is not what should concern you right now—this should—that movie was confiscated from property that does not belong to you. That's stealing. Further, it *may* contain data that is potentially damaging to my client's career and reputation. Therefore, as soon as I leave this office I will file an injunction against you with the Circuit Court of the District of Columbia ensuring that the contents of that disc not be played, shown, inspected, copied, transmitted, or altered in any way."

"You can't do that," Allison exclaimed. "The contents of that disc were produced during the marriage and therefore is marital property, and…"

"Oh yes I can—and I *will*—you better listen to me, Ms. Hues, and listen carefully because I am not playing games here—I don't want to escalate things to the point where they get ugly, but you and your lawyer have brought us to this place, not me. I have no intentions of sitting here and allowing my client to be defamed. Your attorney pulled a stupid move—unfortunately for you, you're the one who will have to live with the consequences."

I reached for the laptop and snapped it shut while maintaining eye contact with Aponi. The sound of plastic impacting reverberated throughout the room.

"The penalty for violating a court-ordered injunction is quite high—you will go to jail, Ms. Hues, I promise!" I paused to let that sink in. "And if you even *think* about doing something stupid with that disc or any other copies that you may possess, I would think long and hard before you act, Ms. Hues.

I promise you, this has the potential to turn ugly like that," I snapped my fingers, "if you don't keep your head straight.

"This meeting, Ms. Matthews, is over. I strongly urge you to counsel your client on these matters. The law, whether you agree with it or not, is on my client's side. We will be in touch!"

With that, I scooped the laptop under my arm and exited the Peace Room, holding my breath and not letting it out until I was on the other side of the thick conference room door, and out of sight…

Eighteen

Vince lowered the sketchpad to the deeply stained worktable and dropped the mechanical pencil as well. He rubbed his beard and scratched at his cheek. The drawing that stared up at him wasn't quite right—Vince couldn't put his finger on it, but it just wasn't the kind of sketch that he was feeling this minute. He sighed, glanced around his studio, and decided that a short break was in order.

It was a little after seven. The sun, he could see from the high windows, was beginning to set. The room in which he stood was an oversized loft, perfect for an artist such as himself. It had high ceilings and aging brick walls that held character and ancient whispers in the darkening mortar. Four high windows were cut into adjoining walls, each one high enough that he had to stand on a stool to reach the sash. A small fireplace was built into one corner of the room; a small pile of wooden scraps lay unburned inside the hearth. A cheap futon laid in the center of the room, one that he had picked up at Ikea a number of years ago—just in case he worked far into the night or just got too tired to head home—not a rare occurrence lately…

On the long wall opposite the two windows and in front of a low coffee table hung his collection of masks—they were suspended in rows from floor to ceiling. There were close to two dozen of them—masks of various shapes, sizes, patterns, and colors. Each one representing someone whom had touched him in some small, yet significant way. A lover, a friend, family member, or even stranger—someone whom had made a lasting impression on Vince's psyche.

The floors of this space were concrete, but Vince had taken a colorful throw rug that contained wisps of red, orange and purple, and placed it across the center of the room, giving the room a touch of class. Along with his masks and a few other knickknacks, it made the space feel lived in and homey. That was important since he spent a great deal of time here, working, thinking, and being artistic and creative.

Vince left the sketchpad on the worktable and walked over to the coffee table, reaching for his cup of java. He sat down on the futon, ran a hand over his hair and reached for his cell on his hip. After taking another sip of coffee, he flipped open the phone and dialed the number he knew all too well.

He was staring at his latest piece as he waited for the connection to be made—the one of Maxi—it hung off to the right about halfway up the brick wall. Vince was happy with it—the mask had come out quite nice—at first it had taken him a while to complete—not knowing for sure what color scheme to apply to the surface of plaster. The lifecasting itself had gone quite well, and the bas-relief that had stared back at him had been unnerving, to say the least. But Vince wasn't sure how this piece was to be finished—a solid dark color—no, that wasn't quite right, since it didn't match Maxi's mood—multiple colors then? Diagonal stripes, thick or thin swaths of alternating color? That was a thought—but he didn't think it would work here. In the end, a tie-dye kind of pattern—bursting out from the epicenter—radiating outwards, the darkness of deep rich browns and reds leading to the lightness of pale gray and yellows. And for the finishing touches, Maxi's lips—those sensuous pieces of flesh that Vince remembered all too well, outlined in a vibrant day-glow kind of orange smear, standing apart from the rest of the mask like a lone Joshua tree in a forgotten desert.

Vince heard the familiar voice and grinned to himself.

"Hey you."

"Hey."

"Angeliqué baby. *Que pasa?*"

"Sorry, lover boy…" And that's when Vince began to suspect that he wasn't talking to whom he thought he was. "…she's not here right now."

"Oh. My bad. I thought this was Angeliqué," Vince mused. "Guess not."

"No harm—most people confuse our voices. This is Amber. And you are Vince." Not a question, Vince noticed, but a statement.

Vince smiled. "Amber, hello. How'd you know?"

"Not too hard," Amber said, "she's only been talking about you non stop… kind of hard to concentrate on anything else…"

"Really?" Vince was intrigued. He directed his mind back to New Orleans for a clue as to the identity of this woman—and then suddenly it hit him like a palm to the forehead—she was the young woman whom he had met when he'd gone to Angeliqué's studio the night of her show—the beautiful model, bare, reclining on the floor—head tilted back, brown hair inches from the ground, darkly rimmed nipples erect, trim body, firm legs and thighs, auburn skin covered with a hauntingly beautiful pattern of *veve*. Vince saw all of her with razor-like clarity—and recalled the way he had been stunned into silence by a shard of recognition, which flowed through him now. He was silenced once again by the thought.

"Are you there?" she asked after the pregnant pause.

"Yes, ah, I'm right here."

"Soooooo—only you, me, and several thousand miles of fiberoptic cable between us…" Amber laughed and Vince felt himself flush.

"Yes. So true."

"Cat got your tongue, I see," she mused. "Not to worry. Guess you were expecting someone else—but listen, go ahead; why don't you throw down your rap, the one you were going to use on Angeliqué, on me instead—let me try it on for size!"

"Hmmm, there's a thought. But I better not."

"Why," Amber teased, "afraid, I'm going to poke holes in your shit?"

Vince laughed. "Naw, nothing like that."

"You sure? I don't mind. I don't have anything else to do tonight!"

"Sorry to hear that, but tell you what—can you just *mention* to Angeliqué that I called? That would be best."

"Oh yeah, I can do that, Vince. Not a problem."

"Cool," Vince said, warming to this woman immediately.

"Yeah, cool," Amber responded, warming to him, too.

Vince was ready to say something else—feeling himself wanting to continue the conversation, launch onto another plane, another topic that had already formed on the tip of his tongue and was ready to take flight—when his cell beeped. He frowned, glanced at the tiny screen and the unfamiliar number, and put the phone back to his ear.

"Amber, can you hold one sec—I've got another call coming in. Don't go away, okay?"

"Sure, not going anywhere."

Vince clicked over and said hello.

"Mr. Cannon, Jr.?" a familiar voice asked.

"Yes?"

"Hey, Vince. It's Desiree! What's up?"

Vince smiled. "Hey you. How ya livin'?"

"Not bad considering…waiting for a brutha to give a sistah a call back and a ride on that beautiful bike. Ya know???"

"Desiree. Sorry, boo. I've been busy and…"

"Yeah, yeah, yeah. Tell it to one of those *uneducated* women you obviously are confusing me with, okay?"

"Damn, Desiree." Vince's thoughts went to that of Amber on the other line. "Listen—I'm on a call right now. Can I call you in a minute?"

"A minute?" Desiree responded, "or do you mean, tomorrow or next week? Don't keep a sistah waiting!"

"I got you, Desiree. I'll call you back." Vince switched back over with a sigh. "Amber? You still there?"

"Yeah, where am I gonna go? Besides, I'm waiting to hear some words of wisdom from you, seeing how you're the writer/philosopher here." Amber laughed and Vince found himself grinning along with her, momentarily forgetting Desiree and her *drama*.

"Writer/philosopher? Where'd you get that from?" Vince asked.

"Please. I'm staring at the cover of your book right now." He heard a rustling noise in the background. "Nice photo, by the way. I dig that jacket. Black suits you well, Vince."

"Thank you, Amber. Okay—you got me on the writer bit, but philosopher? I don't think so."

"Don't be modest. I've been reading you. And I have to say I'm impressed."

"Really?" Vince mused. He wouldn't admit it, but any time someone had something positive to say about his book, he absolutely loved it. Vince never got tired of hearing folks talk about his book. Never!

"I've only recently begun reading it, but yeah, it's good. I'm digging the part about how you found your passions, and how one goes about finding theirs. That has really got me thinking about what makes me tick—and what turns me on."

Vince thought about that. He recalled their brief time together in Angeliqué's studio—watching her as she lay silently as Angeliqué applied the finishing touches of paint to her body. The *veve* glistening as it dried on her smooth skin. And Amber watching him watching her, a peculiar expression on her face.

As Amber continued to speak, Vince listened and found himself intrigued by her words. "Yes—to be truly happy in life, we all need to seek out those things that we're one hundred percent passionate about—and pursue those."

Vince and Amber continued to speak on the subject that Vince loved—helping folks find their way to true happiness. They spoke for close to fifteen minutes—the time whisking by like some amusement park ride, Amber asking many questions, truly captivated by his words, and Vince responding, giving her little anecdotes from the book and his seminars. Vince was enjoying the conversation and impressed that Amber had taken the time to get into his book and explore the essence of his ideas.

"So, Amber, please continue to read the book and let me know of any questions or comments you might have. I'd love to help out in any way I can."

"That would be cool—I mean, like I know the author and got the hook-up, you know?"

"Exactly!" Vince smiled. "This is a journey—one I seriously believe will bring a lifetime of joy. So, enjoy the ride! Anywho—I'm not going to take up any more of your time, Amber. It's been a real pleasure speaking with you."

"Likewise, Vince."

"Take care and hope to talk with you soon."

"You too. Bye." Amber's sweet voice lingered in his ear long after the connection went dead. Vince sat there, thinking about her, replaying the conversation in his head, remembering Amber as he first saw her, reclining on the floor, a certain air of innocence and purity surrounding her being like a shroud. But then he smiled as he thought about certain words and phrases she used this evening, and the way she laughed—and Vince knew that just beneath the surface, there was raw, untapped sensuality, ready to burst forth from her pores like a geyser. Vince smiled. He could feel it. Vince could sense it. He knew…

❈❈❈

It was after eight when Vince returned Desiree's call. The sun had set; the evening was dark and moonless. A pot was brewing, sending a comforting aroma into the room.

Desiree answered on the third ring.

"Hey you. I'm returning your call. It's Vince."

"Greetings," Desiree said with a laugh.

"So, what's up? What are you doing?"

"Not much—finishing up some reading," she said. "How about you?"

"In my studio, trying to do some sketches, but not really feeling any of them—the spark of creativity refuses to light tonight," Vince mused.

"Wow—you have a studio?" Vince could hear the excitement in her voice.

"Well, yeah—you don't think I create my masks on the dining room table, do you?"

"I don't know—I guess I didn't consider it, that's all. Your own studio—now that is the bomb!"

"Thanks."

"So, what kind of sketches are you doing? Nudes?" Desiree chuckled.

"No, not nudes! Get your mind out of the gutter! Damn. I'm doing facial sketches—trying out some ideas for a new mask that I want to do. But I can't quite get it right—this is what happens sometimes—you have an idea in your head—you can see it when you close your eyes, but translating it onto paper or plaster is something else indeed."

"I think that is so cool, that you actually go through this process of creating your art," Desiree said, "as opposed to just flinging paint at a square of canvas and hoping the results turn out great."

Vince laughed as he poured himself another cup of the steaming liquid. "No, I don't just fling paint at canvas, but there's a thought! Thanks…"

"So," Desiree said, her voice getting softer, "perhaps I should come over there *now* and give you something to sketch. Whatdayathink?" She ended her sentence with a sexy kind of laugh—but Vince knew she was dead serious about her proposal.

"Hmmm, there's a thought. But don't you teachers have to get up early? I mean, it is a schoolnight after all."

"Why don't you let me worry about that, Mr. Artist? I'd like to see you again, and it seems like you need some *inspiration*…I think I can provide some of that." She chuckled again; as she did, Vince had a number of thoughts swirling around in his head—he did like her look—he recalled her face from the coffee shop and how that first time he had spotted her he had focused on the lines and symmetry about her face. A face possibly suitable for one of his masks…

"Listen, that's cool with me. Let me give you the address and you can come on down now. That is if you're truly serious?"

"Give me the digits and find out!"

Vince gave her the information and hung up, a smile forming on his face as he did so.

✠✠✠

She showed up thirty minutes later. Vince opened the door and invited her in with a wide sweep of his hand. He took her coat, kissed her on her cheek while admiring her tight jeans and form-fitting white top that revealed her thin, dark waist. He offered her a cup of coffee, which she accepted, as she went to the wall to view his collection of masks.

"These are incredible," Desiree said as she stared in awe at his art. She marveled at the colorful patterns that were laid across the faces of plaster. Desiree had figured that Vince was a weekend artist—one who dabbled when he had the spare time, no more—but looking at the collection set in front of her, she knew she had been wrong.

"Vince, have you sold any of these?" Desiree asked, lightly stroking the raised plaster of several masks, then turning to stare at him.

"Some—I have a relationship with several galleries in town. But to be honest, I'm my worst critic—I never think they are good enough to be sold to the public."

"Well," Desiree said while taking a seat on the futon, "I'm here to tell you they are. Without a doubt. Boy, you could make some serious loot with these!"

Actually, Vince had been thinking long and hard about pursuing the sale of his art. Up to now, it had not been a priority of his to find more buyers for his masks. Vince knew that the interest was out there—all he needed to do was pursue this seriously, make some phone calls, let folks know he was ready to sell, and the tide would carry him onward and upwards…no doubt about that.

"Thank you. Yeah, I need to get some of these out there and hung in galleries."

"For sure—you have real talent!" Desiree took a sip of her coffee and put the mug down. She rose, walked over to his worktable and the sketches that lay in a heap. She glanced through them, taking her time, admiring his work. Vince watched her silently.

"These are very good—what are you talking about?"

Vince rose and joined her, taking his cup with him. "I don't know—I can't put my finger on it, really—I just am not feeling any of them."

"What are you trying to do?" Desiree asked.

"Trying out some designs for my next mask. I'm going for a new look and want to try it out on paper first." Vince stood next to Desiree inhaling the scent of her perfume. It was sweet and heavenly. His eyes scanned her body—her leather boots, jeans that fit her like a glove, the roundness of her ass, her curvy hips and waist—thin and flawless, the tight-fitting tee, swelling of her breasts, strong yet sumptuous neck and shoulders, hair that was soft, dark, and pulled back, highlighting the features of her smooth face. Desiree was a good-looking woman—no, that didn't do her justice. Desiree was *fine*. She was young and her body was flawless, age having yet to play its cruel trick with her form. Vince felt the desire stir in him. He pursed his lips and thought about her, wondering how she moved, unencumbered by clothes, watching as her hips rotated ever so slightly as she shifted weight while reaching out to grasp another sketch, eyes flickering over to him and sensing him observing her silently. And she played the game back, twisting her lip into a smile and creating a sparkle in her eyes, grateful for his stare and interest.

"I should do you," Vince said, without preamble. It came out wrong, he realized, and laughed. "That didn't come out the way I planned. Sorry."

"No," Desiree said, pausing to look at a sketch before she turned to face him. She was inches from Vince. She could touch him easily by raising her arm just slightly. "Don't play that shy routine with me now—tell me what's really on your mind, Vince."

"Desiree," Vince said smoothly, raising his hand to her shoulder. "I didn't mean it that way."

"You said you should do me. What did you mean then?"

"I meant I should do a lifecasting of you," Vince explained, lowering his hand to her waist. "...For a mask," he said as she leaned into him. "You, Desiree, will be my next subject."

Nineteen

Quentin was furious! I found him pacing the length of my office. India had gotten him a cup of coffee—it lay untouched on the coffee table, its tendrils of shifting vapor rising toward the ceiling. I came in, shut the door and flung my jacket onto the back of my chair.

"Q-Dawg—please tell me that ain't you on tape…brutha, please!" I stood before him, hands on my waist, thinking about how fucked up this case had just become.

"Man?" His voice cracked like that of a frog. I thought to myself, *oh, Lord; this shit ain't good at all…*

"Okay—tell me this—we went over this a month ago—I asked you specifically, remember—were there any other women? And you said, 'no.' Remember that, Quentin?"

"Yeah." Quentin sat down and grabbed the coffee, spilling a bit on the table and his wrist. "Shit! Sorry." I went to my credenza and grabbed a tissue to wipe up his spill.

"Dawg—I'm not here to judge you. If you had extramarital affairs that's okie doke with me—but if I'm going to provide the best legal advice and get the best arrangement for you, I need to know the truth. Understand?" He shook his head sourly. None of this shit mattered now.

"Yeah, I'm sorry, Trey. I fucked up. I know it. I didn't think that this would come out. Fuck!" Quentin held his head in his hands. He looked so pathetic hunched over, this oversized guy, larger than life, sitting in my chair, realizing the errors of his ways—but unfortunately, too late…

"Q., how is it possible she found the tape? I mean…"

"It wasn't a tape—I shot it on DV, true, but copied it straight to my hard disk on the laptop and erased the tape."

"Yeah, well, so far so good," I said, with a hint of scorn in my voice, "but obviously she discovered it anyway. Right?"

"Man, I don't know how the fuck she found it. I had all that shit on a separate drive, used PGP to encrypt that shit and…"

"Dawg—if I want technical talk, I'll phone the firm's IT department."

"Sorry—I used this program that scrambles the data. You need a password to get to it."

"Okay, cool. So what happened—you taped the password to the screen?" I grinned but Q. wasn't laughing with me.

"Naw—I know I password-protected that shit. I don't know—sometimes I forget to log off or unmount the disk." Again I was shaking my head. Quentin stood and went to the window, staring down at the street below. "I guess it's possible that I left the drive in a state where she could view it without my password, like after I had already put in the password and just left the machine on. It's not like I shut the fucking thing down every day. Fuck! I don't know what happened, Trey. Obviously, I didn't leave the shit out for her to find. I'm not that stupid!"

I was ready to say something smart but held my tongue. Again, thoughts of Paris Hilton, R. Kelly, Pamela Anderson, and other celebrities who had found themselves in this very same mess sprang to mind.

"Okay. Let's leave this alone. We're not solving anything by focusing on what *may* have happened. The fact is, your wife found it, has copies of it, and Lord knows how many. Hopefully she hasn't shown it to too many folks. We have your career and reputation to think about."

"Fuck!" Quentin exclaimed, his fists clenched by his side.

"Where's the laptop now?" I asked.

"At my crib."

"Here? In the Georgetown condo?"

"Yeah, it's been there since I moved out six months ago." I pondered Quentin's words. Either his wife had known about her husband's infidelity for six months and said nothing or…

"Q. Has Aponi been to your crib since the two of you separated?" He turned from the window to stare at me.

"Naw, Dawg."

"Q.?" The look in his eye told me he was lying.

"What? Okay, yeah, she was there one time—she came to town with some of her friends a few weeks ago and we met to try and work things out." Right. I could just imagine how *that* went down. My mind was whirling with so many questions. Things were getting complicated by the second.

"Okay. Listen to me. Go home. Get some rest. You have a game in two days. Let me ponder all of this stuff and call you with any questions I may have. You gonna be around? I'm going to need to get in touch with you round the clock. Leave me your cell. I have a feeling her attorney's going to be hounding me."

"Yeah. No problem. Can you do anything about the disc?" he asked timidly.

"Don't worry about that—I scared the shit out of them—told them I'm filing an injunction with D.C.'s Circuit Court. Told your wife she'll without a doubt do jail time if those images get into anyone's hands."

"Can you do that?"

"Damn Skippy! This is serious, Q. You don't want that tape floating around. Your career could suffer because of it. Nobody likes a playa who flashes his shit in front of a camera, especially when he's married. If we don't strike and strike hard, that shit *will* wind up on the Internet! Trust me, Dawg, you don't want that…" I put a hand on Quentin's shoulder. "But don't worry, Q., Trey is in 'da house, and on point—I got you covered. Things will work out in the end—you might have to give up that house of yours, though— that may be the only way out of this nasty little mess."

"Fuck," Quentin said, but it came out as a whisper.

Yeah, I thought to myself, *that's what got your dumb ass into trouble in the first place…*

✠✠✠

It always amazes me just how many freaking voice-mail messages I get when I'm not in the office—the amount is staggering. And that doesn't count the messages that India Jasmine Jackson takes for me—for those folks who don't want to be connected to my voice mailbox, or who are technologically challenged, or who would rather speak to a live female. Whatever!

The day after the fiasco with Quentin Hues, it was about two p.m. when I arrived back in the office after some pretty good sushi. I flung my jacket onto the back of my chair, sat down, unlaced my shoes to let my feet breathe, and punched the button on my phone and heard the female voice say in that recognizable tone: "You have *eight* new messages." Eight? In less than an hour? How the fuck was that possible? And so, I proceeded to listen and delete, listen and delete, listen and delete, when in walks Bernard John Marshall. He did not look pleased.

"Bernie."

"It's Bernard." He took a seat. I stared into his hard eyes, my mind relatively calm, not racing, not trying to anticipate or figure him out. Why bother? I'd find out soon enough.

"Bernard." I didn't have time or interest in small talk. Not with this prick who had stolen Calvin's job.

"This *thing* with Quentin Hues."

"Settlement conference," I corrected.

"Didn't go too well, I presume." I stared at Bernard. He obviously had done some reconnaissance work and gotten the 411. "You filed an injunction in District Court."

"Yes. Yesterday afternoon." I had done exactly what I said I would do. Make no mistake. When I say I'm gonna do something, I do it, especially when it comes to law.

"Not a good move, in my opinion."

"Really? Well, *Bernard*, right now my concern is to ensure that this *thing*, as you call it, does not tarnish my client's reputation. The best way to ensure that, in *my* opinion, is to file an injunction."

"By filing an injunction you are doing just the opposite—you draw attention to this thing—instead of focusing on…"

"Excuse me, Bernard," I said, cutting him off. I clasped my hands together, fingers interlocking on the smooth desktop. "I'm pretty busy right now. I sure don't have time to deconstruct every aspect of this case, or any other I'm working on, with you. Perhaps Calvin should have mentioned to you how I operate." I stared at those dead blue eyes, wanting to reach across the desk and strangle his fucking neck until the color drained from his face— but, don't get me wrong—I'm not a violent man...honest!

"And, Trey, let me tell you how *I* operate," Bernard replied calmly, but underneath the unruffled exterior, it was clear that a fire was brewing. "As the new managing partner, it is my responsibility and right to review the strategy of all attorneys in this firm, and to ensure that they are conducting themselves in a manner that is consistent with the overall objectives and direction of this law firm." Bernard paused for a moment to let me take that in. "On a personal level, let me say this—I really don't care how busy you are or whether in your past life you and Calvin discussed every aspect of each case or not. I reserve the right to come in here whenever I damn well please and ask whatever questions I see fit. Furthermore, if, in my humble opinion, I think you are heading down the wrong path, I will let you know. That is my job, counselor. That is my right." Bernard's voice had not increased in volume a single decibel. But it had changed in cadence and in pitch. He was pissed. I could almost see the steam rising off his head. "Are we clear, counselor?"

I was ready to fire back—first off, I don't need this fucking job—I'm damn good at what I do, and can find another gig anywhere in this town—I bring a shitload of money into this firm—second—I retain some pretty heavy-weight clients—so fuck Bernard John Marshall and the horse he rode in on! But then, at the exact moment I was readying to unleash on BJM, my phone rang; I checked the caller ID and saw it was Vince. I glanced up and told Bernard politely, but firmly, "Bernie, I gotta take this one, okay???"

✠✠✠

Five days later, I get a call from guess who? Allison Matthews, Esq., of course. I'd purposely avoided calling her—part of my strategy these past few days—make her wonder what was going through this brilliant legal mind of mine—she already knew I wasn't kidding about the injunction—she and her client had already been served—that much I knew. That had happened on Friday just in time for the weekend. I love it! It was now Tuesday afternoon.

"Counselor, I've been waiting for your call," Allison began, cool, calm, and collected, just like at H20 a week before. My thoughts went back to that evening and I had to smile.

"Ms. Matthews, what a pleasant surprise. Is this to discuss business, or are you calling to collect on that ride I promised you? I'm still interested in getting you on the back of my bike, you know…" *Yeah*, I thought to myself, *on the back of my Indian, legs splayed wide across the hard leather, back arched against the backrest, lovely breasts bare to the elements…*

"I'm sorry, Mr. Alexander, but right now, all you and I have to discuss is business."

"That is a shame," I responded.

"I was hoping that by this point we would have completed our settlement issues and moved on…but I guess not."

"Well, counselor, the unfortunate deviation in the schedule is your doing, not mine."

"Look, Trey, you know damn well that the injunction isn't going to stick in any court—why are you wasting our time and your own?" I could hear Allison getting hot.

"Really? I don't see it that way."

"Let's examine the facts—your client is an adulterer—that much is true. He was stupid enough to tape himself with three women that we know of, and then left the evidence around for my client to find—not the sign of a genius…"

"I'll give you that one, Allison," I quipped, "…*if* it can be proven that is my guy on the disc, which remains to be seen."

"Okay—let's put that aside for a moment. Your client has effectively relocated here to Washington and away from New Jersey where Aponi was born and raised, and made her home."

"Agreed. But the house was his free and clear before he ever laid eyes on your client. He may owe her part of the furnishings acquired during the marriage, but nothing else regarding that premises."

"Look, Trey. I did not call to argue the merits of this case with you..."

"No? Then what did you call me for?" I asked in a smug tone.

"I want to see this thing settled just as quickly as you do. This is a strain on my client, and I'm sure on yours as well..."

"Yes it is—especially when he's in the public eye and being accused of adultery."

"Counselor—can we meet and get this issue behind us? I feel confident that the two of us—you and me—no clients around to complicate things, can make this happen—our cool heads will prevail. I'm certain of it." I had to smile. Allison was good—she was speaking to me, attempting to get back on my good side—after that staggering left hook that came from out of nowhere—and ladies and gentlemen, it was working.

"Okay Ms. Matthews, that sounds like a good idea. Let me check my calendar." I swiveled in my seat and glanced at my Outlook calendar on the screen.

"I was thinking tomorrow or the day after. My schedule is light," Allison was saying.

"Hmmm, the next two days are not good for me," I said, "I'm in court. Let me see..."

"Friday then?" Allison was being more than accommodating—that was evident. And why shouldn't she be—we could have settled this thing last Thursday if it hadn't been for that *thing*. Why was everyone calling Quentin's screen debut a *thing*? Even I had called it that a few times...

"Hmmm, Friday. Oh, that's right, I'm heading out of town this weekend, leaving on Friday. No, that's not going to work." I could hear Allison controlling her breathing on the phone—the frustration was registering loud and clear. My lie about going out of town was to box her into a corner—give her little alternative but to see me one evening after work. "Here's a thought, Allison." My mind was racing—I could ask her to dinner, regardless of what she had said a moment ago about there only being business between us. Get her away from the office one night, perhaps pick her up on the bike—no, she'd never go for that—could meet her at the restaurant via the bike—bring the extra helmet—then she'd have no reason not to take a quick spin—no, she won't go for that either—she'd see right through that charade...

"I have this thing that I do once a month—it's kind of like volunteer work—you'll probably find this hard to believe," I let out a short laugh, "but I assist at a women's shelter here in town. Once a month I cook for the ladies—it's a thing I've been doing for close to a year now—they love it 'cause the food is the bomb, even if I say so myself, and I enjoy it because I get to hone my culinary skills on some fairly demanding folks."

"Why do I not believe you?" Allison asked. "This sounds like some kind of ploy to get me to think more highly of you." She was laughing now.

"What? A guy like me can't give back to the community? Is that what you're saying?"

"Not at all—I just don't buy that *you* would give back to the community, that's all." More laughter transported me back to H20 the week before.

"Well, I guess it shows how little you know about me. Anyway, here's the deal—I'm going to be there tomorrow evening from about four until eight-thirty or so. Why don't you stop by? You can have dinner with us, see me in action, if you doubt what I say, and most importantly, it will give us a chance to talk about the Hues." I was grinning to myself, knowing that she was ambivalent about doing this—on the one hand, wanting to get this case over and done with; on the other, not wanting to spend any social time with me because of a perceived conflict of interest. I loved putting Allison in this spot; it served her right for messing with me the way she did...

"Trey, I don't know...," Allison said uncertainly. I could hear the wheels spinning...

"Allison. This is not a date—I heard what you said about keeping it strictly business, loud and clear—but if we don't do this tomorrow, then it's next week before I'll have time to sit down with you." I let that thought hang in the air, like smoke from incense.

"I don't know..."

"Tell you what—here's the address of the women's shelter. It's not far from the U Street Corridor." I gave her the address and heard her scribble it down. "It will be fun. Plus I can always use another set of hands. You do know how to find your way around a kitchen, don't you?"

"Yes, Mr. Alexander, I do. We'll see," she muttered.

I decided not to push it any further. "Okay. Hope to see you tomorrow evening. Good day to you, counselor," I said, signing off.

"And to you as well."

Twenty

I pulled my coal-black Cadillac Escalade up to the inconspicuous home of The Nona E. Taylor Women's Center at a few minutes to four on Wednesday. I double-parked my *other* phat ride with the gleaming rims— put the hazards on, and got out. It was a beautiful day. I glanced up at the heavens, took in the blue sky and cool breeze that caressed my bald head and face, and thanked God for another lovely day. Walked to the back to begin unloading the food and supplies I had brought from home.

The Nona E. Taylor Women's Center was housed in a four-story brick house on a well-lit and neat street in Northwest D.C. All well-kept row houses, each one different in terms of size, color, and façade, giving the block that down home "neighborhood" feeling. In fact, one would be hard pressed to even pick the center out from any other residential property, save for the small brass plaque that hung next to the doorbell, which was located up the stone steps on the second floor.

I used my remote to unlock the back and grabbed the first of a dozen large trays and Tupperware containing various dishes and ingredients. Walked up the stairs and hit the buzzer with my elbow and waited. A heavy-set woman came to the door a minute later, glanced through the lace that covered the beveled glass and opened the door.

"Trey Alexander, look at you!" I flashed a smile at Yolanda Taylor, founder and director of the center. "Put that tray down and give me some sugar!" I obeyed and went to her willingly, feeling her bosom meld around my own body. Yo and I had known each other for two years—I met her through a friend; she had been searching for someone to do some pro bono work for the center—I wasn't looking to get involved, but this friend urged me to give Yo a call, just to hear her story—and I did so after weeks of him hounding me—and I'm glad I did.

Yolanda was the color of chocolate syrup, possessed twisting dreads, a soft, youthful face, and a heart the size of her black coffee thighs.

"How ya livin', Yo?" I said, standing back to look at her.

"Life's a blessing, Trey, you know that."

"Yes, I do."

"Come on in. I've got sixteen women with hearty appetites—they are ready for you, boy."

"Any good looking ones, Yo? I could use a fall project right about now," I said, eyeing her with a smirk.

"Boy, you know I'll pop you, you mess with my girls."

"Just checking, Yo. Maybe next month."

"Boy, you too much!" I observed her smile—the way her full lips curved upward and showed her teeth—that wonderful smile and the way her eyes narrowed and held a tinge of sadness in them. Yolanda's sister, Nona Elizabeth, had been in an abusive marriage for a number of years. After two years of violence and neglect, after Yolanda tried repeatedly to get her younger sibling to leave and get the help she desperately needed, Nona's husband shot her dead one evening, in this very house, because he had come home several hours late from work, and dinner wasn't served hot, to his liking…

He was now serving a life sentence for first-degree murder at a correctional institution in Tennessee. Yolanda had purchased the house from the estate and turned it into a shelter for battered women, vowing never again to find herself in the position of not being able to extend a hand to another woman in need.

Yolanda had told me that story one fall day, the two of us strolling around the neighborhood, a cloudless sky overhead not unlike today, and me thinking to myself, I have no choice—I *need* to give something back to these women, *hope*—and what better way than to serve them. Me: Trey Alexander, with all of my superciliousness.

I handed Yolanda the tray, told her she better not drop it, and retreated to get the others.

Fifteen minutes later, all of the food was in the first floor kitchen and the Escalade was parked safely in the alley out back—Yolanda had graciously offered to let me use her spot so I could keep an eye on my shit. I strolled in the back door, wearing jeans and boots, and a thin pullover black sweater. Without fanfare I donned a heavy cotton personalized apron from Williams-Sonoma, one of my favorite stores, and a matching bandanna, and went to work.

The center's kitchen was fairly large and functional—not equipped with all of the latest appliances for any kind of serious cooking, like mine, but it would do. The range was gas, thank God, and Yolanda had put in a double oven a few years back. A large, center island made of wood was where I did most of the food preparation work. This meal was something that I planned meticulously several weeks in advance. I thought long and hard about the menu, always vying for something different, a theme, if I could swing it, not wanting to just feed these women, but dazzle them with culinary excellence. That's what food was anyway, at least in my mind—more than just nourishment or sustenance—a means of teasing one's palate, tempting the senses with wonderful aromas and tastes. I had settled this month on an age-old holiday favorite—a beef tenderloin roast, pan-fried with rosemary and garlic, served with deep-roasted fall vegetables, a salad, freshly baked bread, and for dessert, several scrumptious pies that I would bake here. All of the ingredients I bought myself—never asking for contributions or financial assistance—not that I needed it—plus, the whole idea was to give these women one night a month of dining in style—Trey style!

It's hard to explain—I've tried over the years, with my friends staring at me in awe when I tell them what I do, once a month, this way of giving back to the community—and they all have the same reaction—nigga please... you? The Trey we know? Cooking for a women's center??? PU-LEASE!

The truth—my job is filled with long hours and mountains of stress—for months I had been searching for something to help me release the tension (besides sex). I thought about something physical, and do work out on a regular basis. In fact, Vince and I try and get to the court for a game of pickup basketball when we can. But that isn't enough. No, I wanted something that wasn't so damn cerebral…practicing law meant that you were always on your toes—dancing with your opponent, the game of chess—surveying the kaleidoscope of moves—eight to ten steps ahead. Always thinking, or outthinking your opponent. It became tiring. But quick…

Cooking—it releases one from the normal confines that holds us to our daily lives—cooking allows us to dream, to experiment. When I cook, I forget about my problems or those of others. In the kitchen, it is as if I am in some other place that only I hold the reins to. I feel free, alive; creating the way I know Vince must feel when he fashions a piece of art—a testament to those who have come before him, a celebration of the past and present.

And, on a more superficial level, I cook and serve because I *can*. I consider myself one of the lucky ones. I've been educated and found a trade that I'm damn good at, and they pay me a sizeable salary for my wares. I'm lucky—I've had choices all my life—some folks are not that fortunate. Or smart. Or gifted. Or, for whatever reason, find themselves in this shelter, at this sanctuary, on this quiet street, for just one day or a week, because someone close to them took their dignity away…

I began with the roast and the pies, since they would take the most amount of time. Some of the dishes I'd already prepared at home, such as the piecrusts and the bread. Some of the women from the center came downstairs to meet and watch me work. There were all kinds here—a sanctuary from the "elements", a calm in a storm—Yolanda's warm smile and nonjudgmental heart comforting—black women, Latinos, a few white women, all ages and sizes from a barely legal girl impregnated by her young overconfident boyfriend to a middle-aged, educated white woman with thick red welts on her cheeks and neck.

I made small talk as I set the beef roast out on the counter surface, and tied the rosemary sprigs lengthwise along the meat with kitchen twine in two-inch intervals. I rubbed the meat down with garlic and seasoning while I fielded questions from the onlookers—how old I was, how'd I learned to cook that good, how much money could a lawyer make, and was there a missus waiting for me at home…

Switching gears to the pies for a moment, since they needed to bake for a good forty minutes or so—I had settled on two of my favorite—wild blueberry-peach pie made from wild Canadian blueberries that I had FedExed to me the day before, and a mixed berry tart, using the leftover wild blueberries, fresh raspberries, blackberries, and strawberries. Treats, I just knew the ladies would love.

I pulled out the previously made dough, kneaded it between my black hands, while a young Latino with a thick accent, a dazzling smile, and twin black eyes watched me curiously.

"Papi, I hope your hands are clean!"

"Didn't you see me just wash them after handling that meat?"

"Naw."

"Pay attention then." I went back to my work as she sucked her teeth, but made no move to leave.

I proceeded to roll the dough into thin slivers, using generous amounts of flour and getting much on my black apron. Oh well, that's what aprons are for. The Latino snickered in the corner while I sucked my teeth at her. Grabbing a fresh mound of dough, I divided it in half and pressed each half into two pie dishes. I then grabbed a steel bowl that I had brought from home, and used it to combine the wild blueberries, cut peaches, cinnamon, and sugar into the pie filling. I divided this evenly between the pie dishes and then carefully draped the rolled-out pie dough over the filled pie dishes, trimming the edges, brushing the tops with heavy cream and sugar, and ending with cutting three slits equidistant from each other with a sharp knife. Perfection!

I had also planned on serving pasta—Capellini, or angel hair pasta, with fresh tomatoes and basil. I brought a large pot of water to boil and fetched the ingredients for this dish—plum tomatoes that I had already diced, cut basil leaves, ground pepper, and virgin olive oil. I loved pasta dishes—they were one of my favorites—the sauce was something I was always trying to improve upon.

Then back to the roast—I heated a large oval skillet with vegetable oil and began browning the roast, about four minutes each side. The kitchen filled quickly with the aroma of the rosemary and the cooking meat—Yolanda and a few of her ladies came to take a peek just as I was transferring the meat to the top oven where it would roast for a good fifty to fifty-five minutes. Meanwhile, I directed my attention to the sauce that would cover the meat like a warm blanket—dry red wine, minced shallots, and soft unsalted butter, boiling the concoction for ten minutes until it was reduced to less than half a cup. Soon now, I would be pouring this lovely sauce over the beef for a mouthwatering meal. The anticipation, I could see, was growing.

The water boiling, I threw in the fresh capellini, checked on the roast and my pies, which all were coming along nicely. I yelled for Yo to set the table. She replied back from the next room that they were already on it!

At five forty-five p.m., the ladies and I sat down to dinner. The oversized table fashioned from several pieces of rich oak was covered with a yellow cloth and fresh flowers that Yo had collected this morning on her rounds to several florists. Yolanda used her good china—this being a special occasion, and I did the honors, waiting for all of the ladies to be seated at the table before serving each entrée with a flourish.

Yolanda said grace. It was customary and obligatory—not to be messed with or hurried in this house. As I glanced around the oversized table I took in each woman—their attire—nothing formal—this not being the place or the time for that—most of these ladies had escaped with what they could carry or worse, what they had on their backs—nothing more—some came to the table barefoot and in jeans—others, a simple dress or pair of leggings. Regardless, they were each beautiful in their own way—they held their head up with pride, bruises and all. I grinned as I faced each woman in turn and felt satisfaction—I was pleased that I had chosen to spend my evening with these courageous ladies—women who found the strength to stand up and say, "enough is enough," and search for a better life…

Yolanda thanked me for my efforts. This was the one time where I found myself humbled. Humbled because my part in all of this—preparing tonight's meal, was the easy part. What these women faced every single day was difficult, and something, I wondered if I could cope with as well.

After grace, we began to eat. The food, if I may say so myself, was the bomb! The beef tenderloin roast was to die for, the vegetables, roasted to perfection, the capellini, well, what can I say—I have overheard folks say I make the best spaghetti sauce west of Sicily! We broke bread, the ladies and I, and feasted like there was no tomorrow. Even the security guard, a middle aged, oversized black man named Ernie, threw down. I made sure he got a plate and sat down with us. We made small talk—never speaking of one another's tragedy—there was a time and a place for that, but not tonight. No, on this evening it was about other, lighter things—the weather, shows on TV, any interested cases I could share—and of course, in my business, there were always interesting cases to discuss...

I glanced at my watch. Seven-fifteen. I wondered if Allison would show. For a split second I thought about sharing the unfolding drama between Quentin and his wife with the group—but that would be bad form—especially if Allison did indeed show up. Yolanda asked about my friends—she had met Vince and Erika before when they had come by to help months ago—and so we caught up on that, the latest gossip, what she was doing with the center—never revealing too much about her personal life—as if that, too, was off-limits, or in some way offensive to her girls.

I served the pies around seven-thirty while Yolanda poured strong coffee. The wild blueberry-peach pie was the hit of the evening—when I carried it over to the table, held snuggly between my oven mittens, the purple-blue-yellow filling was overflowing from the bursting slits and meandering down the golden brown pie crust like lava. The aroma struck everyone at once—it damn near brought a hush to the room. Of course, I snatched the opportunity to present this delicacy to the group with the most pomp and circumstance I could muster. Not an ordinary dessert—no, ladies, this one was commissioned especially for this group. Be careful, ladies—several spoonfuls of this delectable pastry and you undoubtedly will be hooked—an addict for life!

I sat back, stuffed, wiping my bald head with my hands, sipping coffee, looking around at the satisfied faces. Feeling good about my life and where I found myself this particular moment. At the top of my game, in the zone—a successful attorney, clients whose life in the majority of cases gen-uinely improved, due to my talent and skill…great friends, my health, a sex life that most men would give their left nut for, a fly crib, phat rides…and at the end of the day—I was a good man, regardless of the shit I pontificated on endlessly about every day, because I gave back—I made these ladies smile, even if for just a fleeting moment, like a pebble dropped into a pond, the ripples fan out for a meager moment, and then the waters grow still again…

And then, out of nowhere, I felt this sudden rush of emotion—it began down low, in the bowels of my stomach, and rushed like an avalanche through my veins, turning my blood into ice water, smarting my heart.

The sad truth: I was alone. I didn't have the comfort of warm flesh, a part-ner, or lover for more than a fleeting hour or so—a soul mate who could take the chill away when I felt cold. I glanced around the table; some women were holding hands while conversing. There was laughter. There were hugs. And I felt my eyes water and sting as the tears began to well under my eyelids. Using my forearm and elbow, I quickly wiped them away, mindful that no one here would spy my weakness, and think less of me.

I was a lucky man, true—successful, talented, good looking, with many things that I could call my own. No question that there were many bless-ings in my life. But I was alone…

I turned my head and glanced toward the kitchen. Beyond the back door and windowsill lay my ride. I got up quickly, began walking towards it, as my vision distorted into a kaleidoscope of shifting patterns and colors…

Twenty-One

Desiree lay back on the futon, eyes closed, waiting for Vince to begin. She was breathing regularly, which surprised Vince, since she was, at this point, shirtless.

"Is this going to hurt?"

"Please! Do you think I would have gotten all these other folks to pose for me if it did," Vince responded, sweeping his arm toward his collection of masks. He glanced down at Desiree, took in her dark skin, the black lace underwire bra that held the two mounds of lovely flesh barely contained. She was spilling out, the roundness of both breasts perfectly symmetrical above the lace. A hint of nipples could be seen if one looked very carefully, but Vince didn't want to get caught staring.

The surface of the futon was covered with a clean, off-white dropcloth. Her hair draped behind the back of the couch; it lay still, like her hands that remained in her lap.

"Can I get you anything before we begin?" Vince asked softly.

"No, I think I'm fine. I'm anxious to begin."

"Good. You're going to do just fine—I can tell." Vince smiled as he gathered the lifecasting materials at his feet behind her. Desiree glanced over at him, her eyes flicked upwards; they danced for a moment before settling on the ceiling, and growing out of focus.

"Let me pull back your hair." Vince gingerly took the length in his hand and tied it back with a red bandanna. It covered her from the beginning of her hairline halfway back. "Don't want to get any mess on your lovely hair."

"It's okay—I'll just make you wash it." She gave Vince an impish grin.

"I just might hold you to it."

Vince moved behind her, bent down and said quietly, "Let's begin."

He reached for an oversized jar of petroleum jelly, raked two fingers worth of the gel onto his digits and slowly began applying it to Desiree's face. He worked slowly, methodically, stroking her face beginning with her forehead, and applying a thin layer of jelly to her skin. Desiree closed her eyes and smiled, moaned for effect and said: "Oooh, this is nice—I didn't know massages come with the package!"

Vince paused for a moment, looked into her eyes and said, "Depends on the package, darling...now hush!"

He continued—spreading a coating of Vaseline on her cheeks, rubbing the gel into her skin and around her cheekbones, using both fingers at once to knead the bridge of her nose. Vince worked slowly, taking his time, watching Desiree as he worked, leaning over and reaching for her chin, coating that angular rock of bone and flesh with gel until she glistened like a beacon. Once he was done, Vince stood back, admiring his work. He forked out another two fingers of Vaseline and reapplied his digits to her face, smoothing the blob of gel and creating an additional layer. He rubbed her eyelids gently, careful not to get any on her eyelashes; worked his way down around her nostrils, highlighting her full dark lips with the gel as if it were lip gloss, caressing her mouth as if she were his lover. Vince watched her as he worked, gazed at the rise and fall of her breasts, her eyelids that fluttered like leaves in an autumn breeze, her tongue that peeked out as if there were a mouse in a quieted house, searching for morsels of food.

Next Vince applied the alginate; the gel-like substance that once applied would harden within six to eight minutes. He spoke softly as he worked, explained the process as he went, telling her how he had mixed it with warm water and that she would feel a lukewarm sensation on her skin as he applied it. She was doing well, Vince told Desiree, reminding her that if she needed to move or stretch, now was the time to do it. Desiree was relaxed, Vince could tell—she had succumbed to this artist—allowing him to do what he wished in the name of art and creativity.

Spreading the alginate didn't take much time at all—he began with her forehead, used the fleshy tips of his fingers as a brush, painting her with the substance that would form the base of the mask. Vince next covered her cheeks and nose, leaving the nostrils for last. He encased her chin with the material, then told her to hold still and not to worry as he applied the gel to her lips. Lastly, he covered her nostrils with the gel, after inserting two short straws for her to breathe.

At this point her entire face was covered with the white substance. Vince bent down, studied his handiwork, told her that she was doing great, and that there were only a few minutes left to go. He rubbed her shoulder with his elbow, moved down her forearm, then moved close to her ear and pointed out that his hand was inches from her breasts. Desiree's arm came up as she tried to swat him away. Vince just laughed.

Behind the futon, on the floor, in a metal tray was a bunch of one inch wide plaster strips. Alongside the tray was a bowl of warm water. Vince reached for a strip, dipped it in the water and applied it to Desiree's face, gingerly laying it across the drying alginate. He explained to Desiree that the plaster would give the mold that he was creating more weight and actually speed up the drying process. He asked again if she was okay—she raised her hand and waved.

Applying the strips was one of Vince's favorite parts—it always brought back thoughts of those old Mummy movies that he'd watched as a kid. Vince used different sized strips that he had precut to lay over the alginate. He'd apply a strip to the hardening substance, and apply light pressure so that the plaster would bond more quickly. About three minutes after he began, her face was covered with plaster bandages, and the process was near completion.

"Okay, Desiree—you are doing great—now, we wait, let me see…" Vince reached for her face and stroked the cast lightly. He could feel that in some places it was already hardening. "About two more minutes and we will be through. Cool?" He smiled and glanced down her torso again. Damn—she was a fine woman, no question. Trey would love to be here right now—God he could imagine just what his boy would do to this woman in her compromising situation…

Three minutes later he tested the mold with his fingers and satisfied, told Desiree to sit up slowly. He reached for her hands and placed them carefully against the mold. Then grasping her forearms, he pulled her to him, telling her to bend forward and let the weight of the cast come off in her hands. He used his fingers around the edges and guided it into her hands. The mold came off easily and without any fuss. He held it within his hands, and gingerly carried it over to his worktable where he inverted it and placed it on top of a folded towel. He returned to the futon with a warm facecloth lathered in soap, and tenderly began to wash Desiree's face. He got off as much as he could. Then, when most of the Vaseline had been removed, Desiree stood up and went to the worktable, a towel curved around her neck as she marveled at the mold that lay before her.

"My God, Vince, that shit worked!" she exclaimed as she studied the casting that lay on the table. It was always eerie for the model to see for the first time the cast—witnessing the clarity and detail that the lifecasting process afforded. "Wow, that's me—no two ways about it! Damn!" Vince smiled, rubbed her back and told her that she could finish washing up in the bathroom. There wasn't anything more to do until the mold was completely dry—a day or two away.

Desiree returned a few minutes later—even though she wore no makeup, the glow had returned to her face and neck. She joined Vince once again in front of the worktable, staring down at the mold of her features. Vince rubbed her bare back. She reached over and kissed him on his cheek.

"This has been so exciting for me, you just don't know. I'm thrilled that you are creating a mask of me."

"For me, too, Desiree—every mask holds a unique experience—this has been fun—and actually, once the mold dries the real fun begins, because that's when the creative juices take over and art burst forth!"

"I can't wait," she said.

"You'll be part of the process. I promise," Vince said.

"I wouldn't have it any other way!" Desiree responded. They stood there, the two of them, marveling at the creation on the table, each wondering where this piece of plaster would carry them.

✠✠✠

Three nights later, when Desiree arrived back at Vince's studio, the plaster lifecasting was hung in the center of a four-foot-square canvas and displayed on an easel, which stood in the center of the room, illuminated overhead by a single halogen lamp. Vince greeted her with a hug and a kiss to her lips… a kiss that lingered for a moment before he pulled back, glancing downward, happy to be seeing her once again.

"Good to see you, girl," Vince mused, his smile lighting up the darkened interior.

"You, too, my brutha." Her gaze swept past Vince to the easel and her likeness in bas-relief, under spotlight. "Damn, Vince, this is the bomb!" She rushed past him, left Vince standing by the open doorway, and screeched to a halt by the unfinished mask. Running a hand lightly over the face of the plaster, she found herself catching her breath and touching her own flesh, comparing it to the plaster and marveling at the similarity—the lines and depressions, captured as if redrawn perfectly by the hand of a divine spirit.

"Vince," she said softly, "I can't believe how good this came out. I mean, it is so damn lifelike."

"Yes, that's one of the things that attracted me to the lifecasting process—the way it captures the *essence* of a person's being—many folks who see themselves for the first time captured and memorialized in plaster find it quite unnerving."

"I can see why," Desiree said, stepping back from the easel.

"Of course," Vince said, "we are only halfway through—the best part, as far as I am concerned, is yet to come."

"And that is?" she inquired, turning to him.

"Creating art," he said, joining her by the mask. "Filling the crevasse of plaster with paint, allowing the mask to breathe; to take wings and live."

"I feel you."

Desiree glanced at his worktable that was covered with dishes of colorful paint. Vince took her hand and led her to the table.

"This is what I was thinking—let me know your thoughts—you said something last time about flinging paint onto a canvas in a haphazard kind of way. Well, I was thinking that we could put a single color on as a base and then try that—see what comes of it!"

"Are you serious?" Desiree exclaimed, walking back to the easel and touching the mask. Vince eyed her silently. She stepped back, then returned to the worktable. "Yeah, I'm feeling that! Yeah, that'll work!"

"Alrighty then," Vince exclaimed. "Let's do this."

They selected a color for the base of the mask—Vince suggested something bright, to match Desiree's mood and personality—orange or red. She was feeling something of a darker color—a muted brown or jet-black. They settled on indigo. Vince used a wide brush to apply the paint while Desiree watched. He applied two coats to ensure that the paint saturated the plaster and soaked into the material's crevices. Once that was done, he reached for a clean brush, something thinner than the last one. He told Desiree that they should select a bright color, dip the brush into the paint and then fling it onto the mask, creating their art. Desiree asked that he begin the process, for she didn't want to mess up the mask with her *inexperience*.

Vince grinned and dipped the brush in some orange paint, stood about two feet from the easel, and lightly snapped the brush in the direction of the mask. Little streams of paint, colorful blobs of orange hit the mask's surface like raindrops, the heavier one cascading down as if tears. He concentrated on the eyes first, then selected a crimson red color and flung the paint at her nostrils and mouth. A blob of paint made contact with the plaster just to the right of her plaster lips—then it smeared and dripped down toward the chin. Desiree was enthralled.

"Let me do some, Vince!" He handed her the brush and stepped out of the way. She selected a greenish-blue hue first; then a pale-yellow shade, flinging the paint with abandonment, giggling like a schoolgirl as drops of paint attached themselves to her mask. Thirty minutes later they were done. The mask was awash with color—streams of paint, pinpoints of various shades adorned the plaster turning the once virgin mask into a dazzling creation of fine art. They stepped back together, admiring the creation. Vince was pleased. Desiree stood and gawked, silent at first, then raising her voice as she pointed to the various areas of still drying paint.

It was close to nine p.m. when Vince moved the easel over toward the high windows where the mask could dry. He cleaned up his workspace and washed up while Desiree made a pot of fresh coffee. They relaxed on the futon, staring silently at their creation. Desiree was impressed, Vince could tell. For his part, he was feeling it, too, and her as well, the time spent together over the past week as they gave this mask life, giving him a fresh insight to this young woman. They sipped their coffee and talked, enjoying each other's company. Suddenly Desiree put her mug down and jumped up.

"Vince, I know you're going to think I'm crazy, but I've got an idea."

"Speak!" he commanded her, but winked as he laughed.

"What if…" she exclaimed, waving her arms in the air in an animated sort of way, "what if we did a casting…oh never mind!" Desiree slumped to the couch and reached for her cup. Vince stopped her.

"No, go on. I want to hear this."

"Okay. What if…I was thinking…we could do a casting…of my torso. There. I said it!"

"Torso?"

"You do know what a torso is, don't you?"

"Yeah, I recall that part of the anatomy from my freshman biology class— course, that *was* a long time ago!" Vince put his mug down on the coffee table and looked at Desiree. She was motionless, watching him for a reaction. He nodded slowly.

"I *could* do that."

"Vince, here's the thing—I was thinking—we do a torso casting, say from here…" She held her hand just below her neck, "…to say about here…" and used her other hand to trace a line slightly below her navel. "You could then take that casting, paint it the same way as we did tonight, and then somehow either attach it to the mask or better still…" She paused to ponder this point for a moment before continuing, "mount it on a frame like the others but leaving this space of perhaps four inches between the mask and torso. What do you think???"

Vince eyed her—watched her irises dance among the pupils. Excitement dripped from her pores like sweat. Vince grinned.

"Damn, girl, I like it! I honestly do!" He stood, went to the still drying mask and observed it silently. Turning to Desiree, he said, "Yeah, I like it a lot!"

Desiree was nodding her head rapidly.

"So, you're cool with me taking a casting of your…" He paused to consider the right word. "…*unclothed* upper body?" Eyebrows raised, waiting for a response.

"Well, hello! I'm the one who suggested it!"

"Cool. Just checking."

Desiree stood, drained her coffee in several gulps and slammed the mug down.

"Vince, let's do this!" she exclaimed while her eyes glittered. "Let's do this shit right the hell now!"

Twenty-Two

Ernie strolled in fifteen minutes later with Allison Matthews in tow. I was in the kitchen supervising the clean-up—one thing about Yolanda— she did not play when it came to chores around the center—she didn't ask for much in return—it cost the ladies nothing to stay here since most of her funding came from state and federal monies, the remainder handled by private donations. But she was adamant about everyone pulling their weight— a house this size meant that there were always things to do—cleaning, cooking, laundry, etc…The deal was that when I came every month to do the cooking, the ladies would clean up after supper.

I had my back to the wooden island, orchestrating the women putting what little remained of the meal into Tupperware bowls. There was a lot of dish washing to be done; the dishwasher had been filled ten minutes ago and a wash started. Carmen, the young Latino lady, eyed me curiously as I directed the troops. She was by far the most voluptuous of the bunch, and was attempting to flirt with me. I was standing there, arms folded, thinking to myself—under any other circumstances, I'd give this girl the ride of her life…

And then Allison strode in.

She wore a devilish smile—like the one she flashed that first night at H20 when I had strolled up to her and gave her a taste of Trey's game. She wore a black suit—slim pencil skirt with a center slit and matching jacket, nylon- less showing off her nice legs, black pumps, and a blouse of graphic design done in black and white—black diamonds amidst a sea of alternating black, then white waves. Hair pulled back, all business-like, and large gold hoop earrings that came down nearly to the bottom of her jaw. A black leather bag hung from her shoulder. Allison looked quite beautiful and I fought the urge to go to her and kiss her on that sensuous mouth of hers.

"Hey, Ms. Matthews," I said, grinning while I wiped my hands with a kitchen rag.

"Counselor," she replied, nodding at the women who stared curiously at her. "I wanted to see if you really could cook—or if you were just yanking my chain." She smiled for a moment and then held out her hand to the others, introducing herself to the women in the kitchen. Carmen eyed her as she shook her hand, then said, "Are you his wife?" as she gestured toward me.

"He wishes!" Allison said and I feigned injury.

"Hmmm. Girlfriend then?" Carmen continued.

"No, not girlfriend either. We are at work together on a legal case."

"Hmmm," Carmen replied again. She was staring at me, licking her lips, consciously or unconsciously, I don't know. "You got a woman at home, Papi?"

"Who wants to know?" I shot back. "Besides, no one here could handle these goods!" I exclaimed, hands on my hips. Yolanda, who was in the next room, let out a short yelp while the rest of the ladies rolled their eyes.

"Hmmm," Carmen grunted before drying her hands and leaving the kitchen in a huff.

"So, Allison," I said, turning my full attention to her, "can I get you a plate—there's still some excellent eating left."

Yolanda walked in, shook hands with Allison and said, "You really should grab a plate; Trey didn't hold back this time—tonight's meal was a real treat."

"No thank you," Allison said.

"No?" I asked, feigning surprise, "after all the smack you said about me, you're not even going to try my cooking—oh no, we can't have that."

"No, really, but I do believe you—since there are witnesses present, and that's the only reason."

"Whatever!" I snorted. I began to grab my utensils, dishes/bowls, and left-over ingredients, and made ready to put them in the back of the Escalade. "Well then, don't just stand there looking all pretty; give me a hand with these things!" Allison obliged as Yolanda leaned against the doorframe and smirked at me while shaking her head. She knew what I was up to—it was as plain as day to her.

A few minutes and several trips later, all of my things were securely stored in the back of my ride. Allison and I were standing by the back bumper staring at the sky, the colors of sunset—reddish-orange purple tinge—painting the sky like swaths from an enormous brush. A light wind had picked up, rustling the leaves on the trees. It was going to be a beautiful night.

"Care to grab a cup of coffee, Trey?" Allison asked. "I was hoping we could talk about our case."

"I have a better idea—why don't you follow me home. I've got to drop these things off—I don't want them to stay too long in the back seat. Let me drop them off at home and then I'll put on a pot of coffee that will make Starbucks shiver."

"I don't know…"

"Allison—are you always this indecisive? Listen, I don't bite, okay? Follow me home—I live three minutes from here. We can have the food put away in five, I'll fix you a plate and a cup of Joe, and we'll discuss our case." I moved toward the front of the SUV. "Where you parked? Let me pull around front and then you can follow me." I hit the remote and opened the door, got in and shut the door before Allison could say anything or argue the point further. I watched her through the mirror as I started the engine and slipped a Maxwell CD into the changer—indecision was etched on her face. The power windows came down and I leaned out and said with a smile and a wink, "Honestly, I don't bite, baby…unless you like it like that!"

✠✠✠

All this time together and I haven't provided you all with the details of my crib—shame on me! As I mentioned when we first met, I live in D.C. right off of 15th and U Streets. It's a bad crib—two-story condo on the ninth and tenth floor of this really upscale building, walking distance from Republic Gardens, Bar Nun, and Utopia. Parking is underground and we've got our own doorman. Oh yeah, you know by now how we do!

Allison followed me in her silver Nissan Altima as we pulled into the garage.

I wound down to the P-2 level, parked in my spot and directed her to visitor parking. I grabbed a cart by the elevator and began unloading my stuff. A few minutes later, after Allison had joined me, we were done and riding up in silence.

The gleaming doors opened onto my floor. I let Allison pass, checking out her ass and tight legs as she moved past me, before pushing the cart to the right and toward my condo entrance. I unlocked the door, opened it, and stepped aside, letting Allison enter first.

I still recall the first time I walked into my condo two years ago—the building's renovation had just been completed and the paint on the walls and ceiling was still wet. My breath was taken away by what I saw.

When you walk in, the first thing you notice is the enormity of the open space and slanted ceilings. The first level is made up of the living and dining rooms with a large open-air kitchen to the right, the latter separated from the former by teak countertops. There are dual skylights cut into the slanted ceilings. Large sliding-glass windows are cut into one wall with a cement balcony beyond. Like my office, colorful African-American art adorns the walls. As you walk in, you immediately step down into the sunken living room—a thick buffalo-brown couch and matching love seat are off to the left by the window. Directly across from the couch on one wall is a huge plasma TV and state-of-the-art stereo system. A thick, dark-brown throw rug sits diagonally in the middle of the living room. To the right is the kitchen. Moving further to the right of that is the dining room, equipped with a cherrywood table set for eight, a clear vase containing fresh flowers in mid-center, the fragrance permeating the air.

Allison drew in a breath as she glanced around. "Wow," she managed to say after a moment.

"Yeah, kind of takes your breath away at first, doesn't it?" I asked, being sincere.

"Sure does—how long have you been here?"

"Two years—found it by accident and damn glad I did—can't imagine living anywhere else."

"It's beautiful." I had painted the walls of the living room a light golden brown; the dining area was a rich red, and the kitchen off-white. It worked, though.

"Have a look around while I put this stuff away." I watched her walk toward the back rooms and then up the winding staircase to the upper floor. I was done putting everything away by the time she returned.

"I have to say, Trey, I am impressed. This place is beautiful—and you've really done a wonderful job decorating it, although I can't believe you did all this by yourself—you *had* to have some help—a woman's touch, no doubt—there's no way you came up with all of this on your own."

"See, herein lies your problem, Allison—you just refuse to believe how great a package I am," I said grinning from ear to ear. "I mean, you can't accept the fact that I've got skills in the kitchen, regardless of the fact that we just left sixteen very satisfied women. Second, you come into my home…" I said, holding my arms out wide, "a home that I decorated with my own two hands, *without* assistance, and yet you still refuse to acknowledge the obvious—what is staring you straight in the face!"

"And what might that be, counselor?" Allison asked, taking a seat on the couch and crossing her legs.

"Simply that I am, without a doubt, the most amazing specimen of a man that you've ever met—past, present, and future, baby!" I threw my head back and laughed at the vastness of my own ego—even I had to chuckle at that one—then went to the kitchen to pour some wine. I put on a pot of coffee to brew and returned with two bluish wine stems filled with Luna Di Luna Merlot-Cabernet. The wine was a dark purple against the colored glass. Allison accepted the wine with a nod and took a sip.

"Oh my, that's nice."

"Yes it is. As requested, I'm brewing some coffee. Now, let me fix you a small plate of food." I turned toward the kitchen.

"Trey, don't go out of your way, really." I stopped in mid stride and spun around.

"Woman," I began, walking toward her. "You are plucking my last nerve—you will try some of my food, you hear me, you will. I've gone to a lot of trouble—at least have the decency to take a bite!"

Allison frowned. "Okay, I didn't realize you were so sensitive…"

"Women!" I said in an exasperated tone, but smiling as the word escaped my lips. I observed Allison remove her jacket and drape it on the arm of the couch. Her thin tank sweater was sexy in that it showed off her curves and slender arms. I was looking at her breasts underneath the sheer material, fantasizing about her nipples and what they must look like unencumbered by a lace bra.

I pulled out some leftovers to fix a plate for Allison—a small portion of the beef tenderloin and a generous helping of the angel hair pasta, made with the fresh tomatoes, basil, and my special sauce. I could have zapped the food in the microwave and saved some time, but that just wouldn't do. I pulled out a skillet to braze the beef, and a bowl to boil water for the pasta. I poured the pasta sauce in a smaller skillet and began to warm it under a low fire.

"Come here," I said to Allison, who rose off the couch and came to the kitchen willingly, her glass of Merlot-Cabernet in hand. Her shoes were off and I took in her red polished toenails. Nice. She slid next to the counter-top where she could watch me, crossing her legs and curling her toes on the tile. "So," I said, while turning the beef and stirring the pasta sauce in the skillet, "let's talk about the case."

"Okay. As I was saying on the phone, Trey, I really think that this issue can and should be resolved without much fanfare. I mean, your client is a successful basketball player. My client was married to him for two years. She's not looking to clean him out—only to get what's fair and equitable…"

"The main residence is not fair game, Allison," I said, turning to stare directly at her. "We've gone over this before—the residence was bought *before* he married her."

"I understand that. But don't you think that this latest development changes everything?"

"No."

"Well, I do." Allison took a sip of wine and placed the stem on the counter. "Come on, Trey—the guy's screwing other women under his wife's own nose and then gets caught. This changes everything—the Hues would still be married if it weren't for his infidelity, for God's sake!"

"Not according to my client," I quipped.

"Trey—let's stop playing games here—my client is out of a perfectly good marriage. Now she's only looking for something that she can call her own. The main residence is located in the area of Jersey where she grew up—she has family there. Your client doesn't. He no longer lives in the area. He no longer plays for New York. There is no reason for him to keep that house. If my client wasn't asking for it, he'd probably have it on the market in no time!"

"Perhaps, perhaps not." I continued to stir the sauce and watch the beef tenderloin with a close eye.

"Why are you dragging this out? This I don't understand. We have solid evidence of your client's infidelity and no court in the land is going to enforce your hastily filed injunction—you'll see. Then we'll be in a position to ruin your man's reputation, hell, the tabloids and talk shows will make a field day out of this—all because he refused to play fair."

Allison shook her head and moved across the tile to the range where I was standing. She leaned against the counter and looked up into my eyes. "Is that what you want, Trey? A sensational trial—lurid tales of infidelity, wild interracial sex caught on tape by the star forward of the Washington Wizards himself?"

I stopped stirring the sauce and put the wooden spoon down on the stove. "Allison—are you aware that Quentin is in high-level talks with Pepsi for a multimillion-dollar endorsement deal? No? Well, he is. And what do you think is going to happen when the good folks at Pepsi get wind of this *thing* you're speaking of? I'll tell you what's going to happen. There will be no endorsement deal. Period. End of discussion. And you don't have to possess a degree in mathematics to know that zero divided by two is still zero." I paused to let this sink in. Took a sip of my wine before continuing.

"This deal, if I had to guess, and I'm taking into account other players who have had similar endorsements, will run on the average of five to ten million dollars for a relatively unknown like Quentin. He's no Michael Jordan, but the boy has skills, is good-looking, and commands a presence in front of the camera. Now, for the sake of argument, let's say he gets eight million. Eight divided by two is four—that's how much money your client will be entitled to." I took another sip, swished the wine around my gums before swallowing. Allison was watching me intently.

"Four million dollars, Ms. Matthews—not bad cheddar for the former Mrs. Hues who didn't do shit to earn it…"

Allison began to protest but I held up my hand.

"Hold it—I know what she's entitled to. What I'm saying is this—go public with this *thing* and everyone loses—my client and yours. Especially yours. My client's reputation will be tarnished. Yes, that much will be true. He will lose any chance of future endorsement deals. He may lose his contract. But he will, at the very least, have a skill that can be put to good use in some other city, on some other day when the smoke clears. Your client, on the other hand, has nothing other than her good looks. She's a young girl with no education and no plans for getting one—Quentin was her plan. Her way out. Screw with Quentin and his future, and she cuts off the hand that feeds her…Not a good strategy, Ms. Matthews, nor would I want to be the attorney who counseled her client on that course of action… "

Allison was silent. I glanced down, watching her toes curl. I concluded that she must do that when she's nervous. She, too, was looking down—then her head raised and she exhaled forcefully. "So, Mr. Alexander, what do you want?"

I took a moment to turn over the beef tenderloin. It was sizzling in the pan, sending its wonderful aroma around the kitchen. The pasta sauce was beginning to slowly bubble, so I turned off the heat and moved it to the back burner.

"Simple—the disc and all copies destroyed, and a signed statement from your client, and anyone else that she may have shared her story with, that they will not discuss the contents of that disk—ever. And I mean *ever!* In turn—she gets the main residence. Then, we divide up the remaining assets as normal, and our clients go their separate ways. If the endorsement thing comes to fruition, then your client gets half, no questions asked. More than fair. If not, no harm no foul. With me so far?"

"Yes." Allison was staring off into space—I could see the wheels turning. This was a good deal and she knew it.

"Yes what? Is this acceptable to you? Do we have a deal?"

"It's acceptable to me. I, of course, have to run it by my client…"

"Wait a second, Allison—I thought you wanted to resolve this quickly—just the two of us—isn't that what you said to me yesterday? So let's resolve it. Right now. No clients, just us lawyers, as you indicated."

Allison walked across to the counter, picked up her wine stem, and took a long sip. I watched her tilt her head back and swallow. Watched her close her eyes for a moment as she enjoyed the wine warming her insides. Opening them, she stared straight at me and said with a wicked grin, "Okay, counselor, you've got yourself a deal."

"Excellent. I trust I can count on you to get me that disc and all copies ASAP. And we'll need to get your client and anyone else she talked to about Quentin's wanderings into my office at once."

"I'll take care of it. You have my word on that."

"Good. I knew you were reasonable, Allison." I scooped up a spoonful of sauce and placed the tip of the wooden spoon to my lips. I scrunched up my eyes and groaned. "Oh my God, this is soooo damn good!" Allison stood there with a smirk on her face. "What?" I asked, "you don't believe me?" I dug up another spoonful, blew on it, and walked over to her, my left hand underneath the spoon so I wouldn't drop any on the tile floor.

"Prepare to be dazzled," I said, as I reached her. Allison put down her wine glass, leaned back on the counter, arms extended on either side. She closed her eyes.

"Fire away," she said, and opened her mouth. I was giggling as I extended the spoon toward her open orifice.

"Open wide," I said. The spoon touched her bottom lip and I tilted upwards, watching as a bit of the sauce slid sensuously into her mouth. She began to swallow, her lips closed on one another causing the spoon to shift on its axis slightly. Before I could react, a blob of sauce slid off the spoon and dropped, rebounding on her thin sweater above her left breast, and then dropped to her dark skirt right above the center slit. "OH SHIT!" I yelled. Allison's eyes snapped open in horror. She dropped her chin and glanced down.

"OH FUCK, Trey! Fuck, this is my favorite top!" Allison spun away from me as her hands went to the fabric. "Goddamn it!"

"Allison, NO!" I yelled, dropping the spoon on the counter and grabbing her hands. "Don't touch it—listen to me—you'll make it worse." I ran to the sink, grabbed a paper towel and ran back. I lightly dabbed the towel on the fabric of her top and skirt, soaking up the mass of the sauce. Allison had this look of horror on her face.

"I can't fucking believe this—sorry, I can't believe this shit—this is one of my favorite outfits…" She reached out to grab the towel from me, but I moved my hand back, resisting her.

"Allison—listen to me—this is what we are going to do." I bent down so she was eye level with me. "Follow me—we're going upstairs. I'm going to give you an oversized tee shirt that you're going to change into…"

Allison began to shake her head and protest. I reached up and lightly grabbed her chin.

"No, Allison—you're going to take these clothes off now and I'm going to clean them. I've got this stuff that works wonders on stained fabric that can't be washed—but we need to do it now before the stain dries." I bunched up the sauce-laden paper towel in one hand and grabbed Allison's hand with the other. I gestured for her to follow me. Silently, with a dejected look on her face, she did.

Twenty-Three

A fire burned leisurely, but not silently, the flames spitting flickers and sparks into the brick-lined chimney. The lights were extinguished—no need for them, the firelight providing ample light and comfort to Desiree who lay topless and prone on the blanketed floor, and for Vince, who knelt over her, a smile lodged on his face. The oversized jar of Vaseline lay beside him. His fingers were covered with it and he paused as he admired her form—smooth dark skin, perfect breasts that swelled to chocolate peaks, a thin curvy waist and seductive navel, which like sexy lips, seemed to speak to him when he probed and massaged her brown flesh.

Taking his time, Vince coated her skin, rubbing her neck and clavicles, descending to her breasts, rubbing around the base of her mounds, then taking the nipples in his hands, between fingers, lubing them up, feeling them become pointy and hard as Desiree worked hard to control her movement and her soft moans, the fire dancing behind them creating patterns on the walls and ceiling. Moving downward, to her flat belly and navel, massaging and coating her taut skin with jelly until her entire body shined. And then as Desiree watched him, speaking softly and with shortness of breath as he worked, Vince proceeded with making a casting of her torso—for him, the very first time he had attempted this—the thought had been rolling around in his head for months, but not having the right person to try it with, he had put it on the back burner. Angeliqué would be the perfect person to *experiment* with—but, well, Angeliqué wasn't here...and hadn't returned his call from the previous week...but Desiree was and so the opportunity had presented itself...

The alginate went on next, and Vince enjoyed spreading the gel over her body—his fingers and palms reacquainting themselves with her lovely flesh and nipples—before applying the plaster strips and waiting for those to dry. He had her sit up and move to the futon when he was done, as she had done before, wanting to ensure that her breasts be properly *represented* in the plaster, not giving gravity a chance to interfere…

When they were done—the alginate and plaster hardened, he could strike the firm cast with his knuckle and be rewarded with a hollow response—Vince had Desiree sit forward as before so that he could remove the casting. He did this gingerly, since the cast was twice the size of his usual masks. Desiree watched silently as the cast came off, revealing her still perky breasts (Vince had opened the windows earlier to ensure the room remained nippy—no pun intended)… He carried the cast with both hands to his worktable and laid it out so that it could dry. Desiree followed him, unconcerned with her topless state, astonished once again at ability of the lifecasting process to capture the essence of human flesh. Together, they stared in silence at the casting, reflecting on its meaning and the innumerable possibilities once paint was applied.

Revisiting the futon a few moments later, Desiree sat back and Vince returned moments later with a bowl of warm soapy water and a warm washcloth. Kneeling in front of her, he asked, "May I cleanse you?" Desiree nodded, her eyes sparkling like the fire burning behind them. He reached for her with the washcloth and using slow, gentle strokes, removed all remnants of the alginate and petroleum jelly, and then washed her the way a parent does his or her infant. She followed him closely with her stare, watching him as he cleansed her, and Vince silently admired her form and splendor, rubbing her flesh, feeling her the way a lover does. And finally, when she was all-clean, and Vince decided that he could no longer stand being mere inches from her body without taking her—a piece of succulent fruit that longed to be consumed—he reached for her mouth with his own, and took her, right then and there—his tongue invading her mouth, teeth scraping against enamel as the intensity between them ignited like a flame, hands finding breasts, soft to the touch as he kneaded them between fingers,

Desiree responding to Vince by giving herself to him without question, leaning in, opening up, his hands on her thighs, rubbing the tight denim, grasping her legs, she reaching for his back and pulling him to her, mouths on each other, latching on, connecting—tongue to tongue, mouth to mouth, flesh to flesh—and she reaching back, grasping for his shirt and pulling upward, until it came off and landed on the floor several yards away from them. Then them resuming their connection of flesh—mouths finding one another again, and now, breasts to breast, nipples to nipples, as he pushed his weight against her, his breath hot on her neck. He found the cleft between her legs, the sweet spot, and rubbed her there, as she moaned and guided his hand, as if he needed the help, which he did *not*. Her jeans came down, peeling like a cornstalk, until they, too, like his shirt, laid crumpled on the floor. Clad in only her black panties, she looked uncompromisingly beautiful, with the firelight flickering off her naked form. And then, without further ado, using a slight tug from both hands, her panties slid downward—thighs, then knees, then ankles, and then off into space, and he parted her legs like the Red Sea, using both hands to spread her wide, her head flung back and eyes closed, as he lowered his head and found the epicenter, her molten core.

Vince fed like a cat, lapping up her milk, her sweet juice, licking her folds that quivered with excitement as his hand rushed along her skin, gliding across every inch of softness, making his way from her neck to her ankles, ensuring he explored every delicious inch of her being as she held her legs in the air. Desiree opened her mouth and told him what she was feeling, let him know that this loving was so damn good—exciting her soul, making her yell out in ecstasy, the passion infusing her interior and whipping her into a frenzy. By the time he had pulled back to take a breath, Desiree had come twice—the juice of her sex glazing his mouth and chin, and painting her thighs and ass with its sinful wake.

Vince returned moments later, naked, his manhood erect and wrapped up tight in a latex condom. He knelt before her, kissed her passionately before leaning forward and entering her effortlessly. Desiree moaned on contact, reaching for him, pulling him to her, ensuring she was filled up completely, his balls pressed solidly against her vulva. As firelight danced off their undulating form, Vince found his rhythm and settled into a groove, grasping for the spot where her neck and chin rested against the futon, holding on, pumping against her, feeling her squeezing him and sucking him in, her sex like a vortex, swallowing him, consuming him with her passion. They found their groove together and moved to it, a song they both knew; Vince reaching for her breasts and squeezing, bending forward and consuming the areolas with his mouth, painting a wide swath with his tongue. Desiree felt so good to him, her body so tight and well defined, almost body-building material—Vince was turned on just by glancing down at her lovely form, observing her curves and the way she moved to him, thrusting against him as he impaled her with his cock—the feeling wonderful and yet, Vince thinking to himself, isn't it amazing how the simple act of loving in a singular kind of fashion—something that is repeated over and over again, a million trillion times over the course of a lifetime, can be so unique and utterly *individualistic*, as if he were experiencing this feeling, like an adolescent, for the very first time.

Vince paused and pulled out slowly, groaning as he did, then guided Desiree over, her knees on the futon, breasts and chest pressed against the back of the couch as he re-entered her and pummeled her with newly found enthusiasm. Desiree shrieked, reached back and pulled him into her, screaming his name, demanding he fuck her good and even harder than before, and Vince complying, closing his eyes, giving in completely to this woman, ensuring that this *experience* would be one that she would remember, recorded in the journal for all times, even though he knew he couldn't last much longer, the feeling much too sweet, like nectar, way too intense for him to continue any longer, and yet, wanting to hold out—not for her, but for himself—the feeling so *intense*, as good sex always turns out to be, but then in the end, giving in, resigning himself that the feeling that began rising from the base of his sex and shot through him like an avalanche—carrying with it all of the energy and passion of a sudden thunderstorm in summer.

Vince came—one minute he was contemplating the mere existence of an orgasm and whether he could hold out for a few minutes longer—and then it was *here*, now—and Desiree, in an instant, joined him, her entire body vibrating, fingers, hands, legs and thighs—each part of her body reacting as if it were a guitar being strummed—the flesh heaving, as if it had a mind of its own, shaking as she unleashed her passion—the two of them, their waves slamming against each other, Desiree's head thrown back and her eyes rolled back, her voice hoarse from screaming and moaning—"Oh God, Vince, I fucking came!"—the tendrils in her digits tight, the muscles in her neck and shoulders—taut like a bow.

And when he had ceased his thrusting, and slowed to a stop, Desiree sighed, one gigantic breath that was expelled as she turned to him, feeling him exit her warm, wet place, and together flopping onto the futon...

Finding each other,

Wrapping legs and arms around one another,

As if they were twine around a Christmas package,

Resting their heads on each other,

As their heartbeats slowed,

And they reveled,

In the afterglow,

Of wild, unrestrained sex...

Twenty-Four

Fifteen minutes later Allison and I were back where we left off—in my kitchen. Only now, Allison was clad in an extra-large gray Georgetown University sweatshirt. She was leaning against the counter watching me as I poured her more wine. I smiled fiendishly, handed the glass to her and toasted her silently with my own stem. I observed her taking a sip before I took one myself. She placed the glass down on the counter and sighed.

"Allison—I told you, the stains will come out—trust me. I just checked on it—they're almost gone. Give it thirty more minutes and you won't even know a stain was ever there. I swear!"

"I hope so."

"You'll see. So..." I said, putting my stem down and walking over to her. I reached for her glass, placed it on the table, and then before she could react, I reached for her waist with both hands and hoisted her up onto the counter. "You'll be safer here—trust me!" Her legs parted as I pulled back and I spied a hint of white panties. Allison frowned at me for a moment but then smiled, grabbed the wine and took another swig. I watched her, my eyes never leaving hers. Then I let them roam downward. She looked damn sexy sitting there on my counter, clad in an oversized sweatshirt, legs smooth and sculpted, toenails painted, a hint of white cotton visible when she rocked backwards or arched sideways to put down her wine glass.

"Allison," I said, wiping the smile off of my face. "We are going to try this again," I said, turning toward the stove and the still uneaten pasta sauce. I grabbed the spoon, stirred it in the skillet as I heard Allison say, "No, Trey," emphatically.

I ignored her purposely; stirred it a bit more, took a taste—satisfied, I loaded up another spoonful and carried it gingerly over to the counter.

"Trey! Remember what happened the last time!" Allison exclaimed.

I reached her, lifted my chin to her and said, "Open wide!"

"No." She shut her mouth and rocked backwards. I flicked my eyes down and gazed at her panties. The part where the fabric met skin was oh so smooth… Allison closed her legs with a smirk.

Raising the spoon to her lips, I again said softly, "Allison, open." This time she did. I moved in, her legs parted and I found myself nuzzled between her thighs. She arched backward, the sweatshirt riding up— unconcerned, she grabbed the wine stem and took a swig, rolling her eyes back as she swallowed. Her mouth opened and I slid the spoon partway in. She swallowed, opened her eyes and said, "Damn—I take back every bad thing I've ever said about you, Trey—give me some more!"

I flashed a smile while moving in once again with the spoon. Touched her bottom lip, tilted upward, waiting in anticipation for the tip of her tongue to come out, probing the air cautiously, seductively, the motion reminiscent of a serpent.

"OUCH!" Allison bellowed. I glanced down. A blob of sauce had landed on her inner left thigh—a mere inch from her pantyline. Allison's eyes were wide. She said nothing. I didn't speak. Instead, I gazed at her parted legs and that spot of red delicious sauce. Glanced back up. Allison was watching me silently. Without warning, I kneeled down, my eyes never leaving her. Shifting my gaze, I found myself eye level with her crotch, the spot of homemade sauce inches from my nose. My heart was racing. The blood, I could feel, coursed through my veins like a water hose on full. I leaned in and touched my lips to that spot. Felt, more than saw Allison open her legs ever so slightly. Tasted my creation—my mouth opening slowly, the blob of pasta sauce in contact with my tongue, its mass smearing my lips as if gloss. I glanced up briefly, made eye contact with Allison—and before any words could be spoken, my gaze dropped back down. My nose followed, brushing against the centerline of her panties. Slowly and methodically, I moved my nose around her crotch, rubbing against the cotton of her panties, inhaling her scent. I had opened my mouth, sucked up what remained of the sauce, and swallowed it in one gulp before running a wet tongue over her flesh by the side of her pantyline, licking up any lingering remnants of my delicious pasta sauce.

My head tilted upward, searching her face—Allison was watching me silently, her eyes unwavering, lips unmoving, neither a smile nor a frown painted upon her mouth. Then both her hands found my head, palms connecting with flesh, and I understood what needed to be done.

Beginning at her ankles, my hands grasped her lower legs and moved upward, slowly feeling the smooth flesh. Reaching her knees, I paused, felt around the bone with my fingers while my head moved from left to right and back again, my nose brushing against the dampening cotton fabric of her panties. Reaching behind her knees, I felt for the hollow space and tickled her flesh before moving upward to her thighs. Then grasping them with my hands, I spread her legs wide and felt her arch backward, while simultaneously lifting my chin, forcing my nose into the cleft of her center. I heard Allison groan as my mouth reached the edge of her now damp panties. My teeth found the fabric, gripping it, and tugged it aside.

Eyes opening, I saw her core, the axis of my desire and hers—Allison's lovely pussy—thin outer lips, a small entrance to her love tunnel—light brown pubic hair that radiated out from that spot, but controlled—cut, trimmed, like a well-kept lawn. At the bottom of her inner vulva, a single drop of juice—wetness, poised at the slit and gleaming like freshly fallen snow. Following her flesh lines upward to the top of her sex, darker than the rest of her skin, the convergence of pussy lips and hooded knob—and set in the middle—a thin, golden loop which pierced the center of her clit, with a tiny dark green stone that swiveled around the loop of metal, like an earring or a piece of artwork.

Not being able to contain myself one second more, I moved in—my lips colliding with hers, my tongue flicking at the drop of freshness as if it were salt, sloshing it around the tip of my tongue before, in one slow movement, I licked her sex from bottom to top. Allison responded by groaning. She gripped my head tighter and I attacked her pussy with all of my mouth—

slowly at first, using my tongue as a probe to pierce her cunt like a fork does raw meat, alternating with wide swaths from my wet tongue across her lips and inner thighs—but then abandoning any semblance of slow, coordinated movement, losing myself inside of her sex—ditching any strategy that called for working her into a frenzy—no, at this point we were too far gone for that mess. *Fuck that*; I wanted to taste Allison, *NOW!* And so, I grabbed her thighs, hoisted her legs back toward the counter and like one devours an oyster, I took Allison's entire cunt into my waiting mouth, slurping it up in one giant gulp, swishing it around like sushi, shaking my head rapidly and violently, feeling the clit piercing between my teeth—then exhaling and opening my mouth, allowing her engorged pussy to slide out, like a baby from a birth canal, all shiny with spittle.

Drunk now with the liquor of Allison's sex, I reached for the wooden spoon, drew it across her pussy lips before she could react, sketching a red swath of warm sauce, painting her hole in all of its glory. The spoon found her clit, decorated her pierced clit with more paste before I moved it down her cleft, spinning the wood in my hands, watching it glide from one pussy lip to the other, leaving sauce in its wake. Then finding the hole and probing lightly, around the edges, lightly dancing along the opening, like a gymnast does on a balance beam, one foot in front of the other, hands held wide, before turning/diving into the vortex—sticking the wide mouth of the sauce-laden spoon deep inside of her.

The end of the spoon stuck out a good six inches in a perverse sort of way. Head held back, Allison was too far-gone to notice. And I wasn't telling…

Turning my attention to her clit, I flicked my tongue along the thin gold ring as Allison squirmed on top. Tugged at it with my teeth—side to side, up and down, inserting the entire thing into my mouth, sucking at it like it was some kind of hard candy that tasted so damn good, vacuuming up the sauce, tapping the ring against my teeth and tongue until Allison was bucking her hips and moaning incessantly. I raised my hand to her clit and rubbed the piercing with my thumb. Ran it lengthwise along her pussy lips and the embedded spoon handle, gripping the end, moving it around inside of her pussy, yanking on it and watching her give birth to it before I discarded it on the tile floor like trash. Then my tongue reacquainted itself with her cunt as I replaced my thumb where the spoon had gone, twisting my hand clockwise and feeling her insides swell around me. Allison squashed her thighs against my ears hard, making a mess—sauce and pussy juice combining, splashing against my nose, cheeks, and hand. And for a moment I heard my ears ring before I pried apart her thighs and slurped her cunt once again into my waiting mouth, not caring about my chin, which was covered with sauce and Ally juice. My dick was straining against my jeans. I let one hand snake down to feel myself. Hard as a stone. I was ready.

The next few minutes were a blur to me. I stood up, hands reaching underneath the sweatshirt and finding her lovely breasts as I assaulted her lips with my mouth. Our tongues intertwined and twisted around one another like branches on a vine. Slipping my hands underneath her bra as if my skin was lotioned, my fingertips found her nipples firm. Grasping them, tugging at them, I ground against her wet pussy with my hips. And then, my jeans were down—whether through Allison's help or not, I don't know. What is clear is that my dick found her opening like a missile finds its target, and I pressed home, into her wet slit as she sucked in a breath and reached for my back. I slid in, tip to balls, Allison's cunt expanding as I greeted her with my member, filling her up completely. I came to the end, paused for a microsecond and then began pulling out, the feeling of her pussy constricting around me so overpowering that I thought I might come quickly, like a high-school kid. And then Allison was pushing me away—my dick plopped out, shiny and wet, as she reached for it with her hand and gave it a firm tug.

"Wrap it up, Trey," she said seductively, her eyes shimmering with anticipation, "and then you can fuck me…"

Twenty-Five

I mages of candles flickering against dark skin, and Miles' horn cutting through the haze of incense and cigarette smoke rushed through Vince's psyche as he sprinted down the jetway to the waiting DC-9. His garment bag cut into his left shoulder, yet he smiled—remembering Angeliqué as she flung cool paint against his flushed skin. The way they made love that night on the floor of her studio was indescribable—the sudden rush of feelings and emotions simmering against their colliding flesh in a delicious kind of way—almost causing his step to falter with the intensity of it all. Vince reached the jet, flashed a grin to the flight attendant who greeted him as he took his seat in first class.

It had begun with a fleeting thought as he lay in his bed the night before unable to sleep, the trick the mind plays on itself as one stretches his or her limbs under the weight of covers—and for Vince, he found himself imagining Angeliqué as he shifted around in his bed, her lovely form caressing him lightly from above, the way the covers did to his nude, pulsing form, causing him to swell with anticipation, and with pain. And that feeling, at the edge of that place where consciousness crosses over the divide and sleep takes over, was haunting. Yet just before he slipped into the fathomless pit, he found a thought and forged it into cold, gleaming steel—Vince decided that night that he would go to her, just as she had prayed to Ezili Freda, the voodoo goddess of love, the one who was fond of pink and pale blue candles, that he would.

So here he was. Eighteen hours later. Heading south on a whim...

The plane made a slow roll skyward as the force of the engines pushed him back into his leather seat. He glanced outside his window as the city of Washington veered away to the right. Soon blue sky and sunlight was streaming onto his dark face, causing him to squint. He thought about what he was doing—heading to New Orleans to surprise Angeliqué. He hadn't seen her in a while—they'd talked on the phone—less frequently than when he'd first returned, but every time he heard her voice—the breathless way she called his name or used vulgar language to describe how she was feeling, and more importantly, what she intended to do to him once he was back in her town, made him crave her even more.

Vince was heading to New Orleans on a Friday afternoon to surprise Angeliqué. She had no clue that he was coming. He hadn't told her. His heart and mind raced with the possibilities of surprising her later that night. It tickled away at him and made him excited.

The jet banked left and followed the meandering shoreline southbound toward Angleique's home. Vince tilted his head back and closed his eyes. Immediately Desiree's smile replaced the picture of Angeliqué's wild, frizzy hair. The thought chilled him. He had spent an evening with Desiree just a fortnight ago. She had made him laugh over dinner at this West African place on 18th Street. As they sipped martinis and filled their bellies with spicy food, Desiree talked non-stop about her friends and their crazy drama. The one whose man was caught cheating with a woman from his church, or the other who told Desiree in a hushed tone that her cat was fond of licking her under the covers, and that she was growing to enjoy it way too much! Vince sat there and laughed as Desiree told him these stories and more, and he found himself thinking about her and their relationship— barely two weeks old. He enjoyed Desiree—she was good-looking, smart, and feisty—girlfriend definitely had plenty to say—there wasn't any dead air between them—and yet, he recognized after making love to her recently and spooning her body in his, that the *feeling* that he felt when they were together was *different* than that which he recalled between Angeliqué and him.

Not better, not worse…just *different*.

Vince tried to sort out the data that were his feelings and analyze the results.

He was having trouble seeing it clearly. But what his heart was telling him so far was this: He enjoyed his time with Desiree. She was fun to have around, like Maxi (he reminded himself), then pushed that thought down, out of sight. Desiree was intellectual and could always be counted on for a lively debate. The sex was nothing to shake a stick at either—hell, there were no problems in that department, with her young, tight body and her angular features that caused him to stare sometimes without saying a word. But, as he pondered the similarities and differences between her and the voodoo lady he recalled how down in New Orleans Angeliqué had stirred something deep inside of him...something that had remained in his heart and in his soul, to this day...

He remembered the way he felt staring into Angeliqué's eyes as they dined at Brennan's, the way she moved as they walked hand-in-hand down Toulouse, her hip lightly bumping against his as they moved, the sophisticated, yet sensuous way Angeliqué carried herself as her wild hair caressed her face and neck—almost with a mythical, surreal quality, Vince thought. Was that right, or was this some kind of hoodoo-voodoo shit that he was conjuring?

His mind whirled as the plane leveled, the flight attendant bringing him a rum and Coke with a smile that Vince returned, momentarily suppressing thoughts of Angeliqué, Desiree, and even Maxi, as he made small talk about the weather and the coming of winter.

Then they were back—those three women who tugged at Vince's heart-strings in different ways. He allowed himself to remember with vivid recall the times he had spent with Maxi—the way she smiled, and her eyes that lit up a room. The way they moved as they danced in sync, that night at The Saint, in time to the music that seemed to wrap around them and sweep them away. Those sweet images came and went, replaced by those of Desiree— her thin, smooth form in his studio as he hovered over her with fire in his eyes, preparing for the lifecasting. Then, days later, flashes of the two of them playing chess as they conversed, Desiree clad in an oversized University of Maryland sweatshirt and not much else, the rising swell of her sweet, bare ass uncovered as she reached over to capture one of Vince's knights.

But it was Angeliqué Vince's psyche kept returning to—it was something about her that was *different*. When he was with her, he felt something else—he couldn't put a finger on it, but he noticed his pulse quicken with the thought of gazing upon her again tonight—the stirring in him, radiating outward, warming with its fire-like intensity.

Like a sudden thunderstorm that swoops in from out of nowhere and darkens the sky, Desiree came flooding back into his thoughts, pushing the voodoo lady aside.

Here she was, a chocolate-coated vibrant young thing who looked damn good on his arm, and was at his beck and call. What was there not to like? But, he had had similar thoughts regarding Maxi, too. Vince had made a quick getaway from her only months after they began dating because it didn't feel right, because she was not the *one*—and Vince was afraid that he was about to do the same thing to Desiree. This time he needed to make sure—there had been several times recently when he wondered if he had done the right thing in letting Maxi go. He had been thinking about that just the other day, pondering those thoughts and letting them marinate as he watched Desiree prance around his studio as she shoveled Chinese takeout into her waiting mouth; he even picked up the phone and dialed Maxi's number after Desiree had left, fully satisfied from the food and the sex—the call went to voice mail and Vince sighed with relief but left a short message anyway because he knew she'd see the number on Caller ID.

Maxi hadn't returned his call yet.

With a whoosh Desiree was replaced by thoughts of Angeliqué. It was a powerful sensation that began in his toes and rose upwards until he felt his spine tingling in anticipation.

Was it all a dream? Vince asked himself again. Or did Angeliqué possess some kind of supernatural power that she wielded over him, waving her wand from a thousand miles away to command him with a strength that he felt even from here? Was it the Creole magic, the spells and incantations, the ritual prayers to voodoo priests and priestesses, the altar in the corner of her Quarter studio, littered with dolls and candles, playing cards and chicken claws, that drew him to her?

This trip, Vince knew, was his way of finding out.

He wasn't about to make further changes to his social life until he was sure. Not yet. No need to rush things. He had acted hastily last time. He had lost Maxi in the process. Did he regret that? Perhaps. This time he needed to slow his roll.

Vince thought about the way he was acting, juggling these women as if they were balls that he tossed up and arced into the air—he knew it wasn't right—Trey, of course, would be proud, Vince acting like the true dawg that Trey hoped he'd grow up to be, but that wasn't him—never had been. Vince appreciated women. He treated them with respect and as equals with feelings.

What was he doing then, keeping Desiree on hold, in effect, while flying off to spend the weekend with some other woman?

Vince brushed the thought aside as the flight attendant refreshed his drink with her painted-on smile.

✠✠

The night air caressed his back—it was a wonderful sensation, to be back in New Orleans this time of year, the rest of the country hunkering down for winter, and yet, here in Louisiana, the flowers were still in full bloom, and birds were still singing, not yet having left for warmer pastures.

The flight had been uneventful. He had caught a taxi from the airport to his hotel, unpacked, taken a quick shower, and put on fresh clothes. He selected a pair of black baggy trousers and a gray mock turtleneck—then changed his mind, replacing the mock with a button-down gray silk. Black loafers completed the ensemble, but it took Vince another fifteen minutes to decide whether he wanted to wear socks or not—in the end, he opted for loafers sans the socks, and headed out to his woman.

His first stop was to the concierge desk where he was directed to a florist three blocks away. Vince picked up some carnations, vibrantly red, and proceeded to Angeliqué's home.

He walked leisurely through the French Quarter, taking his time—it was close to eight o'clock—the sun had just gone down, but the sky was clear. The forecast that evening called for light winds and low sixties—he had thought about bringing a jacket, but left it back in the hotel room instead. He walked past shops and restaurants, enjoying the light breeze as it billowed his silk shirt, and the live music that emanated from open bars; the throng of young people that traversed Bourbon, searching frantically for beads—Vince followed them for a bit before heading onto a side street where it was peaceful.

He had thought about calling ahead, after all, this was a Friday night, the beginning of the weekend, and there was always the possibility that she wouldn't be home. But Vince weighed his options heavily in his head, ultimately deciding not to call—he'd just show up and take it from there.

Vince turned onto St. Philip, and immediately felt the pang of anxiety that coursed through him. As he passed the two-story homes with their shutter-covered windows and balconies draped with twisting ivy, Angeliqué's corner studio/home now coming into view, he felt angst—butterflies fluttering inside his stomach, and he exhaled slowly to calm his breathing. His grip tightened on the flowers he carried. He paused to check himself. This was ridiculous, Vince told himself—he looked fine; besides, he was going to visit someone whom he had shared something special with. There was no reason to feel apprehensive.

Nevertheless, Vince crossed the street, fading deeper into the shadows of the night. Light from the gallery windows flooded the street and he wanted to make sure he wasn't seen—not yet. Sounds from various night creatures were more pronounced here—away from the masses of yelling, inebriated people. Vince came to a stop directly across the street from the broad expanse of glass. He peered in, noticed that the place was empty save for a lone woman who sat at a desk toward the rear of the building, her head down as she attended to some paperwork. He scanned the interior walls, observing from the shadows Angeliqué's art, the *veve* of the voodoo spirits—the elaborate designs surrounded by colorful hues and shades of the Haitian art.

Vince took a breath and crossed the street, cutting a diagonal line toward the gallery entrance. He spotted the courtyard entrance off to the right, a heavy wrought-iron door that hung open. He headed for that.

Coming upon the entrance, he slowed his gait and peered inside to what lay beyond. The courtyard was bathed in shadows; it was exactly as he remembered. The red brick wall was covered with thick ivy and he could hear the trickling of water from the oval pond. Vince reached for the black metal and then stopped dead. To the left by the table where he had laid his wine stem months before, he saw them—a couple caught in embrace. The shock of frizzy hair was unmistakable. Angeliqué was facing Vince, but shielded from view by the other person whose head she was grasping gingerly between her hands. Angeliqué kissed the person—it was not a long kiss, but what Vince witnessed froze his heart.

Angeliqué was in the arms of a woman.

Twenty-Six

I'm always down for a party, y'all! So when Q. called me on Tuesday talking about how he was having this thing for his birthday on Saturday evening at Home, and that he had put me on the guest list I said, hell yeah, you know I'll be there. Home is this spot that's patterned after some of the new trendy clubs in South Beach, with actual beds and shit—I kid you not—and you have to reserve those bad boys—but it's all good, 'cause some fine-ass honeys roll in there looking for someone to share their covers with. And you know this brutha ain't mad at any of them!

I got there close to midnight. Not one to arrive early, I made damn sure I pulled my shit up to the curb just as a big-ass line was wrapping itself around the block. They had been promoting the hell out of this party on the radio all week—talking about how all of these ball players, rappers, and video stars would be there. Oh yeah, Quentin got it like that—he's young, good-looking, and on his game—with the exception of his little legal troubles, he'd be on top of the world. But Q. wasn't one to let the soon-to-be-former Mrs. Hues bring him down. Not on his birthday. No! So he rented out Home on a busy Saturday night, invited everyone who was anybody, including the entire Wizards team and his former teammates from New York, and made sure all of Washington, D.C. knew about it. And judging from the way the bouncers were handling the crowd, only fly looking folks were being allowed in. They were acting like this shit was Studio 54, pointing to this fine honey over here in the short red dress with the thigh-high boots, and that fine sistah over there with her painted-on jeans and Victoria's Secret sequined bra, letting them and others like them in, while telling the rest of the folks to push the hell on back! Oh well, I hate it when that happens!

I had thought about bringing someone with me to this shindig—thought about that shit for all of five seconds, before deciding that flying solo was best. As I'm fond of saying, "Why bring sand to the beach?" Ya know???

I waltzed in, past the mad throng of people, after making sure my ride was safely tucked away, sandwiched between a bright yellow H2 and a midnight-black 740il. I had decided to dress down tonight, opting out of my normal fly attire—slick designer suit and power tie that are my trademark—instead going casual: brown suede pants that were hand-made for a brutha, a silk print shirt open halfway down my chest, and lizard boots the color of an African desert. Oh yeah, y'all, I was looking *funky fresh*, ya heard me, not at all like the high-priced divorce attorney that I am—but that was the whole idea. It was a Saturday night, and I was in the mood to play—Trey in Play, y'all. Grrrrr!

I found Quentin on one of the upper floors, VIP section of course, looking dapper in his well-tailored suit, sipping on Hennessy and toting a fat Cuban. These niggas crack me the fuck up—they all smoke cigars like they invented the shit, acting all serious like they're connoisseurs—please! You know damn well not one of them bruthas knows a humidor from a matador! Believe that!

"Yo what's up, Mr. Clean?" Q. yelled in a loud, boisterous voice while eyeing my threads. Around him the music swirled, Ciara belting out her latest jam, and not more than six feet away was some hip-hop producer extraordinaire whose name escapes me, lounging on a velvet couch surrounded by honeys and video hoes, looking exactly the way he does in his music videos. I gave Q. a hug as I shouted above the thumping sounds.

"Happy birthday, my brutha, how ya livin'?"

"Sheeit! You know how we do! Check you out," he said, grasping my silk shirt gingerly. "Dayum, bitches gonna lose their mind up in here when they see your shit!"

I grinned as I palmed my bald head. It felt as smooth as a baby's ass. "Q., dawg, you *know* how we do. I'm gonna handle my business, just like I know you will handle yours...it's what us bruthas gotta do!" Quentin grinned while pulling me toward the couch to introduce me to the producer. I shook hands with the man, nodded to the girls to his left and his right even though no one moved to tell me their name. That was cool—I wasn't trying to mess with brutha man's stable.

"So, you're Q.'s lawyer?" he asked me as he laid down a joint in an onyx ashtray on the coffee table where his legs were crossed. He wore baggy jeans, an oversized Phillies jersey, and white Air Force Ones. He eyed me curiously from under his Phillies baseball cap.

"That's right."

He pushed one of the honeys off the couch—gave her a slight nudge as he leaned in and whispered in her ear—a lovely thing, young, Latino, with big tits that glistened under the house lights, and a succulent ass barely contained in low ride jeans. He motioned for me to sit.

"Yeah, your boy's been telling me about his legal shit. I sure hope you can hook a brutha up."

"Yeah, well, I'm gonna take real good care of Q. No worries." I grinned at Quentin who pointed at me for a split second before hooking the waist of some honey who giggled as she was reeled in. The Latino chick retuned with a brandy snifter half filled with Hennessy. She handed it to me silently. I grinned and mouthed a "thank you" to her.

"Word," the producer said while taking a deep drag on his joint. We chatted for a few minutes about what he was up to—he had just returned from Brazil where he had shot a video, and the various rappers and hip-hop artists whom he was working with. I asked him about the biz and which celebrities he had spotted up in here tonight.

Moving on, I sashayed through the crowd, grinning to women as I glided by. A lot of folks I knew or at a minimum had seen before—if you socialize as much as I do, you can't help but run into the same mutha fuckas day in and day out. It's like that in this town. I made small talk with many of the players—Arena, Haywood, Jamison, Storey, Ruffin, Thomas; paying my respects, you know, I pick up a lot of business by mingling with these cats— it was all about networking, and if your shit was good (and y'all know mine is tight), then folks are gonna talk. I don't care who you are—black, white, rich or poor, sooner or later, you're all going to need a divorce lawyer.

Heading downstairs to the main level, I moved past the main bar, scoping out the talent—I was determined to get some pussy tonight—it had been a few days and the pipes needed to be flushed…I needed to be cleansed. But not one to rush things, I make sure I check the place out first, see who is there, and more importantly, let them see me in all of my glory. I grabbed the hand of some unsuspecting female and led her to the dance floor silently. Did my thing out there moving my body like it was a serpent—all sensuous-like, letting them know that a brutha could move. She was grinning from ear to ear as we danced to the new Snoop cut, and I could see out of the corner of my eye that people were talking about me. Oh yeah—let the hushed conversations begin—"who's that?—Oh, I hear he's some big-time attorney—look at him prancing around here like he owns this damn place—yeah girl, but he *is* fine, look at him—and I bet he can get us into VIP—shush—here he comes, maybe he'll ask *me* to dance!"

An hour later I was sweaty from shaking my stuff on the dance floor. I had pocketed four cards from various honeys—not bad—one every fifteen minutes—a bit slow for me, but hey, the night was still young. Besides, I wasn't ready to leave with anyone yet. So, I bid farewell to my latest dance partner, told her I'd give her a call next week to do lunch, and headed back upstairs to VIP where it was less crowded, and the big ballers played…

I spotted a low couch that was being shared by two women. I took the corner edge after freshening up my drink, and made small talk with them. One was a Wizards dancer. She was short and squat but had a killer body in her skin-tight polyester black pants and wife beater. The other, her friend, a statuesque redbone "model" from New York was clad in a pair of smart tan slacks, matching boots, and an off-white top that fit her torso to a T. It seemed that everybody was a model these days—I swear, every other woman I met nowadays did some kind of modeling. Well, that was cool with me. They both were fine as hell, so Trey here had no problem resting his ass with them for a minute. They were asking me about what I did, and that got us into a conversation about high-profile divorce cases—I was sharing with them some juicy stories from around the water cooler—and they were starstruck, just sitting there listening to a brutha talk casually about some well-known people who were going through some nasty shit, courtesy of their spouses.

Off to the right, something caught my eye. It was less the movement than the splash of color on this fine-ass frame that caught my attention—I glanced up, in mid-conversation with the lovely ladies, and had to pause in what I was saying. It took me a split second to look her over—her fine, chiseled features; perfect skin, shiny hair done in a thin braided ponytail that went halfway down her back, a pair of tight trousers that were an explosion of color: red, blue, indigo, and green—a kaleidoscope that shone off her package like a beacon—and a loose fitting white top with a plunging neckline that was worn midriff. Topped off by a pierced navel that sparkled and looked sexy as hell. This chick looked like a piece of mouthwatering candy, gliding along on pointy toed boots, with her three girlfriends in tow. Aponi Hues, Quentin's soon-to-be ex-wife had just made her grand entrance. Looking like she owned this spot, looking like she damn well belonged, which she damn well did *not*!

"Uh-oh," I said in a low voice to the redbone honey model who had her wrist leisurely hovering along my thigh. She stroked me absentmindedly as she leaned in, hooked on every bit of wisdom I was imparting this particular evening. I had already decided that I was going to take this honey home and fuck the living shit out of her, just as soon as I finished my drink. But just as I spotted Aponi everything changed. I glanced around searching for Quentin. I knew he would not be amused. Aponi's grin said it all as she waltzed in past a dozen players who eyed her with disdain—they knew exactly who she was and what she was up to. Aponi was here to fuck with a brutha, on his birthday, no less.

Dayum—things were about to get ugly up in this piece…

✠✠✠

"What's wrong?" The redbone, whose name eluded me, whispered in a harried voice—names come and go with me—they stream in my ears and head right back out again unscathed. Her hand had ceased to pet my suede-covered thigh. I gingerly patted her hand and moved it closer to my crotch as my stare locked with hers—she read my meaning loud and clear.

"Nothing to be alarmed by, darling," I said, all debonair-like. "Don't look now, but the birthday boy's ex just walked in, and knowing Quentin the way I do—he's a client—he's gonna be none too pleased."

"Ouch," she replied, leaning into me, letting me feel the warmth and full-ness of her breasts. My hand snaked from her knee to her inner thigh and squeezed as we nuzzled up against one another. I was getting hard quick, and my mind and pulse raced—delicious images sprinted through my psy-che as I planned the culmination to this redbone's seduction. I would fuck this honey on my dining room table. Yeah…*Tonight*. I'd splay her legs over my shoulders while kneading her nipples in one hand and fingering her clit with the other.

But I couldn't fantasize in peace. Off to my left I spied Quentin talking to a female, glancing down at her sweetness and licking his lips as he would in anticipation of a juicy New York strip—I watched him at the exact moment that he spotted Aponi—saw as his words died on his lips, his mouth down-turned into a frown as he set his drink down—the woman whom had hung on every word a moment ago suddenly forgotten. He left her standing there without a second thought and breezed past me, the anger boiling in his veins.

"Uh-oh," I repeated, setting my own drink down on the coffee table in front of me as I smoothed out my pants and readjusted my erection. "I need to go handle this—don't go anywhere, Precious—okay?" Redbone looked at her friend who just shrugged.

Aponi was moving toward Quentin as if he didn't exist. She casually threw her head back and laughed at something one of her friends had said as she neared. I stood up, calling Quentin's name as he made a beeline for his wife. I could see his hands clench and knew there was about to be trouble. I heard him address Aponi above the drone of the music even though I was ten yards behind him.

"Who the fuck let you in?" Quentin bellowed to Aponi who brushed past him like he was a mere annoyance. One of his teammates had reached Q. before me and was tugging on his arm, begging him to back off. Quentin just shooed him away as if he were a fly. When Aponi didn't answer he stepped in front of her, blocking her way. Before anyone could react, he had placed his hands on her shoulder blades, pushing her sharply back.

"This is my party, *bitch*, and nobody invited your ass!" he hissed. Aponi smacked his hands away, her face turning into a snarl.

"Boy, you better get your big ass outta my face before I have you arrested, mutha fucka." Her friends were by her side raising their manicured fingers into his face. "I've got as much right to be here as any of these hos," she quipped, flipping her hand up into the air. She looked Quentin up and down before sidestepping him and bumping into a woman whose drink went crashing to the floor.

"Bitch, watch it!" the woman hissed, but backed away, not wanting to be in the direct line of fire. Aponi didn't have time to turn and react before Quentin had grabbed his wife by the hair and yanked *hard*, pulling her head to the side as if she were some sort of ragdoll. Aponi screamed, as all hell broke loose. Hands and fists started to fly, and bodies were pushed as I reached Quentin and grabbed his hand, yelling for him to calm down. He released Aponi's hair as he eyed me, a terrible snarl that had replaced his normally sedate face. His wife's hand, or someone else's hand, reached up and slapped Quentin across his face. I heard the rancor and watched in shock as his head flew back from the force. I maneuvered myself in between Aponi and her ex—feeling her body pressed against me as I struggled to keep Quentin from beating the shit out of his own wife—and going to jail for assault and battery.

Several of his teammates were successful in pulling him backwards, but not without a great deal of effort—I've got to say this—when a brutha is pissed, it takes a whole *village* to calm him down—that's no lie. And Q-Dawg was pissed as hell. Having his ex interrupt his party was one big-ass mistake.

I used the moment to grab Aponi by the arm and lead her away from Quentin. Her girls were all in my face now, yelling for me to get off of her.

"Hey!" I yelled to get their attention, "I'm a fucking attorney, Quentin's attorney, in case you don't recognize me." This got Aponi's attention but quick. She stopped her struggle, ceased wiggling beside me in an attempt to escape my grasp as I led her through a hallway and into another room. Folks parted for me as if I were Moses. "Calm down, Mrs. Hues, just calm on down," I said to her once I could see she was regaining her composure. She kept glancing behind us, her stare wide-eyed. She was genuinely terrified—this I knew with one hundred percent certainty. It was as if the thought of Quentin, all six-foot-six, two hundred thirty-five pounds, lunging at his own wife whom was at best ninety-eight pounds when *wet*, never entered her mind until a split second ago.

"You've got to get out of here—you hear me?" I said, close to her ear as I continued to grip her by the elbow. "It's not safe," I added as I locked stares with her. "Get your girls to take you home now."

Aponi was shaking her head as I led her down the back stairwell. "Naw, me and my girls just got here—besides, they've been talking about this party for over a week." She glanced over her shoulder as her friends followed us down. There was chatter between them that was lost on me.

"Well, you can't stay here—I'm serious. Quentin is sure to follow and I don't think I can control him when he's this upset." We had rounded a landing and stopped for a moment so Aponi could catch her breath. Her girls were on her, hands at her back and hair, asking if she was okay. Aponi shrugged them away, bent down and started to cry. I looked at the girls helplessly.

"Can't you take her home?" I asked the one closest to me.

"It's her car—ask her," she replied, gesturing to the other. That one was fidgeting like a junkie, and I could tell she had no intentions of leaving any time soon. Aponi glanced up, wiped the tears away with the back of her hand, and centered her gaze on me.

"That mutha fucka's gonna pay for grabbing me. Believe that!" My heart began to plummet as she reached for her cell phone and punched in 911. I snatched the phone from her before she could complete the call.

"Fuck it," I said, as much to myself as anyone else. I reached for Aponi and lifted her up. Her mascara was smeared and she wiped at the corner of one eye with a finger, making it worse. I smiled to her sheepishly, thinking to myself, she still looked fucking good, even though she just had gotten a beat-down. "Listen to me, Mrs. Hues—you are not going to call the cops. Not here and not now. You are going to get out of this club and go home where you can think about your own actions first." I led her to a fire door that warned of alarms and fines if opened in anything other than an emergency. I turned to her friends who remained by the bottom stairwell. "Y'all can go back to the party. I'll take Mrs. Hues home. We need to talk anyway about the legal ramifications of what she just did." I eyed Aponi seriously as I said this, her stare locked on mine, but saying nothing. I was lying my ass off as only Trey can do—hey, that's why I'm so good at what I do, and get paid the big bucks—I knew damn well that my words were baseless—Aponi had done nothing wrong. She definitely suffered from the disease known as poor judgment, but hey, so did a lot of folks these days. Besides, poor judgment wasn't against the law, last time I checked.

Her friends conversed with Aponi as I watched. She was okay, she knew they wanted to stay; she was no longer *feeling* this place and needed to get out. Yeah, she'd be cool with me. They looked me up and down as I shrugged.

For my part, I was pissed. Not only had I just given up some seriously fine pussy, but I didn't even know the honey's name or number. Damn! I thought about running back up there, leaving Aponi alone for a moment, but knew that wouldn't do. Quentin was upstairs, he would spot me immediately, would demand to know where Aponi was. I wasn't ready to deal with Q. yet—not until I talked to Aponi, and calmed her down. Going to the police and filing charges were the absolute last things my client needed right now. His dumb black ass knew not just how much trouble he was in…

✠✠✠

I placed my hand on the cold steel of the emergency exit door, sucked in a breath and pushed…

Nothing. No sound, no alarm.

It figures, I thought as I took Aponi's arm and ran down the darkened alley toward the lights of the street. We reached the sidewalk, cut left, slowed to a brisk walk as I stopped dead in my tracks.

"Shit."

"What?" Aponi asked, staring up at me.

"My car—it's back the other way—in front of the fucking club."

My mind raced. I searched left, then right, trying to make a decision.

"Stay here," I commanded. "Let me run and get the car—I'll be back in a flash. Don't leave, Mrs. Hues—we need to talk."

"Fine, but stop calling me Mrs. Hues—that's the last thing I want to be called."

I returned five minutes later, having to drive completely around the block since the street where Aponi was standing was one-way. She remained in the shadows until I honked the horn. She ran to the passenger side door of the M3 and got in.

"Nice ride," she remarked as I fell into late-night traffic.

"Okay," I said, willing myself to calm down from the rising anger I felt at this woman for interrupting for me what was destined to be a sure fucking thing. *Literally...*

"Where to?"

Aponi was quiet for a moment, her gaze staring straight ahead. "Hello?" I said, "Where to? We can't just ride around all night." Actually we could, but I wasn't a freaking babysitter—that's the last thing I had counted on this Saturday night.

"I don't know—I can't go back to the hotel. Quentin knows where I'm staying. He'll come there for sure. I know him." I could see the fear in her eyes as she glanced at me. I swallowed hard. *Great,* I thought to myself. *Trey tries to be the nice guy and look where it gets him.*

"Look, I'm sure things will be fine. Let me drop you off there, I'll give him a call on the cell, talk to him, explain that the last thing he wants to do is come to the hotel and confront you." Aponi was shaking her head.

"Shit, you don't know Q. He's beyond reason when he's upset. You saw the look on his face; you saw how he tried to kill me!"

"Mrs. Hues—Aponi, please. Quentin isn't trying to kill anyone—he's pissed because you showed up to his party, unannounced and clearly uninvited. That's wasn't a particularly smart thing to do considering the allegations of infidelity you've lobbed at him." Aponi jerked her body around in the seat and squared off at me.

"You've got to be kidding me—my husband's fucking hoes in my own home, *our* home, and his dumb ass puts the shit on tape. You don't think I have a right to fuck with him by going to his party? Shit, if he didn't want me to show up, he should've had it at a private location, and not announced the shit on KYS-FM!"

She had a point there.

"Okay—listen, Quentin is not trying to hurt you. I know this. I know Q. He's upset and rightfully so. This is a very bad time for both of you," I said, my mind jumping to Allison Matthews and what she would say if she found out that I was with her client "unsupervised." "You need to take a step back, Quentin, too, regroup, think about what you want and what you are planning to do. My counsel to you, as an attorney, is to do nothing rash—think long and hard about your actions before you involve the police or the legal system because you may regret the outcome."

I was trying to sound all legalese and scare her. The thing was, Aponi was already scared, and royally pissed off to boot! A dangerous combination…

"So," I said, softly, as I made a right onto Constitution, not knowing where to take her. "Where's your hotel?

"Four Seasons, but we're not going there. I'm telling you that right now!"

Aponi's chest heaved as my eyes flickered quickly over her delectable form. There she was: sitting all snug in my tight ride, breath all harried, hair out of place, and makeup in need of serious refresh, but looking so damn sensuous that I felt a wave of pleasure course down my back and shoot for my legs. I sighed deeply as I cut a right onto 17th Street and headed for my crib…

Twenty-Seven

In the less than ten minutes that it took me to drive to my condo, I weighed the pros and cons of fucking Aponi. I was still very horny—I mean, my shit had been interrupted literally moments before I was ready to make my move—take that redbone home and give her some *Trey Steak*, you know, the kind that comes with the special sauce (and I'm not talking A-1), or better yet, not even wait until we made it to my crib—no, take her ass by the hand, head to the nearest bathroom where once in a stall I'd pull them panties down by my teeth and fuck her doggie style—think I wouldn't?

Instead I found myself babysitting my client's ex—a fine piece of ass, no doubt, but to make matters worse, the client of the attorney I had just recently fucked. Not good…on the other hand, look how fine she was, sequestered in the soft leather of my M3, obviously enjoying the ride and her knight in shining fucking armor, that being *moi*. No, this is a mistake, I'd already gone too far with Allison, and this could spell trouble. Yeah, but look at it this way— SHIT! My dick was calling the shots here, and under normal circumstances that would be okey-doke with me—but tonight things were getting thicker by the moment. For real!

Damn, damn, dayum!

That's what Aponi said as she crossed the threshold and saw my crib for the first time. That's what I whispered as I followed her sexy black ass into my condo.

"Your place is off the heazy," she said, awestruck like a teenager. "You must be making mad cheddar as a lawyer. I hope you are charging the shit out of my lame-ass husband."

"I'm doing okay," I said awkwardly as I smiled, flashing her my white teeth. "Come in and make yourself comfortable," I said, closing the door behind us. She moved into the sunken living room and squatted on the couch, leaning back, showing me those perky young breasts. Her taut nipples were visible under her top. "I have to tell you," I said, "I don't think this is a particularly good idea, you coming here, seeing how your husband is my client, and your attorney won't be pleased." I was both hoping she'd take the hint and leave, but also stay. *Well, at least I made the disclaimer, for the record*, I told myself.

"You got anything to drink up in this piece?" she asked as she threw off her shoes, and folded her legs underneath her, making herself right at home. I returned a moment later with two glasses and a fifth of Johnnie Walker Black. Pouring two fingers, I handed her a glass and raised mine to her.

"What are we drinking to?" she asked, and then continued, "Oh, I know, how about to niggas who fuck with mutha fuckas and get theirs in the end."

"Mmmn, I was thinking something a bit less…I don't know…*violent* sounding…"

Aponi shrugged and tipped the glass to her lips. I followed, silently. The liquor stung, and if I were smart, I would have realized that it was serving as a warning to me—of things to come—uncomfortable things—but you know my dumb ass didn't pay attention to the signs. I just let the hot liquid shoot down my throat and warm my belly as I eyed Aponi from a few feet away, the way she glanced my way as she drank, her initial serious stare replaced by one of devilish intent. I sighed, thinking things were about to heat up if I didn't take control…

"You know what, Aponi, it's getting late," I said, checking my watch, noting the time. It was close to two a.m. "It's been a long evening for both of us. I suggest we get some sleep. I've got a spare bedroom you can sleep in. Why don't we turn in and we can talk in the morning when both of our heads are clear."

"I don't know what you're talking about," Aponi said, downing the last of her drink and reaching for the bottle, pouring herself another one. "I'm feeling fine—my head is clear. Don't know about you…," she said as she took another swig.

"Okay, cool." I finished my drink in one gulp and reached for the bottle, pouring another myself. This little young thang wasn't gonna show me up in my own crib! Oh hell no!

"You don't look like a lawyer," Aponi said, eyeing me curiously.

"How so?"

"Check out your dress—suede pants, those boots—please! You look more like a model or a playa to me." Aponi smirked and I smiled back.

"I guess I should take that as a compliment." I could see her eyes were beginning to glaze over. Her fingernails were tracing circular patterns along her thigh. The movement was not lost on me. The battle raged within me— should I or shouldn't I? I was having trouble deciding. And Aponi wasn't making it any easier. I felt myself lengthening inside of my pants with every breath I drew, and I reveled at the sensation. This was a dangerous game I was playing, right? I took another sip and lost my train of thought as I swallowed hard.

I stood up and stretched, downing the rest of my drink. Aponi watched me silently. "Let me get you something to sleep in. A tee shirt or jersey," I said, heading for the spiral staircase. "The spare bedroom is right down that hallway," I said, pointing toward the opposite side of the room. "There's also a spare toothbrush and other toiletries that you might need in the bathroom next to the bedroom. Be right back," I said as I climbed the stairs. Aponi followed my movement but said nothing. I felt my pulse quicken as a thousand different scenarios raced through my head. The redbone was gone. Replaced by a young half-Indian, half-black vision of loveliness that fucked with me without even uttering a word. I reached the top step, sighed deeply, still undecided as I moved out of sight.

✠✠✠

Once inside the confines of my bedroom, away from the chick that was messing with a brutha like it was going out of style, I reached for one of my many jerseys and came to a decision. As I held the garment between my hands, looking at the colors, New York's colors, stuffing that one away and grabbing another, the purple and gold of Miami Heat, I decided, right then and there, to leave Aponi alone. For once I was going to think with my head—the big one; not the little one—and do the right thing. I was gonna leave it alone. As horny as I was, and let me tell you, I reached down and gave the big guy a squeeze; I swear to God I thought I heard him groan, I shook my head sadly. With resignation written all over my mug, I realized that in a few moments I'd be back here jerking off, while a lovely goddess lay one floor beneath me, her perfect body untouched by age and imperfection. But this was what was best. I knew that. Knew it from the moment I spied her at Home, knew it from the moment she slid into my phat ride. Leave the shit alone, I decided, before things got out of control and all fucked up.

I glanced at myself in the mirror to the right of my oversized bed, patted the package, *my* package, and winced as I felt it full of life. I sighed heavily as I moved out of my bedroom to return to Aponi.

✠✠✠

I was at the top of the winding staircase and preparing to step down when I glanced toward the couch. Aponi wasn't there. I paused. Felt my heart skip a beat. Where was she?

Glancing over the railing, I searched the living room area (not there), the dining area (not there) and the entrance to the kitchen (doubtful she would be there). I took a step down, paused again, and called out her name.

No answer.

I called her again.

I caught the movement below me, behind the interconnections of wrought iron. I stared downward, toward the junction of living room and hallway, and saw her glide into view. She was totally nude, her fine body shining with the glow usually reserved for angels or queens. I kid you not—I hadn't seen anything that close to perfection in a long, long time. Her hair had been wet down and rebraided. Her breasts were perfect round orbs of loveliness with taut dark nipples that were already distended. The smudge of mascara was gone. My eyes roamed downward to her sex, which was shaved clean, save for a pencil-thin line that ran straight down to her pussy. Aponi glanced up at me. Our eyes locked, the stare unwavering. I was speechless. She, too, said not a word. She drew in a breath; I watched her breasts rise as she did so. Then she spoke.

"I don't need anything to sleep in."

I nodded silently, the garment falling from my hand effortlessly. It floated down to the floor below me.

"Trey," she began, nothing moving save for the rise and fall of her chest from her breathing, "let's stop this charade. Temptation has been with me all my life, but I stuck to my vows, as a wife should, even when my husband disrespected me in my own house." She glanced down at herself for a moment, hands down by her sides as she lost herself in silent thought. "I did what I was raised to do. But that ends tonight. I'm no longer Mrs. Hues, Trey. I'm no longer married to *him*."

Aponi took a step forward into the light, and the totality of her loveliness consumed me in a single gulp.

"Tonight I get what's been missing for a long, long time," she whispered, glancing up at me with a seductive smile. My heart was beating so fast I thought it would short-circuit my insides. "Tonight I get what's mine…"

✠✠✠

"Okay, one last time, Quentin," I said, eying him over the steaming mug of coffee as I sat on the couch in my office. Quentin Hues sat across from me, the rage from the weekend's affair long gone, replaced by a look of anxiety. I checked the Breitling and saw we had three minutes left. "I'm telling you for the last time, I want you to walk in there, sit down quietly, study the grain in conference table, and not say a fucking thing…you hear me?"

"Yeah."

"Quentin—you have a lot to lose. Your wife could walk in here this morning and charge you with assault. I doubt that's going to happen—I talked to her Saturday evening and hopefully got through to her. But you know you fucked up. Fucked up bad. Now, it's time to put this behind you and move on. You're a ball player, at the top of your game. Don't let this thing bring you down. Are you listening to me?"

Quentin tipped his head up and sighed. "Yeah, Trey, I hear you."

"I sure hope so. Q.—let me handle my business. Okay—your job is to sit there and not say shit. We're going to dispense with the settlement agreement this morning and get the hell out of there. Agreed?"

"Yeah."

I stood, smoothed over my tie and buttoned my jacket. "Let's go," I said as I put down my coffee mug and headed for the door.

✠✠✠

Allison Matthews turned from the oversized window when we came through the door. She was not amused to see either one of us.

The scowl on her face shone like a searchlight.

I said "good morning" to her and she returned what sounded like a grunt.

Aponi Hues was sitting at the opposite end of the conference room table, same as before, dressed conservatively with her hair pulled back. Her hands were folded in front of her on the table, and she looked so damn good just sitting there, like fresh sunlight that warms your skin. I tried not to focus on her, but I couldn't help it. My eyes roamed over her face, lingering for a moment as thoughts from Saturday night invaded my mind. She stared back at me and smiled.

I sat quickly to hide my growing erection.

"Mrs. Hues," I said, making quick eye contact with her before turning my attention to her counsel. Allison cleared her throat and began.

"I trust this won't take very long, gentlemen, since I'm sure we all have better things to do." Allison's cold stare attacked me as these words wafted from her lips.

I wanted this over and quick. But I was having trouble concentrating. My mind raced—wondering if she *knew*.

Did Allison know?

Scenes from Saturday night invaded my brain and I was powerless to stop them.

Aponi, her lovely caramel breasts hovering inches from my face as I devoured them, one delicious inch at a time.

Those hard nipples, that elicited squeals when I pinched them.

The way she lay on my bed, head turned back as she watched me work, and the single slow lick beginning at the crack of her crescent-shaped ass, traveling downward until I tasted her sugary core.

The way she licked my balls and tugged on my shaft until I came.

The way we did it, over and over again until we were both sore…

Allison's words snapped me back to reality. "My client has made me aware of recent events that transpired this past weekend. These events concern *everyone* in this room."

Oh shit…

Allison continued. "The fact that Mr. Hues has assaulted my client, his wife, in public, is inexcusable and, frankly, counselor…"

"Ms. Matthews," I said, "let me…"

"Excuse me," Allison exclaimed, interrupted me, her ice-cold stare cutting deep, "I believe I have the floor. As I was saying, your client's behavior is inexcusable and against the law. There is no excuse for this kind of behavior and I am not interested in entertaining one. Are we clear?" Allison didn't wait for an answer.

"My client has further informed me that if it wasn't for the fast actions of counselor Alexander here, who knows what further harm may have come to her. For that, Mr. Alexander, we are grateful."

I did a slow exhale.

"*However*, let me be clear—your behavior, *counselor*, in terms of advising my client was less than professional. You should have called me, regardless of the hour, since she is my client, not yours."

I nodded silently.

"We could press charges this very morning; I hope you have made Mr. Hues aware of this fact."

"I have, Ms. Matthews."

"Good. We have decided not to. We will move forward and put this unfortunate business behind us. Agreed?"

"Yes." Quentin looked up and nodded. He quickly dropped his head back down.

"Mr. Hues, look at me, because I want there to be no misunderstanding on this point—if you ever lay a hand of my client again, I will personally make it my life's work to see you incarcerated for a very long time. Do I make myself clear?"

Quentin cleared his throat and said, "Yes ma'am."

"Good." Allison smiled, pulled two documents from a manila folder, separated them, and slid them across the shiny surface to Quentin and me. "A revised copy of the settlement agreement, the terms that Mr. Alexander and I discussed last week. I trust you will find that everything is in order."

I scanned the multi-page document and told Allison to give me a moment to read it. I glanced right; Quentin stared at the table as ordered; I then snuck a peek left—Aponi watched me and smiled. I turned my head back to the document as Allison's stare alternated between Aponi and me. I felt my temperature begin to rise.

I read on. So far everything looked as we had discussed.

Cool. A few more minutes and then we could leave this room that had suddenly become very stuffy...

I finished reading the settlement agreement. Everything that we had discussed and agreed to was there. I nodded to Allison, then slid the non-disclosure agreement I had drawn up over to her for her review and signature.

The CD-ROM, the one featuring Hues & Ho in their debut performance, was turned over to me.

There was silence as all parties completed the signing of documents.

Allison put down her pen and stood up. "That's it then."

"Yes," I said, relieved that this meeting was over.

She didn't know...

Thank you, Lord!

Aponi stood, walked over to me and took my hand. I shook it as we both smiled. There was a sparkle in her eyes. My heart was beating, and I wondered if Allison could hear the sound. Aponi brushed past Quentin without a word. I turned to leave, but Allison stopped me.

"A word, counselor?"

"Of course. Quentin, could you wait outside for a moment?" Quentin stood and exited the room silently. I shut the conference room door and faced Allison.

"Come here, Trey," Allison gestured. I maneuvered around the huge table, wondering if Allison was planning on giving me a kiss or another tongue-lashing. I walked up to her and gave her my best Trey-smile. That's when her hand flew up and smacked me dead in my face. HARD. The rapport seemed deafening.

"You son of a *bitch*," Allison hissed at me as I held my cheek in hand. "You think I don't know what you did with my client—your client's wife. You *fucked* her, Trey—I know it as sure as I am standing here."

I was stunned into silence. I reeled back, my mouth opened in shock, but nothing, no words or sounds emerged.

"As an attorney, I am astounded that you would blatantly violate the ethical behavior that as a lawyer you swore to uphold." Allison leaned in to me. "And, as a woman, the very same woman who shared her body with you not more than a week ago, Trey, I am aghast; no, that word doesn't do justice to the way I feel right now." Allison reached up and grabbed her hair with both fists. Her eyes were mere slits. "You have no fucking idea how this makes me feel. I can't even…" She paused, wrung her hands tightly, and looked as if she were readying to beat them against my chest. I moved back, out of range.

"You know what—fuck it, Trey." She grabbed her things and straightened her jacket. Allison sidestepped me and headed for the door. Her footfalls echoed loudly. As she rounded the table she stopped, spun on her heels and nearly lunged back to where I was standing by the window. Her trembling finger found my face.

"If you ever touch my client again or even get close enough to *breathe* the same air as she, I swear to fucking God I will take this matter to the D.C. Bar. I'll make sure you never practice law in this town again."

"Allison," I said, my hands coming up in self-defense, "let me…"

"NO, Trey!" Allison quipped, shutting me down, but quick.

"And if you even think about uttering a single word to me ever again, I'll…," she said, jabbing her fingers into my chest. "I know this—I won't be responsible for my actions…"

Allison moved quickly to the door.

"I thought I was getting to know you," she said, her voice lowered as her hand rested on the doorframe. "I thought I caught a glimpse of the kind of human being you were, but you know what? You're not even human," Allison whispered before exiting the room.

"You're a snake, Trey," I heard her say as the Peace Room door slammed, reverberating in my ears. "Nothing more than a fucking *snake!*"

I looked down at the floor, dejected. I was losing steam, like a deflating balloon. My head throbbed and my face, well, it hurt like hell. I heard the door open, and looked up, expecting to see Quentin Hues. Instead, Bernard John Marshall walked in, a smirk painted on his face.

"Judging from those choice words from opposing counsel," he said, a smug tone to his voice, "not to mention that handprint on your face, my assumption is that things aren't going too well…"

Twenty-Eight

The monotony of repetitive motion from the Elliptical Trainer was soothing. Vince's legs were moving rapidly, knees rising up and down as he pumped his arms in time to the music in his ears, a DMX CD. He had begun with something a bit more mellow—some smooth jazz he had brought along, but the jazz just wasn't cutting it. Not now—he needed something with "in-your-face" lyrics and hard-hitting drum and bass hooks— DMX *delivered…*

Vince thumbed the volume until his ears hurt. Ignoring the pain, he wiped the sweat that popped from his brow with a forearm and increased the pace of his workout.

Fuck the pain. I need this…

Vince still couldn't believe it—was it a dream? Was what he had witnessed real? For a moment he closed his eyes and thought hard, as if the action would somehow erase what was etched into his retinas and his mind—Angeliqué in the arms of a woman—kissing her the way she had done to him…

Vince shook his head in disgust and moved faster against the rising strain in his chest.

No, this was no dream.

What he had observed was real.

Vince had watched for no more than several seconds—feeling the earth under his feet begin to heave. He dropped the carnations, partly due to the need to reach out to steady himself, partly because the fragrant flowers suddenly felt heavy and alien in his hand.

Vince had turned on his heels, sucked in a breath as he moved away from the courtyard entrance, increasing his pace until he was sprinting like he was back in college. How he made it back to the hotel was a mystery. But he did.

And here he was, going on sixty minutes on the machine, feeling as if his lungs were on fire, but not caring, as if sweating out the pain would somehow make what he was feeling go away.

But it didn't.

Nor did it make the image fade from his mind's eye.

That scene was locked in his psyche and not going anywhere soon.

Thirty minutes later, he stumbled off the Trainer, gulped down four cups of water and toweled off his face. He returned to his hotel room where he showered and then sat on the bed unable to contemplate his next move.

What to do?

Vince experienced a variety of emotions, from raw, uncut anger to intense hurt. He stared at his cell phone, a million thoughts traversing his cortex—should he call? No, definitely not. At this point he had nothing to say.

This surely wouldn't work—"Hey baby, you're not gonna believe this, but I was in the area and decided to stop by—guess what I saw?"

No.

Perhaps he should call home—speak to his boy, Trey.

Nope. Trey would only make light of the situation—"Damn, dawg, if it was me, I'd bum-rush the both of them and bend one over while making the other lick my balls…"

Perhaps, Erika—he dialed her number but hung up when it went straight to voice mail. She probably was working tonight. Besides, he wasn't sure he was ready to talk with her or anybody else right now.

His stomach began to grind—checking his watch, Vince saw that it was coming up on 10 p.m. He was famished.

Ten p.m. on a Friday night in the Big Easy…alone…

So much for surprising his woman.

Vince snatched up the phone with a heavy sigh, and ordered room service before he made himself sick.

✠✠✠

Vince awoke at seven. He tried to sleep in, attempted to roll onto his side, squeeze his eyes shut and make the pain and hurt go away, at least for another hour more, but it didn't work like that. He lay there instead, staring up at the pattern etched in the ceiling for close to forty-five minutes before he cursed out loud and got up.

The first thing he did was call the airlines. He changed his return flight to later on that afternoon, a two p.m. departure. That was the earliest non-stop out of this town; Vince wasn't in the mood to fly to Atlanta or Charlotte and sit around in a terminal waiting on a connecting flight. So he put the charge on his AMEX Blue and hung up the phone.

Next he threw on a pair of sweats and a tattered Howard University tee shirt, and ran for an hour. The Quarter was miraculously empty this time of morning. Vince headed for the river, past stone churches, an open square that was home to several hundred pigeons, closed-up restaurants, and antique shops. A few folks were out enjoying the air. Vince neither eyed nor spoke to any of them—he ran to clear his head and his heart. For twenty minutes or so, it worked.

Returning to the hotel, Vince showered and changed into a pair of jeans, a light sweater, and a comfortable pair of Nikes. Grabbing some breakfast at the hotel restaurant downstairs, he contemplated his next move before making up his mind. Glancing at his watch, he saw he had enough time.

He quickly packed his clothes—actually stuffing them back into the garment bag was more like it. That took fifteen minutes. Vince was back on the street, showered, clothed and fed, and ready to do what he needed to do by ten-thirty.

He arrived at her residence fifteen minutes later. The street was as quiet as it had been the night before. The gallery was closed, and the wrought-iron gate to the courtyard was shut and locked. Vince peered into the gallery window, saw no signs of activity, and without fanfare rang the bell.

It took about five minutes for the door to be answered. He saw the gray sweats and the Saints jersey before he could make out her face. She came to the door, squinted through the glass as she brushed the hair from her eyes. Recognition lit up her face as the door swung open.

"Vince?"

It was Amber.

He smiled weakly, sensing again that they had met someplace before. "Hey you—ummn, Amber, how are you? I hope I didn't wake you?"

"Well," Amber replied, looking past him skyward before returning his gaze with her own, "actually, I was sleeping, but it's cool—what time is it anyway?"

"Almost eleven."

"Oh, well, it's Sunday—girls are allowed to sleep in on Sundays, ya know what I mean?" Amber smiled and Vince felt his apprehension decrease a notch.

"Listen, is Angeliqué around? I was hoping to speak to her, ummn, for just a moment." Vince shook his head slightly, knowing his words weren't on point as they usually were.

Amber eyed him curiously. "Wow—you know—she's not here. She—ah, left a while ago. That's a drag that you missed her. I can't believe you're here, Vince. You really should've called to tell us you were in town." Amber smiled as he shifted uneasily on his feet. Amber sensed his discomfort when he didn't respond immediately. "Hey, is everything okay?" she asked, touching his forearm. Vince stared down at his sneakers for a moment, deciding how best to answer the question. "You want to come in?" Amber asked. "I can throw on some coffee. You look like you could use a cup."

Amber reached out for Vince's arm, and guided him gently inside.

❊❊❊

The scent of coffee was strong. Vince took a moment to shut his eyes and inhale the sweet scent, letting it invade his body and still him. He took a sip and savored the hot liquid as it warmed his insides. Amber was facing him. They sat in the first-floor dining room, a large art-filled room facing the courtyard. Sunlight streamed in creating bright diagonals on hardwood floors. A gray Siamese cat stretched and as she eyed the visitor curiously.

"So, Vince Cannon, Jr., famous author, philosopher, and motivator, what brings you to our fair city?" Amber asked, setting the mug into her palms.

Vince was silent as he watched the cat move. He took another sip before responding. "Well, I was hoping to surprise Angeliqué." Vince paused, seemingly lost in thought. "Looks like I'm the one who got surprised." His forehead creased and Amber's eyes grew narrow.

"What do you mean?" Her eyes locked with his, but her stare was soft and serene. Vince sensed comfort in her gaze. He sighed heavily and told her.

"I showed up here last night—unannounced." Vince paused to let that sink in. "I came here, hoping to see Angeliqué. I saw her last night all right." Vince emitted a short laugh. "Yeah, she was here—with a woman. They were kissing…"

Vince took another sip of coffee and leaned back watching Amber. Her face had changed—the smile was gone, replaced by a frown that seemed to radiate outwards. Her limbs appeared to hang from her frame. She was not the same woman whom he had watched recline on the floor months earlier, the *veve* covering her body like some exotic pelt.

"Oh my God—I don't know what to say, Vince. I'm sorry." She reached for his forearm across the table and stroked it.

"You don't need to say anything. I guess I came here to try and make sense of this whole thing. To speak with her before I left, seeing how there's no reason for me to stay now."

Amber was deep in thought. She sighed to herself before speaking.

"Vince, listen, I'm sure there isn't anything that I can say that will erase what you're feeling right now. But I want you to know this—Angeliqué, how do I explain this?" Amber glanced up at the ceiling before continuing. "I know she is feeling you—I know this because she speaks of you often. She's always commenting on how she misses you, and how special that night was to her."

"Well, she sure has a funny way of showing it," Vince quipped.

"Vince you have to understand Angeliqué. She's not like most people— she follows her own drum. She's the kind of person who lives very much for today—I think she's been hurt deeply before and thus doesn't put too much stock in tomorrow. This person, this woman you saw her with—I don't think it means much…"

"Amber—with due respect, come on! She was kissing the woman. What does that tell you?"

"Vince," Amber struggled to find the words, "I think Angeliqué is the kind of person who possesses an extremely social and personable soul. I think she connects with folks on a variety of levels. She connected with you. Very much so. But you're not here—and she had no idea when she would see you again. I believe Angeliqué takes things one day at a time—she lives for today, because that's what feels safe for her. "

Vince pondered her words. "Whatever the case, it doesn't change what I saw, and it doesn't change how I *feel*." Vince drained his mug and set it on the table.

"Again, I'm sorry."

Vince patted her hand as he stood up. "I'm not gonna take up any more of your time. Thanks for the coffee and the conversation—it's what I needed, Amber."

"Vince, why don't you stay for a while? I know Angeliqué will want to see you. She *is* missing you badly…"

Vince shook his head. "I don't think so."

"Please?"

Vince shook his head as he smiled at Amber.

"How about this then—where are you staying? Perhaps Angeliqué can swing by to see you when she returns."

"I'm staying at the Fairmont, but it doesn't matter—I'm going home in a few hours."

Amber was silent in thought. "Oh, I thought perhaps you were here through the weekend."

"I was," Vince said softly.

As he headed for the door, he said, "You know what? You are wise beyond your years. I admire that. And you have a perspective on life and on people that I find refreshing. Whatever you do, don't change."

Vince reached for the door.

"Will we see you again?" Amber asked nervously.

"I honestly don't know. But I do hope that you and I can speak again. If nothing else I find your words and presence comforting."

"I'd like that."

As Vince emerged into the brilliance of a Louisiana morning, Amber reached for him; he turned as she leaned in, kissing him lightly on the cheek. Vince stared at her for a moment, taking in the lines of her face as they both smiled, before heading deeper into the Quarter, away from unruly tourists searching for beads, blues, and beer...

✠✠✠

She swept in to the lobby of the Fairmont, her skirt billowing as if caressed by an autumn breeze. It was the hair—bronze and unkempt that got the attention of the male attendant at the desk.

"May I assist you?"

"Yes, I'm looking for a Mr. Vince Cannon, Jr. Can you tell me what room he's in?" Angeliqué asked. She raised her sunglasses onto her head and wiped the hair from her face.

"We aren't allowed to give out room numbers for our guests, but I can ring him for you. Just a moment," the clerk said, flashing his best smile at the pretty lady. Angeliqué returned the smile weakly and then glanced at her watch.

Twelve-eight p.m.

The clerk consulted a computer screen for a moment before frowning. "It appears that Mr. Cannon has already checked out."

Angeliqué bit her bottom lip. "When? Can you tell me how long ago he checked out?" she asked, her voice rising in pitch.

"Looks like you missed him by oh, fifteen minutes or so." The clerk adjusted his tie and said nervously, "I'm sorry, Miss. Perhaps I can be of further assistance?" But when he glanced up, the pretty lady had vanished into the wind...

Twenty-Nine

Thursday night, nine p.m. at the stylish Tryst in Northwest D.C., and the coffee bar was jumping. Not a free table in the house. Thankfully, Erika and her crew of three had secured a table prior to the evening rush—actually, they'd stood at the bar drinking Cosmopolitans for close to forty-five minutes before spotting a group that was leaving, and bum-rushing the table before anyone else could claim it!

It had been close to a month since Erika and her girls had gotten together. Chalk it up to conflicting schedules—school, work, and their *mens*—so it was nice to finally have all of them sitting together in the same room—regurgitating conversations over and over by phone or e-mail just didn't cut it, and got old but quick!

They had a cramped table by the window overlooking 18th Street. Adams Morgan was filled with youthful crowds, even though winter was rapidly descending upon the city. Folk streamed past their window—shades and hues from various countries the world over, and it made Erika feel proud to be living in a city that had diversity as its middle name.

"Girl, I just love your hair!" Tianna, a thick boned, rich chocolate sistah said to Naomi, a leggy woman the hue of creamy butterscotch. She ran a hand over her shortly cropped brown hair, marveling at its texture.

"Thank you!" Naomi said, all smiles.

"Yeah, girl," added Angie, a squat Cuban with dark eyes and matching hair, "what happened to make you lose those twists?"

Naomi shrugged. "I don't know—change of pace, I guess."

"Well, it looks good on you, girl," Erika said, patting her hand. "And I bet your man is loving this new look of yours, am I right?"

Naomi's look turned serious. "Who? Michael? Please! I sent that bama packing after I caught his black ass two-waying some ho at one in the morning. You know a sistah don't play that!" She high-fived her girlfriends in rapid succession.

"I know that's right!" Tianna exclaimed. "What is wrong with these bruthas anyway?"

"Oh please, don't get me started, mommy," Angie said, "'cause they're ain't enough hours in the day!"

"I feel you," Erika declared, laughing as she reached for her martini.

"Besides," Naomi continued, holding up her pinky finger, "the nigga wasn't much use to a sistah anyhow! You feel me?" Squeals of laughter rolled around the table as folks turned to see what all the commotion was about.

"Oh no he didn't," said Tianna, a look of shock on her face.

"Oh yes he did!" Naomi responded. She waggled her finger, and the girls cracked up again.

Things became quiet as the four turned to their drinks. Angie glanced at Erika and spoke. "So, girlfriend, how are things with that anchorman of yours? Don't think I don't watch Channel Four every damn day to get a glimpse of his fine-ass in those dapper suits!"

Erika smiled while running her fingers lazily through her hair.

"Ummn…what can I say? The brutha is fine, right?"

"Oh yes he is!" Tianna said. "Don't let me get that sexy ass man alone—I'll show him what real love is about—you know what they say—'the darker the berry…' "

"Trick, you *best* stay away from my man, unless you want a beat-down!"

"So, girl, seriously, how are things???" Naomi asked.

Erika cleared her throat as she thought about the best way to answer that question… honestly.

The truth—on the one hand, things with James were picture-perfect—he was the consummate gentleman, sending her flowers, taking her out to lunch, cooking for her, and above all else—listening to her—not dominating their conversations with discussions of "me, me, me," but being genuinely interested in her and how she spent her day. That got him major points. So, what was there to complain about? Erika had a man who attended to her every need, was caring and smart, good-looking (oh yes, thank you, Lawd!), and great in bed...save for that little problem...

Erika sighed.

"What's wrong, Erika?" Naomi asked, concern etched on her face.

"Nothing." Erika sighed again. "Things with James and me are fine. He took me away this past weekend. Planned the whole thing and made it a surprise—it was sooooo nice!"

"Really? Do tell..."

"Well, he called me up on Thursday night saying that he was taking me somewhere for the weekend and to be ready Friday afternoon. So, I was packed and waiting when he shows up in this *bad* stretch limo around four! Yes!" She grinned. "Can you believe it? We were then driven to this quaint bed & breakfast in Annapolis two blocks from the harbor. It was so romantic."

"Oh my goodness, that brutha is bad!" Tianna exclaimed.

"You got that right—can some of James rub off on Hector?" Angie asked, cutting a glance over to Erika.

"Ummmn, I don't know about that. Anywho—you should have seen this place—the room was so nice—king-sized, four-post bed, fireplace, window over looking this beautiful garden, drinks in the ornate living room, and being waited on hand and foot all weekend."

"Damn!"

"For real. James took me to dinner at this wonderful seafood place overlooking the harbor. Afterwards, we walked Main Street and window-shopped while we held hands." Erika paused in remembrance. "It was all so romantic and just what a girl needed, you know?"

All smiles around the table.

"We had a wonderful weekend. It was so nice to get away and just spend time with him. It was as close to perfect as perfect can be..." Erika sipped her martini and glanced out the window. Naomi watched her silently before speaking.

"So…why do I get the impression that something's missing?"

"I don't know," Erika responded, but the words seemed washed out like a faded sweatshirt.

"Erika," Tianna asked, locking her gaze on her friend's, "what's the real deal—we're your girls—you can tell us."

Erika put down her drink and sighed. "See, y'all are gonna think I'm tripping if I tell you." She frowned as her mind wrestled with how much detail to spill.

Angie smiled as she reached for the back of her hand. "It's okay, girl—we're not here to judge, you know that."

Erika sucked in a breath. "Okay. I don't know how to explain this, so I'm just going to come out and say it. All right?" Nods. "James is a great lover—we have a great time in bed. But he can't come!" Erika looked away for an instant before settling her eyes on each woman in turn. "There, I said it."

"What you mean, he can't come?" Tianna asked. "Like he can't get it up?"

"He can get it up all right—that's not the problem. No, James' trouble is that he can't orgasm. We've been together for several months now—the sex is the bomb—I'm getting mine, for real, but he doesn't come. And it's really getting to me." Erika took another sip, and then downed the rest of her drink. She caught the attention of the waitress, and swirled her hand about, signaling another round.

Naomi asked, "Have you spoken to James about this?"

"Yeah. I've mentioned it several times." Erika recounted how she first approached James early on in their relationship, and his measured response to her—not to worry; that it was the condoms; yada yada yada. But Erika knew that wasn't it. During the previous weekend, in the private confines of the B&B as a fire crackled and sparked, Erika lowered herself onto James sans a condom and rode him bareback—it was the first time, but they had been dating for a while now, so she trusted him, and more importantly, she needed to be sure. On that Saturday night, Erika made sweet passionate love to James on the four-post bed, reveling in the warmth and glow from the fire, as shadows danced across their writhing forms. The feeling that she experienced from having him inside of her unencumbered, unsheathed, was out of this world—she lost track of how many times she came that evening—but one thing was clear—regardless of how much James panted and moaned, he failed to ejaculate that night…

And that fact, coupled with the disturbing incident at his home with the videotape left her feeling, well, less than a woman.

"I don't know," she continued, "part of me says that it's not a major problem. I mean, we've only been dating a few months, and besides, I know it's not anything I'm doing." She paused, glancing around the table to read her friend's expression. "But lately, I'm wondering if it *is* me—that maybe I'm doing something wrong…"

"Trick, please!" Tianna said, cutting her off with a wave of a hand. "Look at you—you're a beautiful sistah who is definitely in control. Listen to me—it ain't you. Know this!" she said, jabbing a finger in Erika's direction.

Erika smiled. "I know, I know, but it does makes you wonder, right?"

"I agree with Tianna," Naomi said. "I hate to say it, but there are a lot of bruthas out there who can't deal with an intelligent, sophisticated sistah whose got her shit going on. For some, it's a major turn-off—they're used to these silly hos with their only claim to fame being the fact that they can shake their ass on cue!"

"Tell it, mommy!" Angie shouted.

"I'm serious. With due respect to James—you may be dating a brutha who is used to dealing with women who aren't his equal. His past relationships may have been with immature, demure girls filled with low self-esteem. For some guys, it's a power trip—they love being in control. It might be that now that James has met his equal, it's messing with his head—the big one and the little one!"

Erika laughed as her cell phone rang. She reached for her purse, pulled out the cell, and flipped open the clamshell.

"What up, boo—how ya livin'?" It was Trey.

"Fine—what's up with you?" she asked.

"Chillin'…how come you ain't answered my calls—damn, a brutha's gotta track you down?"

"Naw it ain't like that, but I've been busy." The girls chatted among themselves as Erika stole a sip from her martini glass.

"Whatever, ho. Where you at?" he said.

"Out with the girls—why?" Erika excused herself, walked toward the door, and leaned against the thick glass, pushing it open. Cold air blast onto her face causing Erika to shiver. "Hurry up, Trey, it's cold as shit out here. What's up?"

"I need to talk with you, that's what's up! I've been calling you for two days. Damn, boo, you didn't get my messages?"

"Trey, I can't talk. Not now, and probably not later," she replied, checking her watch. "I have a feeling we're going to be here for a while."

"Erika," Trey said, the seriousness in his voice coming through the connection loud and clear, "we need to talk—some shit's come up. I need ya, boo."

Erika hugged herself as the wind whipped around her frame, flinging her hair about. "How about tomorrow? I don't have to be at the hospital until six. We could do lunch if you're not too busy."

"How about later on tonight? You could swing by the crib after you finish your business with your girls."

"Trey, I can't. It's getting late, and I haven't seen my girls in over a month. I don't want to cut our get-together short. Let's shoot for tomorrow, okay? I promise you my undivided attention."

"All right," Trey responded, the disappointment obvious in his inflection. "When and where? Make it someplace we can talk."

Erika head for the door and pulled on it. "How about B. Smith's. I'll make the reservation."

"A'ight—if it can't be tonight I guess tomorrow's gotta do. Don't be late!"

"Whatever! You are not the boss of me!" Erika clicked off as she moved to their table and sat down. Her mind raced, back to the conversation at hand—James. Should she tell her girls abou the incident that remained in the forefront of her mind, out in the open where it messed with her every chance it got—that James had come…*once*…and the circumstances surrounding that episode?

No.

She wasn't ready to share that aspect of her personal life with her girls just yet…

Thirty

Vince glanced around quickly before taking a seat at the dark wood bar. The bartender, a busty brunette with a pierced eyebrow, took his drink order and sashayed away, swishing her hips from side to side. Vince failed to notice the move. He was lost too deep in thought.

It was a Wednesday night, a few minutes to eight at e-Citie, a thriving spot in Tysons Corner that catered to the after-work crowd—mostly ex dot-comers and IT folks. He took a swift look at his watch, hoping no one would notice his anxiety.

Would she show?

Unknown.

She had finally responded to his calls with a short-to-the-point response on his voice mail. Yes, she would meet him.

Vince sipped his Corona and brushed away the appetizer menu with a flick of his wrist. He swept his glance around again. The place wasn't very crowded. A few pockets of casually dressed people sitting around tables talking loudly. Not too many black folks in here, but no one was giving him the eye, which was good.

Stop feeling trepidation, he told himself. *There's no need*…yet, he couldn't stop the emotions he was feeling.

The last few weeks had played havoc on his emotions. They had been on a roller coaster of ups and downs since New Orleans. And why shouldn't they? The image of purity that he had held was gone—shattered by the realization that the woman whom he was falling for was gay. Or bi. Whatever her orientation, it didn't fit in with his plan. And that troubled Vince. Deeply.

Purity—that wasn't quite right. Angeliqué was far from pure. Vince knew that. But there had been something about her that had drawn him in, the way water spirals down a porcelain sink. The attraction, he had suspected, was very much mutual. They had connected on some deeper level; he knew that. So, why then, had things gone so horribly wrong?

Angeliqué had been calling for two weeks now. Attempting to connect with Vince. Trying, he presumed, to explain her behavior…

As if that kind of thing could be explained.

He had yet to return her calls. Vince hadn't fully sorted out his feelings. Besides, what difference would it make? Things had fundamentally changed. The image he held was shattered.

That's all that mattered now.

Then there was Desiree to consider. Was this thing with her just a mini-vacation for him—a jaunt with a feisty young woman, full of spunk and energy, but lacking a deeper connection that was needed for anything more than what they had now? Vince didn't know. And that was part of the problem…

Someone moved up beside him. Vince turned and found himself face to face with Maxi.

✠✠✠

It was the eyes he noticed first. Nia Long eyes. Dark and piercing; lovely orbs that cut right through him.

Vince felt himself shiver.

"Hey you—you made it."

"I said I would," Maxi said, placing her handbag on the bar stool beside him. Vince looked her over. She wore a fashionable beige leather jacket with whipstitch and dark blue jeans. Underneath the jacket, a crocheted cardigan was tight, showing off her breasts. Her hair was pulled back tight and shiny. Perched atop smooth dark cheeks was a new pair of designer glasses—thin, lightweight frames the color of titanium. Vince stared for a moment too long.

"Wow, check you out, Maxi, you look wonderful!" Vince reached over to kiss her. He was aiming for her lips, but Maxi turned her face, presenting him with her cheek instead.

"Thanks," she said, and sat down. Vince pivoted toward the bar, got the attention of the bartender by holding up two fingers. She came over and smiled at them.

"What can I get you?" she said, slipping a square napkin onto the smooth bar surface.

Maxi opened her mouth to speak as Vince leaned in.

"Get her a Cosmopolitan, if you would," he said, grinning at Maxi. The bartender said, "Sure," and reached above for a martini glass.

"Actually," Maxi said, raising her voice a notch, "I'll have an Absolut Heaven." Vince cut a glance over to her. Maxi shrugged. "It's my *new* drink."

Vince leaned back, feeling dejected. Thirty seconds into their reunion and things were not going well. "So, Maxi, thanks for meeting me. I hope you've been well."

"I have, Vince. And you?" she asked, smoothing her hair.

"Fine. Good, real good, thanks for asking." Vince was fumbling and he knew it. It always amazed him—here he was—a professional motivational speaker—he did this shit for a living—getting up in front of people and talking about issues he was passionate about. But, put him in a personal situation like this—and Vince felt himself on shaky ground...

"So, Maxi—I need to say something first. Get it out of the way," Vince said, turning to give her his full attention. "I am sorry for the way things ended." Maxi opened her mouth, but Vince raised his hand. "Let me finish—there are a hundred ways to break up with someone; I chose a shitty way to do it with you. I'm sorry for that, Maxi. There isn't any excuse for my behavior." Vince paused, reading her face, looking for signs. She stared back at him, not communicating anything with her expression, waiting instead for him to go on.

"Maxi, it's hard to explain the place I was in back then—sorting through the various emotions, trying to ascertain what I was actually feeling. I have to tell you, it was a blur to me, and I was confused. Not really knowing for sure what it was I was searching for." He paused to take a sip of his beer.

"You don't have to do this, you know," Maxi said. "I've had time to get over what transpired between us, and what's done is done. I'm not the kind of person to dwell on the past. You, of all people, should know that."

"Yes, you are indeed correct."

"I'm not going to lie to you, Vince—you hurt me. I thought that what we had was special. And I thought we had come to the same place, feeling each other the way we did—I guess I was wrong."

Maxi's drink arrived and she took a sip. "Ummm, this is good," she remarked.

"That's just it, Maxi," Vince exclaimed, "I don't want you to think that I wasn't into you, because that's the furthest thing from the truth. I *was* feeling you." He dropped his voice a notch. "I still am…"

"Vince, I'm not sure what you want me to say."

"I don't want you to say anything, Maxi. I'm here to say I am sorry. And that I hope we can move forward. Be friends or move down whatever road our relationship chooses to take us."

Maxi smiled, but Vince could tell it was the kind reserved for those situations when you felt sorry for someone. "Listen, Vince, you are a wonderful guy. And I enjoyed the time we spent together. But as you said, you were confused and not clear about what it was you were searching for. Well, I don't have that problem." Vince cringed. "I don't mean to be harsh, so forgive me for sounding that way. But I *do* know what I want. And I need a man who is on the same wavelength as me. As I said, you're a great guy; you just need to sort through your issues and then you can move forward." Maxi took another sip and gathered her things. She reached for her purse and dropped a twenty on the counter.

"Hey, you leaving so soon?" Vince asked, staring at the money. "I thought perhaps we could have dinner and catch up."

"Another time, maybe. I've got plans and have to run." Maxi stood up, and bent down to run her palms over her thighs. Vince glanced at her bent-over form. Red g-string panties peeked out from the back of her jeans. Vince felt a twinge of jealousy. Maxi was lovely, no denying that. He had fucked up. He had acted prematurely and it had come back to haunt him. She straightened up and smiled at him. "It was good seeing you, Vince. Stay well, okay?" she said, reaching out to stroke his beard. He returned a weak smile.

"At least put your money away; I'm the one who invited you."

"No, I insist, Vince." She pivoted away from the stool as Vince reached for her arm.

"Would it be possible for us to get together one day soon?" he asked, trying not to show the desperation in his voice that he felt in his heart.

Maxi turned back to him. "Tell you what, I'll give you a call one of these days. Bye, Vince; I really have to go." Vince watched her leave, before turning back to the bar and eyeing her drink that remained largely untouched. He sighed heavily as his cell phone chirped. He grabbed it, cut a glance at the Caller ID, and pressed the phone to his ear in a rapid motion.

"Yeah?" he said in a gruff voice.

"Vince. It's Angeliqué," she said slowly. "Hi, I've been trying to reach you for…"

"Give me a call back in five minutes, would you? I'm in the midst of something," he said, before snapping the phone shut without saying goodbye. He took a swing of his Corona and rose off the bar stool, heading angrily for the restroom.

Outside, Maxi had rounded a corner of the building before pausing besides a wall. Pressing her back into the concrete, she tilted her head up to the sky as she reached for her phone. She drew in a deep breath as she punched in a number.

"Hey girl, it's me," she said forlornly a moment later.

"Hey—so, spill it—how did it go?"

"As you figured—he apologized profusely and basically wants me back."

"I knew it! *Please* tell me you didn't fall for that playa shit, Maxi."

"No," Maxi said, "I followed your orders to the T."

"Good. You do not need no man who is wishy-washy."

"Yeah, but you should've seen him—he looked so damn fine," Maxi said, shaking her head with the memory of him sitting at the bar looking too cute. She began to move toward her car.

"Forget that—how about you? Did you dress the bomb, like I told you?"

"Oh yeah, his eyes practically fell out of his damn skull!"

"Good enough. Let him contemplate that shit!"

Maxi sighed as she opened her car door and got inside, starting the engine.

"Seriously, Maxi—you've already moved on. Don't head backwards," her friend opined.

"Yeah, I know. I know I'm doing the right thing," Maxi said, "but answer me this: Why then, do I feel so damn awful???"

✠✠✠

The tan Lexus coupe accelerated past the intersection as Vince steered the automobile onto the Beltway. He slid in a CD—something smooth—George Duke—to ease his mind. He was pissed. Not at Maxi, but at himself. He should have left it alone. Calling her was a mistake. He had fumbled the situation with her and came out looking like a fool.

A desperate fool.

Vince shook his head miserably. Why didn't he just stay away? He had Desiree and things with her were going fairly well. Why, then, did he feel the need to dredge up the past by trying to reconnect with Maxi?

Angeliqué, that's why.

Ever since he had spotted her in the arms of another woman, Vince had felt that nothing in his life made much sense. Here he was, seemingly heading in one direction, so he thought, but then the rug had been pulled out from under his feet, and he had gone flying, landing flat on his black ass, glancing around, dazed and confused.

Stop it, he told himself. *Get it together. You are Vince Cannon, Jr. There is no need for this shit. Lord, if Trey could see you now, he'd shake his head in disbelief and disgust. So stop tripping over something that wasn't meant to be. Something that never even got started…*

The chirping of his cell phone brought his thoughts back to the present. He cleared his throat and answered the phone.

"Me again." It was Angeliqué.

"Hey," Vince answered, softer this time.

"Is *this* a better time?" she asked cautiously.

"Yeah, it is." He thought about apologizing for his earlier behavior, but then decided against it. He was still fuming from his encounter with Maxi, and images of Angeliqué and her female lover didn't appease his mood one bit.

"So, I've been trying to call you—I guess you know that," she said. "Vince, I want to talk to you. We haven't spoken since prior to you coming back down to New Orleans. I am sorry, Vince, for what happened. I never meant to hurt you; I hope you know that."

Vince had rehearsed this conversation over in his head a million times. But all that he could come up with now for a response was a half-baked grunt.

"You have a right to not want to see or speak to me, but I hope that you won't do that."

Vince was silent.

"Vince, are you still there?" Angeliqué asked.

"Yes, I'm here. And I'm listening."

"How are things with you, Vince?"

Vince emitted a short chuckle. "Angeliqué, please. Is that it? Are we done talking about your encounter with the female?"

"The female—she happens to be somebody to me. I said I'm sorry for hurting you. But I'm not sorry that it happened. Terry is someone who is special. She is a wonderful human being. I'm not sure there is anything further to say."

"Oh, I get it. So I guess all this talk about how much you missed me was just bullshit, right?"

"No, it's not bullshit, Vince…"

And I guess," Vince said, interrupting her, "that what we had, what we felt that weekend doesn't amount to shit!"

"Vince," she interrupted gently, "You can't expect me to sit here and put my life on hold for someone whom I have no idea if I'll even see again. Yes, we vibed—yes, we had a wonderful time. I don't deny any of that at all. But if you're expecting me to sit here and wait around for something that probably will never amount to anything, well, I think you've got the wrong girl."

Vince's mind whirled. This was not what he expected…

"Vince?"

"Yeah."

"I'm thinking about heading up to Washington for a few days. Think we could get together?"

"Well, Angeliqué, you had an opportunity to be with me, but instead, you decided to spend it with your tongue down some female's throat. So why the sudden interest in seeing me?" Vince was livid and no longer interested in hiding his growing anger.

"That's not fair, Vince, and you know it—I had no idea that you were coming down. If I'd have known…"

"What? You'd have made plans to *fuck* her after I left???"

The phone grew silent. Vince knew he had gone too far, but made no move to correct his mistake. A moment passed. Then another. Vince heard Angeliqué sigh and knew she was still on the phone.

"Vince, I'd like to know if you'll see me when I come to Washington. It's a simple question. 'Yes' or 'no' will suffice."

Vince grew still. His mind raced as he processed her words. He felt torn—on the one hand, what he had witnessed in New Orleans had snapped in two the bond he shared with Angeliqué. On the other, he desired to see her again, if for nothing more than to try and rekindle the flame, even though that didn't seem like much of a possibility now.

"I don't know, Angeliqué," he said.

"Okay, Vince. I understand."

Vince's chest rose and fell heavily. What a night—first Maxi and now Angeliqué. Too much drama for one man to take. Then all of that swept away, like a sudden onslaught, replaced with images of Angeliqué and him in her studio, their bodies caressed by candlelight and dripping with paint as he melted inside of her on the floor…

Vince smiled with the memories. Although short-lived, it was a wonderful time that they had shared.

Vince closed his eyes as he tried to erase the present and move backward, into the past…

Thirty-One

B. Smith's restaurant in Union Station is open-air and vast. Perfect for whatever Trey needed to discuss with Erika. She arrived at eleven forty-five a.m. sharp, and was seated at a table for two by the enormous floor-to-ceiling panes of glass overlooking the street. Their table was across from a large pillar, in a section behind the main dining-room area; it offered up privacy, yet one could still see the main section from where they were seated. Erika had just ordered a drink when in strode Trey, still shaded in his rose-colored glasses, bald head shining as always, his charcoal-gray, double-breasted suit impeccable, with a light-blue shirt and matching silk tie, polished black lace-ups, and sterling silver cufflinks that sparkled as he moved. B. Smith's was already busy with the lunchtime crowd—waiters scrambling about to fill drink orders and returning with appetizers and entrees—but even with all the commotion, folks still paused in conversation as he strolled by. Trey had it like that. Everywhere he went, people noticed him.

He came up and gave Erika a peck on the cheek before sitting down.

"Hey, Sassy, check you out. Girlfriend's looking fly as usual." Erika smiled. She wore dark jeans, a tan sweater, and matching boots. A choker adorned her neck with an Indian head nickel hanging from a single leather cord.

"You too, boo. Only about twenty women checked out your entrance this time!"

Trey cocked his head to the side, peering around the column as he adjusted his tie. "For real? Only twenty? Damn, I must be losing my touch!" A waiter came up beside them and took Trey's drink order.

"So, what is the big emergency, Trey? I mean, damn, a girl doesn't call you back within twenty-four hours and you go all mental. What's up with that?"

"Please—it ain't like that! Besides, I thought you were my boo—I mean, if you don't want me to share my innermost secrets with you, then forget you, I'll go find someone else." Trey removed his shades and pocketed them in his breast pocket. "Hmmm, I'm famished—let me see if they got any soul food up in this mutha fucka!"

"Trey, please—stop acting so damn ghetto—you know this is a nice spot!"

"That remains to be seen." The waiter brought Trey's drink and set it down on the table. Trey glanced up. "How's the salmon today, my man?" he asked.

"Very good, sir. I highly recommend it!"

"Well then, that's what I'm gonna have." Trey folded his menu and handed it to the waiter with a flourish.

"Excuse me," Erika quipped, cutting a stare at Trey. "But, what happened to 'ladies first'?"

"Oh, my bad."

Erika shook her head as she sucked her teeth. The waiter gave her an apologetic shrug. "I'll have the glazed pork chops."

"Excellent choice," the waiter responded.

"Oh, and bring my boy here some manners if you would," she declared.

"I'll see if we have any left in back," the waiter said as he moved off.

"Everybody's got jokes," Trey quipped.

"So, Trey. Seriously, what's up?"

Trey cleared his throat. "Not much—actually, a whole lot—it's been a crazy-ass week. Let me tell you." Erika nodded. "Where to begin…let's see. Oh yeah, I didn't tell you, since you didn't return my *phone calls*, but there was some serious drama last Saturday night at Home."

"Really?"

"Oh yeah—you remember Quentin Hues; he plays for the Wizards. He's a client."

"Yes, you told me."

"Yeah, well, he was having a birthday party there and we're all up in the VIP just chilling when in waltzes his wife, soon-to-be-ex with her girls like she owns the spot! All hell breaks loose, a fight ensues, and guess who has to handle the situation?" Trey is grinning as he breaks off a piece of warm bread.

"Let me guess?"

"You got it, baby! Me—Trey to the rescue—Red Cross up in the shit!"

"What?" Erika asked.

"Oh yeah, *moi* had to escort the lovely fine-as-she-wanna-be Ms. Hues to safety." Trey was glancing down at his nails as he pursed his lips. Erika smirked.

"Oh boy—let me guess—safety being the backseat of your ride? What'd you do, Trey? Please don't tell me you took advantage of your own client's wife? Trey, please!"

Trey grinned but said nothing.

"Oh my God, Trey, this is fucked up, even for you—Quentin's wife?" Erika shook her head fiercely.

"What? The girl needed a ride out of there but quick—she was about to get a beat down from her own husband. I'm a hero, and all I get is static from you? That's messed up!" he said, spreading his hands wide.

"Trey, please. Sleeping with your client's wife is unethical. How can you look Quentin in the eyes after doing something like that?"

"Whatever! Besides that brutha's a bigger ho than me, believe that! Anyway, get this—we had our meeting a few days later to finalize the settlement agreement, right? Quentin and me; his wife and her attorney, Allison—you remember that honey from H20—I told you about that situation, right?"

"You mean the fact that you *fucked* her, too! Yeah, you mentioned that. Trey, you're incredible. The only one *not* getting fucked is Quentin—when are you going to show him the pipe? You might as well give him some, too!"

Trey laughed. "Ha, ha, that's a good one—listen up—Allison figured out that I'd been boning Aponi, so she went ballistic on me. Like I owe her a fucking explanation or something. Like we had something going on... Please, we fucked. *Once*. Hello. It doesn't mean she's ready for an engagement ring."

"Trey," Erika said, reaching for his hand. "You are going to do what you want to do. You always have. But listen up. One of these days, your whoring around is going to come back and bite you in the ass. For real, man. You need to slow your roll, ya hear me?"

"Whatever, Erika—I'm doing my thing, ain't hurting nobody. Besides, and you probably won't believe this, but I wasn't trying to fuck Aponi. In fact, I was hoping she'd just let me drop her off back at her hotel. But let me tell you, she was sweating a brutha, and well, I had no choice but to tap that ass!"

Erika eyed Trey but said nothing.

"Anywho—can we get to the topic at hand? The real reason for this get-together?"

"Sure, Trey—it's your party…"

The food came. They ate in silence for a few minutes before picking up where they had left off.

"So, the firm's got their ten-year anniversary party coming up in two weeks."

"Okay," Erika said, savoring the flavor of the chops.

"Yeah, this is big—huge. I mean, they're making a very big deal about this—black-tie and everything. Renting out Sequoia on the waterfront for this party. Can you imagine? Shutting down Sequoia on a Friday night for a private party? Sheeit!"

"So your firm is the bomb; they got it like that…what else is new?"

"Girl, you don't understand. This is serious—everyone is expected to attend. I mean, to not show is a career-limiting move, I kid you not."

"Okay," Erika said, "so obviously you're gonna go—you've been burning up the phone lines to tell me *this*???"

"Erika," Trey said, wiping his mouth with the cloth napkin, "if you weren't my girl, I'd reach over this table and smack you dead in your chops, and I don't mean those on your plate! You don't get it, do you? I need a date! I *have* to show up with a fine honey on my arm—I've got a reputation to uphold. This is all about image, for real—I can *not* go solo."

"So, get a date. I'm sure you can come up with someone to accompany you in less than fifteen seconds, all them females you know!"

"Erika, I'm serious. Man, this is bugging the shit out of me. Who am I going to take? It can't be just any ole ho…no, girlfriend's gotta have class, look damn good, and be able to carry on a conversation with folks—I mean, the partners are going to be there in force." Trey reached inside his jacket pocket and extracted a folded piece of paper. He flattened it on the table and glanced up at Erika. "I've been giving this a great deal of thought. In fact, I've been thinking about nothing else for the past week."

"You're kidding," Erika asked incredulously.

"Nope. In fact, look at this. I had India put together a spreadsheet to help me prioritize my options. Here," he said, sliding the printout over to her. Erika picked up the paper and looked it over, shaking her head.

"Trey, you *are* for real. Poor India…you don't pay her enough!" She glanced over the list. There were close to three-hundred names accompanied by notes—distinguishing characteristics or tidbits of data that would help Trey recall them all, along with phone numbers if he possessed them. "What—what is this?" Erika asked.

"What does it look like? A list of the eligible women. At least those I can *recall*…"

"And?"

"And nothing. I'm having trouble figuring out which one to take. I mean, some of them aren't a good fit for this particular affair. Others probably won't even speak to me 'cause I haven't exactly maintained a *relationship* with them, ya know?"

"Meaning, they haven't heard shit from you since you fucked them?"

"Basically." Trey smiled sheepishly. "Listen, I didn't come here to get a lesson from you on relationships or how to treat women. Okay? I'm soliciting your help because I don't know what to do. I was strongly considering Allison—good-looking, intelligent, fellow attorney, but at this juncture I doubt she'd want to accompany me…There's Aponi, but she's too young and unpolished."

Erika frowned as she shook her head. "You've got to be kidding me! I'm not going to help you with this." She shook her head firmly.

"Boo," Trey said, all smiles, "I *need* your help. Come on, give a brutha a break—please?"

Erika sighed as she glanced down at the sheet. "What about what's her name? The one you met at the Congressional Black Caucus—the tall one? Regina or something? She was nice."

"Naw—I ran into her a couple of months ago. She didn't speak when I said hello. She's still pissed because I never called after our wild night."

"It's no wonder. Okay, let me think." Erika consulted the list. "How about this one: Monica. Says here, 'fine ass and great at her job.'"

Trey snatched the paper and glanced over the list, shaking his head. "Great at her job—yeah, that chick gave a great *blowjob*—that's about the only 'job' she's any good at! Besides, last time I called her she told me she'd gotten engaged."

The two pored over the list —Trey pulled out a pen to make notes; Erika scanned the list and asked Trey pertinent questions. But, fifteen minutes later, no luck, they hadn't reached any conclusion.

"You know what, Erika? There's something very wrong with this picture when *yours truly* can't find a single decent woman to take to a goddamned party. I mean, really! I wouldn't be making an issue of this except for the fact that it is such a big deal!" Trey exclaimed, shaking his head. The waiter cleared their plates, and they both ordered coffee.

"Can I be honest with you, Trey?" Erika asked, but didn't wait for a response. "I think you need to step back and think about what this means… put it in its proper context. What this says to me is that you may have been *intimate* with loads of women, but you hardly know any of them."

Trey's stare locked on Erika's for a moment. For a minute neither spoke. Erika didn't glance away; she wasn't frightened. Erika knew this conversation was long overdue.

The coffee came. Trey and Erika sipped theirs in silence as he reviewed his list. Suddenly Trey's eyes sparkled. "Ah sookie now—I've got it!"

"Yeah?"

"Oh yeah. Hang onto your panties, Erika and check it—you could go with me."

"Me?" Erika asked, her eyebrow rising. She was shaking her head as Trey grabbed her hand.

"Of course, boo—it's perfect. We've known each other for years—and we look *damn* good together, you've got to admit. You are intelligent and can carry a conversation. This way I don't have to trip for the next two weeks trying to figure out who to take!"

"I don't know…" Erika was saying.

"Say you'll go with me, boo. Please? I need this. I can't go solo, and let's face it—none of these women are present tense. They're all past tense!"

"So, what you're saying is that I'm the one you go to when your other hos say no?"

"Naw, baby, you know it's not like that. You're my boo. Honestly, I didn't consider you until this moment, but the more I think about it, the more it makes wonderful sense. You're the one. You're perfect. Besides, we'd have a lot of fun. What do you say?"

Erika sighed. "Trey," she said, "Give me some time to consider this, okay?"

"Meaning what? You have to check with James first to see if it's all right?"

Erika was ready to fire off a response when a movement caught her interest. She glanced to the right; Trey witnessed her change of appearance, as if a fist had suddenly connected with flesh. It was swift and complete. He turned his head, and in that moment, his entire world came to a grinding halt. Trey paused in mid-sentence. Erika was still attempting to process what she saw as her eyes opened wide. They flicked back to Trey for a split second before zeroing in on the object of her attention.

The hair was still long and jet-black, patting her shoulders and back in waves as she moved; the high cheekbones, evident even in profile; the curves to her hips, still shapely and in motion as she traveled the length of the dining room; her face turned to her companion, another woman—but all eyes were on *her*. And Erika could understand why—she was still, after all of these years, *breathless*. Trey's jaw dropped as his eyes literally bugged out. The change in his appearance was drastic. In a split second he had aged ten years. He looked visibly sick, and Erika knew that inside, he was dying.

"Oh shit," Erika whispered as Layla, Trey's ex-girlfriend, the ex-love of his life, and the woman who had *ruined* him, sauntered on by, unaware that she had been spotted by either of them…

To be continued in…
THE FOREVER GAME
by Jonathan Luckett
Coming Soon from Strebor Books International

ABOUT THE AUTHOR

Jonathan Luckett is a native of Brooklyn, New York and has been writing since he was in the seventh grade. Now residing in the Washington, D.C. area, he was educated at Cornell and Johns Hopkins universities. Jonathan is the author of the novels *Dissolve* (2005), *How Ya Livin'* (2004), *Jasminium* (2003), and the self-published novella *Feeding Frenzy* (2002). His work is also featured in *Chocolate Flava* (2004), a collection of erotica. Jonathan has also written various short stories, poetry, and erotic fiction. His work is available on-line at www.jonathanluckett.com.

Available from
Strebor Books International

Baptiste, Michael
Cracked Dreams 1-59309-035-8
Godchild 1-59309-044-7

Bernard, D.V.
The Last Dream Before Dawn
0-9711953-2-3
God in the Image of Woman
1-59309-019-6
How to Kill Your Boyfriend (in Ten Easy Steps)
1-59309-066-8

Billingsley, ReShonda Tate
Help! I've Turned Into My Mother
1-59309-050-1

Brown, Laurinda D.
Fire & Brimstone 1-59309-015-3
UnderCover 1-59309-030-7
The Highest Price for Passion
1-59309-053-6

Cheekes, Shonda
Another Man's Wife 1-59309-008-0
Blackgentlemen.com 0-9711953-8-2
In the Midst of it All 1-59309-038-2

Cooper, William Fredrick
Six Days in January 1-59309-017-X
Sistergirls.com 1-59309-004-8

Crockett, Mark
Turkeystuffer 0-9711953-3-1

Daniels, J and Bacon, Shonell
*Luvalwayz: The Opposite Sex and
Relationships* 0-9711953-1-5
Draw Me With Your Love
1-59309-000-5

Darden, J. Marie
Enemy Fields 1-59309-023-4
Finding Dignity 1-59309-051-X

De Leon, Michelle
Missed Conceptions 1-59309-010-2
Love to the Third 1-59309-016-1
Once Upon a Family Tree
1-59309-028-5

Faye, Cheryl
Be Careful What You Wish For
1-59309-034-X

Halima, Shelley
Azucar Moreno 1-59309-032-3
Los Morenos 1-59309-049-8

Handfield, Laurel
My Diet Starts Tomorrow 1-59309-005-6
Mirror Mirror 1-59309-014-5

Hayes, Lee
Passion Marks 1-59309-006-4
A Deeper Blue: Passion Marks II
1-59309-047-1

Hobbs, Allison
Pandora's Box 1-59309-011-0
Insatiable 1-59309-031-5
Dangerously in Love 1-59309-048-X
Double Dippin' 1-59309-065-X

Hurd, Jimmy
Turnaround 1-59309-045-5
Ice Dancer 1-59309-062-5

Johnson, Keith Lee
Sugar & Spice 1-59309-013-7
Pretenses 1-59309-018-8
Fate's Redemption 1-59309-039-0

Johnson, Rique
Love & Justice 1-59309-002-1
Whispers from a Troubled Heart
1-59309-020-X
Every Woman's Man 1-59309-036-6
Sistergirls.com 1-59309-004-8

Kai, Naleighna
Every Woman Needs a Wife
1-59309-060-9

Kinyua, Kimani
The Brotherhood of Man 1-59309-064-1

Lee, Darrien
All That and a Bag of Chips
0-9711953-0-7
Been There, Done That 1-59309-001-3
What Goes Around Comes Around
1-59309-024-2
When Hell Freezes Over 1-59309-042-0
Brotherly Love 1-59309-061-7

Luckett, Jonathan
Jasminium 1-59309-007-2
How Ya Livin' 1-59309-025-0
Dissolve 1-59309-041-2

McKinney, Tina Brooks
All That Drama 1-59309-033-1

Perkins, Suzetta L.
Behind the Veil 1-59309-063-3

Quartay, Nane
Feenin 0-9711953-7-4
The Badness 1-59309-037-4

Rivera, Jr., David
Harlem's Dragon 1-59309-056-0

Rivers, V. Anthony
Daughter by Spirit 0-9674601-4-X
Everybody Got Issues 1-59309-003-X
Sistergirls.com 1-59309-004-8
My Life is All I Have 1-59309-057-9

Roberts, J. Deotis
Roots of a Black Future 0-9674601-6-6
Christian Beliefs 0-9674601-5-8

Stephens, Sylvester
Our Time Has Come 1-59309-026-9

Turley II, Harold L.
Love's Game 1-59309-029-3
Confessions of a Lonely Soul
1-59309-054-4

Valentine, Michelle
Nyagra's Falls 0-9711953-4-X

White, A.J.
Ballad of a Ghetto Poet 1-59309-009-9

White, Franklin
Money for Good 1-59309-012-9
1-59309-040-4 (trade)
Potentially Yours 1-59309-027-7

Woodson, J.L.
Superwoman's Child 1-59309-059-5

Zane (Editor)
Breaking the Cycle 1-59309-021-8